THE COVENANT OF THE FLAME

ALSO BY DAVID MORRELL

Fiction

First Blood (1972)
Testament (1975)
Last Reveille (1977)
The Totem (1979)
Blood Oath (1982)
The Hundred-Year Christmas (1983)*
The Brotherhood of the Rose (1984)
Rambo (First Blood Part II) (1985)
The Fraternity of the Stone (1985)
The League of Night and Fog (1987)
Rambo III (1988)
The Fifth Profession (1990)

Nonfiction

John Barth: An Introduction (1976)
Fireflies (1988)

Limited edition. With illustrations by R. J. Krupowicz.
Donald M. Grant, Publisher, West Kingston, Rhode Island.

DAVID MORRELL

THE COVENANT OF THE FLAME

WARNER BOOKS

A Time Warner Company

Warner Books, Inc., 666 Fifth Avenue, New York, NY 10103
w A Time Warner Company
Printed in the United States of America
First printing: May 1991
10 9 8 7 6 5 4 3 2 1

Library of Congress Cataloging-in-Publication Data

Morrell, David.
    The covenant of the flame : a novel / by David Morrell.
        p.   cm.
    ISBN 0-446-51563-9
    I. Title.
    PR9199.3.M65C65
813′.54—dc20   90-49445
                                                    CIP

Book design by Giorgetta Bell McRee

To Barbara and Richard Montross,
in memory of Matthew, Saturday nights, and a castle in Spain

CONTENTS

If a man abide not in Me, he is cast
forth as a branch and is withered.
And men gather them and cast them into
the fire.
And they are burned.

—The Gospel according to John

THE COVENANT OF THE FLAME

PROLOGUE

A FURY SLINGING FLAME

ASH WEDNESDAY

Spain, 1391

Archdeacon Ferran Martínez, driven to excess by his fervent Catholicism, preached increasingly inflammatory sermons against all heretics. On March 15, Ash Wednesday, his charismatic hate-filled oratory aroused his parishioners to such a frenzy that they stormed from his church toward the Jewish quarter of Seville. If not for the orderly minded civil authorities, a massacre might have ensued. Instead two leaders of the mob were seized and scourged. But their punishment, far from being a discouragement to fellow bigots, made the leaders martyrs and fueled the fires of their followers' hate. Antiheretical fury spread from Seville to neighboring cities and finally throughout Spain with the terrible consequence that during the summer of 1391 an estimated ten thousand disbelievers were executed, most by beatings and stonings.

Several, though, were put to the torch.

GUARDIANS OF
THE FAITH

France

The religious mania in Spain was not unique. Since the start of the Middle Ages, a heresy derived from ancient Mideastern theology had attracted so many followers that the Church felt threatened. The heresy, known as Albigensianism, maintained that good and evil were balanced forces, that two Gods—not one—controlled the universe, that Satan was equal to, in combat with, and as cunning as the Lord. The body—flesh—was Satan's domain. The mind—the *spirit*—was the path to salvation.

The thought of two Gods horrified the Church. Christ, the physical incarnation of the Blessed Father, could not have been evil. A version of God in the flesh, He could *not* have been part of the Devil's work when, crucified, He sacrificed Himself to redeem His decadent children. The heresy had to be crushed.

The resultant crusade against the Albigensians was merciless. Tens of thousands died. But the heresy persisted. Thousands more died until at last in 1244 at the mountain fortress of Montségur in the Pyrenees of southwestern France, the last stronghold of the Albigensians was surrounded, assaulted, and set on fire.

But there were rumors that the heresy—despite the crusade's brutality—had not been eradicated, that a small group of heretics had used ropes to descend from the mountain the night before the massacre, taking with them a mysterious treasure, and that this core of heretics had impossibly survived to disperse, to burrow deeply, their repulsive errors festering.

THE PLACE OF BURNING

Spain, 1478

    The massacres at Seville and Montségur were but two examples of religious hysteria in the Middle Ages. Jews, Moors, Albigensians, and Protestants became the common target of a papally authorized purification of the Faith, its official title the Inquisition. The northern countries of Europe rejected the Inquisition's influence. But Italy, England, and France committed atrocities in its name.

    Nowhere else, however, was religious intolerance as extreme as in Spain. There the Inquisition, conducted by the sunken-eyed Dominican priest Tomás de Torquemada, resulted in tens of thousands of tortures and executions. The intent was to educate heretics and to guide them toward the true belief.

    Victims had their hands tied behind their back, from which a rope was raised, the pressure on their shoulders excruciating.

"Confess!" they were ordered.

"Confess?" the victims moaned.

"Your heresy!"

"Heresy?" the victims wailed.

"Raise the rope!" the Inquisitors commanded.

Arms were strained. Shoulders popped.

    If the victims survived, they were stretched on the rack, and if they *still* survived but persisted in denying their theological error, the Inquisitors thrust a tube of cloth down their throat. Water was poured. When the victims came near to drowning, the tube—forcibly extracted—brought with it not only water but blood.

These victims had lost both their property and the right to question their accusers. Helpless, they had only two choices: to confess and beg for mercy, but more important, to implicate fellow heretics; or else to insist that they were innocent, that jealous neighbors had lied when informing against them. To confess, even if the victim was not a heretic, brought the chance for freedom. To insist that there'd been a mistake, to refuse to implicate others, caused the harshest penalty.

At the *quemadero*, the place of burning, the accused were dragged from prison for their *auto-da-fé* or act of faith. All wore yellow robes and peaked caps. Those who'd been sentenced to death had black flames—pointing downward—on their garments. The others could still not be sure that they would survive. Only when they climbed to the scaffold would they be certain of the Inquisitors' judgment. Some, a few, were set free. Their confessions had been believed, although penance would have to be suffered. Others were sentenced to prison, a reprieve of a lingering death.

Still others were strangled.

But the worst offenders were burned alive at the stake. Their ashes were scattered, along with those of suspected heretics who'd died before the Inquisitors could question them. Even after death, those suspected heretics were not immune, their bodies exhumed and purified by flames.

This zealous protection of the Faith persisted for a longer period of time than is generally realized. For centuries, from the close of the Middle Ages into the Renaissance and then to the so-called Age of Enlightenment, the Inquisition enforced its beliefs. Only in 1834 was the institution finally disbanded.

Officially, at any rate. But there were rumors.

ONE

CAUSES AND CONSEQUENCES

THE LORD IS MY WITNESS

1

Senate Clean-Air Battle Looms

WASHINGTON, D.C., June 10 (AP)—In this year's most tense confrontation between Democrats and Republicans, the Senate today begins its debate on the controversial Barker-Hudson clean-air bill, which advocates that the nation not only adopt but exceed the stringent atmosphere-control policies recently adopted in California.

"Our air's as foul as the smoke from a field of burning tires," Senator Barker (Dem, New York) announced in a smoggy press conference on the steps of the Capitol Building yesterday. "Take a deep breath. That is, if you're brave enough. Try not to gag. We ought to be wearing gas masks."

"And stay indoors," the bill's cosponsor, Senator Hudson (Dem, New Hampshire), added. "My wife and I went

out for a stroll last night. Five minutes was all we could bear. We rushed back home and made sure all the windows were closed. I gave up smoking a dozen years ago. Might as well not have bothered. According to my statistics, the atmosphere's so filthy we inhale the equivalent of two packs of cigarettes every day. If you don't care about yourselves, then at least protect your children. We've got to stop destroying their and your lungs.''

The Barker-Hudson bill advocates a complete ban on smoking in all public places, an exorbitant fine for car and truck manufacturers if they fail to reduce emissions within two years, an equally exorbitant fine for industries that fail to reduce atmospheric pollution within the same length of time, a surcharge on automobile license fees for owners of more than one vehicle, a mandatory air-exhaust filtration system outside restaurants, dry cleaners, and . . .

2

Georgetown, Washington

As was his custom, the Republican senior senator from Michigan, Roland Davis, woke at six A.M., careful not to disturb his wife. He went downstairs, made coffee, fed his cat, leaned out the front door to pick up the *Washington Post,* and carried the folded newspaper into the kitchen. The June sunrise shone dully through a smog-hazed bay window onto the table. Davis sipped his steaming coffee, put on his glasses, spread open the paper, and scanned it for any mention of his name.

He didn't have to read far. The headline referred to the Barker-Hudson bill, and in the ensuing two-column story, Davis was frequently cited as the leader of the Republican Party's opposition to "an extreme, repressive, radical, and economically suicidal approach to a temporary, admittedly serious problem that requires time and care to be corrected."

Davis nodded, approving both his rhetoric and the reporter's accuracy in quoting him. He was fifty-eight, tall, with a full head of distinguished-looking gray hair, a patrician's face, and a photogenic slender body that he kept in shape by a half-hour daily workout on a stationary bicycle. Better get peddling, he thought. Got a busy day coming up. Besides, he was eager to watch the early morning news.

But first he wanted to finish the story in the *Post*. Barker and Hudson made more apocalyptic statements about "poisonous air pollution contributing to the greenhouse effect and the depletion of the ozone layer . . . increasing rate of skin cancer . . . risk of drought . . . melting polar ice caps . . . rising ocean level . . . state of emergency." Sounded like a plot for a science-fiction movie.

Davis snorted. Those Democrats didn't stand a chance of getting their bill through the Senate, although he had to give Barker and Hudson credit—they knew how to get the attention of the media, and that wouldn't hurt come election time, at least with the liberals in their districts. Or maybe their tactic would backfire. Nobody wants to re-elect losers, and Barker and Hudson were sure to lose today. Clean air? Great idea. The trouble was, Americans didn't like making sacrifices. What they preferred was for the people down the street to make the sacrifice. Every smoker, multiple-car owner, factory worker worried about his job, *everyone* whose lifestyle or pocketbook would be affected by the bill would urge his senator to vote against it.

Hadn't Barker and Hudson ever heard of compromise? Was *moderation* not in their vocabulary? Didn't they realize you had to approach a problem one step at a time instead of jumping on it all at once?

Davis finished the story, pleased that he'd been quoted once more near the end, the voice of reason: "I think we'd all agree, the air's not as clean as it could be. We've got a problem, yes, at least in some big cities, at least in June through September. Conditions will improve, though, when the weather gets cooler. That doesn't mean I recommend we sit on our hands. But we can't change society

13

overnight, although my distinguished colleagues seem to want to do just that. What we need instead, and what I intend to propose as soon as I've evaluated all the statistics, is a balanced, moderate, carefully implemented, nondisruptive solution. Time. Air pollution took time to develop, and it requires time to be reduced.''

Excellent, Davis thought. The *Post* gave me plenty of space, and I'm sure to get even more press in Michigan. The smokers in my constituency will feel less put-upon. So will two-car families threatened with a surcharge on their license fees. But most important, Davis thought, the automobile manufacturers will be awfully grateful when they don't have to worry about meeting new restrictions on exhaust from their cars and their factories.

Awfully grateful.

And mighty generous. Yes, indeed.

The doorbell rang. Davis frowned at the digital clock on the microwave across from him: 6:14. Who'd be here so early? At once the obvious answer occurred to him. An eager reporter. In which case, I'd better make sure I look presentable. Davis used his hands to neaten his hair, tied his housecoat securely, left the kitchen, and did his best to look cheery when he opened the front door.

Abruptly he scrunched his eyebrows together, because no one was there. He scowled up and down the hazy street lined with elegant town houses, but except for a car disappearing around a corner, he saw no activity.

Who the—?

Why the—?

Suddenly an object on his doorstep attracted his attention. A large manila envelope. Frowning harder, Davis picked it up, peered once more along the street, went back inside his house, and locked the door behind him.

Couldn't have been my assistant, Davis thought. Susan would have called first if she had something important for me to look at this early. Even if she didn't have time to phone, she wouldn't merely have left this envelope and rushed away without an explanation.

Troubled, Davis unsealed the envelope and pulled out several documents. Too curious to wait to go into the kitchen and sit down to read them, he quickly scanned the first page, but managed to complete only half of it before a moan escaped him.

Jesus.

Oh, dear Christ.

He rushed to finish the page and flipped through the others.

Fucking mother of—!

The documents provided dates, places, names, and amounts, every bribe he'd ever received, every illegal campaign contribution, every expense-paid vacation, every . . . !

And after the documents, there were photographs that made Davis grope for a wall to steady himself, afraid that his sudden chest pain meant he was having a heart attack.

The photographs—clear, glossy, professional-looking black-and-whites—depicted Davis and his gorgeous young female assistant naked on the deck of a yacht and not simply having sex but performing several illegal versions of it, including sodomy and cunnilingus.

Davis vividly remembered that exquisite summer afternoon. He and his assistant had been alone. Taking care that they weren't followed, each had traveled separately to the small, private Caribbean island owned by one of Davis's most powerful constituents. They'd been assured that the island would be deserted, but just to be extra cautious, Davis had taken the yacht out to sea, where no one could spy on them. No Gary Hart screwups for him.

But someone *had* spied on them!

From the downward angle of the photos, Davis concluded that they'd been taken with a long-distance lens from a plane. And the photos were so sharply defined that Davis and his assistant almost appeared to be posing. Certainly their faces were easily recognizable, except when Davis had the back of his head to the camera while he hungrily burrowed his mouth between his assistant's legs.

And damn it, there was more!

After the photographs, which made Davis's chest heave no longer in pain but rage, he shuddered at the sight of an unsigned typed note, its implied threat as chilling as it was proportioned:

DAVID MORRELL

WE SUGGEST
THAT YOU RETHINK
WHICH WAY YOU'LL VOTE
ON THE BARKER-HUDSON BILL.

Davis tore the documents, the photographs, and the note into halves, quarters, then eighths. The clumps became so thick that he had to subdivide them as he kept tearing. All the while he cursed with furious quietude so he wouldn't waken his wife.

Cocksuckers! he thought, dimly aware of the irony that *one* cocksucker, the evidence about whom he wanted desperately to destroy, was his female assistant. At the same time, he was also aware that no matter how many times he shredded the damning evidence, his frenzy was useless—because whoever had sent this package wouldn't have been so foolish that they hadn't kept copies.

Yes! Whoever! But there wasn't any doubt who *they* were.

Barker and Hudson!

Davis shook with indignation. Junior Democratic senators threatening a senior *Republican* senator? Had they no conception of the power that a seasoned politician such as Davis could muster? I'll—!

Yes? You'll—?

What? Exactly *what* will you do? Confront them? Reinforce the validity of their accusations? No matter what you do to *them,* it's nothing compared to what *they* can do to you if they decide to reveal what was in this package. Your career will be finished, ruined, a joke! *Then what are you going to do?*

"Dear?"

Davis flinched as he heard his wife coming down the stairs. In a rush, he shoved the torn evidence into the envelope.

"Did I hear the doorbell?" Davis's wife appeared at the bottom of the stairs. Her wrinkle-rimmed eyes were baggy. Her pudgy cheeks and belly sagged. Her white hair was in curlers.

"Yes, love," Davis answered. "It was nothing. Just a messenger with some last-minute information about the clean-air bill."

"Oh my, how tedious. I wish they wouldn't bother us this early."

"I know, sweet," Davis said. "But it *was* important. It made me rethink my vote. I'm beginning to sympathize with Barker and Hudson. The children, dear. We have to protect the nation's children. We have to insure them clean air so they can have clean lungs."

"But what about—?"

"My generous supporters in Detroit? I guess I'll just have to make them understand, dear." Davis thought about the photographs, about the arousing smell of his assistant. "Yes, that's right. I guess I'll just have to make my generous supporters understand."

3

The Amazon Basin, Brazil

A haze filled the sky. Juanita Gomez, wearing a long black dress, fought to maintain her strength as she squinted through tears and a veil toward her husband's makeshift coffin. Yes, be strong, she thought, her soul aching. You must. For Pedro. It's what he would have wanted. Around her, she knew, her husband's mourning followers watched her as intensely as they did the coffin. If she lost control, if she gave them the least cause to suspect that her grief had weakened her resolve to continue her husband's work, then her husband's enemies would indeed have accomplished what they'd hoped to achieve by killing him. For Pedro! she thought. Be strong!

Juanita was twenty-five, short and thin, with a narrow face and tawny skin. She wasn't beautiful, she readily admitted, and had never been able to understand why Pedro had chosen her. Her single attractive feature was her shoulder-length dark hair, which despite the poverty of her diet had a sheen. How Pedro had loved to stroke it. How he'd bragged that their two infant children had inherited

17

Juanita's lovely hair. What am I going to do without you? Juanita thought, barely able to restrain the trembling in her legs. But the answer—

—it seemed she heard Pedro's impassioned voice inside her brain—

—instantly made her stand straighter.

Have courage, Juanita. Don't give up. Make sure I didn't die uselessly. Take my place. Inflame my discouraged followers. Say the words! Give the speech!

Yes, Juanita thought, and raised her angry eyes toward the thickening haze that obscured the sky. The speech. Since her husband had been shot two days ago, Juanita had felt an overwhelming pressure of words inside her. Although she'd never been gifted with her unschooled husband's amazing ability to speak in public and capture a crowd's attention, she'd suddenly known that she had to make a pronouncement at his graveside. It was almost as if she'd been commanded to do so. Throughout the preparations for Pedro's funeral, while his bullet-ravaged corpse lay on precious, hard-to-find ice, Juanita had mentally rehearsed what her compulsion dictated. Last night, too distraught with sorrow to sleep, she'd perfected the words. Soon, when the elderly priest finished droning *his* words over the coffin, it would be *her* turn. She would say *hers*. Pedro, her beloved husband, would speak *in* her, *with* her, *through* her— and provided that she remained strong, her husband's followers would subdue their fear, overcome their discouragement, and persist in their fight to save the land.

Be strong!

The cemetery was ancient, the majority of its wooden crosses listing from decay. The graveyard stood on a barren hill that overlooked the shacks in the village of Cordoba and the silt-choked, mud-colored tributary of the once-magnificent Amazon River. The silt was caused by runoff, Juanita knew, by erosion when the rain washed away the soil that the roots of the former majestic forest could no longer protect.

Because of the fires.

Because of the slash-and-burn tactics of her husband's enemies.

Those enemies had compelled the villagers to cut down the trees, to set fire to them, and to use the cleared land to grow more crops. That was why a thickening haze obscured the sky. Juanita trembled with increasing rage. Because of the fires in the distance, on the rim of the dwindling forest. The soil was extremely thin, even with the ashes from the trees, and after a few years of intensive farming, the soil stopped being fertile. As a consequence, more trees were burned, more land cleared, more crops planted until that soil, too, became infertile—a sickening pattern of progressive destruction.

But there was even more sickening destruction, Juanita knew. For her husband's enemies, who owned the land, forced the villagers to leave and brought in heavy equipment to strip-mine the treeless land to get at the minerals beneath it. In the end, nothing of worth remained. Wherever Juanita looked, barren ugliness surrounded her.

The priest had almost finished his prayers. Juanita felt heat in her soul, a furious need to turn to her husband's followers and say her words, to urge them to persist in their fight. Pedro had organized these villagers, convincing them to refuse to allow the wealthy, greedy, *evil* men in the nation's capital to continue destroying God's creation. Pedro had learned from visiting foreigners—what had they called themselves? ecologists? that the dense smoke from the widespread fires was poisoning the earth's air. The foreigners had also said that this largest forest in the world took something bad (she remembered the meaningless term "carbon dioxide") out of the air and added something good (what was it? oxygen?), that if the forest disappeared, which it would at the present rapid rate of millions of acres destroyed each year, the carbon dioxide in the air would accumulate until the weather changed, the temperature rose, and the rains no longer came.

The world depended on this forest, the foreigners had insisted. The burning had to be stopped!

Pedro had understood what the foreigners told him, but he'd also understood that the peasants wouldn't fight to save the forest merely because foreigners claimed it was important to the world. At the same time, Pedro had known that the peasants *would* fight to save their homes, to preserve the rubber trees that gave them both shelter and the crop from which they earned their living, to protect the river from the muddy erosion that choked the fish they depended on for food. They'd fight. That is, if someone showed

19

them *how* to fight, if someone banded them together, if someone gave them the confidence to realize that in numbers there was strength.

So Pedro had accepted the challenge, and for a time, he and his followers had been successful, forcing the enemy from the land. Apparently too successful, for the evil men in the capital had sent assassins with machine guns to shoot—to *shred*—Pedro's body while he made a speech in a neighboring village, and now the air was again thick with smoke. Once more, the ominous fires burned.

You mustn't give up! Juanita heard Pedro's voice in her head. You *must* continue the fight!

As the priest backed away from the coffin, she spun toward her husband's followers, about to raise her veil, to let them see the furnacelike determination in her eyes, to say her words.

But her impulse was interrupted, her husband's followers distracted, by a long black car that bumped unexpectedly along the dusty road and stopped at the base of the cemetery.

The villagers watched in confusion as a stranger got out. He was a tall, refined-looking man in a suit as black as his expensive car. His tie as well was black, in contrast with his immaculate, gleaming, white shirt, perhaps the only such shirt the villagers had ever seen. With dignified funereal steps, the stranger proceeded toward the rear of the car, opened its trunk, removed a cardboard box, and carried it somberly up the hill through the smoky haze toward the mourners in the dismal cemetery.

"Please, forgive me, Señora Gomez," the man whispered, and bowed in respect. His polished accent and careful pronunciation made it clear that he came from the city. "I deeply apologize. I'm extremely reluctant to intrude at this sensitive, trying time for you. I extend my sympathies and offer a prayer for the soul of your brave departed husband. I would not have troubled you, but a man instructed me—in fact, he insisted—that I do so."

"Man?" Her back muscles rigid, Juanita studied the stranger with suspicion. *"What man?"*

"Alas, I do not know. My client never told me his name. Yesterday he arrived unexpectedly at my office. . . . I own a limousine service in the city. He paid me a generous amount to drive

20

to this village and deliver this package . . . this gift, he said . . . at this precise moment.''

With greater suspicion, Juanita stared at the box. *"Gift? What is it?"* Her immediate thought was that the evil men in the city had sent a bomb to destroy her in such a dramatic fashion, during her husband's funeral, that Pedro's followers would surely lose their will to fight.

"My client would not reveal to me what was in the box. In fact, he warned me that if I unsealed it prematurely, he would discover my transgression and punish me severely. He assured me and instructed me to assure *you* that the gift is not a danger, that instead you'll find it a comfort.''

Juanita squinted harshly. "To drive all this way . . . and on such a mysterious mission . . . you must have been paid very well.''

"True, señora. As I confessed, the fee was generous." The man looked embarrassed, as if comparing his fine clothes with the poverty around him. "With the stranger's compliments, señora.''

Juanita reluctantly accepted the box. Its size reminded her of a cake box. But its contents, which made a thunking sound, were much heavier than a cake.

Troubled, Juanita stooped to set the box on the ground beside her husband's humble coffin. She tried, but when her trembling fingers couldn't break the seal, a villager stepped forward and used his knife to open it.

Compelled, Juanita pried up the flaps, then gazed warily inside.

At once she gasped. The villager who'd used his knife to unseal the box gasped as well. With equal suddenness, Juanita moaned, but not in shock, instead in triumph. She eagerly thrust her hands inside the box and held up its contents.

A human head. The severed skull of one of the evil men in the city who'd ordered her husband's death. The head—its features contorted grotesquely—vividly communicated the agony that the man had suffered while being decapitated. The skull was wrapped in a plastic bag, the bag evidently intended to prevent the jagged neck's blood from soaking through the cardboard box.

With a wail of victory, Juanita yanked off the bag, grasped the skull by the hair, and jerked it as high as her arm would permit so

21

that all her husband's followers could see the wondrous gift that her unknown benefactor had sent.

The messenger stumbled back in horror, a hand raised to his mouth as if he might vomit. Nearly toppling him, the villagers surged forward to get a better look.

"Fight!" she screamed. "For Pedro! For yourselves! For the land!"

The villagers shouted with determination.

Juanita swung the head toward Pedro's coffin. "My husband, my beloved, can you see your enemy? Dear father of our children, you didn't die in vain! We won't be beaten! We'll fight! We'll *continue* fighting! We'll *never* stop fighting! Never! Until we're victorious! Until the day the *fires* stop!"

4

The Coral Sea, the South Pacific

The *Argonaut*, a supertanker carrying crude oil from the Persian Gulf to a refinery near Brisbane on Australia's eastern coast, was three hours ahead of schedule. Clear weather and smooth seas all the way. A completely uneventful voyage. Can't ask for better than that, the captain thought. His name was Victor Malone. A twenty-year veteran of the ocean, most of which time he'd spent in the service of the Pacific-Rim Petroleum Corporation, he was forty-eight, of medium height, with receding brown hair and a stocky build. Although while at sea he seldom left the interior of his vessel, his somewhat puffy face had a ruddy complexion. In the super-tanker's bridge, which despite its windows had lately caused Malone to feel claustrophobic, he checked the weather, sonar, radar, and navigation instruments. Nothing unusual. Another ten hours and we'll be in port, he thought. Certainly by tomorrow morning. Confident of a routine evening, Malone told his watch officer that he was leaving the bridge. "If you need me, I'll be in my cabin."

Five minutes later, after locking the door to his cabin behind him, Malone *un*locked a drawer in his desk and removed a half-empty bottle of vodka. A condition of Malone's employment was that he abstain from alcohol while commanding a Pac-Rim vessel, and for most of his career, Malone had abided by that rule. Guilt-ridden, puzzled, he wasn't sure when or why he'd begun to bend and had finally broken the rule.

Perhaps it had been the trauma of the divorce his wife had demanded three years ago after falling in love with a salesman in the real-estate office where she worked in Boston, a man who, she'd angrily explained, wouldn't abandon her for months at a time.

Or perhaps it had been the lonely nights in foreign ports that had long ago stopped being glamorous.

For whatever reason, a sip now and then before he went to sleep had turned into periodic secret binges in which Malone tried to counteract the boredom of too many lengthy voyages. Aware that his vice was getting out of control, he'd tried to exercise discipline on *this* voyage and had indulged his need for alcohol only when absolutely desperate.

Even so, he'd come close to finishing all eight bottles that he'd smuggled aboard. Amazing how they go so fast, he mused as he poured two inches of vodka into a glass and leaned back in the chair behind his desk.

He wished he had ice and vermouth, but tomorrow morning after docking at the refinery, as soon as his obligations were completed, he would go ashore, find an isolated bar where he wouldn't be recognized, and at last be able to enjoy a martini again.

Several martinis.

He'd rent a room to sleep off his drunkenness and the next day return to work with no one suspecting.

That was the beauty of vodka. It didn't taint his breath.

After what seemed a few sips, Malone was surprised to discover that he'd emptied his glass. Confused, he squinted blearily, assessed the situation, and decided, what the hell, we're almost in port. This'll be my last chance before we dock. A routine assignment. No problems coming up. Why let the rest of the bottle go to waste? So

23

Malone poured another two inches into his glass, and by the time he fell asleep a half hour later, the bottle and the glass were drained.

Abruptly his watch officer's gravelly voice roused him. "Captain?"

Malone struggled—and managed—to raise one eyelid.

"Captain?"

Malone, through his half-opened right eye, sought the source of the voice and gradually realized that it came from the wall, from the intercom.

"Captain, we're having some problems with our sonar reception."

With difficulty, Malone raised his head. He shook it to try to clear his thoughts, opened *both* eyes, and blinked, his vision blurry. His glass fell off his lap as he lurched to his feet and groped for the intercom's speaker button. "Uh, yeah, what? Uh, what was . . . ? Tell me that again."

"Captain, I said we're having problems with the sonar."

Malone rubbed his throbbing forehead. "Problems? What kind of . . . ?"

"Intermittent fade-outs."

Malone's tongue felt thick. He strained not to slur his words. "Sounds like . . . an . . ." *That* word was a tough one. His lips were rubbery. "An electrical short."

"That's what it seems to me, Captain. I've ordered a maintenance crew to look into it."

"Good. Yes, good. A maintenance crew. Good. Let me know what they report."

"Captain, I think you'd better get up here."

"Absolutely. I was having a nap. I'll be there shortly. As soon as possible." Too many *s*'s, Malone nervously realized despite his grogginess. He picked up his glass, rinsed it in his cabin's sink, and set it on a counter. Next he placed the empty vodka bottle inside his desk and locked the drawer.

Better brush my teeth.

Better gargle and wash my face.

But when Malone scowled in the mirror above the sink, the stupor in his bloodshot eyes appalled him. Come on! he thought. Wake up!

He washed his face with hot, then cold water and swallowed two aspirins. With alarm, he noticed that his shirt was wrinkled. Better change it, he thought. Look alert!

From the intercom, the watch officer's gravelly voice blurted, "Captain, the sonar has failed. It's"—garbled voices in the background—"completely dead."

Malone somehow didn't waver as he crossed his cabin and reached the intercom, pushing its transmit button. *"Completely?"*

"The screen is blank."

"Switch to the backup system."

"I did, but it's not working either, Captain."

"Not . . . ?" Malone inhaled. Dear God. "I'm coming right up." With trembling fingers, he fumbled to change his shirt. As a last-moment thought, he splashed his face with after-shave lotion on the off chance that a crew member might somehow smell the supposedly undetectable vodka.

God was merciful. No one saw Malone stumble from his cabin, grasp a bulkhead, straighten himself, and waver onward.

"Status report!" Malone demanded when he entered the control room with what he hoped was convincing authority.

"The same," his watch officer replied. "Both primary and secondary sonar systems are not in operation."

"Give me the navigation charts."

"I assumed you'd want them ready for you, Captain. Should I stop the engines?"

"No! Not yet! Not until we have to!" Malone glared toward his officers. What the hell was wrong with them? Didn't they realize how long it would take for the huge, heavy *Argonaut* to coast to a stop and after the sonar was repaired, to regain maximum speed? "Three hours! We're *three* hours ahead of schedule! The refinery's expecting us. We'll probably get a bonus for being so efficient. But all we'll get is *shit* if we stop to fix a minor problem with the sonar and we show up God knows *how* late!"

The lingering effects of the vodka were making him overreact, Malone realized, but he couldn't help himself. He'd counted on reaching the refinery by tomorrow morning, eager to relieve himself of his obligation, to escape this massive vessel, the walls of which had lately seemed to close in on him.

Most of all, he'd counted on his reward. The *martinis*.
He could almost taste them.

"But Captain, without the sonar . . ."

"It's just an electrical problem," Malone insisted. "The maintenance crew will find what it is and repair it." He spread the navigation charts on a table and studied them, noting the varying depths of the ocean and the pattern of reefs.

Yes! These waters were just as Malone remembered! To avoid the reefs in the Torres Strait to the north, he'd guided the *Argonaut* around New Guinea, then southward through the Solomon Sea into the Coral Sea, carefully skirting the Great Barrier Reef along Australia's northeastern coast.

Once past the Great Barrier, except for a few smaller reefs, the ocean was clear all the way to Brisbane.

"What was our position when the sonar went out?"

"Right here, Captain," the watch officer said, naming a latitude and a longitude, pointing at the chart.

"Perfect." Malone's skull felt as if a spike had been driven through it. "No problem. Then all we have to do is make sure to avoid these two reefs." Striving to maintain his balance, he turned from the chart. "Twenty degrees starboard."

"Aye, aye, Captain," the watch officer said. He repeated the course correction to the helmsman, who acknowledged his instructions by repeating them as well. "Twenty degrees starboard."

Malone's hands shook as he lit a cigarette. "Now let's get that electrical problem fixed." He'd amazed himself by thinking so clearly, given his hangover. "And order some coffee up here. It'll be a long night."

Ninety minutes later, Malone requested confirmation of the *Argonaut*'s speed, determined the tanker's position on the chart, satisfied himself that the first reef had been avoided, and turned to order another course correction. As he did so, he bumped his cup of coffee, knocking it onto the floor. "Shit! Get someone to clean this up! Ten degrees starboard!"

"Aye, aye, Captain. Ten degrees starboard."

The control room became tensely silent.

The sonar screen flickered.

"Captain, the maintenance crew has located the problem. We're ready to . . . There. The sonar's functional."

"I told you. A minor problem. No need to stop."

Malone and his officers leaned forward to study the suddenly glowing console.

"Jesus," someone said.

Malone clasped a hand to his mouth.

The outline of a reef flashed before him. At the same time, a sickening, rumbling crunch shook the supertanker's hull. As Malone lost his balance and fell to his knees, the coffee he'd spilled soaked his trousers. Legs wet, he gaped down in shock as another crunch shook the tanker. The coffee. So dark. So much like . . .

5

"Good evening. This is Dan Rather, CBS News. The worst oil spill in history continues to become more catastrophic. Since striking a reef off Australia's eastern coast yesterday, the *Argonaut*—a Pacific-Rim Petroleum Corporation supertanker—remains in danger of sinking while efforts to contain its cargo have been alarmingly ineffectual. An estimated thirty million gallons of crude oil now pollute the formerly pristine Coral Sea. Prevailing currents direct the spill toward one of the world's finest natural wonders, the thousand-mile-long Great Barrier Reef. Ecologists predict that, unless a miracle occurs, the delicate microscopic organisms that form the basis of the reef will be destroyed, and along with those organisms, the Great Barrier itself will be destroyed. As our correspondent in Brisbane explains, yet another magnificent and irreplaceable glory of our planet is about to cease to exist."

6

Australia

Captain Victor Malone, trembling, haggard, left the Brisbane courthouse where he'd been interrogated throughout the day about the mistaken directions he'd given his watch officer to avoid the reef that the *Argonaut* had struck. "Ten degrees *port*," he'd insisted he'd told his subordinates.

But ten degrees *starboard* is what his watch officer and helmsman insisted they'd heard. Fools! No, *cowards*! That's what they were! Damned disloyal *cowards*! They didn't have the guts to stand by their captain! Some of them even claimed they suspected he'd been drinking!

A good thing no one had thought to test his blood until twelve hours after the accident. The chemical analysis would be inconclusive. If a small trace of alcohol did show up in his blood, Malone could always claim that he'd had a drink to steady himself after the helicopter had flown him ashore.

As Malone left the courthouse and photographers snapped his picture, he raised his arm to shield his face and stumbled angrily down the courthouse steps through the crowd toward the car he'd hired to take him away. His muscles shuddered. A vodka martini, he kept assuring himself.

All I need is . . .

If I can manage to escape these bastard reporters . . .

A martini!

That'll set my mind straight!

Malone jabbed his elbow into a photographer's chest, shoved the doubled-over man aside, oblivious to his anguished moan, and reached the hired car. But the dark sedan was empty. Where the hell was the driver? Sure, Malone thought. The son of a bitch. He ran! The crowd made him panic! He's a coward, the same as my officers!

Malone lunged behind the steering wheel, slammed the door shut, jerked the ignition key, stomped the accelerator, and roared from the courthouse.

While he veered around a corner, grinning, free, eager to taste his martinis, his body erupted, as did his car.

The explosion—which he never heard—sprayed blood, bone, hair, and chunks of metal for thirty yards in every direction.

The site of the blast had been perfectly chosen. As Dan Rather explained the next evening, "It appears that the method was deliberate and selective. No one else was injured. Only the *Argonaut*'s captain died."

7

Hong Kong

Chandler Thompson, chief executive officer of the Pacific-Rim Petroleum Corporation, strained not to squint from the glare of television lights while he stood authoritatively straight behind a podium on a platform, addressing a throng of reporters in the conference room of Pac-Rim's headquarters. Forty-eight, with stern, chiseled features, he'd been extremely reluctant to agree to this press conference, but the mounting furor about the disaster left him no choice. He had to diffuse the controversy and bolster Pac-Rim's devastated reputation. His thousand-dollar suit was impeccably pressed. He'd made sure to button its coat before he strode with military bearing into the room and onto the platform.

"Were we aware that Captain Malone had a drinking problem? . . . No. It's stringent corporate policy that all of our crewmen abstain from alcohol while on duty and for twenty-four hours prior to boarding a Pacific-Rim vessel. . . . Do we test samples of their blood to insure that they abide by the rule? It's never seemed necessary. Our officers are rigorously screened before they're hired. We have utmost confidence in our personnel. Captain Malone's violation of the rules was a singular exception. There's no reason to question the professionalism of our other officers, but yes, from now on, we do intend to administer random blood tests to check for alcohol and drugs. . . . Have we any idea who's responsible for the murder of Captain Malone? The police continue to investigate. It would be premature for us to make unwarranted accusations. . . . Our delay in responding to the oil spill? *What* delay? The containment team snapped into action the moment we learned of the accident. . . . Insufficient staff? Lack of training and preparation? Minimal equipment? Nonsense. We were ready for any emergency. . . . One at a time, please. I didn't hear the question. . . . That's true. Several members of the containment team were at home asleep at the time of the accident, but our night-shift supervisor immediately alerted them. I assure you, from now on, our night crew will operate at the same strength as our day crew . . . . No, unfortunately we haven't been able to prevent the *Argonaut* from discharging more of its cargo. . . . Thirty million gallons to date? I regret to say that's correct. Efforts to keep the oil from spreading have so far proved futile. Portions of the Great Barrier Reef, to my great sorrow, have indeed been contaminated. . . . Repeat the question, please. . . . Yes, some containment equipment did malfunction. Rumors of disorganization? Confusion? A twenty-four-hour delay? Why didn't the *Argonaut* have a reinforced double hull so the reef couldn't rupture the cargo's interior wall? Before I answer further questions, I want to assure you that the Pacific-Rim Petroleum Corporation is a responsible, public-minded . . .''

Harried movements on Thompson's left distracted him. A nervous Pac-Rim executive stepped onto the platform, hurrying forward with a folded note. The executive's face was ashen. You idiot, Thompson thought. You'll ruin . . . ! For God's sake, don't you know enough not to interrupt me? We have to keep up a show of confidence. I was just about to . . . !

Repressing a furious scowl, Thompson took the note and mentally vowed to fire the executive the moment the press conference ended.

"Excuse me, ladies and gentlemen," Thompson told the reporters. Straining to look dignified, he opened the note, scanned its typewritten message, and instantly forgot his rage. His heart pumped so fast that he felt dizzy. He grasped the podium for support. The note seemed to swirl.

>Our Brisbane office reports Kevin Stark,
>director of containment planning,

Stark! Yet another executive whom Thompson planned to fire. The bastard's preparations for controlling a major oil spill had been abysmally inadequate. It was *Stark's* fault that containment procedures had been delayed because of insufficient staff and ill-maintained equipment. It was *Stark's* fault that the oil had reached and was killing the Great Barrier Reef.

>was found an hour ago, drowned, his body
>upside down in a barrel of oil.

Reporters responded to Thompson's evident shock and crowded toward him, shouting further questions. Still dizzy, suddenly thirsty, he groped for a glass of water on the podium. As Thompson swallowed the water, he noted its bitter aftertaste and abruptly gasped, fire coursing through his stomach. His legs felt knocked from under him. Photographers flashed more pictures. Video cameras whirred while Thompson dropped the glass, fell to his knees, clutched his stomach, gasped again, and pitched forward, dead before he hit the platform, but not before blood spewed from his mouth, spattering the front row of reporters.

8

Houston, Texas

Virgil Krause, the newly appointed chief executive officer of the Pacific-Rim Petroleum Corporation, urgently thrust documents into his briefcase, about to rush from his top-floor office in Pac-Rim's American headquarters. An hour from now, he was due at Houston's Intercontinental Airport, where a company jet made frantic preparations to speed him to Hong Kong. Krause was forty, in excellent health, known for his energy and resilience, but already the shock of his sudden promotion had made him breathless. He'd been able to spare just five minutes to phone his wife and explain his new responsibilities. She would join him in Hong Kong as soon as possible. Meanwhile, Krause anticipated an intense, mostly sleepless flight during which he would not only have to review the mistakes that had caused the *Argonaut* disaster but would also have to come up with solutions for cleaning the spill and avoiding another one.

More to the point, Krause wouldn't get much sleep on the flight because he feared that the promotion he'd so often prayed for would be his damnation.

Malone, Stark, and Thompson. Their brutal deaths had been as startling as the *Argonaut* disaster.

Will I be next? Krause thought, his hands trembling as he shut his briefcase.

A secretary intercepted Krause as he darted from his office. "This telegram just came for you, sir."

Krause crammed it into his suit-coat pocket. "Got to hurry. I'll read it on the plane."

"But the messenger said it was urgent. He insisted you read it as soon as possible."

Krause faltered, yanked the telegram from his pocket, and tore it open.

The three sentences made him more breathless.

Mistakes demand punishment. Don't let the *Argonaut* happen again. The Lord is your witness.

"GOD BLESS"

1

Manhattan

In her office on the fifteenth floor of a soot-dinged building on Broadway near Thirty-second Street, Tess Drake set a reproduction of a painting onto her desk. The painting, by an early nineteenth-century artist, was a colorful representation of a wooded slope in the Adirondack Mountains in upper New York State. Typical of his time, the artist had idealized the wilderness, making it so roman- tically lush, so idyllic and gardenlike that the painting seemed an advertisement for pioneers to settle there, an American Eden.

Next to the painting, Tess set a photograph, dated 1938, of a similar section of the Adirondack Mountains. Because of limitations in color photography during that period, the hues weren't as brilliant as in the painting. A further contrast was that the photograph didn't idealize the landscape but rather presented the forested peaks real- istically, the cluttered, chaotic woods more impressive as a con- sequence.

Finally Tess set down a photograph, taken last week, of the

slope depicted in the 1938 photograph, and now the contrast was startling, not because improvements in color photography made the hues vivid. Quite the contrary. The image was alarmingly drab, disturbingly lusterless. Except for a hazy blue sky, there were almost *no* colors. No green of lush foliage. Only a muddy brown, as if something had gone wrong when the film was developed, and indeed something *had* gone wrong, but it hadn't happened in the processing lab. It had happened in the air, in the clouds, in the rain. This section of the forest had been killed by acid in the water that was supposed to nourish it. The trees, denuded of leaves, looked obscenely skeletal, the grassless slope cursed.

Tess leaned back in disgust to study the sequence of images. They made their depressing point so effectively that the article she was preparing to write to accompany them couldn't possibly be as strong, although of course the article had to be written, just as she'd written God knew how many others on related environmental disasters, in the hope that people would at last respond to the global crisis. Her commitment explained why, despite lucrative employment offers from such mainstream publications as *Cosmopolitan* and *Vanity Fair*, she'd chosen to work for *Earth Mother Magazine*. She felt an obligation to the planet.

Granted—she readily admitted—it wasn't any sacrifice for her to be idealistic. At the age of twenty-eight, while most of her contemporaries seemed obsessed with money, she had the benefit of a trust fund from her late grandfather that gave her the freedom to be indifferent to the temptation of high-paying jobs. Ironically, that trust fund provided not only independence but a motive for her to devote herself to environmental causes, for the considerable money in that trust fund had come from her grandfather's extremely successful chemical factories, the improperly discarded wastes from which had killed rivers and contaminated drinking water throughout several sections of New Jersey and Pennsylvania. It gave Tess satisfaction to think that she was doing her best to make amends.

She was statuesque, five feet nine, with cropped blond hair, attractive glowing features, and a sinewy, sensuous figure that she kept in shape with a daily workout at a health club near her loft in SoHo. Her eyes were crystal blue, her only makeup a slight touch of lipstick. Jeans, sneakers, and a cotton pullover were her favorite clothes. She reached toward an apple in a well-stocked bowl on her desk, savored the taste of the fruit, sensed someone behind her, and turned toward a man in the open doorway to her office.

"Working late again?" The man's eyes crinkled. "You'll make me feel ashamed for going home." His name was Walter Trask. The editor of *Earth Mother Magazine*, he had his suit coat draped over the arm of his wrinkled white shirt. His top button and his tie were open. Fifty-five, portly, he had gray, thinning hair and paler-gray, sagging cheeks.

"Late?" Tess glanced at her watch. "Good Lord, is it seven o'clock already? I've been putting together my piece on acid rain. I guess I got so involved I—"

"Tomorrow, Tess. Give yourself a break and do it tomorrow. The planet will manage to survive till then. But *you* won't last much longer if you don't go easy on yourself."

Tess shrugged self-consciously. "I suppose I could use a swim."

Trask shook his head. "How I wish I had your energy."

"Vitamins and exercise."

"What I need is thirty less years. Have you read the papers? The murders at the Pac-Rim Corporation after the spill. What do you think?"

Tess raised her shoulders. "It's obvious."

"Oh?"

"The spill pissed somebody off."

"Sure." Trask sighed. "That's not what I meant. Do you think we should do a story on it?"

"*Earth Mother Magazine* isn't a tabloid. The spill's the story. Not the murders. They're a sidebar. A *small* one. Fanatics hurt our cause. Too many people think that *we're* fanatics, exaggerating the threat to—"

"Sure," Trask said again. "But our profit-and-loss statement's in the red. If we could . . . Well . . . Never mind. Lock up when you leave, will you, Tess? And *soon*, okay?"

"Word of honor."

"Good. See you tomorrow, kid." His shoulders stooped, Trask walked down the hallway, disappearing.

A half-minute later, Tess heard the elevator descend. She finished her apple, assessed the artwork for her article, and decided that Trask was right—she needed a break. But the trouble was, she knew that after her swim at the health club, after a shower, a walk home, a salad, a meatless tomato sauce on pasta (with plenty of mushrooms, onions, and green peppers), she'd still feel compelled to work on the article. So in spite of Trask's advice, she packed up her artwork and two boxes of research, slung her purse across her shoulder, hefted both boxes as well as her clipboard of legal-size yellow notepaper, used an elbow to shut off her office light switch, and proceeded along the hallway, elbowing other light switches as she passed them.

A further nudge of her elbow turned on the intruder alarm. Stepping back from the infrared beam, she fumbled to open and close the door, which locked behind her automatically. In a small waiting area, she nudged her arm against the elevator's button, sagged against the wall, heard the elevator rise, and finally admitted she was tired.

Fatigue, or fate. For whatever reason, when the doors hissed open and Tess stepped into the elevator, she lost her grip on her clipboard. It fell to the floor, dislodging the gold Cross pen she'd clipped onto it. The pen, a gift from her father on the day she'd entered college, had bittersweet significance—her father had never lived to see her graduate.

With a mournful twinge, she pressed the button marked LOBBY, felt the elevator sink, and stooped with her purse and boxes to grope for the clipboard and pen. Bent over, her hips angled into the air, she tensed when the elevator unexpectedly stopped. As its doors slid open, she peered backward, up past her knees, and a man loomed into view, casting a long shadow over her. Her awkward, undignified pose made Tess feel vulnerable, at the very least embarrassed. Nothing like presenting my better side, she thought.

But the man's good-natured smile put her instantly at ease. With a sympathetic shrug, he picked up her clipboard and pen, and although Tess realized it only later, his act of courtesy changed her life. In nightmarish days and weeks to come, Tess would compulsively reanalyze these next few moments and wonder if she'd never

37

dropped her clipboard and pen, maybe they'd never have started talking. Maybe none of the pain, grief, and terror would ever have happened.

But her conclusions were always the same. Events had controlled her. No matter the horrifying results, she couldn't have changed a thing any more than she'd have been able to repress the immediate attraction she felt toward this man. Absurd? Illogical? Yes. Call it chemistry, or call it vibrations. Call it a confluence of the planets or a merging of the stars. Whatever the explanation, her knees had felt weak, her groin warm, and she'd briefly feared that she might faint. But instead of sinking, she'd managed to straighten, face the man, and keep herself from wavering.

The man was tall, six feet one at least, and Tess, who was also tall, appreciated men whose shoulders weren't even with her own. He had healthy, glowing, tanned skin, and square-jawed, rugged, classically handsome features. His body was perfectly proportioned, muscular yet trim. His clothes were similar to hers. Sneakers, jeans, a blue cotton shirt, the collar of which projected from a burgundy cotton pullover. But his eyes, though. *They* were what Tess most noticed. They glinted with a radiance that seemed to come from his soul, and their color was unusual, gray, a tint that Tess had encountered only in the heroes of arousing romance novels that she'd read with guilty pleasure during her middle teens.

As she tried to look dignified, the stranger's good-natured smile persisted. "Tough day?"

"Not bad. Just long," Tess said.

The stranger pointed toward the boxes she held. "And apparently about to get longer."

Tess blushed. "I guess I try to do too much."

"That's better than doing too little." The stranger pressed the elevator button marked LOBBY and narrowed his eyes toward her pen. "Gold Cross," he said, noting the manufacturer's name. The words seemed to have particular significance for him. He attached the pen to the clipboard and gave them to her.

Briefly their hands touched. Static electricity must have leapt, for Tess's fingers tingled.

"You work for *Earth Mother Magazine?*" the stranger asked.

"How did you—?"

"The labels on those boxes."

"Oh, of course." Tess blushed again. "And you? You came from the floor below mine. There's only one business on that floor. A TV production firm. Truth Video."

"Right. By the way, I've read your magazine. It's excellent. In fact, I'm putting together a documentary that's related to your work—a video on the lack of sufficient safeguards at nuclear-waste sites. Between your work and mine, I can't think of anything more important."

"Than trying to save the planet?" Tess nodded, despondent. "If only more people felt the same way."

"Well, that's the problem, isn't it?"

"Oh?" Tess frowned. "I see so *many* problems. Which one do you—?"

"Human nature. I'm not sure the planet *can* be saved."

Tess felt surprised by his response.

The elevator stopped.

"Do you need help with those boxes?" the stranger asked.

"No, really, I can manage."

"Then let me hold open the lobby door."

They emerged to frenzied pedestrians, blaring traffic, acrid exhaust fumes, and a smog-dirtied sunset.

"This is what I mean." The stranger shook his head, sounding mournful. "I'm not sure the planet *can* be saved." He helped Tess hail a taxi, peered around as if in search of someone, told her "God bless," and walked briskly away, blending with the crowd, disappearing almost magically into it.

Tess's fingers still tingled.

2

The next morning, standing in the lobby waiting for the elevator, Tess glanced toward the right, noticed the stranger enter the building, and felt her cheeks flush.

"Well, hello again," he said.

Flustered by her attraction to him, doing her best to hide it, Tess managed a pleasant smile. "Nice morning."

"Isn't it, though? When I went for my run, a breeze cleared the air. There's still not much smog yet."

"You run?"

"Every day."

"Hey, so do I," Tess said.

"It shows."

Tess felt her cheeks flush even more.

"Good for the body," the stranger said, "good for the soul."

"I try."

They lapsed into silence.

The silence lengthened.

"This elevator." Tess sighed.

"Yes. Awfully slow. But I do my best to take everything as it comes."

"Sort of like 'patience is a virtue'?"

The man debated. "Let's call it a discipline."

The doors slid open.

"There. You see?" The stranger pointed. "Everything in time."

They entered the elevator.

"I promise not to drop anything," Tess said.

"I was pleased to help."

"But I didn't have a chance to thank you."

"Not necessary," the stranger said. "You'd have done the same thing for me."

Tess watched him push buttons for his floor, then hers, and noted with satisfaction that he didn't wear a wedding ring.

The stranger turned. "I suppose—if we're going to keep bumping into each other—we ought to introduce ourselves."

Tess loved the way his gray eyes twinkled. She told him her name, or at least her *first* name. By habit, she deliberately didn't mention that her last name was Drake because people occasionally associated it with her well-known father, and she felt upset whenever she had to talk about the brutal way he'd been killed.

"Tess?" The stranger cocked his head and nodded. "Beautiful. That's short for . . ."

"Theresa." Again she didn't tell the stranger the full truth. Although "Tess" was sometimes used as a shortened form of "Theresa," her nickname resulted from her father's teasing practice of calling her "Contessa Theresa" when she was a child. He'd finally shortened it lovingly to just "Tess."

"Of course," the dark-haired, strikingly handsome man said. "Theresa. The Spanish mystic, the originator of the Carmelite Order of nuns."

Tess blinked, surprised. "I didn't know. That is . . . I wasn't aware of "

"It doesn't matter. I've got a knack for collecting all sorts of useless information."

"And *your* name?" Tess asked.

"Joseph."

No last name, Tess noted, just as *she* hadn't volunteered hers. The elevator jerked to a stop.

"I guess it's time again for my penance," Joseph said.

"It can't be *that* bad. Last night, I got the impression you enjoyed your work."

"Documenting the decay of the planet? That's hardly enjoyable. Still, I do get satisfaction from trying to accomplish some good." Joseph left the elevator and turned to her, his face glowing. "God bless."

As the doors slid shut and Joseph disappeared, Tess's stomach sank, but not from the upward motion of the elevator.

3

The next day, Friday, Tess became so absorbed in her article that she worked through her lunch hour. At quarter after two, the rumbles in her stomach made her finally decide that her concentration would suffer if she didn't get something to eat.

When she entered the elevator, she thought of Joseph. Descending, it stopped at the floor below hers. Again, she tingled. No, she thought. This is just a coincidence.

But her knees went weak when the doors slid open and Joseph entered.

He grinned, apparently not at all surprised to see her. "Looks like we're destined to keep bumping into each other." He pressed the button marked LOBBY. "How's your penance?"

Standing close to him, feeling his arm against hers, Tess tried to control her breathing. "Penance?" Abruptly she remembered that he'd used that expression yesterday. "Oh, you mean my work. I'm doing an article on acid rain. It's going well."

"Can't ask for better than well."

"I . . ."

"Yes?"

"Don't you think it's odd, to say the least, that you and I decided to take the elevator at . . ."

"The same moment?" Joseph shrugged. "The world's an odd place. Long ago, I decided to accept fate instead of questioning it. Some things are meant to happen."

"Like kismet or karma?"

"Providence." Joseph's gray eyes glinted. "Late lunch?"

Tess smelled his after-shave lotion and couldn't keep her voice from quavering. "I lost track of time."

"Me, too. *Clock* time anyhow. There's a deli across the street. Care to join me?"

Gooseflesh prickled Tess's arms. "Only if it's Dutch treat."

Joseph spread his hands. "Whatever you like. But for me, it'll still be a treat."

Outside, on the noisy sidewalk, they waited for a break in traffic and darted across toward the deli. The afternoon was humid, the struggling sunlight dull with exhaust haze. As Tess reached the opposite sidewalk, she glanced toward Joseph and couldn't help noticing that, just as the first time she'd met him, he peered around as if searching for someone in the crowd. Why? She repressed a frown, wondering—influenced by her father's habits—did Joseph think that he was being watched? Come on, she told herself. This isn't a secret meeting. Get real.

The brightly lit deli, after the noon-hour rush, was only a quarter full.

"Our pastrami's very good today," the waiter said.

"Thanks. No meat, though," Joseph said. "I'd like your to-mato-sprouts-and-cucumber sandwich."

"Coleslaw? How about a dill pickle?"

"Might as well. And a bottle of mineral water."

"Sounds good," Tess said. "The same for me." When the waiter left, she studied Joseph. "No meat? You're a vegetarian?"

"It's not a big deal. Meat just doesn't agree with me. Besides, this is Friday."

Tess—a Roman Catholic—thought she understood the reference. Years ago, Catholics had not been allowed to eat meat on Friday. But only elderly, extremely conservative Catholics still obeyed that outmoded rule, and Joseph, like her, was young enough that he couldn't have been conditioned to abstain from meat on Friday for fear of committing a sin.

"The reason I asked"—Tess subdued her puzzlement—"is that I'm mostly a vegetarian, too."

"Well, that's something else we share in common."

"Like being Roman Catholic?"

Joseph frowned. "What makes you think I'm a Catholic?"

"No meat on Friday."

"Ah," Joseph said. "I see. No, I don't belong to that religion."

"Sorry. I apologize. I guess I'm asking too many questions."

"Don't worry about it. I'm not offended."

"Then as long as I'm . . . If you don't mind, let me ask you something else," Tess said.

"I'm waiting."

"Why did you look so nervous when you crossed the street?"

Joseph laughed. "In New York? With all the junkies and crazy drivers? Who *doesn't* look nervous?"

"One more question."

"Sure."

". . . Would you like to see me tomorrow?" Tess's boldness surprised her. Her heart skipped.

"Would . . . ?" Joseph concentrated, peered down at the table, toyed with his knife and fork, then focused his intense gray eyes upon her. "Of course. I'd enjoy your company very much."

Tess exhaled.

"But I have to be honest."

Damn, Tess thought. Here it comes. This is what I was afraid of. A man this gorgeous, he's probably going to tell me he's involved with someone.

"By all means." She straightened and pressed her hands on the table, preparing herself. "I appreciate honesty."

"We can only be friends."

"I'm not sure what . . ."

"What I mean is, we can never be lovers."

His frankness startled her. "Hey," Tess said, "I wasn't making a proposition. It's not like I asked you to go to bed."

"I know that. Really, your behavior's impeccable." Joseph reached across the table and tenderly touched her hand. She noticed he had a jagged scar on the back of his wrist. "I didn't mean to offend or embarrass you. It's just that . . . there are certain things about me you wouldn't understand."

"I think I *do* understand."

"Oh?"

"You're gay? Is that it?"

Joseph laughed. "Not at all."

"I mean, it wouldn't bother me or anything if you *are* gay. I'd just like to know. I don't want to make a bigger fool of myself than I already have."

"Believe me, Tess, I'm *not* gay, and you haven't made a fool of yourself."

"Then maybe you've had some kind of accident, and . . ."

"You mean, have I been emasculated? Hardly. The truth is, I'm extremely flattered that you want to spend time with me. But I have certain . . . well, let's call them obligations. I can't explain *what* they are or *why* I have to abide by them. You just have to trust and believe and accept. The point is, I welcome your friendship."

"Friendship?" Tess squirmed. "I once got rid of a persistent boy in high school by telling him that I only wanted him as a friend."

"But this isn't high school," Joseph said. "If you want my companionship . . . and I'd enjoy yours . . . I hate to sound formal, but those are my terms."

"Listen." Tess bit her lip. "Maybe we ought to forget it."

"Why? Because you can't imagine a male-and-female relationship that doesn't result in sex?" Joseph asked.

"God, I feel like such an idiot."

"Don't," Joseph said. "You're a healthy, intelligent, attractive woman with normal desires. But I'm"—Joseph's gaze intensified—"totally different."

"You'll get no argument. And maybe that's why . . ." She couldn't believe she was saying this. "I want to *be* with you."

"Platonically," Joseph said.

"All right. Sure. For now. But who knows . . . ?"

"No, Tess. Not just for now, but always. Trust me, that way is better."

"Why?"

"Because it's eternal."

"You're the strangest man I ever met," Tess said.

"I'll accept that as a compliment."

"Okay." Tess increased her resolve. "What time tomorrow?"

"Ten A.M.?" Joseph suggested. "The upper East Side. Carl Schurz Park. Off Eighty-eighth Street. Next to the mayor's house."

"I know it."

"There's a jogging track beside the river. Since we exercise every day, we might as well do it together."

"Swell," Tess said. "So we jog, and I work off my attraction to you?"

"Exercise works wonders, my platonic friend."

"Maybe for you."

Joseph grinned with good nature. "It's like a cold shower."

"I have to warn you," Tess said. "I'll do my best to tempt you."

"It won't do any good," Joseph said. "Really, I'm untemptable."

"I consider that a challenge."

4

Even at ten A.M., the jogging track off the wooded park next to the East River was crowded. The absence of commuter traffic freed the air of smog and exposed an unfamiliar glorious sky. Senior citizens sat on benches, enjoying the weekend's peace. On the left, in a court past a waist-high, wrought-iron fence, teenagers played basketball. Sunbathers spread blankets on grass, enjoying the unusually intense June sun. People walked dogs among the trees. What a gift, Tess thought. What a beautiful day. How rare.

She'd worn a blue jogging suit that complemented the turquoise color of her eyes. Although loose, it managed to reveal her figure, her lean, lithe body and firm, upwardly tilted breasts. A red sweatband encircled her forehead, emphasizing her short blond hair. She leaned her taut hips against the railing that separated the jogging track from the river and studied the runners surging past, many of whom listened to earphones attached to miniature radios strapped to their waists. Her own preference was not to be distracted by music but instead to devote herself exclusively to the high she gained from prolonged exercise. The Zen-like pleasure on the runners' sweating faces made her eager to join them. Soon, she thought. Joseph will be here anytime.

As she waited, she continued to be amazed by her irresistible attraction to him. Certainly he was good-looking, but Tess had gone out with many good-looking men and had never felt so intense an identification with them. Most had been so aware of their looks that she couldn't bear their egos. She'd discovered that one had been seeing three other women while pretending that Tess was the only woman he cared about. Another had been an up-and-coming TV executive whose primary interest in Tess was having someone to tell him how great he was while he gained power.

For the past six months, she hadn't gone out with anyone. Maybe that explained her attraction to Joseph, Tess thought. A combination of overwork and loneliness. But the more she considered that explanation, the more she dismissed it. There was something—she couldn't find the proper words—different about him. A handsome man who wasn't in love with his handsomeness, who treated her with deference, who was easy to talk to, who related to her as a human being, not a potential sexual conquest. All of that certainly counted. Even so, she'd never before been this insistent and candid to a man about her interest in him. Why? There was something *else* about him. What *was* it? The unfamiliar sensation not only puzzled but disturbed her.

She didn't know which direction Joseph would come from, right or left, or straight ahead through the wooded park, so she turned her gaze often, watching for him. We should have chosen a specific spot to meet, she decided, and continued to scan the crowd. Still, there's no one nearby on either side of me. Joseph shouldn't have any trouble noticing where I am.

Because she'd looked forward to spending time with him, Tess had arrived here early, at quarter to ten, but now as she glanced at her jogger's watch, she was troubled to see that it was quarter *after* ten.

Had they failed to see each other?

She studied the crowd more intensely. Then her watch showed half past ten and with frustrating slowness eleven o'clock, and she told herself that something important must have delayed him.

47

But when her watch showed eleven-thirty, then noon, she angrily understood the explanation for his absence.

This had happened to her only once, in her junior year of college, her date having gotten so drunk at a Saturday-afternoon frat party that he'd become too sick to take her to a movie that night and hadn't bothered to phone to explain he wasn't coming. That had been the end of *that* relationship.

And now Joseph, too, had stood her up. She couldn't believe it. Disappointment fought with fury.

Fury won.

The son of a . . . ! He'd seemed too good to be true, and that's exactly what he *was*. Tess, we can only be friends? Well, buddy, you blew it. We're *not* friends.

Seething, Tess joined the stream of joggers, too distraught to bother with the preliminary ritual of stretch and warm-up exercises, her anger so fueling her long, urgent stride that she outdistanced the fastest runners.

Bastard.

5

Sunday was dreary. A dismal rain reinforced Tess's depression. Barefooted, wearing the shorts and rumpled T-shirt that she'd slept in, she sipped from a steaming cup of strong black coffee and scowled from a window of her loft in SoHo. Three floors down, across the street, a drenched, pathetic cat found shelter under a seesaw in a small playground.

Behind her, the television was on, a Cable News Network anchorwoman somberly reporting the latest environmental disaster. In Tennessee, a train pulling twenty cars of anhydrous ammonia, a toxic gas shipped in the form of a pressurized liquid and used in the manufacture of fertilizer, had reached a rural section of ill-maintained tracks and toppled down an embankment. The tanks had burst, and the cargo had vaporized, spewing a massive poisonous cloud that so far had killed the entire train crew, sixteen members of families on local farms, dozens of livestock, hundreds of wild animals, and thousands of birds. A northeastern wind was directing the dense white cloud toward a nearby town of fifteen thousand people, all of whom were fleeing in panic. Emergency workers were powerless to stop the cloud and unprepared to organize so huge an evacuation. At last count, eight motorists had been killed and another sixteen critically injured in car accidents due to the chaos of the town's frantic attempt to escape. Eventually, the anchorwoman reported, the heavy gas would settle to the ground, but paradoxically, although anhydrous ammonia was used to make fertilizer, it wouldn't benefit the land. Not unless diluted. Instead, its present, extremely concentrated nitrogen level (82 percent) would sear hundreds of acres of woodland as well as destroy crops and become absorbed into streams, wells, ponds, and reservoirs, poisoning the town's water supply.

Tess drooped her shoulders, turned off the television, and frowned up toward the monotonous unnerving gusts of rain on her skylight. She shuddered with the realization of how even more disastrous, almost unimaginably so, the accident would have been if it had happened near a major urban area. *One* day, though, that's exactly where it *will* happen, she knew. Because of carelessness, poor planning, badly maintained equipment, government lethargy, greed, stupidity, overpopulation, and . . . Tess shook her head. So many reasons. *Too* many. Piece by piece, the earth was dying, and there didn't seem any way to stop it.

A line from one of Yeats's poems occurred to her: "Things fall apart; the center cannot hold." She felt exhausted. Abandoning her plan to go to her health club this morning, she decided she needed a long hot bath. I've been pushing myself too hard. What I ought to do is curl up in bed and read the Sunday *Times*.

But the news would only depress her further, she knew.

Then watch some old movies, she told herself. Rent some Cary Grant screwball comedies.

But she doubted that she'd do much laughing. How could she

laugh when . . . ? Without minimizing the gravity of what had happened in Tennessee, she admitted, reluctantly, that part of her depression was the consequence of her bitterness that Joseph had failed to meet her yesterday.

Her anger still smoldered. Why would he—?

Joseph hadn't seemed the type to be rude. Okay, I admit, I came on awfully strong. I kept trying to get him to say that we could be *more* than friends. I overreacted. I probably scared him away.

In that case—her indignation flared—the least Joseph could have done was *phone* and explain that he'd had second thoughts and didn't plan to show up. He didn't need to keep me waiting.

Phone you? Tess suddenly thought. Your number isn't listed! And even if it were, you never told him your last name! For all you know, he had a legitimate reason not to meet you, but he didn't have a way to get in touch and tell you about it.

Should I swallow my pride and call him?

Dummy, you don't know *his* last name any more than he knows *yours*.

6

Monday, self-conscious, Tess almost expected to see Joseph enter the lobby while she waited for the elevator, but *this* time, a coincidence didn't happen. In her office, she tried to concentrate on her article, glancing frequently from her computer toward the telephone.

Whenever it rang, she tensed, hoping it would be Joseph, disappointed when it wasn't. By eleven-thirty, frustration made her check the yellow pages for Truth Video's number. She picked up the phone, only to slam it down.

What's wrong with me? I'm the one who got stood up. Why should I call *him?* Have I lost my pride? Do I need to *beg* for an apology?

At two, when she went for lunch, she again wondered if she'd see him in the elevator, but the car passed Truth Video's floor without stopping. On impulse, she decided to eat at the deli across the street. No sign of Joseph.

Thinking of him, she ordered what both of them had eaten on Friday: a tomato-sprouts-and-cucumber sandwich.

She didn't see him waiting back at the elevator, didn't receive a call from him in her office, and didn't cross paths with him when she left the bulding just after seven.

Screw him! He'd had his chance!

But Tuesday, when she still didn't see him and he *still* didn't phone, she banged down the gold Cross pen she'd been using to edit the printout of her manuscript and decided that an apology was exactly what she wanted.

In fact, she demanded it!

Not on the phone, though. No, by God. She wanted to see him squirm.

She wanted him to

The son of a bitch had to apologize in person.

7

Truth Video had a narrow reception area separated from its offices by a thick glass wall and door. A secretary peered up from a desk and spoke to Tess through a slot in a window, her hand poised to press a button that would free the electronically controlled lock on the door. "May I help you?"

Tess's determination wavered.

Don't be a fool! He'll think you're—

Think I'm *what?*

Chasing him? He should be so damned lucky!

Taking a breath, Tess forced herself to look businesslike, not at all angry.

Inwardly, though, she smiled. When I see the creep, when the secretary hears what I tell him and the gossip gets around . . .

"By all means, yes. I'm looking for a man who works here. I don't know his last name, but his first name's Joseph."

The receptionist nodded, although her eyes looked puzzled. "There's only one Joseph who works here. You must mean Joseph Martin."

"Martin?" Tess mentally repeated the name. "Early thirties? Tall? Trim? Dark hair? Gray eyes?"

"Yeah, that's him, all right."

"Well, if he hasn't gone to lunch, would you kindly tell him I'd like to speak with him?"

"Sorry." The receptionist frowned. "I don't know if he's having lunch, but he certainly isn't here."

"Great. Then I'll try again later. Any idea when he'll be back?"

"Well, that's the question, isn't it?"

"I don't understand."

"Joseph hasn't reported for work since he left the office on Friday."

"What?"

"We haven't seen him yesterday or today," the receptionist said. "He didn't call in to tell us he was sick or had a family emergency or . . . He just never showed."

Tess felt off-balance.

"The editing department's been frantic to meet a deadline without his help, and . . ."

Tess's anger no longer mattered. She pressed her fingertips against the window. "Why didn't you phone him?"

"That's another problem. If he's got a phone, he never put his number on his employment sheet." The receptionist studied her. "Are you a friend of his?"

"In a strange sort of . . ."

The receptionist shrugged. "It figures. Joseph's strange

enough. Look, if you run into him, why not give us a break and tell him to call? We can't find his notes for the project we're working on. The editing department's climbing the walls to find those notes and meet their deadline.''

"But didn't anyone go to Joseph's home?"

The receptionist strained to look patient. "I told you we can't find his notes. But the messenger we sent over says that no one lives at the address Joseph gave us.''

"What's the address?"

"It doesn't matter," the receptionist said. "Believe me, it won't help.''

Tess again raised her voice. "I asked you, *what's the address?"*

The receptionist tapped her pen against her chin. "You're wasting your time, but if it means that much to you . . .''

"It does mean that much to me.''

"You *sure* must be a friend of his." The receptionist exhaled, flipped through a Rolodex, and gave an address on Broadway.

Tess scribbled it down.

"I'm telling you, though," the receptionist said. "It's . . .''

"I know. A waste of time.''

8

But when Tess got out of the taxi to confront the blaring horns and noxious fumes of congested traffic on Broadway near Fiftieth Street, she began to wonder. Comparing the address on the dismal building before her to the numbers she'd written on her notepad, she understood—with belated apologies to the receptionist—why she'd been told she'd be wasting her time.

The building had a tourist-trap, overpriced camera-and-electronics shop on the bottom floor. The second floor had a dusty window with a sign: SEXUAL EDUCATORS. The third-floor windows were all painted black. God alone knew what *they* hid, but Tess braced her shoulders, determined to find out. Because the address she'd been given had specified a number on the third floor.

She stepped around a drunk, or more likely a junkie, passed out on the sidewalk, entered a hallway that stank of urine, climbed equally foul-smelling stairs, mustered the confidence to ignore the oppressive absence of lights, and reached the gloomy third floor. The names of businesses on various doors reinforced her increasingly despondent certainty that this building was strictly commercial, that neither Joseph nor anyone else would have an apartment here.

But then why, she brooded, convinced that something was wrong, had Joseph told his employer that this was his address?

She found an open door with a number on its grimy frosted glass that matched the third-floor number on her notepad.

Inside, she studied a frizzy-haired woman with too much lipstick who sat behind a desk. The woman chewed gum while reading a paperback. On every wall, from floor to ceiling, there were eight-inch-square cubicles with closed metal hatches that had numbers and locks.

Tess haltingly approached the desk.

The woman kept reading.

"Excuse me," Tess said.

The woman turned a page.

Tess cleared her throat. "If you don't mind . . ."

The woman splayed her book on the desk and frowned upward.

"I'm looking for . . ." Tess shook her head. "There isn't a sign on the door. What kind of business *is* this?"

The woman gnawed her gum. "A mail service."

"I don't . . ."

"Like a post-office box? The mailman brings it. I sort it. I put it in those slots. The customers pick it up."

"Have you ever heard of . . . ? I'm looking for a man named Joseph Martin."

"Sorry. It doesn't ring any bells."

"Maybe if I described him?"

"Honey"—the woman raised a chubby hand—"before you get started, I'm just a temp. The regular gal got sick. Appendix or something. I don't know any Joseph Martin."

"But he told his employer that this is where he lives."

The woman chortled. "Sure. Maybe he sneaks in at night and sets up a cot. Come on, I told you this is a mail service. What this Martin guy probably meant was this is where he wanted his check sent."

Tess's pulse quickened. "If he's one of your customers . . ."

"Maybe yes. Maybe no. I just started this morning. No one named Joseph Martin came in."

"But if he *is* a customer, could you find out if he picked up his mail on Saturday or Monday?"

The woman squinted. "Nope."

"Why not?"

"Because that information's confidential, honey. When I started this morning, the guy who hired me made sure I got two points. First, I have to get ID from customers before I let them unlock their box. And second, I'm not allowed to give out information about the clients. There's too many process servers." The woman eyed Tess with suspicion.

"I'm not a process server."

"So *you* say."

"Look, I'm just worried about my friend. He's been missing since Friday, and . . ."

"You say. Me? I have to protect my buns. If this gal I replaced gets sick enough to quit or die or something, maybe I can make this a permanent job. So why not get lost, huh? For all I know, you work for my boss and he sent you here to check out if I'm doing what he told me. So look for your friend somewhere else."

9

In a taxi on the way back to work, Tess trembled, frustrated. She tried to assure herself that she'd done her best. If Joseph had decided to quit his job and drop out of sight, that wasn't her concern, she told herself.

But despite her insistence, she couldn't ignore the queasy churning in her stomach. Suppose Joseph's disappearance had something to do with *her*.

Don't kid yourself, she thought. Nobody quits his job just to escape a woman who was too insistent about starting a relationship.

Anyway, Joseph *didn't* quit his job. The receptionist at Truth Video said he never called in to explain why he wouldn't be at work.

So what? That doesn't prove a thing. Lots of people quit their jobs without calling in to say they've quit. They just never show up again.

But Joseph didn't seem that irresponsible, Tess thought.

Sure, just like he didn't seem the type to stand you up? Stop being naive. You met him only three times. You really don't know anything about him. You admitted—in fact you told him—he's the strangest man you ever met. Even the receptionist at Truth Video called him strange. And maybe that's why you're attracted to him.

Tess bit her lip. Admit something else. You're concerned because you think something might have happened to him. For all you know, he's sick at home, too weak to phone for help. That explanation would certainly soothe your wounded pride.

Tess sagged in the backseat of the taxi.

What's wrong with me? Do I actually hope he's too sick to make a phone call?

On the taxi's radio, an announcer gave a tense update about the toxic-gas disaster in Tennessee. Three hundred dead. Eight hundred critically injured. Fields littered with thousands of dead animals and birds. Already the forests and crops were turning brown from the caustic effects of the poisonous cloud's searing nitrogen. The Environmental Protection Agency, among many other government agencies, had rushed investigators to the nightmarish scene with orders to search for the cause of the train's derailment. Their conclusions so far—according to an unnamed but highly placed informant—indicated that budget cuts at the financially troubled Tennessee railway had resulted in understaffed maintenance crews. The railway's owner could not be reached for comment, although rumors suggested that his recent divorce—costly and caused by an affair with one of his secretaries—had distracted him from crucial business decisions. As well, the foreman of the maintenance crew was reputed to have a cocaine addiction.

Jesus, Tess thought. While I'm worrying about a possibly sick man who stood me up, the planet gets worse.

A gruff voice intruded on her thoughts.

"What?" Tess straightened. "I'm sorry. I didn't . . . ."

"Lady." The taxi driver scowled. "I told you we're here. You owe me four bucks."

10

Surprised to discover that she'd been gone from the office for almost two hours, Tess tried to concentrate on the revisions she'd made in her article, but as she jotted notes for a possibly stronger last paragraph, she found herself staring at her gold Cross pen. She remembered the day her father had given it to her and how dropping it had been the catalyst that brought Joseph and her together.

Abruptly she stood, left her office, proceeded along a row of other offices, and stopped at the end of the corridor, at the open door of the final office. With equal suddenness, she felt her determination wither. Because what she saw was Walter Trask, the fif-tyish, portly, avuncular editor of *Earth Mother Magazine*, hunched over his desk, rubbing his temples and shaking his head at what looked like financial statements.

Tess turned to leave.

But Trask must have felt her presence. Shifting his worried gaze toward the open door, he changed expressions and smiled. "Hey, kid, how are you?"

Tess didn't answer.

"Come on, what's the matter?" Trask leaned back and raised his hands. "You're always so cheery. It can't be *that* bad. Get in here. Sit. Stretch your legs. Talk to me."

Tess frowned and entered.

"What is it?" Trask raised his eyebrows. "Trouble with your article?"

"Trouble? Yes." She sank toward a chair. "But not with the article."

"Which means it might be . . . ?" Trask raised his eyebrows higher.

"Personal." Tess felt a greater hesitation. "This is embar-rassing. Maybe I shouldn't have . . ."

"Nonsense. That's why my door is always open. Personal problems always result in *professional* problems. When my staff's unhappy, the magazine suffers. Talk to me, Tess. You know I'm fond of you. Think of me as a confessor. And I hope I don't need to add—anything said in this room, believe me, goes no further."

Tess tried not to fidget. Given her late father's background, she knew she ought to be more sophisticated about certain matters. "What I wanted to ask . . . You know these companies that hold mail for people?"

Trask narrowed his gaze, emphasizing the furrows around his eyes. "Hold mail for people?"

"Sort of like post-office boxes, except they're not in a post office."

"Ah, yes, now I . . . mail services. Sure," Trask said. "What about them?"

Tess's stomach hardened. "Who uses them? Why?"

Trask leaned forward, considered her, then ordered his

thoughts. "That all depends. Quick-buck mail-order outfits for one. The kind that advertise in the back of supermarket tabloids and sex magazines. You want a genuine World War Two Nazi bayonet or an inflatable, life-sized, anatomically correct female doll? What you do is send your check to such and such an address. The creep who placed the ad picks up his mail at one of those services, lets the scam last three or four months until he figures his customers are impatient enough to call the police, and then he skips town with all the cash. Of course, there were never any bayonets or inflatable dolls."

"But . . ." Tess gripped her thighs. "Why make it so complicated? Why not just use an official post-office box?"

"Because"—Trask raised his shoulders—"I know this is hard to imagine, *some* people who read those ads in the tabloids and magazines are smart enough to smell a scam if the company they're tempted to send the check to doesn't have a permanent-looking address. Besides, those con artists risk being charged with mail fraud. The last thing they want is to go near a post office, where a clerk might wonder about hundreds of letters addressed to vaguely suggestive names. World War Two Collectibles and Home Anatomical Education."

"Okay." Tess frowned. "In a sick way, that makes sense. But surely there are other reasons to use these places." She suddenly remembered what the frizzy-haired woman had told her. "To stay away from process servers?"

"You figured that out? You bet," Trask said. "A guy who's afraid of being served with a summons to testify in court, or who's running from a lawsuit, or who hasn't been paying his child support and doesn't want his wife to know where he lives."

Tess considered and shook her head. "I still don't . . . Wouldn't a process server merely wait around until his target came in to get his mail?"

"Process servers get paid for results," Trask said. "They know a mail drop's trouble. I mean, they could wait around for days, maybe *weeks*, and still not . . . If someone's really nervous about being found, all he has to do is pay to have the service forward his mail to another address. Mind you, there *are* legitimate reasons to use a mail service instead of a post-office box."

Tess waved her hands for Trask to continue.

"Why is this so important to you?" Trask asked.

"Please!"

"Okay, so maybe your job takes you out of the country a lot, and you don't want to depend on the post office to forward your mail. Or maybe you live in another state, but for legal reasons, you need a corporate address in New York City. Or maybe you own a legitimate mail-order business, but you're well aware of the resistance that potential customers have to temporary-looking post-office-box numbers. There are *many* legitimate reasons. But basically, in my experience, seven times out of ten someone uses a mail service because—"

"They don't want anyone to know where they live."

"You got it," Trask said.

Tess stared at her gold Cross pen. "Thanks."

"Whatever your problem is . . . Listen, kid, I don't want to pry, but I hate to see you looking so dejected. Since I've answered *your* question, return the favor and answer mine. I might be able to help. Why is this important to you?"

Tess slumped, shaking her head. "I . . . It's just that . . . Well, I found out a friend of mine . . . at least, *sort* of a friend . . . uses one of these services."

"A 'friend'?" Trask assessed the word. "Are you saying this friend's a man?"

Tess nodded glumly.

"Oh." Trask's voice dropped.

"I was supposed to meet him on Saturday, but he didn't show up, and he didn't report for work this week."

"Oh." Trask's voice dropped lower.

"And now I'm trying to find out why."

"Be careful, Tess."

"I can't help it. My pride's involved. I need to know what happened to him."

"Well, maybe . . ." Trask sighed.

"What?"

"This is just a guess. But it could be you don't want to hear."

"Tell me."

"Maybe, if he didn't want someone to find him, *whoever* he

didn't want to find him—an ex-wife who hasn't been getting her alimony, for instance—might have gotten too close. It's possible your friend was forced to move on.''

Tess shoved her pen in her purse. "I'm sorry I interrupted you. Thanks, Walter. I've taken too much of your time. I'll let you get back to work.'' She stood.

"No, Tess, please, wait. I told you I might be able to help. Perhaps you didn't know, but before I founded *Earth Mother Magazine*, when I worked for the *Times*, I was their expert in tracking down reluctant sources.''

"Then how do I find him?''

"Top line first. Given the implications of the mail service your friend used, are you absolutely sure you *want* to find him? Think it over.''

"Yes, I'm sure.''

"Should I take it that means you're in love with him?''

Tess hesitated. "Yes. No. Maybe.'' She swallowed, despite a constriction in her throat. "I'm so confused. God help me, what I do know is I'm worried about him and I want to be with him.''

"A clear enough answer. Okay, my friend, I could write down a list of people and places for you to check. But you'd find it exhausting and time-consuming, not to mention a pain in the ass, to go through them all. Besides, you're a good enough reporter that you've probably already thought of them. So I'll save you the hassle and cut to the bottom line. I'm going to let you in on a secret. Because you confided in me, *I'll* confide in you. But just as I'll keep *your* confession in confidence, I take for granted you'll keep *mine*. Word of honor?''

"Yes.''

"I know I can count on you. This is the reason I was so legendary at the *Times* for being able to track down reluctant sources.'' Trask wrote two words on a piece of paper.

Tess frowned at them. " 'Lieutenant Craig'?''

"He works for Missing Persons. Central Division. One Police Plaza. Just mention my name. If he doesn't cooperate, tell him I said to remind him of nineteen eighty-six.''

"Nineteen eighty—?''

"Six. I doubt you'll have to remind him, though. He owes me

a favor he's well aware he can't ever completely repay, and unless he's had a lobotomy, he'll stop whatever he's doing and give your problem his full attention. But if he doesn't, let me know. Because in that case, I'll send him a copy of a letter—along with some audiotapes—that'll give his memory one hell of a jolt, I guarantee.''

11

Lieutenant Craig was a tall, beefy man, late thirties, with tousled hair, a ruggedly handsome face, and sharply creased cheeks that gave his mouth a pinched expression.

When he heard Trask's name, his dour look intensified. ''Swell. Just swell. The finishing touch on a crummy day.'' Craig wore a rumpled suit that matched his haggard features. ''That leech is a . . . Never mind. You don't want to know my opinion of him. My language would ruin *your* day. So what's that bloodsucker got in mind *this* time?'' Squinting toward Tess, Craig gestured toward a stout wooden chair in front of his cluttered desk.

Tess sat, trying to ignore the phones that rang constantly at desks behind her, detectives answering the calls while pecking at typewriters and computer keyboards. ''Well, actually''—she tasted bile, ill at ease—''Walter, I mean Mr. Trask, doesn't want anything.''

Craig closed one eye and squinted more severely with the other. ''Then why did he tell you to mention his name?''

''I guess because''—Tess clutched the arms of the chair, needing to steady her hands—''he figured you'd give me extra help.''

Craig laughed, a crusty outburst that sounded like a cough. ''Hey, I'm here to serve the public. No kidding. I'm really a devoted civil servant. Rich or poor, young or old, male or female, white, black, Chicano, Christian, Jewish, or Muslim—did I touch all the bases?—regardless of race or creed, et cetera, everyone who shows up in this office gets my full and complete attention. Unless of course they're relatives of politicians, and then I *really* snap to attention." The lieutenant laughed again and abruptly did cough. "Damned allergies. So, fine, you need my help and Walter sent you here. So what can I do for you?"

Tess glanced toward the ceiling.

"Look, whatever it is, don't let it embarrass you. I've heard it all before and then some, believe me."

"It's not that I'm embarrassed exactly," Tess said.

"Then . . . ?"

"It's just that . . . Now that I'm here, I'm not sure . . . I mean . . ."

"Hey, it's almost six. I'm supposed to be off duty. *Why did you want to see me?*"

"It seemed awfully serious a couple of hours ago, but involving the police . . ."

"Sure, I understand. There's serious, and then there's *serious*," Craig said. "The thing is—count on me—it's my job to tell the difference. So long as you *are* here, you might as well explain why you're clutching the arms of your chair so tightly. Hey, lady, take advantage of the taxes you pay. Unburden your soul. What's the worst that can happen?"

"You can make me think I'm wasting your time."

"Not likely," Craig said. "The truth is, I love it when people waste my time. It gives me enormous satisfaction to tell the taxpayers they're worried for nothing. Think of it this way. After you talk to me, I could reassure you enough—it's possible—that you might even get a good night's sleep."

Tess felt her stomach harden. "But suppose what I tell you gets a friend of mine in trouble with . . ."

"The law? Look, the way we do this is, first we discuss your problem. *Then* we decide what's next. But if I understand the reason Walter sent you here, it's not to make waves but to smooth the waters. So if it's possible, let's keep the law out of this. That's not a guarantee. What I said was, if it's possible."

Tess nodded, surprised that she'd grown to like this man. "All right, I'll give it a try." Amazed, she released her hands from the arms of the chair. "There's a man I know . . ."

It took her awhile.

"Don't stop. Keep going," Craig said.

With delicate prompting and a welcome cup of coffee, Tess finally finished her story.

"Good." Craig set down his pen. *"Better* than good. Impressive. An excellent description. But after all, you work for Walter, so I take it for granted you're a skilled reporter with a wonderful memory." The lieutenant studied his notes. "Yes. Gray eyes. Extremely unusual. . . . And the last time you saw him was Friday? . . . And he uses a mail service? . . . And his employer doesn't have his home phone number? . . . And he has a habit of glancing nervously around him?"

"Yes."

"If you don't mind, I have one, no, *two* more questions."

Tess felt exhausted. "What *are* they?"

"Your home and work addresses. And your telephone numbers, both places."

Tess wrote them down.

"A day or two, and I'll be in touch."

"That's it? You'll be in *touch?*"

Craig coughed again. "What do you think, I use a crystal ball or a Ouija board? For starters, I've got to phone the hospitals, the morgue."

"Morgue?"

"You mean you never . . . ?"

"I've been trying not to think about . . ."

"Well, it's always a possibility. That's where we start. Of course, there are *other* possibilities, *other* reasons why a man would disappear. You put me in an awkward . . . Hey, there's always . . ."

"What?"

"Always hope." Craig straightened the files on his desk. "But in conscience, I ought to warn you . . ."

"About?"

"A man who keeps checking behind him?" Craig stood. "Never mind. We'll talk."

"All of a sudden"—Tess stood as well—"I don't want to."

"Yes, that's what my former wife used to say. But you and I *will* talk. Soon. I promise. In the meantime, I suggest you see a movie, get drunk, whatever'll help you relax enough to sleep."

12

Tess seldom drank, and this hardly seemed a good time to start to rely on alcohol, but a long swim and a fifteen-minute sauna did relax her, loosening her tension-knotted muscles. At nine, when she returned to her loft, she felt exhausted enough that, after a salad, she went to bed. But her mind wouldn't shut down. She kept recalling, reexperiencing, the troubling events of the day. Joseph? What had happened to him?

Why had he guarded his privacy so much?

When would Lieutenant Craig phone?

Tense again, she tried to read but couldn't concentrate on the new Ann Beattie novel. She turned on the television and frequently switched channels, impatient with the forced cheery conversations on what seemed an endless stream of talk shows. It wasn't until after two that she finally managed to sleep, but her dreams weren't restful.

At work Wednesday morning, she had a headache that aspirins did nothing to soothe. Regardless, she strained to focus her thoughts on her new assignment, an article about the overuse of herbicides and pesticides on Midwestern farms and the recent discovery that those poisons had passed through the soil and now were present in alarming quantities in the water supply of various cities. Each time the phone rang, she lunged to pick it up, hoping to hear Joseph's voice, simultaneously dreading what she might be told if the voice wasn't Joseph's but instead belonged to—

"Ms. Drake?"

"Speaking." Tess winced, recognizing the gravelly voice.

"This is Lieutenant Craig."

"Yes?" She squeezed the phone with one hand while using the other to massage her throbbing forehead.

"I promised I'd call as soon as possible," the lieutenant said. "Are you free to take off work and go for a drive?"

Tess felt dizzy and closed her eyes.

"Ms. Drake?"

"Call me Tess, please." Yesterday, Craig hadn't commented on her last name, apparently not associating it with her father. To simplify matters, she didn't want him to make the connection, which he might if he repeated "Drake" often enough. "Have you found something?"

"Why don't we talk about it in the car? Is fifteen minutes too soon? I'll pick you up outside your building."

"Fine." Tess's throat cramped. "Sure. That's fine."

"Don't look for a cruiser. To keep you from feeling self-conscious, I'll use an unmarked car. Just wait at the curb."

Tess set down the phone and shuddered.

Outside, on the busy, noisy, exhaust-acrid sidewalk, she paced. Ten minutes later, exactly when promised, a brown Chrysler sedan stopped in front of her, the lieutenant waving for her to get in.

The moment she sat beside him and buckled her seat belt, Craig steered out expertly into a small break in traffic.

Tess studied his face, trying to read his thoughts. "Well?"

The husky lieutenant coughed. "Rotten throat. My doctor says I might have asthma. No wonder, this crummy air."

"You're avoiding my question."

"Just making conversation. It never hurts to be pleasant. Okay, here's the thing. What I've got is good news and maybe bad news."

"I believe," Tess said, "that my line's supposed to be, I'll take the good news first."

"Right. That never hurts either." Craig turned off Broadway, heading east on Thirtieth Street. "I checked all the hospitals. You never know—your friend might have had an accident, been hit by a car, maybe had a stroke, a heart attack, whatever, and be in a coma. If he wasn't carrying a wallet at the time, the hospital personnel wouldn't be able to identify him.''

"And since this is supposed to be the *good* news," Tess said, "I gather you didn't find my friend at any hospital."

"Plenty of coma patients, but not anyone who matches your description of him."

"Well, that's some reassurance, at least."

Craig raised a hand from the steering wheel. "Not necessarily. I checked only the hospitals in the metropolitan area. If your friend took a trip this weekend, to New Jersey, let's say, or Pennsylvania or up to Connecticut, and if he did have an accident that put him into a coma, I wouldn't know about it yet. These days, almost everything's in computers, but it still takes a while to get access to those other states' hospital records. I've got someone working on that, incidentally. But my hunch is, gut feeling, we'll come up negative. That's not a promise, mind you. Just a—"

"Hunch. I note and appreciate your qualification."

"Simply being cautious," Craig said "Long ago, I learned the hard way: seldom affirm, seldom deny. People often don't pay attention to what I'm telling them. They hear what they *want* to hear, and later they claim I was more positive than I . . ."

"This reporter understands cautious statements. Please, get on with it," Tess said. "I'm waiting for the other shoe to drop. The possible *bad* news."

"Yes, well . . ." Craig stopped the sedan in a blocked line of traffic on the narrow confines of Thirtieth Street. Ahead, at the crowded intersection of Lexington Avenue, a policeman waved cars around a stalled pizza truck. "My next choice was the morgue."

"Is that why we seem to be heading toward First Avenue?"

Craig frowned in apparent confusion.

"If we keep going in this direction," Tess said, "we'll reach the New York University Medical Center, and next to it, across from Thirtieth Street, is the Medical Examiner's Office."

"So. I was hoping to prepare you. Yes, that's where we're going. Over the weekend, then Monday and Tuesday, there were several unidentified guests of the medical examiner." Craig peered ahead and resumed driving as the traffic cop on Lexington Avenue supervised the removal of the stalled pizza truck. "Most of the corpses didn't match your description of your friend. But a few, though . . ."

"What about them?"

"A floater in the Hudson River. Same height. Same apparent age. Same body type, with allowance for bloating. I hate to add graphic details."

"I don't shock easily, Lieutenant. I was in Ethiopia during the recent famine. I've seen my share of . . . too many . . . corpses."

"Sure. No doubt that was bad. I'm just trying to prepare you. It's possible you haven't seen corpses like these. The problem with floaters is the water clouds their eyes so we can't tell whether the color was green or blue or in this case what we're looking for, gray. There's also a junkie we found in an alley. Overdosed on heroin."

"Joseph isn't a drug addict." To keep her hopes up, Tess insisted on using the present tense.

"That might be, but it's not always easy to tell, and as you explained, your friend has a habit of keeping secrets. The point is, this junkie's description is the same as your friend's. Except for his eyes. No help there, either. Rats ate them out."

Tess inwardly cringed. "I get the idea."

"If you're as determined as you told me yesterday . . ."

"I *am*."

"I could show you photographs. That's the usual procedure and a lot less traumatic. The problem is, as vivid as the photos are, they still don't give the same perspective as . . . In cases where the face has been damaged, it's often difficult to make a positive ID unless . . . Are you . . . ? This is a terrible question. Are you willing to look at the . . . ?"

"Corpses? Yes." Tess shuddered. "For my friend, I'm willing."

13

Despite her various experiences as a reporter, Tess had never been to the New York City mortuary. Uneasy, she expected something like in the movies, a wall of refrigerated steel cubicles, a shiny hatch being opened, a sheet-covered corpse being pulled out on a sliding table. Instead Craig escorted her along a hallway to a small room where she faced a large window, beyond which was a dumbwaiter shaft.

Craig gave instructions into a phone, set it down, and explained, "To save time, I made arrangements earlier. The staff's got everything ready. Tess, it's still not too late to change your mind."

"No. I have to do this." She trembled, not sure what would happen next, bracing herself.

A half minute later, she flinched, hearing a motor's drone. Apprehensive, she watched cables rise, a platform being lifted. As the platform stopped beyond the window, she found herself staring at the swollen, lead-colored face of a corpse with filmy eyes and skin that seemed about to slip off its cheekbones. Although the skin was gray, its texture reminded Tess of a split, peeling, parboiled tomato. Turning away, she felt nauseous.

Craig gently touched her shoulder. "Yeah, I know. For what it's worth, as many times as I've been here, I always feel queasy."

Tess fought to restrain the insistent spasms in her stomach. "Thanks. I think . . ." She breathed. "I think I'll be okay. Apparently I'm not as tough as . . ."

"Nobody is. The day I get used to looking at corpses in as bad shape as this is the day I quit my job."

"The sheet that comes up to his neck. It covers the stitches from the autopsy?"

"Right. This is gross enough without . . ." Craig hesitated. "Is it him? Your friend?"

Tess shook her head.

"Are you positive? From being in the water so long, the face is disfigured. You might not be able to . . ."

"It's not disfigured enough that I wouldn't recognize him. This isn't Joseph."

Craig sounded awkward. "That must be some relief to you."

Tess felt clammy. "So far, so good."

"So far. That's the trouble. Unfortunately there are others. Do you think you can . . . ?"

"Hurry. Let's finish this."

Craig picked up the phone and gave new instructions.

Again Tess heard a drone. Still averting her gaze from the window, she imagined the platform descending, the corpse disappearing. "Can I—?"

"Yes. It's gone. You can turn around now."

Tess slowly pivoted, her legs unsteady. Her breath rate increased. Once more, the drone of the rising platform made her flinch. She became light-headed and mustered all her discipline, forcing herself to study the next corpse that stopped beyond the window.

Craig had warned her that rats had eaten the eyes, but she wasn't prepared for the further damage that the rats had inflicted. The corpse's lips had been chewed away, exposing teeth that seemed to grin. The nose was gone, leaving two grotesque slits. There were jagged gaps in the cheeks, a shredded oval hole beneath the chin, like an obscene second mouth, and . . .

Tess spun away. "Get it out of here!"

Despite the pounding behind her ears, she heard Craig speak into the phone and in a moment, mercifully, the drone of the descending platform.

Craig gently touched her arm again. Tess felt him waiting and sensed his hesitation, the uneasiness with which he tried to think of a sympathetic remark before he'd be able to ask . . .

"No, it isn't Joseph." Tess shook. "The forehead's too narrow." She breathed. "The hair's the same length, but the part's on the right instead of the left. Thank God, it isn't Joseph."

"Come over here. Sit down."

"I'll be okay."

"Sure. All the same, you look pale." Craig guided her. "Come on, take a rest. Sit down."

Tess obeyed, leaned back, closed her eyes, and felt cold sweat on her brow. "Is that the end?" Her voice was a whisper. "In the car, you mentioned only those two corpses. I want to know about my friend, but I hope to God there aren't any more."

Craig didn't answer.

Slowly, nervously, Tess opened her eyes.

Craig glanced toward the floor.

"What?" Tess asked with effort.

Craig pursed his lips.

"Tell me." Tess frowned, her voice regaining strength. "Are there others? You're . . . What are you holding back?"

". . . There *is* one more."

Tess exhaled.

"But I don't think the victim can be identified. Not *this* way anyhow. Not visually. Probably only by bone X rays, dental records, and . . ." Craig gestured, ill at ease. "He was burned. Over much of his body, especially his face. I don't know what use it would . . . I really question whether you should look at him "

"It's that hopeless?"

"Definitely worse than what you've seen. I doubt that viewing the body would accomplish anything, except make you sick."

"You mean sicker than I already am."

Craig grimaced. "I guess that's what I mean."

Tess debated, concluding with relief, "If that's your opinion. I want to do everything possible to learn what happened to Joseph, but if . . ."

"The only reason I even mentioned the victim is . . ." Craig peered toward the floor again.

"You're still holding something back."

"Is where he died."

Tess felt a worm of fear uncoil in her stomach. *"Where he died?* What are you trying to say, Lieutenant?"

"You mentioned you were supposed to meet Joseph on Saturday morning."

"Yes. So what?"

"To go jogging."

"Right." Tess straightened.

"On the upper East Side. At Carl Schurz Park."

"Damn it, I asked you, what are you trying to say, Lieutenant?"

"That's where this victim was found. At three A.M. on Saturday night. In Carl Schurz Park."

Tess surged to her feet. "Jesus. How did he . . . ?"

"Get burned? We're not certain yet. The victim might have been a derelict, sleeping in the park. It closes at one A.M., and it's supposed to be patrolled, but sometimes street people sneak in and manage to hide. The victim was doused with gasoline and set ablaze. The autopsy shows he died from the flames, not from a knife wound or a gunshot that a fire is sometimes used to conceal. The blaze destroyed his clothes, so we can't tell if he *was* a derelict, but as we know, sometimes kids get their kicks by tracking down vagrants while they sleep and setting them on fire. That neighborhood doesn't see much trouble, so near to the mayor's house. The gangs tend to stay farther north and west. All the same, the scenario I just described is consistent with what happened."

"But do you *believe* that scenario? You wouldn't mention this victim unless you thought there was a chance"—Tess could hardly say the words—"he might be Joseph."

"All I'm doing is pointing out a common denominator."

"Carl Schurz Park."

Craig nodded. "But it's probably just a coincidence. Your friend wasn't a derelict. What would he be doing in the park at three A.M.? Especially *that* night."

"What's so unusual about last Saturday night?"

"On Sunday it rained, remember?"

"Yes."

"Well, the storm began around two in the morning. Even if your friend couldn't sleep and felt tempted to take a walk, is it reasonable to believe he'd have gone out after he saw it was raining? And if he did, why would he have left the street to climb the fence of a park that was locked for the night?" Craig shrugged. "The scenario that doesn't raise questions is the one I described. A derelict

72

snuck into the park to find shelter. Kids followed him and set him on fire.''

Tess bit her lip. "All the same, I don't have a choice."

"Excuse me?"

"I have to look at the body, to try to assure myself it isn't Joseph. Otherwise I'll never stop wondering."

"I meant what I said. It's much worse than the others."

"*Please*, Lieutenant."

Craig studied her. "Why don't we compromise?"

"I don't"—Tess swallowed—"understand."

"I admire your loyalty to your friend. But why not do yourself a favor? This time, look at photographs. Since visual identification is almost hopeless, the difference won't matter, and you can still put your mind at rest."

She thought about it, dismally nodding.

"I'll be back in a minute," Craig said.

Alone in the room, Tess waited nervously, darting her eyes toward the window and the horrors she'd seen beyond it. She wondered what greater horror she would soon—

Lieutenant Craig reentered the room, carrying a folder. He opened it, then hesitated. "Remember, the fire disfigured most of the body, especially the face. *All* of the body would have been disfigured, but it seems that the victim had strength enough to run through the rain and get to a pool of water. He managed to roll in it and put the flames out before he died."

Tess reached for the folder. She slowly removed what felt like six photographs, discovering that they were frontside down. A short reprieve. Tense, she turned the first one.

She gasped.

What once had been a head now resembled a roast that had been seared, scorched, blackened, charred, and . . .

"Oh, my God." Tess jerked her eyes away, but the image of the grotesque mutilation remained in her mind. The blistered skull had no hair, no features, nothing that could possibly resemble Joseph's handsome face. Soot-filmed bone protruded from dark whorls of crisped . . .

Her voice quavered. "Lieutenant, I'm sorry I doubted you."

"Here. Let me . . . There's no need to torture yourself any further." Craig reached for the photographs.

Tess shook her head fiercely. "I started this. I'll . . ."

She turned the next photograph. Another head shot, equally repulsive. In a rush, she set it aside. Only four more to go. Hurry, she thought.

She wasn't prepared for the next photo. The corpses on the platform beyond the window had each been covered with a sheet to the neck. But now she winced at a full view of a naked, almost totally charred body. Only the legs to the knees and the left arm below the elbow hadn't been scorched. However, what Tess noticed most, with mounting nausea, were the bulky stitches that ran from the pelvis up to the rib cage, then right and left, forming a Y, where the pathologist had closed the body after the autopsy had been performed.

I can't take much more. Tess inwardly moaned, hands shuddering, and flipped another photograph. Whatever horror she'd dreaded she would see, she discovered—exhaling sharply, reprieved—that she was staring at the corpse's unburned left leg and foot. Thank you, Lord. Now if only . . . She turned the next-to-last photograph and again exhaled, reprieved, viewing the corpse's unburned *right* leg and foot.

One more to go.

One last photograph.

And if I'm lucky, Tess thought.

She was.

At the same time, she wasn't, for although the final photograph wasn't threatening (indeed it was predictable, given the logic of the sequence—a shot of the corpse's unburned left arm below the elbow), something in it attracted her shocked attention.

Abruptly her memory flashed back to when she'd talked with Joseph in the delicatessen last Friday afternoon.

"We can only be friends," he'd said.

"I'm not sure what . . ."

"What I mean is, we can never be lovers."

His frankness had startled her. *"Hey,"* she'd said, *"I wasn't making a proposition. It's not like I asked you to go to bed."*

"I know that. Really, your behavior's impeccable." Joseph

had reached across the table and tenderly touched her hand. *"I didn't mean to offend or embarrass you. It's just that . . . there are certain things about me you wouldn't understand."*

And while he'd said that, Tess had glanced down at the back of the hand, the *left* hand, that Joseph had placed on hers.

Just as Tess now glanced at—no, *riveted her eyes upon*—the back of the left hand in the photograph.

She felt as if she'd swallowed ice cubes, as if her stomach were crammed with freezing chunks of . . . !

A choked sound escaped from her throat. She slumped back in the chair, forced her eyes away from the photograph, fought to speak, and told Craig, "It's him."

"What?" Craig looked surprised. "But how can you be . . . ? The corpse is so . . ."

"On Friday, when we ate lunch, Joseph touched my hand. I remember glancing down and noticing he had a scar, a distinctive jagged scar, on the back of his left wrist." Weary, heart sinking with grief, Tess pointed toward the photograph. "Like *this* scar on this left wrist. He's dead. My God, Joseph's . . ."

"Let me see." Craig grasped the photograph. As if clinging to Joseph, she resisted. The lieutenant gently pried at her fingers and carefully removed the photograph.

Craig scowled down, frowning, nodding. "Yes. An old scar. Judging from its thickness, the wound was deep. No one mentioned this to me. Otherwise I'd have told you about it and saved you the pain of looking at the other photos." He raised the picture closer. "Not a knife scar. Not jagged the way it is. More like a wound from a broken bottle or maybe barbed wire or . . . Tess, are you sure?"

"In my mind, I can see his hand on mine as vividly as I see that photograph. There's no way to measure them. But yes. . . . I'd give anything not to be. . . . I'm sure. The scars are identical. This is Joseph. Joseph is . . ." Tess felt pressure behind her ears, in her stomach, but most of all, around her heart.

Her voice sank. Abruptly she felt numb. "Dead. Joseph is . . ."

"Tess, I'm sorry."

"Dead."

14

In the mortuary's parking garage, Tess's walk became more unsteady. She was barely conscious of Craig helping her into the car, then going around and sitting behind the steering wheel. She fumbled to put on her seat belt, again barely conscious that Craig snapped it into place for her. With unfocused eyes, she stared toward the blur of other vehicles in the dimly lit garage.

At last Craig broke the silence, coughing. "Where shall I drive you? Home? After what you've been through . . . You're trembling. I don't recommend that you try to go back to work."

Tess turned to him, blinking, only now fully aware of his presence. "Home? Work?" She crossed her unsteady arms and pressed them hard against her chest, restraining her tremors. "Would you . . . ? This'll sound . . . Do me a favor?"

"I already promised I'd help as much as possible."

"Take me to where he died."

Craig furrowed his brow. "To the park?"

"Yes."

"But why would you . . . ?"

Tess hugged her chest harder, wincing. *"Please."*

Craig seemed about to say something. Instead he coughed again, turned the ignition key, put the car in gear, and drove from the garage, emerging onto First Avenue, following the one-way traffic northward.

"Thank you," Tess said.

Craig shrugged.

"Tomorrow, first thing, I'll make a point of telling Walter how cooperative you've been," she said.

"Walter? Hey, you've got the wrong idea. I'm not doing this for *Walter*. I'm doing my *job*. Or *have* been. But at the moment, I'm doing this for *you*."

"I'm sorry. I apologize." Tess almost touched his arm. "I

didn't mean to sound insulting, as if I thought you were only paying back a debt or . . ."

"You didn't insult me. Don't worry about it. But I like to make sure things are clearly understood. Not many people would have gone through what you just went through for a man they'd only met a few times but considered a friend. Loyalty's a rare commodity. You'd be amazed how many people *don't* care when someone's missing. I admire your persistence—your sense of obligation—so if you tell me you want to go to the park, fine, that's where we go. The office will just have to do without me till this afternoon. Joseph Martin must have been special."

Tess thought about it. "Different."

"I don't understand."

"It's hard to explain. He had a . . . Sure, he was handsome. But more important, he had a kind of . . . *magnetism*. He seemed to . . . the only word I can think of is . . . he seemed to glow." Tess raised her chin. "And by the way, in case you've been wondering, there wasn't anything sexual between us."

"I never suggested there was."

"In fact, the reverse. Joseph insisted that we could *only* be friends, that we could never have sex."

Craig turned to her, frowning.

"I know what you're thinking, and so did I. Wrong. He didn't say that because he was gay or anything, but because . . . How did he put it? He said a platonic friendship was *better* because it was *eternal*. That's how he talked. Almost poetically. Yes." Grief squeezed Tess's throat. Sorrow cramped her heart. "Joseph was special."

Craig concentrated on driving but continued frowning. They crossed the intersection of Forty-fifth Street, passing the United Nations building on the right, heading farther northward.

"So." Tess quivered and straightened. "What happens next?"

"After the park? I talk to Homicide and tell them we've got a tentative identification of the body."

"Tentative? That scar is . . ."

"You have to realize, Homicide needs more than that to be absolutely certain. They've sent the fingerprints they managed to get from the left hand to the FBI. Even with computers, though, it can take several days for the FBI to search its files for a match to those prints, especially given the backlog of cases. But now, with a possible name for the victim, they can speed up the process, go to Joseph Martin's file, compare prints, and . . . Who knows? It could be the scar is coincidental. You might be wrong.''

"Don't I wish. But I'm not." Tess felt dizzy.

"I'm just trying to give you hope."

"And I'm *afraid* that hope's as rare as loyalty."

Tess's breathing became more labored the closer they came to Eighty-eighth Street. Tense, she watched the lieutenant steer right, cross two avenues, and just before the final one, manage to find a parking space. With greater distress, she got out of the car with him, locked it, and in hazy sunlight faced the opposite side of East End Avenue.

To the left, partially obscured by trees, was the six-foot-high, stockadelike, wooden barrier that encircled Gracie Mansion. One of the first New York City houses along the East River, it had been built by Archibald Gracie in 1798. Huge, with many chimneys and gables, as well as numerous verandas, it had once been the museum for the city but was now the well-guarded mayor's residence.

Straight ahead, however, compelling Tess, was the wrought-iron fence that encircled the woods and paths of Carl Schurz Park.

"You're certain you want to—"

Before the lieutenant could finish his question, Tess clutched his arm and crossed the avenue. They passed through an open gate (a sign warned that no radios, tape players, or musical instruments were permitted between ten P.M. and eight A.M.) and proceeded along a brick walkway. Thick bushes flanked them. Overhanging branches of densely leaved trees cast shadows.

"Where?" Tess sounded hoarse.

"The guards at Gracie Mansion saw the flames at three o'clock Sunday morning. Just about . . .'' Craig glanced around. "There." He pointed toward a cavelike contour in a granite ridge behind bushes to his right. "The mayor's guards are pros. They know, whatever happens, they don't leave their post. After all, the flames might have been a diversion, a trick intended to draw them away

78

and expose their boss. So they called the local precinct. In the meantime, the mayor's guards saw the flames streak from *here"* — Craig indicated the cavelike contour, then gestured ahead past bushes toward a miniature amphitheater beyond an overhead walkway—"to *there,* toward that statue."

Tess wavered, approaching the human-sized statue. It increased in definition, becoming a bronze child, knee raised, peering sideways, downward, toward the brick surface in the middle of the fifty-foot perimeter of the circular enclosure.

The statue resembled a nymph. Perversely, it reminded Tess of Peter Pan.

"And?" In the stone-lined basin, Tess heard her voice crack as she swung toward Craig.

"Remember, you asked to come here."

"I haven't forgotten. *And?*"

"The officers from the local precinct found . . . The rain had pooled on these bricks. The victim . . ."

"Yes, you told me. He tried to roll in the water and put out the flames. *Where?*"

"Behind the statue, Tess." Craig raised his hands and stepped closer. "I don't recommend . . ."

"It's necessary." Tess slowly rounded the statue.

And sank to her hips on a ledge at the statue's feet.

The contour of a man, lying sideways, his knees pulled toward his chest, had been blackened into the bricks.

"Oh."

"I'm sorry, Tess. I didn't want to bring you here, but you kept insisting."

With a sob, Tess stooped toward the dismal dark shape on the bricks. She touched where Joseph's heart would have been. "Do me another favor?" Her voice broke. "Please? Just one more favor?"

"Take you away from here?"

"No." Tears streamed from Tess's burning eyes. Through their blur, she begged him silently.

Craig understood. He opened his arms, and sobbing harder, she welcomed his embrace.

15

Memphis, Tennessee

Billy Joe Bennett couldn't stop sweating. Moisture oozed from his scalp, his face, his chest, his back, his legs. It rolled down his neck. It soaked his shirt. As he nervously drove through one A.M. traffic in this bar district of the city, he felt as if he'd sat in a puddle. The problem was that he didn't sweat because of the hot, humid night. In fact, he had the windows of his Chevy Blazer rolled shut and the air-conditioning on full blast. Still, no matter how much he shivered from the cold air rushing against him, he couldn't stop sweating. Because he shivered from something else and sweated for the same reason. Two reasons actually. The first was tension. After all, he was due to testify before a shitload of government investigators this morning. And the second was a desperate need for cocaine.

Jesus, he thought. How could anything that made you feel so good when you snorted it put you through this much hell when you didn't have it? Billy Joe's insides ached as if every organ scraped against the other. His muscles contracted so forcefully that his cramped hands seemed about to snap the steering wheel. God Almighty. The glare of headlights stabbed his eyes. The blaze of neon lights over taverns made him wince. If I don't get some nose candy soon . . .

He kept glancing furtively toward his rearview mirror, desperate to make sure he wasn't being followed. Those damned government investigators were worse than bloodhounds. Since Sunday, they'd been tailing him everywhere. They had a car parked on his street when he was at home. Each day since the train's derailment, they'd forced him to give them urine samples, the tests on which he'd passed, because Billy Joe wasn't any dummy. No, siree, boy. He read the papers, and he watched the news on television, and months ago he'd realized that random drug testing would soon be required for anyone who worked in transportation. So he'd planned for the day when *he* might be tested. He'd paid his brother, who never touched cocaine, to piss in a sterile jug for him. Then he'd taken the jug home, poured urine into several plastic vials, and hidden them behind the toilet tank in his bathroom. The second he'd heard about the derailment, he'd gone to the bathroom, smeared Vaseline over one of the vials, and inserted it—Lord, that had hurt!—up his rectum. And sure enough, Sunday, a government investigator had knocked on his door, shown him a court order, handed him a glass container, and requested a urine sample.

So Billy Joe had said, "Of course. I've got nothing to hide." He'd gone into the bathroom, locked the door, removed the plastic vial of urine from his rectum, poured the warm fluid into the glass container, returned the vial to his rectum, and came out of the bathroom, telling the investigator, "Sorry, I don't piss so good on demand. This is the most I could coax from my bladder."

The investigator had given him a steely look and said, "This is all we'll need, believe me."

"You're wasting your time."

"Yeah, sure, we are."

After that, Billy Joe hadn't gone anywhere without a Vaseline slicked vial of urine up his rear end. Talk about cramps and pain. Man, oh, man. But he was a railroad worker, broad shouldered, big chested from twenty years of lifting rails, shifting ties, and hefting a sledgehammer. He was tough, he told himself, right on, no two ways about it, and if those government investigators thought they could scare him, those pansies in their cheap suits had another think coming.

At the moment, though, Billy Joe did feel scared. Because on Monday, he'd used up his carefully hidden stash of cocaine, and the first day without it hadn't been too bad, a slight case of the shakes is all, but the *next* day his stomach had started to squirm, and the day after that, he'd thrown up and couldn't stop sweating. Now at one A.M. Thursday morning, soaking wet, trembling, doing his best to drive without wavering, he feared he'd go fucking out of his mind if he didn't get a jolt of coke soon.

Dear God in heaven, he couldn't testify before those government investigators this morning if he looked and shook and sweated like this. He couldn't keep his thoughts straight. He wouldn't be able to concentrate on their questions. He'd stammer or worse, maybe even babble, and they'd know right away that he wasn't just nervous, like from stage fright, but suffering from withdrawal, and that would be that. He didn't know what the government could do to him if the investigators proved he was an addict, but this much he did know—he wouldn't like it one damned bit. Three hundred people were dead because that section of track had given way, toppling the train. Twenty cars of anhydrous ammonia had split open, and ever since Sunday, the newspapers had been full of stories about possible criminal negligence, even manslaughter. Shit, man, they put you *away* for that.

So all right, as foreman of the maintenance crew, he'd checked those tracks, and they'd looked okay to him. Granted, maybe he hadn't checked them as thoroughly as he could have, but it had been late afternoon, and he'd been eager to get back to town and snort some coke. It wasn't *his* fault that the jerk who owned the railway had mismanaged the business because he was too busy dipping his wick in his secretary. The dummy's wife had caught him, kicked him out of the house, divorced him, and taken him for millions. Hell no, Billy Joe thought, it wasn't *my* fault that the railroad was forced to cut back on its maintenance fund so the jerk could pay his divorce settlement. If there'd been more guys checking the tracks, the accident wouldn't have happened.

But that's not *my* problem. No way. Not now. Never mind fixing those tracks. *I'm* the one who needs fixing, so I don't fall apart eight hours from now when those government investigators try to crucify me.

Again Billy Joe scowled at his rearview mirror. He'd been driving at random, watching if headlights behind him took the same routes. He'd made sharp turns, run red lights, veered down alleys, done everything he could think of, remembering all those detective and spy movies he liked to watch and the way the heroes got rid of tails. Satisfied that he hadn't been followed, he drove hurriedly from the bar district, heading toward the river. He didn't have much time. Each night at one-fifteen, his supplier set up shop for five minutes—and *only* five minutes—at a secluded parking lot next to a warehouse close to the Mississippi.

Wiping sweat from his eyes, Billy Joe glanced at his watch. Christ, it was almost ten after. He pressed his trembling foot on the accelerator. The dark parking lot looked deserted when he steered past the warehouse and stopped. No! Don't tell me I'm late! It's one-fifteen on the button! I *can't* be late!

Or maybe *he's* late. Yeah, Billy Joe decided, heart pounding. That's what it is. He just hasn't got here yet.

At once, the headlights of another car turned into the lot. Billy Joe relaxed, then shook with sudden worry that this wasn't his supplier but government investigators who'd been tailing him. Fighting not to panic, he told himself, there's no crime in taking a drive to the river. Hey, all I have to do is tell them I couldn't sleep, I needed to relax, I felt like watching the lights of the barges on the water. Sure, no problem.

He didn't recognize the blue Ford that stopped beside him. Not a good sign but maybe not a bad one. His supplier often took the precaution of switching vehicles. But when a tall, thin man wearing a T-shirt got out of the Ford, Billy Joe didn't recognize him either, and that for certain was not a good sign.

The man knocked on Billy Joe's window.

Billy Joe lowered it. "Yeah?" He tried to sound gruff, but his shaky voice didn't manage the job.

"You're here to do business?" the man asked.

"I don't know what the fuck you're talking about."

"Cocaine. Do you want to score, or don't you?"

Entrapment, Billy Joe thought. If this guy *was* an investigator, he'd blown his case right there. "What makes you think I—"

"Look, don't waste my time. The regular delivery man had to leave town for his health, couldn't stand the competition, if you get my meaning. *I've* got this route now, and plenty of other stops to make. Four minutes more, and I'm leaving. Make up your mind."

Billy Joe suddenly realized that the Ford had approached the parking lot from the opposite direction that he himself had used. This guy—whoever he was—couldn't possibly have been tailing him.

Billy Joe realized something else, that he was sweating more profusely and shaking so bad his teeth were clicking together.

"Okay, I've made up my mind." Barely controlling his trembling hands, he awkwardly opened his door and stepped out, legs wobbly. "Let's do business. Same price as the other guy charged?"

The stranger unlocked the trunk of the Ford. "No. The feds have been making too much trouble, intercepting too many shipments. I've got extra expenses."

Billy Joe felt too desperate to object.

"But this one time only, I'm being generous, adding more to each package. Sort of a goodwill gesture, a way of introducing myself to my customers."

"Hey, fair enough!"

Rubbing his hands together, Billy Joe followed the man to the trunk of the car and peered eagerly inside. What he saw was a bulging plastic garbage bag that the stranger opened, revealing white powder. "What the—? What kind of way is that to—?"

A sharp, pungent odor reached his nostrils. The trunk smelled like a . . . ? Laundry. That was it. A *laundry?* Why would—?

"All for you, Billy Joe."

"Hey, how come you know my name?"

The stranger ignored the question. "Yes, we brought all of this for you."

"We?"

Car doors banged open. Three men who'd been crouching out of sight in the Ford rushed toward the trunk, grabbed Billy Joe— one on each side and one behind him—bent him over, and shoved his head toward the powder in the plastic bag.

Billy Joe strained to shove back, squirming, twisting, frantic, but even years of hefting a sledgehammer didn't give him the strength to resist the determined men.

"All for you, Billy Joe."

He struggled with greater desperation, but the powerful hands kept pressing him downward. As his head came closer to the white powder, the strong, pungent smell became overwhelming, making him gag. He recognized what it was now. Ammonia. Powdered bleach.

"No! Jesus! Stop! I—"

His words were smothered as his face was thrust against the powder. It smeared his cheeks. It caked his lips.

Then his face was rammed *beneath* the powder. It filled his ears. It plugged his nose. He fought to hold his breath, but as the three men held him down while the fourth man twisted the mouth of the plastic bag around his neck, Billy Joe finally inhaled reflexively and felt the stinging powder surge up his nostrils, spew down his throat, and cram his lungs. It burned! My God, how it burned!

The last thing he heard in a panic before he lost consciousness was, "We know it's not the powder you're used to, but how do you like it, Billy Joe? You let three hundred people die from ammonia. It's time you got a whiff of it yourself."

16

The eastern bank of the Mississippi, ten miles north of Memphis

In the bedroom of his country mansion, Harrison Page huffed and puffed but finally admitted that his frustrating efforts were pointless. The irony of the word wasn't lost on him. *Pointless.* It exactly described his penis. Out of breath, giving up, he rolled off the woman—his affair with whom had caused his wife to divorce him—and lay on his back, staring bleakly at the dark ceiling.

"Sweetie, that's okay," the woman, Jennifer, said. "You don't need to feel your manhood's threatened. You're tired is all. You're under stress."

"Yeah, under stress," Page said.

"We'll try again later, sweetie."

Page had only recently admitted to himself how much her shrill voice annoyed him. "I don't think so. I've got a headache."

"Take one of my sleeping pills."

"No." Page stood, put on his pajamas, and walked toward a

window, parting its drapes, brooding, oblivious to the moonlight glinting off the river.

"Then maybe a drink would help, sweetie."

If she doesn't stop calling me that, Page thought. "No," he said, irritated. "I've got a meeting with my lawyers before I testify at the hearing this morning. I have to be alert."

"Just doing my best to be helpful, sweetie."

He spun, trying to control his temper. The moonlight through the parted drapes revealed her naked body, her dark mound between her legs, her lush hips, slender waist, and ripe breasts. *Over*ripe, Page bitterly thought. They're like melons so swollen they're about to go rotten. And her skin, when he stroked it, had lately begun to make him cringe, because beneath its smooth, once-arousing softness was a further softness, like jelly, like . . . fat, Page decided. The way she lies around all day, watching soap operas, eating chocolates, she'll soon be as fat as . . .

Although he stifled the angry thought, another thought insisted. How could I have been such a fool? I'm fifty-five. She's twenty-three. If I'd kept my dick in my pants where it belonged . . . The first time, after we screwed, when she started calling me sweetie, I should have realized what a mistake I was making. We don't have anything in common. She's incapable of an intelligent conversation. Why didn't I stop right then, give her a bonus, transfer her to another office, and thank God I hadn't ruined my life?

But the fact was, Page dismally admitted, he'd let his dick control his brain. He *had* ruined his life, and now he didn't know how to salvage it. "I'm going downstairs. I've got some testimony to prepare before I walk into that hearing."

"Whatever, sweetie. Go with the flow, I always say. Just remember, I'll be waiting."

Yes, Page thought, subduing a cringe. Isn't that the hell of it? You'll be waiting.

He put on slippers and left the bedroom, shuffling along a corridor, gripping the curved banister of a marble staircase, unsteadily descending, relieved to be out of her presence. Her excessive perfume—like the smell of flowers at a funeral—had been making him sick.

Except for Jennifer and himself, the mansion was deserted. He'd sent the butler, cook, and maid away, lest they overhear conversations that might incriminate him if the servants couldn't keep their mouths shut when the investigators questioned them. Footsteps echoing, he felt the emptiness around and within him as he crossed a murky vestibule, entered his study, and turned on the lights. There he hesitated, chest heaving, staring at a stack of documents on his desk, the possible questions that his lawyers had anticipated he'd be asked at the hearing and the numerous calculated responses he would have to know by heart.

Weary, he rounded the desk, slumped in his chair, and began reviewing the depressing documents. If only his ex-wife, Patricia, were here, he'd be able to talk with her, to sort out the problem and try to solve it. She'd always helped him that way, listening sympathetically, rubbing his taut shoulders, offering prudent advice. But then he wouldn't have this problem if Patricia were here, because they wouldn't be divorced and she wouldn't have nearly bankrupted him in the settlement and he wouldn't have been distracted from managing the railroad, let alone have been forced to cut maintenance costs so he could squeeze out more profits to make up for the millions he'd been forced to pay his ex-wife. Three hundred people dead. Tens of thousands of acres of forest and pasture turned into a wasteland. An entire county's water supply poisoned. All because I thought with my dick instead of my head.

A noise made him jerk his eyes toward the left. With a flinch, fear burning his stomach, he saw one of the French doors that led to the patio swing open. Three men and a woman stepped in. All were in their thirties, trim, good-looking, dressed in dark jogging clothes.

Page lurched to his feet. His years of being an executive had trained him never to show weakness but to react aggressively when feeling threatened. "What the hell do you think you're doing? Get out of here!"

They shut the door.

"I said, get out!"

They smiled. The woman and one of the men had their hands behind their backs.

Page fought to control and conceal his fright. They looked too clean-cut to be burglars, not that he knew what burglars would look like, but . . . Maybe they were . . .

"Damn it, if you're reporters, you've picked the wrong way to get an interview, and besides, I've *stopped* giving interviews!"

"We're not reporters," the woman said.

"We don't have any questions," one of the men said.

"I'm calling the police!"

"It won't do you any good," another man said.

They approached him. The woman and one of the men continued to hold their hands behind their backs.

Page grabbed the phone and tapped 911, suddenly realizing that the line was dead.

"See," the third man said. "It doesn't do any good."

"I locked those doors! I turned on the security system! How did—?"

"We're handy with tools," the first man said.

"Like *these* tools," the woman said.

They brought their hands from behind their backs.

Page opened his mouth, but terror choked his scream.

While two of the men grabbed Page's arms and forced him flat across the desk, the remaining man held up a railroad spike, and the woman swung a sledgehammer, driving the spike through Page's heart.

17

". . . impaled on a stack of blood-soaked documents that confidential sources indicate were statements that Harrison Page had been prepared to make at the hearing this morning." The bespectacled television reporter paused somberly.

Appalled, Tess sat on a stool at the kitchen counter in her loft, watching the twelve-inch TV next to the microwave. The red numbers on the Radarange's digital clock said 8:03. She'd been trying to make herself eat breakfast—fruit salad, whole-wheat toast, and tea—but after yesterday's ordeal at the morgue and her discovery that Joseph was dead, she didn't have much appetite.

The reporter continued, "In a further grotesque aftermath of the Tennessee toxic-gas disaster, the body of Billy Joe Bennett, foreman in charge of inspecting the section of the track where the derailment occurred, was found early this morning in a Memphis parking lot near the Mississippi River. Bennett had been under investigation for possible negligence due to alleged cocaine addiction."

The television image shifted from the reporter to a harshly lit videotape of stern policemen standing near a warehouse, staring down at something, then a close-up of a garbage bag on the parking lot's asphalt, the bag filled with white powder, then a panning shot of a sheet-covered corpse being lifted on a gurney into an ambulance. Off camera, the reporter explained the grisly means by which Bennett had been murdered.

With renewed pangs of grief, Tess was reminded of the brutal way in which *Joseph* had been murdered.

The reporter came back on the screen. "Police speculate that Bennett and Page were killed for revenge by relatives of victims of the toxic-gas disaster."

A commercial for disposable diapers interrupted the news. Tess rubbed her forehead, peered down at her breakfast, and felt even less hungry.

The phone rang, startling her while she rinsed out her teacup. Who'd be calling this early? Troubled, she left the kitchen, walked to the section of the loft where the furniture was arranged to form a living room, and picked up the phone halfway through its third ring.

"Hello?"

The gravelly voice was so distinctive that the speaker didn't need to identify himself. "This is Lieutenant Craig."

Her fingers cramped around the phone.

"I apologize for calling at this hour," Craig said, "but I won't be in the office, and I wasn't sure I'd have a chance to phone you at work this morning—that's if you feel up to going to work."

"Yes. I'm going." Tess sat, dejected. "I almost decided not to. But it doesn't do any good to brood. Maybe work will distract me."

"Sometimes it helps to be with other people."

"I'm not sure *anything* will help." She slumped, weary. "What can I do for you, Lieutenant?"

"I wanted to know when you take your lunch break."

"Lunch? Why would—? I doubt I'll be eating lunch today. That's why you called? To invite me to *lunch?*"

"Not exactly. There's something I might want you to look at," Craig said, "and I figured if you were going to be free at a certain hour, we could make an appointment."

Tess felt cold. "Is this about Joseph's death?"

"Possibly."

"You're holding back again."

"This might be nothing, Tess. Really. I'd prefer not to talk about it until I'm sure. I don't want to upset you without a reason."

"And you don't think I'm upset already? Okay, one o'clock. Can you pick me up outside my office building at one o'clock?"

"I'll make a point of it. Who knows? Maybe the meeting won't be necessary. That's what I mean. Don't think about it."

"Sure. Don't think. What a great idea."

18

But Tess had *many* things to think about. She kept remembering Joseph's burned corpse and the dark contour of his body seared into the bricks at Carl Schurz Park. In the elevator at work, she shuddered, identifying it with Joseph, numbed that she'd never see him again.

At *Earth Mother Magazine,* she went immediately down the hall to Walter Trask's office and told him everything that had happened.

Trask frowned, more haggard than usual. He stood, came around his desk, and clasped her shoulders. "I'm sorry, Tess. Honestly. More than I can say."

"But who would have done that to him? *Why?*"

"I wish I had answers." Trask hugged her. His features gray, he stepped back. "But this is New York. Sometimes there *aren't* any answers. I'm reminded of the jogger who was raped and nearly killed by that marauding gang in Central Park. The kids who did it weren't raised in a slum. They came from middle-class families. Poverty can't be blamed for their behavior. It doesn't make sense, like too many other things."

"But why would Joseph have been in Carl Schurz Park in the rain at three A.M.?"

"Tess, listen to me. You don't know anything about this man. You found him attractive, but he . . . This'll sound harsh. Nonetheless, it has to be said. When you mentioned that he hadn't given his employer his phone number and he used a mail service, I was worried. The man had secrets. Possibly his secrets caught up to him."

With eerie clarity, Tess recalled what Joseph had told her in the delicatessen Friday afternoon. *"I have certain . . . let's call them obligations. I can't explain* what *they are or* why *I have to abide by them. You just have to trust and believe and accept."*

"Maybe. Maybe he *did* have secrets," Tess said. "But that doesn't mean the secrets were bad, and it doesn't mean I have to turn my back and pretend I never knew him."

"Believe me, I sympathize." Trask put an arm around her. "Really. All I'm asking you to do is try to be objective. Protect your emotions."

"Right now, the last thing I'm capable of being is objective," Tess said.

"Look, perhaps you shouldn't have come in to work today.

Take a break. Give yourself a rest. Go to your health club, whatever relaxes you. We'll see how you feel tomorrow.''

"No," Tess said. "Being alone would make me feel worse. I *need* to work. I have to keep busy.''

"You're sure?''

"The more work, the better.''

"In that case . . .''

"What?''

"I've got something I want you to do.''

Tess waited.

"It'll mean postponing your article on the overuse of herbicides and pesticides on Midwestern farms.''

"But that's an important issue," Tess said automatically. "Those poisons are sinking through the earth and into the drinking water.''

"All the same, there might be a story we ought to do first. The TV news this morning. Did you watch it? The murders in Tennessee? Remind you of anything?''

"I gather you're thinking of the murders at the Pacific-Rim Petroleum Corporation last week.''

There'd been three, two in Australia and one in Hong Kong, after the massive oil spill that continued to endanger the Great Barrier Reef. Victor Malone, captain of the supertanker that had run aground, Kevin Stark, executive in charge of cleanup efforts, and Chandler Thompson, director of the Pacific-Rim Petroleum Corporation, had each been killed following widespread allegations of drinking while on duty, failure to respond to the spill in time to contain it, and corporate refusal to admit its negligence. Malone had been blown apart as he drove from Brisbane's courthouse. Stark had been drowned, his body discovered upside down in a barrel of oil. Thompson had been poisoned when he drank a glass of water during a press conference.

"Remember, we talked about those murders last Wednesday," Trask said.

Tess sank toward a chair, dismally remembering something else. That evening, shortly after their conversation, she'd first met Joseph. She dug her fingernails into her thighs, forcing herself to concentrate on what Trask was saying.

"I suggested we do a story about the killings."

"And I said *Earth Mother Magazine* isn't a tabloid," Tess replied. "We shouldn't add to the controversy. Fanatics hurt our cause."

"Well, now it seems we've got some fanatics in Tennessee."

"No, the parallel isn't exact. The police suspect that Bennett and Page were killed by relatives of—"

"That's what they said on television." Trask scowled. "But I just checked my sources at the *Times*. They're preparing a story that quotes a Memphis policeman who wonders if some nutso ecologists might be responsible."

"What?"

"Already the major environmental-protection groups, like the Sierra Club and Greenpeace, are anticipating the charge, condemning the murders as totally irresponsible."

"But it's absurd to suspect . . ." Tess jerked forward. "Sure, some Greenpeace members were once arrested for taking over a whaling ship in Peru. And it often puts boats filled with people between whaling ships and their quarry. But there's a big difference between seizing private property or risking your life to save an endangered species and—"

"Executing someone you blame for contributing to the destruction of the planet?" Trask raised his eyebrows. "Of course. And don't get me wrong. Greenpeace is a reputable organization. I certainly don't think it would ever resort to violence. But the new director of the Pac-Rim Corporation did receive a note warning him that he'd better make sure another spill doesn't happen, so we know that fanatics were responsible for *those* murders. My point is, I agree with you—extremists hurt our cause. Every time protestors invade a nuclear-power facility or steal research animals from a medical lab or throw blood on a woman who wears a fur coat, the public reacts as if all environmentalists are a bunch of lunatics. The rest of us who believe that education, common sense, and good example are the proper ways to gain converts become guilty by association. So let's not avoid the issue. Let's face it head-on and make clear that the majority of environmentalists are *not* crazed, Looney-Tunes weirdos, that *we* don't approve of excessive protests any more than the public does."

Tess studied her boss and slowly nodded. Burdened with grief, she fought to pay attention. "You know, Walter, the more I think of it . . ."

"Not a bad idea? Of course, if I say so myself. Does that mean you'll do the piece?"

Tess nodded again, pensive, straightening.

"Good."

"I see several possibilities." Her voice sounded cramped. With effort, Tess continued, "While I'm condemning extremists, I'll still be able to emphasize the threats to the environment that make them behave the way they do. Right motives, wrong methods."

"You got it, kid. And if you get deeply enough into the story—you never know—maybe you'll be able to take your mind off what happened to your poor friend."

"I doubt it, Walter. Very much. But Lord knows, I'll try my best." Her eyes misted. "I definitely need distracting."

For the rest of the morning, Tess almost succeeded. Struggling to immerse herself in the subject and stop brooding about Joseph's death, she searched through her files. Determined, she called the reference department at the public library, the *Daily News,* and the *Times.* She jotted notes and quickly made lists. Trask's reference to animal-rights activists prompted her to recall that last year a group of protestors who'd stolen rabbits being used for medical research had destroyed a five-year experiment that might have resulted in a cure for muscular dystrophy. In another case, the animals that were stolen had been infected with anthrax to test a new vaccine. A minor epidemic had resulted before the animals were recovered.

Seeking further examples, Tess recalled what had happened in Brazil last week. Pedro Gomez, a rubber-tree tapper who'd been trying to organize his fellow villagers to stop developers from their slash-and-burn destruction of the Amazon jungle, had been blown apart by automatic weapons while making a speech. At his funeral, his wife had received a "gift," the head of the financier suspected of ordering Gomez's death. The theory was that one of Gomez's followers had killed the financier to get even. Nonetheless the beheading, like the supposed revenge slayings of Billy Joe Bennett and Harrison Page in Tennessee, was related to a major environmental catastrophe, and Tess decided to include the incident as an example of radical behavior ultimately caused by an ecological crisis, and while condemning that behavior, she could still emphasize the crisis itself.

By noon, Tess had a rough outline for her article, amazed by how much she'd been able to accomplish so quickly, given her need to distract herself. But the truth was, a festering corner of her mind continued to brood about Joseph. More and more, she kept glancing at her watch, its hands proceeding relentlessly, with surprising speed yet paradoxical slowness, toward one o'clock and her appointment with Lieutenant Craig. What had he wanted to show her? Why had he been evasive yet again?

19

The lieutenant drove an unmarked *rust*-colored car this time. When he stopped at the curb and Tess got in to fasten her seat belt, she noticed that his creased brow was beaded with sweat. His blue suit coat was lumped beside him. The front of his wrinkled white shirt and the underarm she could see were dark with moisture.

"Sorry." He coughed. The windows were open, but the only breeze on this sultry, smog-hazed June afternoon came from passing cars. "The air conditioner doesn't work."

"I'll adjust."

"Good. That makes one of us."

"Asthma, you said?"

"What?"

"Your cough."

"Oh." Craig steered into traffic. "Yeah, my cough. That's what my doctor tells me. Asthma. Allergies. This town's killing me."

"Then maybe you should move."

"Sure. Like to someplace wholesome? Like to Iowa? What's that line in the movie? *Field of Dreams.* Yeah, that's the movie. 'Is this heaven?' And Kevin Costner says, 'No, it's Iowa.' Cornfields? Give me a break. I was raised here. *This* is heaven." Craig frowned, his voice dropping. "Or at least, it used to be."

He turned east off Broadway.

"We're heading in the same direction we did last time." Tess became rigid. "Don't tell me we're going back to—"

"The morgue?" Craig shook his head and coughed. "I'd have warned you. No, we'll be driving up First Avenue again."

"To Carl Schurz Park? But I don't want to—"

"No, not there either. Let me do this *my* way, all right? So I can explain and prepare you? And don't frown. I swear, cross my heart, you won't see anything gross."

"You're positive?"

"I'm not saying it won't disturb you, but I guarantee it won't make you sick. On the other hand . . . Okay, here's the deal. You told me your friend was different? That's an understatement. According to the FBI, he doesn't exist."

"Doesn't . . . ? What are you . . . ?"

"We sent your friend's name to the Bureau to help them find a match for the fingerprints on the corpse's unburned left hand. They searched their computers for a file on Joseph Martin. No surprise. It's a common name. There are *plenty* of Joseph Martins. What *is* surprising is that *none* of the fingerprints in those files matched the fingerprints we sent to the Bureau."

"But surely not *everybody* has fingerprints in the Bureau's files."

"Right." Craig continued toward First Avenue. "So the next step is to check with social security, to match the number your friend gave his employer with the names and addresses on their list."

"And?"

Craig steered around a UPS truck, its driver hurrying to make a delivery. *"And?* There *is* a Joseph Martin with that number. The trouble is, he lives in Illinois. Or *used* to live in Illinois. Because— and this took several phone calls—the Joseph Martin who has that social security number *died in 1959."*

"There's some *mistake*."

Craig shook his head. "I double-checked. The result came up the same. Joseph Martin—*your* Joseph Martin—should have quit fooling everybody. He should have done the decent thing, stretched out on the floor, crossed his arms, stopped breathing, and been as dead as the Joseph Martin who's in a cemetery in Illinois."

While Craig reached First Avenue and headed north, Tess felt pressure behind her ears. "You're telling me Joseph assumed the identity of a *dead* man?"

"Actually dead *child*. Infant. Remind me—how old did you estimate Joseph to be?"

"Early thirties."

"Let's make it thirty-two," Craig said. "Because that's how old the other Joseph Martin would be today if he hadn't been killed in a car crash along with his parents in '59."

"And I'll bet there were no surviving close relatives."

"Oh?" Craig assessed her. "You understand how this is done?"

Tess spread her hands. "Someone who wants a new identity chooses a community at random and checks the obituaries in the local paper for the year in which he himself was born. He looks for an infant who died that year and was either an orphan or was killed along with his immediate family. That way, he doesn't look older or younger than he says he is, and there's no one who can contradict his claim to be that person. The next step is to find out where the child was born. That information is often in the obituary: 'So-and-so was born in this or that city.' The person seeking a new identity then writes to the courthouse in that city, tells its record office that he lost his birth certificate, and asks for a replacement. People often lose their birth certificates. It's not unusual for someone to ask for another copy, and clerks almost never bother to check if the name on the birth certificate matches the name of someone who's dead. As soon as he gets the birth certificate, the person sends a photostatic copy to the social security office, explains that he lived abroad for many years and didn't need a social security number but now he does. The social security office seldom objects to such a request. With a birth certificate and a social security number, the person can get a passport, a driver's license, a credit card, all the documents he needs to appear legitimate, to enter the system, get a job, pay taxes, et cetera.''

"Very good," Craig said, continuing northward. "I'm impressed.''

"Reporters pick up all kinds of information." Tess certainly didn't intend to add that the real way she'd learned about assuming false identities was by overhearing her father's phone conversations with business associates.

Craig brooded, passing Forty-ninth Street. "With some co-operation from the federal government, I've been able to learn that Joseph began to use his assumed identity in May of last year. That's when he first started paying income taxes and social security. Since then, he's had two jobs, not counting his present one. The first was in Los Angeles, the second in Chicago. Obviously he didn't want to stay in any place too long, and he felt the need to put a lot of miles between one location and another. In each case, he worked for a video documentary company.''

"Okay." Breathing too fast, Tess concentrated so as not to hyperventilate. "So Joseph had something to hide. Everything about him was a lie. That explains why he didn't want me to get close to him. The question is, what the hell was he hiding?''

"Maybe you'll be able to tell *me* when you see where I'm taking you. Certainly *I* can't figure it out," Craig said.

"Figure out what? Where are we going?''

"No. Not yet.''

"What?''

"The problem is . . . See, first I have to explain some other things.''

Tess raised her arms in exasperation.

"Be patient. When I talked to the accountant where Joseph worked," Craig said, "I asked to see the paychecks he cashed. They're too large for a supermarket or a liquor store to accept them. He'd have needed to take them to a bank. And the bank would have sent the canceled checks to his employer's bank, which in turn would have sent them to the employer's accountant. As it happened, Joseph cashed all his checks at the *same* bank. Back there." Craig pointed. "We just passed the bank on Fifty-fourth Street.''

"So you went to the bank, showed them a court order allowing you access to their records, and examined Joseph's account," Tess said.

Craig assessed her again. "You'd have made a good policeman."

"Police*woman*."

Craig ignored her correction. "Yes. That's what I did. I went to the bank, and the address they had for Joseph was the mail service on Broadway. That was *also* the address he told the bank to print on his checks. No surprise. What *was* surprising is that the microfilm records of Joseph's canceled checks show that he hadn't made any payments for electricity or rent. Obviously he had to live somewhere and pay his utilities, so how was he keeping his landlord and Con Edison happy? Turns out, every month he sent a check for thirteen hundred dollars to a man named Michael Hoffman. Now take a guess who Hoffman is."

"An accountant," Tess replied.

Craig studied her with greater intensity. "You're *better* than good. Right. An accountant. Clearly, Joseph was trying to increase the smoke screen that protected his privacy. So I spoke to Hoffman. He told me that Joseph and he had never met. They conducted all their business through the mail and over the phone."

"But Hoffman paid Joseph's major bills," Tess anticipated.

"No compliment this time—you're correct."

"Okay. With Hoffman's records and cooperation from Con Edison, you ought to be able to find out where Joseph lived."

"In theory."

Tess frowned. "Another smoke screen?"

"Right. Joseph's arrangement with his landlord was that the landlord would pay the utilities and Joseph would reimburse him. So Con Edison couldn't help us."

"But the landlord could."

Craig didn't answer.

"Whenever you purse your lips like that . . . What's the matter?" Tess asked.

"The landlord is a real-estate conglomerate that owns thousands of apartments. All their records are stored in a computer. They looked up Joseph Martin's name, gave me his address—in

Greenwich Village—but when I went there, I discovered that the agency had given me the wrong address, that Joseph didn't live there. In fact, the real-estate firm didn't even own that apartment.''

"You mean, someone made a mistake and typed the wrong information into the computer?''

"That's *one* possibility. The agency's looking into it.'' Craig scowled toward a traffic jam on First Avenue.

"One? What's *another* possibility?'' The lieutenant's somber expression made Tess nervous.

"Suppose . . . I keep thinking of smoke screens. I'm suspicious by nature. I keep wondering if Joseph found a way to access the firm's computer and tamper with their records. He might have been *that* determined to keep someone from finding out where he lived. Or maybe he bribed a secretary to falsify the records for him. However Joseph did it, it makes me *more* determined to find out why,'' Craig said.

"But if you don't know where Joseph lived, where are we going?'' Tess rigidly clasped her hands together.

"Did I say I didn't know? I made a few assumptions. One was that since Joseph's bank is on the East Side and he arranged to meet you at Carl Schurz Park—''

"And died there.'' Tess squeezed her eyes shut, repressing tears. "The upper East Side.''

"That maybe Joseph's apartment is in that direction. Of course, his mail service is on the opposite side of town. But given his obsession about secrecy, it's logical for him to break the pattern. So I asked the precincts around here to find out if anything unusual happened from Friday night onward, something that might help us. That's how we caught Son of Sam. While the bastard was shooting his victims, he overparked and got tickets. On the weekend, there were lots of incidents. But after I sorted through the reports and eliminated several possibilities, I read about a fight in an apartment building on East Eighty-second Street. An apparent attempted mugging. One of the tenants, a man, was assaulted. He ran from the building, chased by several men. They made enough noise that several other tenants woke up and peered out their doors, seeing shadows struggling on the stairs. Someone coming in late from a party noticed what appeared to be a gang chasing a limping man down the street.''

"East? Toward the river?''

"Yes.'' Craig sighed. "And this happened on Saturday night—or rather at half past two on Sunday morning.''

"Oh,'' Tess said. "Jesus.''

"I spoke to some of the tenants who were wakened. They said the fight began on the seventh floor. That building has only four apartments per floor. This morning, I got there early enough to talk to the people who live in three of those apartments, but I didn't get any answer at the fourth. The tenants in the *other* apartments said it had been several days since they'd seen the man who rents that apartment. Not unusual apparently. They hardly *ever* see him. He's a loner. Friendly but distant. Keeps to himself.''

Tess frowned, more rigid.

"The name on the downstairs mailbox for that apartment is Roger Copeland. Of course, that means nothing. Anyone can put a false name on a mailbox. The neighbors describe the man as handsome, tall, in excellent physical condition, in his early thirties, with dark hair and a tawny complexion.''

"My God.'' Tess winced. "It certainly sounds like Joseph.''

"The thing is, what the neighbors noticed most were his eyes—gray, with what they described as a glow.''

Tess quit breathing.

"And his unusual way of speaking,'' Craig added. "On the few occasions they spoke to him, he didn't say 'Good-bye,' but 'God bless.' ''

Tess felt a chill.

"Joseph used that expression often, you told me. So I got some keys from the landlord, checked the apartment . . .''

"And?'' Tess fought to restrain a tremor.

"I'd rather not describe what I found,'' Craig said. "It's better if you see it fresh, without expectations. But I really don't understand what I . . . That's why I'm taking you there. Maybe *you* can make sense of it.''

Craig steered toward the side of the road, parking in a narrow slot. Tess all at once realized that she'd been so engrossed by their conversation that she hadn't noticed they'd turned onto Eighty-second Street.

"It's just up the block," Craig said.

"You learned all this since yesterday afternoon?"

"That's why I phoned you early and told you I wouldn't be in the office. I had plenty to do."

"But shouldn't *Homicide* be working on this? Not Missing Persons?"

Craig shrugged. "I decided to keep my hand in."

"But you must have hundreds of other cases."

"Hey, I told you yesterday, I'm doing this for you." With a cough, Craig stepped from the car.

Puzzled by Craig's statement—

—was he saying he'd become attracted to her?—

—Tess joined him, her confusion immediately changing to apprehension as she walked past garbage cans along the curb, approaching the mystery Craig wanted to show her.

20

The apartment building, one of many narrow structures crammed together along the street, looked different from the soot-grimed others only because its brick exterior was painted a dingy white. At each window, a fire-escape ladder led down from a rusted metal platform.

Craig opened the outside glass door, escorted Tess through a vestibule flanked by mailboxes (ROGER COPELAND, 7-C), pulled out a key, and unlocked the inside door.

The interior smelled of cabbage. They proceeded along a hallway and reached concrete steps on the left that crisscrossed upward. An elevator faced them on the upper landing.

"The architect saved costs," Craig said. "The elevator stops at only every other floor."

"Let's walk," Tess said.

"You're kidding. To the *seventh* floor?"

"I didn't get my run in this morning."

"You're telling me you *run* every morning?" Craig asked.

"For the past twelve years."

"Holy . . ."

Tess glanced at Craig's beefy chest. "A little exercise might strengthen your lungs. Can you manage the effort?"

"If *you* can do it, *I* can." The lieutenant stifled a cough.

"Just a guess. Did you ever smoke?"

"Two packs a day. For more years than you've been running." He coughed again. "I stopped in January."

"Why?"

"Doctor's orders."

"Good doctor."

"Well, he's certainly persistent."

"That's what I mean. A good doctor," Tess said. "As long as you stop lighting up . . . Well, it'll take a few more months to get the nicotine out of your system, and a few more *years* to purge your lungs, but you're in the right age group. Late thirties. On balance, you've got a good chance of not getting lung cancer."

The lieutenant stared at her. "Are you always this dismally reassuring?"

"I guess I hate to see people damage themselves the way they seem determined to damage the planet."

"I keep forgetting you're an environmentalist."

"An optimist. I'm hoping if I try hard enough, and if *others* try hard enough, we might actually be able to clean up this mess."

"Well," Craig coughed and gripped the banister. "I'm prepared to do *my* share. Let's go. Seven floors. No problem. But listen, if I get tired, can I lean on your shoulder?"

21

Craig was out of breath, his brow beaded with sweat, when they reached the seventh floor. But he hadn't complained, and he hadn't stopped to take a rest. Tess gave him credit for being determined.

"There. That's my exercise for the month," Craig said.

"Don't break the start of a pattern. Try again tomorrow."

"Maybe. You never know. I might surprise you."

The lieutenant's mischievous grin made Tess suspect that he was trying to make her feel at ease.

To the left, they faced 7-C. There wasn't any name in the slot below the apartment's number. A metal sign on the door said ACE ALARM SYSTEM.

"You'd better put these on," Craig said. He handed her rubber gloves and coverings for her sneakers. "Homicide was here this morning. They took photographs and did a preliminary dusting for fingerprints. But they'll be back, and even though I've got permission to show you the apartment, we don't want to disturb it any more than necessary."

Craig had rubber gloves and shoe coverings for himself as well. After knocking and getting no answer, he pulled two keys from his pocket and unlocked two dead bolts. But when he twisted the doorknob, Tess placed a nervous hand on his arm.

"Is something wrong?" Craig asked.

"Are you sure there's nothing inside that'll gross me out?"

"You'll be disturbed. But I guarantee—this won't be like the morgue. Trust me. You don't need to feel afraid."

"Okay." Tess compacted her muscles. "I'm ready. Let's do it."

The lieutenant swung the door inward.

Tess saw a white corridor. A red light glowed on an alarm box to the left. The alarm was primitive—no number pad, just a switch, presumably because the landlord had economized by installing the least expensive model.

Craig flicked the switch down. The light went off.

They entered the corridor. Beyond the alarm box, Tess saw a small bathroom to the right. A sink, a commode, a tub, no shower stall. The tub was old enough that its rim was curved, oval instead of rectangular, metal feet supporting it. But despite its age, and that of the sink and commode, the pitted white surfaces gleamed.

Tess concentrated so hard that the sound the lieutenant made when he shut the door surprised her, making her flinch.

"Notice anything?" Craig said behind her.

Tess studied the neatly folded, clean towel and washcloth on a shiny metal rod next to the sink. On the sink itself, a toothbrush that looked new stood in a sparkling glass. The mirror on the medicine cabinet shone.

"Joseph was a better housekeeper than *I* am, that's for sure."

"Look closer." Craig edged past her. Entering the bathroom, he opened the medicine cabinet.

Tess peered inside. A razor. A package of blades. A tube of Old Spice shaving cream. A tube of Crest toothpaste. The tubes were methodically rolled up from the bottom and set in an ordered row. A bottle of Old Spice after-shave lotion. A bottle of Redken shampoo. A packet of dental floss.

"So?" Tess asked.

"The basics. *Only* the basics. In fact, for most people, *less* than the basics. In all my years of being a detective, of searching the rooms that belong to missing persons, I've never yet seen a medicine cabinet that didn't contain at least *one* prescription medicine. An antibiotic or an antihistamine, for example."

Tess opened her mouth to respond.

Craig raised his hand to interrupt. "Okay, from the way you describe him, Joseph was healthy, exercised every day, ate right, took care of himself. But Tess, there isn't even an *aspirin* bottle, and everybody—I don't care *how* healthy Joseph was—keeps aspirins. I mean *everybody*. I checked the rest of the apartment. I found vitamins in the kitchen. But aspirins?" The lieutenant shook his head. "The guy was a purist."

"What's so strange about that? He didn't like taking chemicals, no matter how benign they are. So what?"

"I'm not finished yet." Craig motioned for her to follow.

They left the bathroom, continued along the hallway, and reached a kitchen on the left.

There, the stove, refrigerator, and dishwasher were several years old, but like the sink, commode, and tub in the bathroom, they were polished until they gleamed. The worn but bright counter was bare. No toaster. No microwave. No coffeepot.

Craig opened the cupboards. They were empty, except for a plate, bowl, and cup in one and a few spotless stainless steel pots and a colander in another.

Craig opened every drawer. They, too, were empty, except for a knife, fork, and spoon in one and two larger metal spoons appropriate for stirring food cooked in the stainless steel pots. "To put it mildly, Joseph felt compelled to strip things down to the absolute essentials. The vitamins are in the spice rack behind you, by the way. No sage, no oregano. Never mind salt or pepper. Only vitamins. And no alcohol anywhere, not even cooking sherry."

"So Joseph didn't like to drink. Big deal," Tess said. "I don't drink much either."

"Keep an open mind. I'm just getting started."

Tess shook her head, bewildered, as Craig pulled open the fridge.

"Orange juice, skim milk, bottled water, fruit, a shitload of lettuce, tomatoes, peppers, sprouts . . . Vegetables. No meat. No—"

"Joseph told me he was a vegetarian."

"Don't you think he was taking it to an extreme?"

"Not necessarily. *I'm* a vegetarian," Tess said. "You ought to see *my* refrigerator. The only thing different is I sometimes eat fish or chicken but *only* white meat."

Craig gestured impatiently around him. "No cans of food in the cupboards."

"Of course. Too much salt. Too many preservatives. The taste is synthetic."

"No offense, but I hope I never have to eat your cooking."

"Don't jump to conclusions, Lieutenant. I cook very well."

"I'm sure you do, but if I don't get a steak now and then—"

"You'd have less cholesterol," Tess said. "And maybe less weight around your belt."

Craig squinted, then chuckled, then coughed. "I suppose I could use a few less . . . Never mind. As I said, we're just getting started. Let me show you the living room."

Tess followed, leaving the kitchen, proceeding down the corridor.

And faltered.

Except for thick, open draperies at the windows, the room was totally empty. No carpet. No lamps. No chairs. No sofa. No tables. No shelves. No television. No stereo. No posters. No reproductions of paintings. Bare floor. Bare walls. Not even a—

"Phone," Craig said, seeming to read her mind. "Not in the kitchen. Not here. And not in the bedroom. No wonder Joseph didn't give his employer his phone number. He didn't *have* a phone. He didn't *want* one. And my guess is he didn't have any *use* for one. Because the last thing he wanted was a call from someone or to *make* a call. Your friend had reduced his life to bare necessities. And don't tell me that's typical of a vegetarian. Because I *know* better. I've never seen anything like this."

Trembling, Tess opened a closet and stared at a jogging suit on a hanger next to a simple but practical overcoat. No boxes on the upper shelf. Below, on the otherwise barren floor, she saw a solitary pair of Nike jogging shoes.

Trembling harder, she clutched the edge of the closet door to steady herself and turned. "Okay, I'm convinced. This isn't . . . No one lives like . . . Something's wrong."

"But I haven't shown you the best part or, I should say, the worst." With a stark expression, Craig nodded toward a door. "The bedroom. What you'll see in there . . . No, don't cringe. It won't make you sick. I've promised you that several times. But I need to *know*. What does it *mean?*"

His footsteps echoing, Craig crossed the room and opened the bedroom door.

As if hypnotized, Tess stepped forward.

22

The bedroom was almost as empty as the living room. Plain draperies but no carpet. There was something in the corner, but here the draperies had been shut, the room too shadowy for Tess to be able to identify the murky shape.

She groped along the inside wall and found a light switch. However, when she flicked it, nothing happened.

"There's no lamp," Craig said. "And the overhead bulb doesn't work."

"Then how did Joseph keep from stumbling around in the dark?"

Instead of answering, the lieutenant pulled the draperies open.

Hazy sunlight flowed in, making Tess blink as her eyes adjusted. Abruptly she blinked for another reason, because what she saw in the room bewildered her.

The murky object she'd glimpsed dimly in the corner was a mattress on the floor. No. Not even a mattress. A pallet, six feet long, three feet wide, one inch thick, made of woven hemp.

"Joseph didn't exactly pamper himself," Craig said. "No pillow. No sheet. Just that one blanket. I looked. There aren't any others in the closet."

Tess's forehead pounded. With mounting confusion, she noticed that the blanket the lieutenant referred to had been folded at the bottom of the pallet with the same meticulous care as the towel and washcloth that had been hung so neatly on the rack in the bathroom.

"And there's your answer for how he kept from stumbling around in the dark," Craig said.

The pain in her skull increasing, Tess frowned toward where the lieutenant pointed and shook her head. Next to the pallet, a dozen candles stood in saucers.

"Somehow I don't think he was just trying to save on his electricity bill," Craig said.

To the right of the pallet, Tess squinted at a plain, pine, three-shelved bookcase. Feeling pressure in her chest, she walked toward it, examining the titles. *The Consolation of Philosophy, The Collected Dialogues of Plato, Holy Bible: Scofield Reference Edition, Eleanor of Aquitaine, The Art of Courtly Love, The Last Days of the Planet Earth.*

"I guess he never heard of the *New York Times* best-seller list," Craig said. "Philosophy, religion, history. Heavy. I'd hate to have spent a weekend with him. Not many laughs."

"He wasn't boring," Tess said, distracted, continuing to examine the shelves. "Several books about the environment."

"Yes. That's another interest you and he shared."

Trembling no matter how hard she tried to control it, Tess drew her index finger past a book called *The Millennium* and noticed a title that wasn't in English. The volume was bound in well-worn leather and looked very old.

"Can I take it out?"

"As long as you put it back exactly where you found it," Craig said.

With care, she removed the book from the shelf and examined its dry, cracked cover. *El Círculo del Cuello de la Paloma.*

"Looks like Spanish," Craig said.

"Right."

"I'm still working on English. Can you read it?"

"No." Tess exhaled, frustrated. "I took a few courses in high school, but I don't remember the vocabulary."

"Below the title," Craig said. " 'Abu Muhammad 'Ali ibn Hazm al-Andalusi.' " He stumbled over the words. "I assume that's the author's name. It barely fits across the cover. 'Muhammad'? Sounds Moslem."

Tess nodded, wrote the title and author's name on a notepad, then opened the book. Its pages were brittle, the entire text in Spanish. Impatient, she returned her gaze to the bookshelf, in particular toward the Scofield Bible. Earlier, something about it had troubled her. It didn't look right. She cautiously replaced the Spanish book and withdrew the Bible, finding that its covers slanted inward. With a frown, she stared inside and discovered, shocked, that most of its pages had been removed. A straight line showed where a knife or scissors had been used to cut out the pages.

"Why would—?"

"That's one of many things I want to know," Craig said.

Tess read the names of the sections at the tops of the heavily underlined, remaining pages. "He cut out everything except the preface and . . ." She flipped more pages. "John's Gospel, John's epistles, John's Book of Revelation. I don't understand."

"You're not the only one. And this . . ." Craig pointed. *"Whatever* the damned thing is. On the bookshelf. *This* is the weirdest of all."

Tess raised her eyes. She'd noticed the object when she walked toward the bookshelf, but it made so little sense that she'd postponed examining it in the hope that the other things in the room would help her interpret the grotesque image.

The object was a statue, or to be exact, a bas-relief sculpture, one foot tall and wide, fashioned out of white marble. It depicted a long-haired, muscular, handsome man straddling the back of a bull, jerking the struggling animal's head up, slashing its throat with a knife.

Blood cascaded from the wound toward what appeared to be wheat growing out of the ground. At the same time, a dog lunged toward the blood while a serpent sped toward the wheat and a scorpion attacked the bull's testicles.

To the right and left of the grisly scene, torchbearers watched. The torch on the left was pointed upward, the torch on the right pointed downward. And above the torchbearer on the left, a bird—

—an *owl?* hard to tell—

—stared with fixated eyes toward the slashing knife and the cascading blood.

"What does it mean?" Craig asked. "Since I first saw it this morning, the thing's been haunting me."

Tess had trouble speaking. Her mouth tasted bitter. Her shoulder blades felt frozen. "It's . . . Horrible. Repulsive. Disgusting."

"Yeah, just your ordinary, everyday decoration around the house."

Attached to the wall behind the statue, imitating the torches

that flanked the eerie, grotesque scene, were candles in holders, one facing up, the other down. A saucer had been set beneath the latter candle to catch the melting wax when it fell.

"Joseph didn't have a lot of respect for the fire code," Craig said. "If the landlord had known about all these candles, your friend would have found himself and his few belongings out on the street. It's a wonder he didn't burn down the building."

"But this is *crazy*."

"It sure as hell spooked me."

"Look, there's no way I can borrow the Bible and the Spanish book, right?" Tess asked.

"Homicide would have my ass if I let you."

"Well, can I at least take pictures?"

"You've got a camera?"

"Always. A reporter's habit."

"Okay. But I want you to promise," Craig said, "you won't publish the photographs unless you're given permission from Homicide or me."

"Agreed."

"Then be my guest," Craig said.

Tess removed a small 35-mm Olympus from her burlap purse and took several close-up photos of the statue from different angles. Then she opened the Bible and photographed the most heavily underlined pages. Next, after putting the Bible back on the shelf in the spot where she'd found it, she photographed the entire bookshelf and finally the pallet flanked by candles.

She put away the camera. "All set."

"There's one other promise I want you to make," Craig said. "If you learn anything from those photos, I want to hear about it in case it's something we haven't already discovered."

"Word of honor."

Craig fidgeted.

"That look on your face. You're doing it again," Tess said. "Holding back."

"The thing is . . ."

"What?"

"Are you ready for another shock?"

"You mean, there *is* more?"

"In the closet." Craig opened it. "Notice he had few clothes. A pair of clean jeans. An extra shirt. A spare—only one—cotton pullover. A few pairs of socks and underwear on the shelf. And *this*." Craig reached to the right, toward the inside wall of the closet.

"Whatever it is, I don't want to see it."

"I'm sorry, Tess. But it's important. I have to show you."

The lieutenant pulled an object from the closet. The object was a foot-long section of wood that seemed to have been cut from a broomstick. A half-dozen three-foot-long pieces of rope were attached to one end.

Tess shuddered. "A *whip?*"

"With dried blood on the ropes. He . . . I believe the term is . . . flagellated himself."

23

The Tsavo National Park, Kenya, Africa

The hunter waited patiently, clutching his long-distance, high-powered rifle, hunkering with practiced discipline in a shelter of scrub thorn next to a cluster of baobob trees. His view of the water hole was unobstructed. At midday near the equator, the heat was so severe that the targets would soon lumber into view, forced to seek water. Although his wide-brimmed hat and the bushes around him provided some shelter from the glaring sun, the hunter sweated profusely, his khaki hunting shirt dark with moisture. But he didn't dare raise his canteen and drink, lest his motions reveal his position. After all, his quarry was extremely cautious, vigilant against intruders.

Still, the hunter's patience and determination had been rewarded many times before. He simply had to maintain professional conduct. Later, when his hunt was successful, he could afford the luxury of drinking.

His nerves tingled. There! To his left! He sensed more than heard the approaching rumble of huge, plodding feet. Then he saw the dust cloud they raised, and finally the massive animals emerged from a stand of flowering acacia trees, warily assessing the open grassland, nervously judging the water hole.

Elephants. The hunter counted ten. Their wide ears were flared, straining to detect unfamiliar, threatening sounds. With disappointment, the hunter noted that four were tuskless children and that the adults had tusks that were barely—hard to tell from this distance—four feet long. With greater disappointment, he remembered a time, twenty years ago, when the curved tusks had been six, eight, and sometimes ten feet long. On average, the weight of each tusk had dropped from eighteen pounds to nine. As a consequence, it required much more killing to achieve the quota demanded by ivory merchants. Twenty years ago—the hunter mentally shook his head—forty thousand elephants had roamed this plain, but last year, he'd estimated that only *five* thousand remained, and that figure didn't include the two thousand carcasses he'd come upon during his increasingly determined expeditions. Soon the ivory trade wouldn't exist. Because the elephants themselves would no longer exist. Twelve tons of tusks, the harvest from thirteen hundred elephants, were worth $3 million. But smaller tusks meant *less* weight and *more* killing in order to achieve the quota.

His fingers rigid on his rifle, the hunter watched the reluctant elephants finally overcome their nervousness and approach the water hole. They were so magnificent. He focused his intensity, clasped his rifle's trigger, and slowly, angrily, swiveled his vision, scanning the grassland around the water hole.

Again the hunter's nerves tingled, instincts quickening.

To his right, he saw motion. Figures rose from the shelter of waist-high grass. These figures, *too,* held rifles.

Men! Dressed in camouflage khaki, the same as himself!

Other hunters!

But he and they weren't competitors. Not at all. Quite the contrary. They existed in a complex, deadly condition of symbiosis. *Their* purpose demanded *his* purpose, and with angry resolve, the executioner swung his rifle toward those predators.

Even from a distance, he could tell that they weren't using hunting rifles but automatic weapons—M-16s and AK-47s. He'd stumbled upon the evidence of their slaughter too many times before. Entire herds destroyed, riddled with bullets, their carcasses rotting in the sun, their tusks grotesquely hacked from their faces, their meat—which could have been used by starving natives—left for ravaging jackals and swarming maggots.

God damn those other hunters.

To hell!

Which was exactly where *this* hunter intended to send them.

Careful not to reveal himself, he slowly stood, raised his rifle, braced it against his shoulder, intensified his vision through the rifle's high enlargement sights, steadied his finger on the trigger, and with enormous satisfaction, squeezed.

Without removing his gaze from the rifle's sights, he saw— in close-up—the predator's skull blow apart.

Nothing like explosive bullets.

At once, the hunter saw *another* predator surge upward from the grass, recoil in horror, raise his hand to his mouth, and stumble back, fleeing.

No problem.

With a slight shift of angle and focus, the hunter shot yet again. *And blew the second predator's chest apart.*

So how does it feel? the hunter thought. When you died, did you feel like . . . did you identify with . . . did you imagine . . . and regret . . . and feel sorry for . . . the agony you caused so many of God's magnificent irreplaceable creatures? The elephants?

Shit, no. You're incapable of emotion, except for greed.

But you're not feeling *that* now, are you?

You're not feeling *anything*.

Because, you bastards, you're one less curse on the planet.

Native bearers scrambled from the waist-high grass and fled toward a distant ridge. Their panicked outlines were tempting, but the hunter restrained his trigger finger and lowered his rifle. His message had been delivered. He understood—although disapproved of—their motives.

The native bearers needed employment. Yes.

They needed money. They needed food.

But no matter their desperation, they shouldn't help to destroy their heritage! The elephants were Africa! The elephants were . . . !

The hunter's anger diminished. His churning stomach made him want to vomit. As the native bearers scrambled below the curve of the distant ridge, he stood with professional caution, assessed the grassland around him, and regretted that the elephants had been spooked by his gunshots and had retreated from their desperate need to drink from the shallow, muddy water hole, but he felt tremendous pride that he'd done his duty.

It took him five minutes to reach the first of his executed predators. His dead antagonist looked pathetic, the robust man's skull blasted open, his blood soaking into the dirt. But then—

—the hunter reminded himself—

—the dead elephants looked even *more* pathetic. Because when alive, so magnificent, the elephants had been a triumph of creation.

An *example* had to be made.

115

The hunter removed a pair of pliers, knelt, propped open the corpse's mouth, and began the necessary but repulsive work of reinforcing the example.

"Ivory," he muttered, his voice choked. "Is *that* what you want? *Ivory?* Well, here, damn it, let me help you out. I mean, unlike the elephants, you've got all the ivories anybody needs."

With torturous effort, the hunter began to yank out each and every one of the corpse's teeth.

He set them neatly in a pile beside the sunken-mouthed corpse.

He then proceeded toward his other victim.

By every means necessary . . .

Examples . . .

Reprisals . . .

Had to be made!

The slaughter had to be stopped!

24

"I'm sorry," Craig said.

"For what?"

"Really, I didn't mean to upset you this much."

"It's not your fault," Tess said. "I had to . . . I *needed* to see that apartment. *Earth Mother Magazine* won't go out of business because I'm not there. I wouldn't be much good to them anyhow. I've got some thinking to do."

With a troubled expression, Craig double-parked on the noisy, crowded street outside Tess's loft in SoHo. "Well, while you're thinking, remember your promise. Homicide will investigate thoroughly, but if something occurs to you that might help explain what we found in Joseph's apartment, let me know." The lieutenant gave her a card. "That's my home telephone number at the bottom. If it's important, don't wait to call me at the office."

"Hey, don't worry. If I have to, I'll call you in the middle of the night."

Craig grinned. "That's fine with me. I'm a very light sleeper." He coughed. "That is, when I sleep at all."

"Which reminds me." Tess fumbled in her purse. "I almost forgot. While I waited for you to pick me up, I brought you a couple of presents."

"Oh?"

"A copy of our magazine. Maybe *that'll* help put you to sleep."

"I doubt it. If anything, I'm sure it'll keep me awake. You have my word—I'll read it. Cover to cover."

"I'll have a quiz prepared. Also, I brought you this."

She handed him a box of cough drops.

Craig looked amused. "Thanks. People don't often give me anything—except grief." He cleared his throat. "Take care, huh?"

"You, too." Echoing Joseph's words, she surprised herself by adding, "God bless."

Craig nodded.

After getting out of the car, Tess watched the lieutenant drive away. Pretending to climb the steps to her apartment building, she waited until Craig's car disappeared around a corner. Then, instead of entering her building, she walked briskly in the opposite direction. Toward a shop down the street.

25

QUICK PHOTO, a sign said on the window. A bell rang when Tess opened and shut the door. A middle-aged Hispanic clerk glanced up from stacking boxes of film behind the counter. His voice had no trace of an accent when he asked, "Can I be of help?"

Tess hesitated. The clerk's tawny skin . . . There was something about . . . It reminded Tess of *Joseph's* skin. She'd assumed that Joseph's swarthy skin was due to a tan.

But maybe . . .

She wondered, could Joseph have been *Hispanic? That* would explain the Spanish book on his shelf.

"Yes. In your window, you advertise one-hour film processing."

"Of course. But for an extra charge," the clerk said.

"No problem." Tess unloaded her camera and handed the clerk the film. "It's important. I need it back as soon as possible."

"One moment." The clerk took the film through a door behind him and returned a half minute later. "My brother is beginning to process it now." He poised a pen above an order form. "Your name?"

Tess gave him all the information he needed.

The clerk handed Tess a claim check. "Is there anything else I can help you with?"

"Yes. I want more film. Three rolls. Thirty-six exposures each. ASP two hundred." From trial and error, Tess had learned that, for her simple, easy-to-carry, inexpensive camera, an ASP of two hundred was a good compromise for getting clear indoor and outdoor pictures. "I . . . You look . . . Do you speak Spanish?"

The clerk smiled. *"Sí, señorita. Muy bien."*

"Then, if you don't mind, could you tell me what this means?" Tess pulled her notepad from her purse and showed him the title she'd written.

"El Círculo del Cuello de la Paloma?" The clerk shrugged. "The circle . . . or possibly the ring . . . of the neck of the dove."

Tess frowned, disappointed. She'd hoped that the title would give her an indication of what the book contained. "Well, have you ever heard of a book with that name?"

"My apologies, *señorita.* No."

"Then what about this?" She pointed toward the author's name: Abu Muhammad 'Ali ibn Hazm al-Andalusi. "Why is the author's name so long?"

The clerk raised his shoulders. "In Spanish, long names are common. They often include the *parents'* names."

"But Muhammad isn't a Spanish name. It sounds Moslem. Arabic."

"That's true," the clerk said.

"And what about at the end here? 'Al-Andalusi'?"

"That means he comes from Andalusia."

"If I remember," Tess said, "that's in Spain. Right?"

"Yes. The southernmost province."

"I don't understand. Why would someone who's Arabic come from a Spanish province?"

The clerk spread his hands and shook his head. "My former country's history is complicated." He glanced at a clock on the wall. "Your pictures should be ready by five."

"I'll be back. Thank you."

"De nada."

26

Tess hurried to her apartment building, ignored the elevator, and ran up the stairs to her loft. After locking the door behind her, she rushed to pick up her portable phone, tapped some numbers, and went to a closet, pulling out a suitcase.

The receptionist at *Earth Mother Magazine* answered.

"Betty, Tess. Is Walter free? . . . Good. Then put me through. . . . Walter, it's Tess. I need a favor. I can't come into work for the next few days. Can you spare me? . . . Yes, I've been working on the article. This isn't connected. Let's call it family business. The point is, I have to leave town. . . . What? Is this about Joseph? Okay, all right, you guessed it. Are you a mind reader now? . . . Walter, I have to do this. . . . Be careful? Hey, what else? I promise.''

With relief, Tess broke the connection, carried the suitcase toward her bureau, and pressed more memorized numbers on the portable phone. "Public library? Reference department, please.'' While she waited, she tossed a change of clothes into her suitcase. "Reference department? I'm a journalist. I'm on deadline, and I'd appreciate it if you checked your computer for a book I'm trying to find. It's called *The Circle*—or *The Ring*— *of the Neck of the Dove.''*

Waiting again, Tess entered her bathroom and placed an emergency kit of toothpaste, etc., into her suitcase. "No? Thank you.''

But Tess felt hollow as she zipped her suitcase shut. She left the bathroom, reached for her volume of the yellow pages, and finally found what she wanted.

Again she pressed numbers on the portable phone. "Trump Shuttle? I need a seat on the six-o'clock flight to Washington. Yes, I know you guarantee seats. But I don't want to wait if you have to bring out another plane. My Am Ex number is . . .''

She slumped on her sofa, tried to clear her mind, and pressed more buttons. "Mother? I'm coming to town tonight. . . . That's right, it's been a long time. We'll catch up. . . . I'm fine, Mother. Listen, as I recall, you had some influence with the Library of Congress director. Didn't he used to come to father's dinner parties? . . . Good. I want you to call him. Ask him if he knows about and can get me this book.'' Tess gave the title. "Eight, Mother. Maybe later. . . . I'm trying. I just don't know exactly. Don't keep dinner waiting. . . .Yes, I love you, too.''

She pressed the disconnect button, searched her address book, and pressed more numbers. Actually, she jabbed them. "Brian Hamilton, please. . . . That's what I expected. He's *always* unavailable. Tell him Theresa Drake is calling. . . . Yes, *that* Drake.''

The name had magic. Or possibly caused fear. For whatever reason, Brian Hamilton answered quickly. "How are you, Tess?'' His voice was smooth. "It's been a long time.''

"Not long enough. But I want to get reacquainted, Brian. In person.''

"Oh? Does that mean . . . ?''

"You bet. I'm coming to town. Be at my mother's house at eight tonight."

"I'm sorry, Tess. I can't. I'm scheduled to attend a reception for the Soviet ambassador."

"With all respect to the Soviet ambassador . . ."

"Respect. Exactly. We're suddenly allies. I have to—"

"You're not listening, Brian. I need to see you."

"But the Soviet ambassador—"

"Fuck him," Tess blurted. "You promised my father you'd be there if I ever needed help. I demand you honor your promise."

"Demand? You make that sound like a threat."

"A threat? Brian, I don't make threats. I make *guarantees.* I'm a journalist, remember? I know your secrets, just as I knew about my father's. I might be tempted to write a story about them. Unless you want to put out a contract on me."

"Hey, Tess, let's not overreact. You know we don't . . ."

"Just be at my mother's. Eight o'clock."

Brian hesitated. "If you insist. For the sake of old times and your father. I look forward to—"

Tess broke the connection.

27

On schedule at five o'clock, her clothes moist from urgency, Tess carried her suitcase into the Quick Photo store. Again, the bell rang. Again, the middle-aged Hispanic clerk glanced up at her.

Tess eased her suitcase onto the floor and breathed out. "My pictures? They're ready?"

"But of course," the clerk said. "As we advertise, one-hour service." He reached in a drawer. "Here they are."

Tess opened her wallet.

"I'm sorry your friend got angry."

". . . My *friend?*"

"The man you sent to pick up the photographs for you."

"But I . . ."

"A month ago, we gave out some wedding pictures by mistake. In truth, it was *my* fault. I forgot to ask for the claim check. Since then, I don't give out *any* pictures unless . . ."

"Here's the claim check," Tess said. Her hand shook. "You did the right thing. I didn't send . . . What did he look like?"

"Tan. Early thirties. Tall. Well built. Good-looking." The clerk paused, then frowned. "He became quite insistent when I wouldn't give him the photographs. He was so upset that I almost feared he'd *force* me to give him the photographs. I reached under the counter." The clerk held up a baseball bat. "For this. In case he turned violent. Perhaps he noticed my gesture. Fortunately it wasn't necessary. Just then, three customers came in. He left in a hurry." The clerk frowned harder. "What I noticed most about him were his eyes."

"His eyes?" Tess gripped the counter for support. "What about them?"

"Their color was unusual."

"Gray?"

"Yes, *señorita*. How did you—?"

Tess gaped. Feeling sick, she dropped money on the counter, grabbed the package of photographs, and mustered the discipline not to tremble. She rushed toward the door to find a taxi.

"You're certain I did the right thing, *señorita?*"

"Absolutely. From now on, you get all my business."

The overhead bell rang as Tess lunged out. Scanning the smoggy street, she suddenly realized, her stomach burning, that she wasn't just looking for a taxi.

The man the clerk had described sounded like Joseph. But Joseph was dead!

How could—?

As she hailed a taxi and scrambled into it, Tess surprised herself by assuming one of Joseph's habits. Nervous, she darted her eyes in every direction to see if she was being followed.

URGENT FURY

1

LaGuardia Airport

The grim-faced man in the taxi's backseat leaned forward rigidly, straining to keep the taxi ten cars ahead of him in sight. He was thirty-eight, of medium height and weight, with brown hair and unremarkable features, so average that no one ever remembered him. He wore a conservative, moderately priced, nondescript suit, a cotton-polyester-blend white shirt, a subdued striped tie. His briefcase looked no different from thousands of others.

"Which airline?" the taxi driver asked.

The passenger hesitated, watching the taxi he was following.

"Hey, friend, I said, which airline?"

"Just a moment. I'm checking my tickets."

"Don't you think you should have done that a little sooner?"

Ahead, the taxi the passenger studied turned to the right off the busy ramp, rounded a curve, and sped past a crowded parking lot. A sign said, TRUMP SHUTTLE, DELTA, NORTHWESTERN, PAN AM SHUTTLE.

"Turn right," the passenger said.

"You waited long enough to tell me. Which airline?" the driver repeated.

"I'm still checking my tickets."

"Hey, if you miss your flight, pal, don't blame me."

The passenger squinted forward, noticing that the taxi he followed steered around the parking lot, passed the signs for Pan Am, Delta, and Northwestern, and approached a large new building on which a huge red sign announced TRUMP SHUTTLE.

"Up here will do," the passenger said.

"Well, finally."

When the driver stopped behind a limousine in front of the terminal, the passenger had already checked the taxi's meter. He added the cost of the bridge toll and a 20-percent tip, shoved several bills toward the driver, grabbed his briefcase, and hurried out his door.

"Hey, buddy, you want a receipt?"

But the passenger was gone. As he walked toward a set of automatically opening doors in the shuttle complex, he glanced unobtrusively to his left, seeing the woman he was following get out of her taxi, pay the driver, and carry her underseat suitcase toward another set of doors.

They entered the terminal simultaneously, moving parallel to each other, separated by a throng of arriving travelers. The brown-haired, nondescript man paused next to a group of similarly ordinary-looking businessmen and pretended to inspect his ticket while he watched the woman hurry toward a line at a counter.

The line moved quickly—Trump guaranteed promptness. Nonetheless the woman looked impatient. When she got her turn, she urgently presented a credit card, signed a voucher, grabbed a folder that presumably contained a ticket, and rushed past the counter toward where the attractive female clerk pointed.

Excellent, the chameleon thought. He veered through the crowd, following his quarry. She'd already passed through the security station by the time he arrived there. Strictly speaking, no one without a ticket was allowed beyond this point. No problem, though. The chameleon always carried a bogus ticket with him, and in his considerable experience, few security personnel actually bothered to check that ticket.

He set his briefcase on the conveyor belt that led into the X-ray machine. A uniformed attendant nodded for him to proceed through the metal detector. The chameleon, by habit, carried no metal, not even coins or a belt buckle when he was working. His watch was made of plastic. The metal detector remained silent as he stepped through and picked up his briefcase on the other side of the X-ray machine. The briefcase, of course, contained nothing that would arouse suspicion. Only innocent, boring documents. Certainly no weapons. His expertise was surveillance, after all. The chameleon had no *need* of weapons, although on a very few occasions, emergencies had forced him to defend himself, his average height and weight deceptive, his martial-arts skills impressive.

He increased his speed, climbing a moving escalator, just another of many harried businessmen in a rush to get on a plane.

Ahead, on the spacious upper level, his quarry walked faster. Again, no problem. The chameleon didn't want to catch up to her but only keep her in sight. He glanced at his watch. Five minutes to six. Peering ahead, he saw his quarry present her boarding pass to an attendant and disappear quickly through an open door toward the tunnel to her plane.

The chameleon waited until the door to the tunnel was closed, then proceeded toward a window, and watched the plane pull away from the boarding platform. But he still wasn't satisfied. Experience had taught him that he had to wait until the plane left the ground.

Five minutes later, the chameleon had to give Trump credit. As advertised, the shuttle left on time. Turning, he walked toward a counter near the passenger door. On a board behind the counter, he noted the plane's destination.

"Excuse me," he asked the attendant. "What time will that flight arrive?" Hearing the answer, he smiled. "Thank you."

He had only one more thing to do. At a bank of phones, he used a credit card to contact a long-distance number. "Peter, it's Robert."

Both names were fake, on the slim chance that this phone

would be monitored or that someone on a neighboring phone would overhear. Never take chances.

"I'm sorry to have kept you waiting, but our friend had trouble making connections. I know how much you want to meet her. She's on a Trump shuttle to Washington National Airport. She'll arrive at seven oh seven. Can you—? . . . That's what I thought. Peter, you're a pal. I know she'll be glad to see you."

His work done, the chameleon hung up the phone. Clutching his briefcase, he retraced his steps through the concourse. But on second thought, his work was *not* yet done. Not at all. It never ended. *Never.*

Not that he objected. His duty was too important. It occupied . . . indeed it possessed . . . his mind and his soul.

First, as soon as he returned to Manhattan, he would quickly arrange to have a tap put on the woman's phone. That hadn't seemed necessary until today, until her visit to the apartment on East Eighty-second Street made it obvious that the woman continued to be obsessed with the death of her friend. If her phone had been tapped earlier, yesterday while she'd been at the morgue, for example, the chameleon might have learned that she'd made arrangements to fly to Washington, and his task of following her would have been less complicated. That oversight in his surveillance of her would now be corrected. Her trip to Washington might have nothing to do with the death of the man called Joseph Martin, but the chameleon couldn't depend on "might have." He needed to know everything that *she* knew.

Next, he would check with the members of his team to learn if they'd been successful in tracking down the man who'd tried to intercept the pictures that the woman had left to be developed at the photo shop near her apartment building. The chameleon had been one of three people who'd entered the store while the man was arguing with the clerk. As a consequence, the chameleon had gotten a good look at the man when he stormed from the shop, enough to give a thorough description to the members of his team. In particular, what had interested the chameleon—intensely so—were the man's gray eyes.

Finally, while the chameleon waited for his contacts in Washington to warn him when the woman would be returning to Manhattan, he would occupy his time by following someone else. The detective, Lieutenant Craig, was showing unusual interest in this matter. After all, the investigation should now belong to Homicide, not Missing Persons. Perhaps the lieutenant's *real* interest was in the woman. The chameleon didn't know. Yet. But he *would* know. Soon. *Everything* about the detective. Because anyone as persistent as Lieutenant Craig had become might learn things that were very, very useful.

2

On the Trump Shuttle 727 to Washington, Tess did her best to ignore the drone of the engines and concentrate on her priorities. She always felt discomfort after takeoffs and now rubbed her forehead while she opened and closed her mouth, trying to relieve the aching pressure in her sinuses and behind her ears. Nonetheless the photographs in her purse insisted. She wanted to seem casual, however. Not attract attention. Be cool. She was still disturbed that someone had tried to steal the pictures. Only after glancing at the passenger next to her did she decide to open her purse. The passenger was reading *USA Today,* the front-page sidebar of which said that a third of all species of North American fish were in danger of extermination. The next paragraph indicated that for every tree that was planted, four others were killed by acid rain, dried streams, or commercial development.

Angered by the article, her frustration intensifying, she opened her purse, removed the package of photographs, and studied them. The close-ups of the titles on Joseph's bookcase immediately attracted her attention.

With equal immediacy, she noticed that the seat-belt sign was off and stood to walk up the aisle toward a row of phones mounted on the bulkhead at the front of the cabin. Using her credit card, she put a call through to New York and her favorite bookstore, the Strand, on lower Broadway.

"Lester? How's it going? . . . Me? How'd you guess? Is my voice that distinctive? . . . Well, yeah, a little fuzzy. I'm on a plane to Washington. . . . No, just family business. Listen, can you do me a favor? I assume my credit's still good. It *better* be good, I drop a fortune in your store every month. So pay attention, okay? I've got a list. Are you ready?"

"Always, sweetheart. Anytime you want to . . ."

"Lester, will you give me a break?"

"Just trying to be friendly, my dear. Let's hear the titles."

"The Consolation of Philosophy, The Collected Dialogues of Plato, The Millennium, Eleanor of Aquitaine, The Art of Courtly Love, something in Spanish called *The Circle of the Neck of the Dove."*

"Never heard of that one, dear."

"Well, I've got plenty more." Tess recited them.

"No authors, sweetheart?"

"From what I'm looking at, I can barely read the titles, let alone . . ."

"You sound in stress."

"Stress? You don't know the half of it. Just get me those books as soon as possible."

"Got it, sweetheart. I'll check our stacks. As you're well aware, we've got just about everything."

"Send them to . . ." Tess almost said her loft in SoHo, but all at once, suspicious, remembering the incident at the photo shop, she told him the address for *Earth Mother Magazine* up from the Strand's location on Broadway.

Stomach cramping, she replaced the phone and returned to her seat, ignoring the curious glance of the passenger who set down his *USA Today.*

Tess closed her eyes—

—in truth, squeezed them tightly, painfully shut when she anticipated—

—dreaded—

—her arrival at Washington National Airport and her eventual meeting with her mother.

Not just her mother. Her dead father's nemesis.

That son of a bitch.

That murderous bastard.

That fucking Brian Hamilton.

3

Alexandria, Virginia

Although the sun had just begun to set, every downstairs window of the colonial mansion was brilliantly lit, every outside floodlight gleaming. As the taxi steered through a tall, open, metal gate, Tess scanned the shrubs that bordered the fence, then directed her gaze toward the spacious, upwardly sloping lawn, the numerous, elaborate flower gardens, the magnificent, towering oaks (from one of which she'd fallen and broken her arm as a child; with painful fondness, she remembered her father rushing to help her), the fountain that she'd loved to wade in (what a tomboy I was, she thought, and managed a smile).

At once her smile dissolved as the taxi continued along the extensive curved driveway, approaching the mansion and a silver Rolls Corniche parked below the white stone steps that led past columns to the huge double-doored entrance.

The Corniche had government plates. A chauffeur (bodyguard?) stood alertly next to it, his hands at his sides while he squinted toward the taxi.

No doubt about it. Brian Hamilton had arrived.

Tess paid the driver and got out of the taxi, staring at the chauffeur when she passed him, giving him a good look at her.

Brian had presumably told the man what she looked like. With a nod, he stepped back, ignoring her, directing his attention toward the taillights of the taxi as it continued around the semicircle of the driveway and disappeared down the quiet, tree-lined street. Yes, definitely a bodyguard, Tess thought.

She carried her suitcase up the steps and hesitated beneath the portico, finally ringing the doorbell.

Ten seconds later, a butler in livery answered.

Tess hadn't been here in so long that she didn't recognize him. "I've come to see my mother."

"I know, Ms. Drake. My name is Jonathan." He gave her a solemn smile. "Welcome. You're expected. If you please, let me carry your suitcase." He shut the door when she entered and with echoing footsteps, escorted her across the large, lofty, marble-floored vestibule toward the drawing room on the right. On the way, Tess noticed that a new Matisse had been added to the collection of paintings along the wall.

The drawing room's sliding oak door was closed. When the butler pulled it soundlessly open, Tess tried to appear calm the moment she saw her mother rise from a French Regency sofa to the left of the fireplace.

"Theresa, dear, how *wonderful* to see you." Her mother had never approved of her father's calling her Tess. Trim, tall, in her sixties, her mother looked ten years younger due to numerous face-lifts that nonetheless gave her aristocratic features a pinched expression.

As always in the evening, she wore a formal dress, this one made of expensive amber silk that whispered when she walked, and considerable jewelry: a diamond necklace, matching earrings, a ruby broach, a sapphire ring on one hand, her glinting, impressive engagement and wedding rings on the other (despite her husband's death six years ago, she persisted in wearing them), an emerald bracelet on one wrist, a gold Piaget watch on the other.

"Really, truly, how *wonderful*." Like so many graduates of Radcliffe in the pure old days before that women's college had crassly (God help us, what's the world coming to?) been integrated with the men at Harvard, she walked as if a board had been strapped to her back, and with husky tones reminiscent of Lauren Bacall (who *hadn't* gone to Radcliffe), she tended to emphasize her words. "It's been so *long*. You know how I *miss* you. You mustn't be such a *stranger*."

By then, her mother had reached Tess and with the obligatory, fashionable almost-kiss, brushed her right and then left cheek, barely touching, against Tess's.

"Yes, Mother, and it's good to see you." Tess managed to smile.

"Jonathan will take your suitcase to your room. Come in. Sit down. You must be *exhausted* from your travel."

"Mother, it's only an hour's flight from New York."

"Oh, really? Well, yes, I suppose that's true. Then why don't I *see* you more?"

Tess walked toward the French Regency chair placed across from and matching the sofa. "My work keeps me awfully busy. I barely have time to do my laundry, let alone—"

"Your *laundry*." Tess's mother cocked her head back. "You do your own . . . ? I keep forgetting. You want to be *independent*."

"That's right, Mother." Tess squirmed against the scrollwork on the chair while her eyes searched the room but, disturbingly, found no sign of Brian Hamilton. "Independent."

"And your work? *How* is your little magazine doing?"

"It isn't little, Mother. And I think it's doing some good."

"Well, *that's* what we want." Tess's mother fidgeted on the sofa. "It's about the environment? Something about *pollution?*"

Tess nodded. "And the problem's getting worse."

"Well, of course, at *my* age, I won't live long enough to— Never mind. The important thing is that you're happy."

"Yes, Mother." Despite her confused emotions . . . about Joseph's death, about the man whose description resembled him, the man who'd attempted to steal the photographs she'd taken of Joseph's bedroom . . . Tess managed a genuine smile. She imitated her mother's habit of emphasis. "I *am* happy."

"Well," Her mother smoothed her dress. "In *that* case"— she straightened her necklace—"I suppose that's all that matters." But she didn't look convinced.

Tess felt self-conscious as her mother assessed her sneakers, jeans, and short-sleeved cotton pullover. "I know, Mother. You wish I'd dress like—"

"A *lady*. At the moment, you appear to have come from an athletic event. At the *very* least, you could have worn a brassiere."

"I feel more comfortable this way, Mother. Especially when it's so humid."

"Humid? Precisely. Your pullover's so damp that I can see your . . . I'll *never* forgive myself for allowing you to go to Georgetown University instead of one of the Seven *Sisters*."

Tess bristled. "It wasn't you who let me go. It was Father."

Tess's mother shook her head. "That's an ancient topic. We've discussed it *far* too often. I'm sorry I raised it. Since we see each other so seldom, let's do our best to be agreeable."

"That's all I want, Mother."

"Very well, then, it's settled. We'll be agreeable." Tess's mother smoothed her dress again. "I know you *told* me not to have dinner prepared, but I took the liberty of having Edna prepare some liver pâté. You always *enjoyed* that, as I recall."

"Very much," Tess lied.

"And some *tea,* of course. I think we could all use some tea."

As her mother picked up and daintily jingled a tiny silver bell, Tess peered around again. "Speaking of all of us, I asked Brian Hamilton to meet me here." Tess frowned. "I think that's his Corniche in the driveway, but I don't—"

The door to the drawing room slid open. Tess swung her head sharply. A maid stepped in. She wore a uniform, complete with a bonnet, and carried a silver tray of toast and pâté, placing them on a thirty-thousand dollar antique table.

Someone else appeared, a man who wore a tuxedo and carried another silver tray upon which were teacups and a two-hundred-year-old Japanese teapot. "I apologize for taking so long on the phone, Melinda. I hope you don't mind. I thought I'd make myself useful and help Edna bring in the things."

"Mind? Of course not. I'm sure Edna appreciates the courtesy, and no guest of *mine* can ever do anything wrong."

The man set his tray beside the toast and pâté on the table, then turned to Tess and smiled. He was in his early sixties, but for all that, he was straight backed, trim, solid, with thick, dark, superbly cut hair, and a rectangular, ruggedly handsome face. He photographed extremely well. In newspapers, the captions beneath the photographs usually emphasized his numerous medals from Vietnam and his legendary career as a maverick general in the Marines. His smile exaggerated the crinkles around his eyes and made him look more rugged. His voice was husky but with the smooth cadence of a television announcer. "How are you, Tess?" He held out his manicured, muscular hand.

Reluctantly Tess shook it. His grip was firm. "I've been better, Brian. At the moment, I've got a problem."

"So I gathered on the phone." Brian turned toward the maid, then raised his eyebrows toward Tess's mother. "But before we discuss . . ."

Tess's mother got the hint. "That'll be fine, Edna. We can pour the tea ourselves."

"As you like, ma'am." Edna curtsied and left the room, pulling the door shut behind her.

"There," Tess's mother said. "Now I'm *sure* you wouldn't mind doing the honors, Brian."

"Of course." He picked up the teapot.

"No, wait," Tess said. "Before we . . . I'm really not . . ."

They frowned at her.

". . . thirsty or hungry. I grabbed a pretzel in the airport."

"Pretzel?" Tess's mother looked horrified.

"I'd like to get to the point," Tess said. "And Brian, since you're wearing your tuxedo, I assume that means you either just came from—or still plan to go to—the reception for the Soviet ambassador. I also assume that means you're anxious either to return or arrive there, so I won't keep you any longer than necessary. Believe me, I don't want to waste your time." She tried not to sound sarcastic.

"Tess, you could never waste my time." Brian set down the teapot, came around the table, and faced her. "I told you on the phone, for the sake of old times . . . and your father . . . I want to do everything I can to help."

"Exactly. My father."

"We were friends," Brian said.

"But that didn't stop you from sending him to Beirut."

"Now honestly," her mother said, "if this conversation is going to be *unpleasant,* I don't intend to sit here and—"

"That's a good idea, Mother. Why don't you leave? Brian and I have things to talk about."

"No, Melinda, you stay right where you are. It's time we cleared the air," Brian said. "For all of us." He sat beside Tess's mother and clasped her hand.

At once, for the first time, Tess had the suspicion that they might be having an affair. Her father's best friend? The man who'd sent that best friend to his death? Could that monster possibly be screwing his best friend's wife? The thought of the two of them in bed together made Tess so queasy that she wished she hadn't eaten the pretzel on the way from the airport.

"Okay, the three of us," Tess said. "That's fine with me. Just so long as I get what I want."

"Your father was a committed diplomat," Brian said. "He went to that insanity in Beirut because he thought he could make a difference, help settle the violence among the Christians, the Moslems, and all their splinter groups. In his heart, he believed he could actually stop the killing."

"You sound like you're making a speech," Tess said.

Brian shrugged. "An occupational hazard."

"In fact, that bromide you just gave me, I think I read those same words in the *Washington Post* at the time of my father's death."

"Possibly." Brian looked despondent. "Unfortunately, on occasion, because I'm asked so many questions, I'm forced to repeat myself."

"But what you didn't tell the *Post* was that my father was sent to Beirut to negotiate an arms agreement with the side you wanted to win—the Christians. And you *also* didn't tell the *Post* that your security was so damned sloppy that the Moslems found out and kidnapped my father to stop him from completing the arms deal."

"Now, Tess, that's all speculation."

"Don't treat me like a fool. The Moslems wanted my father to confess about U.S. interference on the side of the Christians. But my father wouldn't confess no matter what they did to him, no matter how much they tortured him. So they beat him, they starved him, and when he *still* wouldn't talk, they slit his throat and dumped him into a gutter. As an example to America not to interfere.''

"Tess, that's your interpretation. Weapons had nothing to do with it. He was there as a well-intentioned negotiator, pure and simple.''

"Nothing about what you bastards do is pure and simple.''

Tess's mother flinched. "I refuse to tolerate vulgar language in—''

"No, let her finish, Melinda. For once and for all, we'll settle this,'' Brian said.

"I know what you ordered my father to do. I know he disapproved of the assignment but wouldn't refuse an order from the White House,'' Tess said. *"How* do I know? Because I overheard his conversations on the phone. And when he brought documents from work, I not only secretly read them. I made copies before he shredded them.''

"If you did, Tess, that's a breach of national security. There are serious penalties for—''

"As serious as what happened to my father? What would you do to me? Put me in jail? Of course not. I'd talk. So unless you want another Iran-contra arms scandal, you'd have to kill me!''

"That's *enough.*'' Tess's mother jerked upright. "That's *all* I intend to hear. Your father was a great man, and I won't listen to you sully either his or Brian's reputation!''

"No, Melinda, wait.'' Brian clasped her hand again, his voice disturbingly calm. "I think Tess is almost finished. I believe she's leading up to something. And when she finally gets to the point, I suspect we'll finally settle the ghost that haunts us. Tess, excuse me, but if I can be allowed to be vulgar, cut to the chase. What in hell do you want?''

Tess inhaled and answered as calmly as she could. "Whenever I see your name in the newspaper, I look away in fury. But I don't live in limbo. I hear things. Despite the change in administration, I gather you're still very much associated with the government.''

"That's correct.'' Brian straightened.

"With the National Security Council, among other things,'' Tess said.

"An unsubstantiated rumor."

"Hey, Brian, we're talking about payoff time! A favor in exchange for my silence! I won't forgive you for what you ordered my father to do, but I swear—God help me—if you do what I want, I'll never raise the subject again!"

The rugged-faced war hero studied her. "That's a tempting offer."

"Then take it."

The diplomat's eyes became more calculating. "So what's your problem?"

Tess's cramped muscles abruptly went limp. "I have . . . That is, I *had* . . . I don't know what to call him. . . . A friend."

Slowly, haltingly, for the next quarter hour, Tess explained, describing her meetings with Joseph, his failure to join her at the park, her grotesque experience at the New York City morgue, her disturbing visit to Joseph's apartment. She ended her stressful account by displaying the photographs of the puzzling objects in Joseph's bedroom.

Brian studied the photographs. "Weird. Are you sure your friend wasn't on drugs?"

"Drugs? No way. And he didn't drink either. He didn't even use aspirin. He was fanatical about his health."

"But he acted as if he might have been followed. And . . ." Brian shook his head. "I honestly . . . What do you want me to do?"

"Use your infuence with the FBI and the CIA. I think that Joseph might have been Spanish. I know he assumed a false identity. The FBI has his fingerprints. Make copies of them and send them to Interpol. Get in touch with . . . Whatever it is you do, *do* it. Pretend the country's been threatened, if that gives you motivation. I want to know Joseph's real identity. I want to find out who killed him! And who tried to steal these photographs! And who might be following me! And—"

"Wait," Brian interrupted. "You believe . . . You're telling me you think you've been *followed?*"

"I'm so confused I don't know *what* to think."

"All right. Calm down. Let me . . . All right, those photographs. Can I borrow them and make copies?"

"Not a chance. I won't let them out of my sight."

"In other words, you don't trust me to keep them safe."

"I'll have copies made and send them to you."

"Very well," Brian said. "Clear enough. . . . I have one more question."

"I've got nothing to hide. Ask it."

"You met this man three times, and only three times, and yet you feel this obligated to find out who killed him. Does that mean you fell in love with him?"

Tess glared defensively. "It's more complicated than that. He was different. Special. Let's say I *cared* for him. So what?"

"Just so I know your motive."

"My motive is justice, Brian. The same motive *you're* supposed to have. As long as it doesn't involve selling weapons in Beirut."

"All right." Brian stood, military straight. "You'll hear from me."

"The sooner, the—"

"Speed isn't always a virtue," Brian said. "But thoroughness? In that, I'm an expert."

"Then prove it," Tess said.

"One day, I hope you won't hate me."

"I don't know why you would care. No." Tess shook her head. "That's wrong. I've got a suspicion, so Brian, if I'm right . . . for my father . . . and your relationship with my *mother* . . . bust your ass."

"Theresa," her mother objected.

"Mother, if you don't mind, keep out of this."

"Oh, my." Her mother clasped her mouth.

Brian extended his hand. "A deal, Tess?"

"If you deliver? Yes, it's a deal." She shook his hand. It was no longer firm.

"As soon as I can."

"Knowing you and your skills . . ." Tess paused.

"*You* should have been a diplomat."

"Far too ugly, Brian."

"Perhaps you're right. Excuse me, Melinda. I've got some work to do."

"Don't forget the reception for the Soviet ambassador," Tess said bitterly.

"I haven't. But I've decided not to go. As you put it on the phone, fuck him. But by all means, with respect."

"Yes, by all means."

Brian Hamilton strode toward the oak door, slid it open, and disappeared.

"Really," Tess's mother said, "did he have to say . . . ?"

" 'Fuck'? Mother, for heaven's sake, he's a war hero. If you're attracted to him, you'd better get used to hearing him use foul language on occasion."

"Good gracious, I hope not."

"Mother, didn't Father ever say 'fuck'?"

"Well, yes, but I ignored it."

"Then you've got a problem. I've changed my mind. Hand me some of that toast. Pour me a cup of tea."

"I'll ring for Edna."

"No, Mother. You'll pour the tea. And incidentally, I hate liver pâté."

4

Parked down the shadowy street from the mansion in this elite district of Alexandria, Virginia, the chameleon's surrogate—his height, weight, and features equally unremarkable, exept that his hair was sandy, not brown—sipped stale coffee from a plastic cup, his empty thermos on the seat beside him, next to his Browning 9-mm semiautomatic pistol concealed beneath his oversize metal briefcase.

The briefcase was open, a cord from an audio scanner plugged into the car's cigarette-lighter receptacle to use energy from the vehicle's battery. The scanner could not detect broadcasts from two-way radios, such as those used by the police and taxi drivers, which operated on a UHF frequency in the range of four hundred megahertz. Instead the scanner was intended to intercept conversations from cellular telephones, such as those used in cars, which broadcast on a much higher frequency, the eight-hundred-megahertz band.

While it was legal to possess equipment to eavesdrop on police transmissions, it was a punishable offense to own a receiver that intercepted broadcasts from car phones. Not that the chameleon's surrogate cared. He'd broken many laws in his career. *This* was the least of them.

Indeed he was prepared to break *many* more laws, and it didn't matter to him how serious they were. After all, he had his orders, a mission to complete, and so far this mission had gone smoothly. He'd had no difficulty in following the tall, blond, attractive, athletic-looking woman from Washington National Airport to here. At the moment, with an equal lack of difficulty, another member of his team was arranging to put a tap on the mansion's telephone system. Eventually the mansion itself would be bugged. Meanwhile this limited electronic surveillance would have to do.

Periodically the man, who wore an ordinary, medium-priced business suit and had a talent for making himself virtually invisible in a crowd, heard a dim conversation from this or that frequency on his scanner. After listening carefully, he decided that their topics did not concern him.

Periodically as well, he turned on his car's engine so that the scanner wouldn't drain the vehicle's battery. Although he directed his stern attention toward the mansion and in particular toward the entrance and the exit from the semicircular driveway, he repeatedly darted his eyes both ahead and upward, in the latter case toward his rearview mirror.

What troubled him were headlights. If he saw any approaching him, he'd immediately shut off the car's engine, disengage the plug from the cigarette-lighter receptacle, place the cord in the briefcase, and close the lid. After all, this exclusive area was likely to be patrolled by police cars, the officers in which might be tempted to stop to ask him why he was out here at this hour.

That was the trouble with trying to establish an automobile

surveillance site in an upper-class suburban neighborhood. Few people, if any, parked on the street. *This* night, however, the watcher had gotten lucky. A half block down from the mansion, someone was having a party—or what in so exclusive a district was probably called a reception—and not all the visiting cars had been able to fit in the spacious driveway. A few Cadillacs and Oldsmobiles sat out here in the street behind him, but although the watcher's dark Ford Taurus didn't blend with those expensive automobiles, the watcher doubted he'd have any problems in convincing a curious policeman that he was a hired driver who'd been forced to use this Taurus when the Cadillac he was to use turned out, he would claim, to have a faulty fuel pump earlier this evening. The watcher's luck remained with him. No police cars had so far driven by.

Abruptly he straightened, seeing a silver Rolls Corniche emerge from the mansion's driveway and head in the opposite direction. After quickly removing night-vision binoculars from beneath his seat, he studied the Corniche and satisfied himself that only a chauffeur and a man in the backseat were inside. The Corniche had a government license plate. Intriguing.

The watcher noted the plate's number on a slip of paper and would later use his contacts to determine who owned the car, but for the moment, since the woman wasn't in the Corniche, his duty was not to follow the car but instead to maintain his surveillance on the mansion.

At once he heard beeps, then buzzes that were interrupted by a voice from his audio scanner, so distinct that it had to be coming from a car phone that was near, presumably in the Corniche.

"Hello," a man said with a formal tone. "Mr. Chatham's residence."

"This is Brian Hamilton. I know it's late. I hate to disturb him, but is Eric home?"

"He is. However, he's about to retire for the evening."

"Tell him who's calling, please. And tell him it's important."

The watcher increased his concentration. Eric Chatham? Chatham was the director of the FBI! And Brian Hamilton, evidently the passenger in the Corniche, was the former secretary of state, currently an adviser to the President, also a member of—among other things—the National Security Council.

My, my, the watcher thought. Heavy hitters.

"By all means. Just a moment, Mr. Hamilton."

The watcher stared toward the red light on his audio scanner and the voices coming from it.

"Brian?" a sonorous voice asked, tired and puzzled. "I was just getting into my pajamas. I've been looking forward to reading the new Stephen King, something that has nothing to do with . . . Never mind. What's going on? My assistant tells me this is important."

"I apologize," Hamilton said. "I came across some information tonight, and I'd like to discuss it with you."

"Now? Can't it wait until the morning? At my office? My schedule's crowded, but I can squeeze you in for fifteen minutes just before lunch."

"I might need more than fifteen minutes," Hamilton said. "In private. Undistracted." The reception became less distinct as the Corniche left the neighborhood.

"In *private?*" Eric Chatham sounded confused.

"Yes. This relates to a case your people were asked to work on. But in truth, it's personal. It has to do with Remington Drake, his widow, and his daughter. I need to ask a favor."

"Remington Drake! Dear God. And this favor's important?"

"To me. Yes, *very* important," Brian Hamilton said.

"A favor? Well, if you're putting it on that basis. You've certainly done enough favors for me, and Remington Drake was certainly my friend. How quickly can you be here?"

"Ten minutes."

"I'll be waiting."

"Thanks, Eric. I appreciate your cooperation."

"Don't speak too soon. I haven't cooperated *yet.*"

"But I have every confidence that you will. Ten minutes."

The transmission ended.

The watcher frowned, trying to interpret what he'd heard. But he'd been concentrating so hard that he'd failed to hear something else, the soft rush of rubber-soled shoes on the street, darting toward his side of the car. Because of the heat, the watcher had left his window open. After all, he couldn't keep his engine running constantly at the risk of attracting attention just so he could use the car's air conditioner.

In alarm, as the watcher—stomach burning—snapped his head toward the rushing footsteps, he gaped at a .22 pistol being shoved through the open window. Startled, he didn't have time to grab his Browning from beneath his suitcase. The .22, equipped with a silencer, made a spitting sound. The watcher groaned from the impact of the .22 bullet against his skull. The close-range wallop was forceful enough to jolt the watcher sideways. Blood spewed. He shuddered and toppled to the right across his audio scanner.

But the small bullet didn't kill him. Shocked, powerless, in excruciating pain, he retained sufficient consciousness to sense, hear, and quiver as the assassin jerked open the driver's door.

The assassin grabbed the watcher's body, twisted it, and shoved it, crammed it, onto the floor below the passenger seat. At once the assassin shut the door, started the car, and drove at a steady, unobtrusive speed from the shadowy neighborhood.

Slumped on the floor, the watcher blinked, unable to see, feeling his life drain from him as his blood soaked the carpet. His skull felt as if a nail had been driven through it. If the assassin had used a more powerful weapon, the watcher would have been killed instantly, he dimly realized. But a large-caliber pistol, even with a silencer, would have made a discernible noise, not much, more like a cough than the .22's spit, all the same perhaps just loud enough that someone leaving the party down the street might have heard and become suspicious. A silencer-equipped .22, though—especially if the ammunition had a specially calculated, reduced, so-called "subsonic" amount of powder—was almost as quiet as a handgun could be.

In a sickening daze, the watcher felt the car turn a corner. As his blood pooled in front of his face, threatening to drown him, he was murkily amazed that he wasn't dead. Through his terrible pain, a weak thought struggled to assure him that he might have a chance of surviving.

Survive?

Hey, who are you kidding?

Give me a break.

With a head wound?

No way.

But he knows I'm still alive. He can hear me wheezing. Why doesn't he shoot a second time and finish me?

An amateur?

No.

God in heaven, *no,* the watcher's fading mind concluded.

Thoughts spinning, the stench of his cascading blood making him gag, he blearily decided, I'm wrong! Not an amateur. When the watcher had pivoted toward the rushing footsteps, he'd noticed that the pistol had an unusual shape, a baffle attached to the top where the slide would normally jerk back and eject the empty cartridge, then snap forward to position a fresh round into the firing chamber.

But the baffle prevented the slide from moving back and forth and allowing sound to escape from the weapon. The baffle was a reinforcement of the silencer. Thus the .22 could be fired only once! That was why the assassin hadn't pulled the trigger again and made sure I was dead!

No! Not an amateur! A professional. Very professional! A well trained, experienced killer!

The assassin was good enough to need only one shot. He's aware I don't have a chance. He knows it's only a matter of time until . . .

The watcher, even more weak and light-headed, began to pray in agony, with fervent desperation. It was all he could do now. He had to protect his soul. His only consolation was that he couldn't be interrogated. Nonetheless, he regretted that he wouldn't be able to prevent the assassin from searching him and taking the ring that he kept hidden in his suit coat.

Abruptly he felt the car stop. He heard the assassin get out and heard another car stop beside the Taurus.

So they're going to leave me here—wherever this is—to die?

Hope made his weakening pulse regain some strength. Maybe I can muster the energy to crawl from the Taurus. Maybe I can find someone to help me, to drive me to a hospital.

But his hope was cruelly destroyed, for the next dim sound he heard wasn't the assassin getting into the other car. Instead he heard liquid being spattered into the Taurus. He felt it soak his clothes and retched from the sharp stench of gasoline.

No!

The last thing he heard was a match being struck and the whoosh as the gasoline ignited. Flames filled the Taurus and swooped across his body. No! Dear God! In absolute torment, he prayed more fervently. Our Father Who art in heaven . . . ! Amazingly his will was powerful enough that he got as far as *deliver us from evil* before the excruciating blaze consumed him.

5

In the mansion's vestibule, as Tess walked toward the huge, wide staircase, her mother said, "Despite the evening's regrettable unpleasantness, I really am glad that you came to visit. I hope a *good* night's sleep will put you in a better mood."

"Thanks, Mother. And it's good to see *you*." Tess drooped her shoulders. "But somehow I doubt I'll sleep much. I've got too much to think about."

"Well, perhaps if you had something to read. That always puts *me* to sleep. Oh, my." Tess's mother halted abruptly on the staircase.

"What's the matter?"

"I completely *forgot*. You asked me to phone the director at the Library of Congress. He found that *book* you wanted and sent it here by messenger." Tess's mother retreated down the stairs. "It's in the drawing room. But he says you made a *mistake* about the title."

"The Circle—or else *The Ring*—*of the Neck of the Dove?"*

"Apparently that's a *literal* translation from Spanish. But in

English, the prepositions disappear and . . ." Tess's mother hurried into the drawing room and came back, removing a tattered book from a package. *"The Dove's Neck Ring.* Yes, that's what it's called."

The book smelled old. Tess quickly opened it, her spirits rising when she saw that it was in English. "Thank you." She hugged her mother, who blinked at so forceful a show of affection. "I appreciate it. Honestly. Thank you."

Her mother looked confused. "I've never seen anyone get so excited about a *book* before. When I paged through it, waiting for you to arrive, it certainly didn't appear very interesting."

"On the contrary, Mother, I expect to be fascinated." Heart pounding, Tess wanted to rush upstairs to her room so she could start reading, but she forced herself to climb the steps slowly, matching her mother's pace. In a long upper corridor lined with paintings by French Impressionists, they paused outside Tess's door.

"Good night, Mother." Tess kissed her cheek. Again her mother looked surprised. "I apologize for making a scene, but you can't imagine what I've been through the past few days. You have my word, I'll try my best not to upset you anymore."

"Dear." With a choked voice, her mother hesitated. "You don't have to apologize. Good heavens, you're all I have. I'll *never* stop loving you. Make as many scenes as you want. You'll always be welcome here. And I promise, I'll do *everything* I can to help solve your problems."

Tess felt pressure in her tear ducts.

At once her mother did an amazing thing. She kissed Tess in return, no casual brush of a cheek against cheek, but an actual kiss, her lips placed firmly yet tenderly on Tess's brow. "Remember what I used to tell you when I tucked you in bed when you were a child? Sleep tight. Don't let the bedbugs bite."

Tess brushed a tear from her eye. "I remember. I . . ."

"What, dear?"

"I don't say this often enough. I love you, Mother."

"I know. I've never doubted it. Stay in bed as long as you want. Phone the kitchen in the morning and tell Edna what you want for breakfast. Then please phone *me.* I'd like to join you."

Tess sniffled, wiping her cheeks. "I look forward to it."

"I wish you wouldn't cry."

"Of course. I remember. Emotion always made you uncomfortable."

"It's not so much *feeling* emotion but showing it," her mother said. "Very early, a diplomat's wife learns the difference."

"Well, Mother, I'm afraid I'm not a diplomat's wife. I'm merely his daughter."

"The daughter of Remington Drake? Not 'merely.' Not at all. Between your father and me, you're made from strength. Obey your heritage. Be strong."

"I will, Mother. I promise."

"I repeat, I love you. And by the way, there aren't any monsters under your bed. I guarantee it."

Tess watched her mother proceed down the corridor, a tired elderly woman whose footsteps faltered slightly but who nonetheless maintained her posture, trying to walk with dignity. Only when her mother stepped into her bedroom did Tess, heart aching, go into her own.

6

The room had been Tess's bedroom for as long as she'd been alive. Turning on the overhead light, shutting the door behind her, she studied the canopied bed, the covers of which a servant had folded down. The servant, presumably the butler, had also unpacked her suitcase, placing her shorts and T-shirt on a lace-rimmed pillow.

With bittersweet emotion, Tess scanned the room, her complex layers of memory making her see it as if transparent photographs had been placed in front of one another, all the different stages of her youth: her childhood bed, her dollhouse (which her father had made), her stuffed play animals, then the larger bed and her baseball glove on the bureau, her bat and ball beside it, the posters of baseball and football stars that had given way to posters of rock stars and her stack of records beside her stereo, the books she'd studied in college (she'd refused to live in a dorm at Georgetown University, preferring to stay at home so she could be near her father).

All gone now. All lost and gone.

With a shudder of regret, she subdued her nostalgia, peered down at the book in her hand, and forced herself to pay attention to why she'd come here.

The Dove's Neck Ring. The title page indicated that the book by Ibn Hazm had been translated from Spanish by A. R. Nykl in 1931. Leafing through the introduction as she walked toward the bed, she learned that Ibn Hazm had been an Arab who'd emigrated from northern Africa to southern Spain in the early eleventh century and had written this book, a treatise on platonic love, in 1022.

Plato.

Tess suddenly remembered *The Collected Dialogues of Plato* that she'd seen on the bookcase in Joseph's bedroom. And she painfully remembered something else: Joseph's insistence that his relationship with her could never be physical, only platonic. "That way is better," he'd said. "Because it's eternal."

Dejected, she turned on the bedside lamp, reached for the switch that extinguished the overhead light, and slumped on the bed, propping pillows behind her, continuing to scan the book.

She could understand why her mother had found it boring. The book was an elaborate essay, not a narrative, and its stilted English translation tried to recreate the feel of medieval Spanish. It was crammed with homilies and abstractions.

According to the introduction, *The Dove's Neck Ring* had been extremely popular in its day, often copied by hand; the printing press had not yet been invented. Eventually the book had made its way upward through Spain to southern France, where in the mid-twelfth century it had been one of the texts that formed the basis for an idealized view of the relationship between men and women, known as courtly love.

The expression caught Tess's attention. She suddenly remembered another book that she'd seen in Joseph's bedroom: *The Art of Courtly Love*. But why had Joseph been fascinated by that subject?

147

Reading with greater curiosity, Tess learned that the notion of courtly love had appealed to and been sponsored by the then Queen of France, Eleanor of Aquitaine (the title of *another* book in Joseph's bedroom!), and later by Eleanor's daughter, Marie de France, both of whom had gathered poets and minstrels around them, directing them to compose verses and songs that celebrated a ritualized, highly polite, and refined set of rules that dictated how men and women should behave toward one another.

Tess scrunched her forehead in confusion. She didn't know how these puzzling details fit together, but Joseph had obviously acted toward her in keeping with the strictest of the codes of courtly love.

While one branch of this ancient tradition treated courtly love as a type of foreplay, a prelude to sex, the other branch of the tradition had maintained that sex was an impure, imperfect form of love. According to the author of *The Dove's Neck Ring,* true love wasn't based on physical attraction but rather on an attraction between kindred spirits, compatible souls. These souls had once existed in harmony, during a prelife that reminded Tess of heaven. When born into the physical world, the souls had been separated and thereafter felt incomplete, compelled to keep looking for one another, never to be satisfied until they met. Just as their original relationship had been pure, in the sense of nonphysical, nonsexual, so their relationship in *this* world should be the same, uncontaminated by the vulgarities of the flesh. This idea of a heavenlike prelife evidently came from Plato's dialogues (Tess again remembered the book by Plato in Joseph's bedroom), and the notion of nonsexual, highly spiritual affection between men and women was thus known as platonic love.

Tess scrunched her forehead harder, a deep corner of her sub-consciousness straining to understand. For certain, she'd felt an instant identification with Joseph the moment he'd entered the elevator when she'd first met him last Wednesday.

Had it been only a week ago?

But her reaction to Joseph had not been merely an identification.

Much more! An *attraction.* Powerful. What romantics liked to describe as love at first sight, but what the long-dead author of *The Dove's Neck Ring* would have called love at *second* sight.

All theory. Speculation. Surely it didn't explain Tess's overwhelming determination.

Courtly love? Plato? Why in God's name had Joseph been so obsessed with these ideas?

Her chest ached. On impulse, she glanced at her watch, surprised to discover that it was almost two A.M.

Although she'd told her mother that she was so disturbed she doubted she'd be able to sleep, she abruptly felt exhausted and decided to get out of her clothes, change into her shorts and T-shirt, and try to sleep.

But as she stood and removed her cotton pullover, she noticed the phone on the bedside table.

The mansion's air-conditioning made her breasts cold, nipples rising.

Still, she hesitated, staring at the phone. I ought to call my loft and check if I've got any messages on my answering machine, she told herself.

No. It can wait till morning.

Sure.

But so much has . . .

I ought to make sure that nothing else has happened.

So she tapped buttons on the phone, listened to the static on the long-distance line, heard a buzz, then another buzz, and finally her voice on the answering machine. "This is Tess. I can't answer the phone right now. Please leave a message at the tone."

Immediately she tapped two more numbers, 24, her birthdate, the security code that she'd programmed into her answering machine that would prevent anyone else from calling her home, pressing two numbers at random, and gaining access to her messages.

A man's gravelly voice was instantly recognizable. "Tess, it's Lieutenant Craig. The time is"—garbled voices in the background—"quarter after five. Call me at the office as soon as you can."

A beep signaled the end of the message.

Curious—shivering because of it—Tess waited to hear if she had any other messages.

"It's Lieutenant Craig again. Half past six. Call me at once."

Another beep.

The urgency in the lieutenant's voice made Tess even more anxious to hang up and phone him, but she resisted the impulse, still needing to know if she had other messages.

"It's Lieutenant Craig. It's almost eleven. Where the hell *are* you? *Call me.*"

This time, there were three beeps, the signal that all the messages had been replayed. Tess broke the connection, removed her wallet from her purse, found the card that Craig had given her, and decided that even though his first message had told her to call him at the office, he wouldn't be there now at two in the morning.

Quickly tapping numbers, she called his home.

Again she heard long-distance static, then a buzz, another buzz, and another.

By the fifth buzz, she began to suspect that Craig *was* at the office. By the sixth, she became certain and lowered her hand toward the disconnect lever so she could try his office. When her hand was an inch from the lever, a crusty voice said, "Hello?" and coughed.

She pressed the phone hard against her ear. "It's Tess. I'm sorry if I woke you, but your messages—"

"Where have you *been?* My God, you had me worried."

"I'm in Alexandria, Virginia." In the background, Tess heard soaring music, an orchestra, a chorus, a soprano hitting impossibly high notes.

"*Alexandria?* What are you doing *there?*" The soprano's voice swooped, then rose again.

"My mother lives here. I caught the six o'clock shuttle."

"But you haven't answered my question. What are you—"

"Trying to explain what we saw in Joseph's apartment. My mother has contacts with the Library of Congress and . . ." Tess hesitated, not wanting to tell the lieutenant about her mother's powerful connections with the government because of her father. "Is that opera I hear in the background?"

"Puccini's *Madame Butterfly.* Just a second. I'll turn it off."

A moment later, the music stopped.

"I didn't know you liked opera," Tess said. "Somehow you don't seem the type to—"

"Listen to me," Craig said. "Don't ever leave town like that again! Not without telling me! You *have* to let me know where I

150

can reach you. When I kept calling and you didn't answer your phone, I got worried that something had happened to you.''

"Well, in a way, something almost did.''

"What?''

"Those pictures I took at Joseph's apartment. I left them at a one-hour photo shop while I packed. When I went back to the shop, the clerk told me that a man who claimed I'd sent him tried to get the photographs.''

"Jesus.''

"The only way the man could have known about those pictures is if he'd followed us when we left Joseph's apartment and he saw me go into the photo shop,'' Tess said with urgency.

"That sure as hell sounds logical to me. *Jesus,*'' the lieutenant said again, and coughed. "That's what I mean. You can't stay out of touch. You've got to let me know where you are and what you're doing. This might be dangerous for you.''

"There's *more*. I don't understand it, but when the clerk described the man, it sounded like Joseph. The man even had gray eyes. Could I have been wrong at the morgue? Could Joseph be *alive?* Could—''

"No, Tess, you weren't wrong. That much I can guarantee. Whoever the man was, he very definitely wasn't Joseph.''

"But how can you be sure? *How do you explain the gray eyes?''*

"Coincidence maybe,'' Craig said. "I don't know, but—''

"You yourself said that the scar on the corpse's wrist wasn't enough for an absolute identification. Maybe that scar's a coincidence, too. Since the FBI hasn't been able to match the corpse's fingerprints with anyone in their files, maybe—''

"No, Tess, we *do* have a match. That's one of the things I tried to call you about.''

"From the FBI?'' Tess asked quickly. "They *know* Joseph's real identity?''

"Not from the FBI. From our own lab. They dusted Joseph's apartment and matched the prints they found there with those from the unburned left hand on the corpse in the morgue. Tess, the fingerprints match. Point by point, they *match,* and they also match fingerprints on Joseph's desk at Truth Video. Your identification's been verified. Joseph died in Carl Schurz Park.''

Tess's knees abruptly weakened. She sank toward the bed and shivered so much that she wrapped a sheet around her. Since the incident in the photo shop, her fear that someone might be following her had been tempered by the hope that whoever it was would be Joseph, that Joseph might somehow still be alive.

But now she suffered a renewed aching surge of grief, her stomach sinking, her chest hollow, her mind off-balance.

"Tess?"

She tried to answer.

"Tess?" Craig emphasized her name, sounding worried.

"I'm here. I'm . . . Yes, I'm all right."

"For a moment, I thought . . . Look, I'm sorry. I guess I could have been more delicate."

"I felt . . . Never mind. I'll be okay," Tess said.

"You're sure?"

"All that matters now is getting even, finding out who killed Joseph and why." Tess shook her head, bitter. "You said the matching fingerprints were *one* of the reasons you tried to call. What else—?"

"It's about the photographs." Craig paused.

"And?" Tess frowned. "You're going to make me ask? What about them?"

"It's a good thing you took them, and a damned good thing the clerk didn't give them to the guy who claimed you'd sent him."

"What's *wrong?*"

"Someone broke into Joseph's apartment. They torched his bedroom."

Tess jerked upright, the sheet falling off her shoulders. *"Torched it?"*

"Almost burned the whole top floor before the fire department put it out. It's a miracle no one was hurt."

"Christ, when did this happen?"

"Four o'clock."

"About the same time the guy was trying to steal my pictures."

"Which are the only record of what we found in Joseph's apartment," Craig said.

"But I thought you said Homicide got there before we did and took photographs."

"I was wrong," Craig said. "What they sent was a fingerprint team. When they saw the bedroom, they decided they wanted pictures. The photographer was scheduled to show up in the afternoon."

"But he *didn't?*"

"Not in time. After all, the apartment wasn't a crime scene. There didn't seem any urgency."

"Oh, shit."

"Just make sure those photographs are safe. Hide them. Have copies made from the negatives," Craig said.

"First thing tomorrow morning."

"*Several* copies. Keep another set. Are you coming back to Manhattan tomorrow?"

"I don't know yet," Tess said. "I still have things to check."

"Then send the other copies to me. Federal Express." Craig gave his office address at One Police Plaza. "There's one other problem."

"I'm not sure I want to hear it."

"After the Fire Department put out the blaze, when they thought it was safe, they let me search the torched apartment. That building has concrete floors. There wasn't any risk of my falling through or of *anything else* having fallen through."

"I don't know what you're getting at," Tess said nervously.

"I had to use a pole to move sections of the toppled ceiling and walls. But I knew where to look, so it didn't take me long to clear the spot I wanted."

"*What* spot? What are you—?"

"Where the bookcase was," Craig said. "Where the *statue* stood on the bookcase. The books were destroyed, as you'd expect. So was the bookcase. Just ashes. But the statue was made of marble, and marble doesn't burn. It might crack from heat, but . . . I kept looking. The statue couldn't have fallen through the concrete floor, and when it toppled from the bookcase, it couldn't have rolled very far. It's gone, Tess. The statue's gone! Whoever torched the apartment must have taken it when they left. I don't know what the hell's happening, but I want you to promise me. Swear it. *Be careful!*"

7

East of Maine, the North Atlantic

The United States Coast Guard cutter *Sea Wolf,* out of Portland, continued its speedy mission through a moderately choppy sea. Clouds obscured the moon and stars, intensifying the night, although even in daylight the *Sea Wolf*'s destination was still too far away to have allowed for a visual identification. On the cutter's bridge, Captain Peter O'Malley could see his objective as a blip on the radar, however, and its implications made him frown.

"Distance: fourteen thousand yards," a crewman said. "Looks like air reconnaissance was right, Captain. Its course is erratic. Minimal speed."

O'Malley nodded. Six hours earlier, a group of Air Force F-15 fighter pilots practicing night maneuvers in a military corridor off the New England coast had noticed the blip on their radar screens. Its unusual behavior had prompted the flight group's leader to radio his commander at Loring Air Force Base near Limestone, Maine, and request permission to contact the vessel. Permission was granted, but all attempts to communicate with the vessel had failed.

"Identify yourself."

No response.

"Do you need assistance?"

No response.

After repeated efforts, the group's leader had requested further permission to change course and descend for a visual inspection. Again, permission was granted. After all, the vessel's radio silence combined with its puzzling, slow, random course and its proximity to United States waters justified concern. At a cautious distance, using intense-magnification night-vision apparatus, the flight group's leader determined that the vessel was a massive fishing trawler. English lettering on the stern indicated that the trawler's name was the *Bronze Bell,* its home port Pusan, South Korea. The English lettering wasn't unusual—many oriental commercial ships used English identification symbols when operating in Western waters.

What *was* unusual, indeed disturbing, however, was that in addition to its erratic, sluggish approach toward U.S. waters, the trawler displayed no lights, not even the mandatory signal lights that maritime law required during night voyages to prevent converging vessels from failing to see each other and colliding.

The troubled commander at Loring Air Force Base insisted on confirmation. The equally troubled flight-group leader repeated that the trawler was totally—"I mean, absolutely"—dark.

The situation became delicate, the potential for an international incident disturbing. A misjudgment could destroy careers.

If the approaching foreign vessel had been military in nature, the United States military would have gone on alert. But since the vessel was civilian, it required a less severe response. The Air Force immediately contacted the Coast Guard and since O'Malley's cutter was the nearest government vessel in the area, the *Sea Wolf* was at once dispatched to investigate.

Now, five hours after having received his orders, O'Malley— a red-haired, twenty-year veteran with a home in Portland and a wife and daughter whom he loved very much—continued to frown at the blip on the radar screen.

"That's it, Captain," a crewman said. "She just crossed the two-hundred-mile boundary. She's in our waters."

"And drifting." O'Malley sounded as if his best friend had died.

"That's what it looks like, Captain."

"And still no response to our radio messages."

"Affirmative, Captain."

O'Malley sighed. "Battle stations."

The crewman pressed the alarm. "Aye, aye, Captain."

Through the cutter's hull, the alarm sounded muffled but effectively shrill. Below, it would be excruciating, the rest of the crew snapping into action.

"You think there'll be trouble?"

"That's the problem, isn't it?" O'Malley said.

"Excuse me, Captain?"

"What *should* I think? Trouble? For sure. Obviously something's wrong. The question is *whose* trouble—ours or that trawler's? I guarantee this: My dear departed mother, God rest her soul, didn't raise her son to be a dummy."

"I second that opinion, Captain."

"Thank you, Lieutenant." O'Malley allowed himself to grin despite his nervous preoccupation. "And I promise you, I'll do everything in my power to insure that every mother's son in my command lives to see his family again."

"We already know that, Captain."

"I appreciate your confidence, but it won't get you a better rating on your duty report."

The lieutenant chuckled.

"I want a boarding party," O'Malley said.

"Yes, Captain."

"Armed."

"Yes, Captain."

"Get the Zodiac ready."

"Aye, aye, Captain."

O'Malley continued to frown toward the radar. Thirty minutes later, the *Sea Wolf*'s night-vision screen revealed the enormous South Korean trawler wallowing in waves a thousand yards ahead, its bulky outline made eerily green by the monitor.

The lieutenant straightened, cocking his head. "The Air Force wasn't exaggerating, sir. I've never seen a darker ship."

"I want every gun manned," O'Malley said.

"Aye, aye, Captain."

"Still no response to our radio messages?"

"Afraid not, sir."

"Pull portside and hail them on the bullhorn."

O'Malley nervously waited as a communications officer crouched protectively beside a housing on the deck and blurted questions through the bullhorn.

"Ahoy, *Bronze Bell!*

"Ahoy! Please, respond!

"You have entered United States waters!

"Please, respond!

"Ahoy, do you need assistance?"

"Fuck it," O'Malley said. "Get a team in the Zodiac. Make sure they're fully armed, Berettas, M-16s and for God's sake, make sure they're fully protected from our deck when they cross to the trawler. The fifty-caliber machine guns. The forty-millimeter cannons. The works."

"Aye, aye, Captain."

The Zodiac, a rubber, outboard-motor-powered raft, sped toward the *Bronze Bell,* its seven-member team holding M-16s at the ready. In the dark, as they reached the trawler and threw grappling hooks connected to rope ladders over the trawler's side, O'Malley said a quiet prayer for their safety and mentally made the sign of the cross.

The team shouldered their rifles, unholstered their pistols, jacked a round into each firing chamber, and clambered briskly up the rope ladders, disappearing over the side.

O'Malley held his breath, regretting that his duty required him to remain aboard while these other men—*good* men, *brave* men— potentially risked their lives.

Something was very wrong.

"Captain?" The two-way radio beside O'Malley crackled.

Picking it up, O'Malley answered, "Reception is clear. Report."

"Sir, the deck is deserted."

"Understood. Remain on battle alert. Establish sentries," O'Malley said. "With caution, check the lower decks."

"Affirmative, Captain."

O'Malley waited the longest five minutes in his life.

"Captain, there's still no sign of anyone."

"Keep checking."

"Affirmative, Captain."

O'Malley waited another tense five minutes.

Flashlights wavered on the trawler's deck. Lights came on. The two-way radio crackled. "Captain, we can't find *anyone.* The trawler appears to be completely deserted."

O'Malley knew the answer to his next question. The team would surely have reported the information. But he had to ask it anyhow. "Did you find any corpses?"

"No one alive *or* dead, Captain. Unless they're hiding some-where, the vessel's been abandoned. It's kind of spooky in a way, sir."

"What do you mean?"

"Well, Captain, the television's on in the crew's recreation area. There's a radio playing in their quarters. There's food on plates in the galley. Whatever it is happened, it must have been fast."

O'Malley frowned. "What about damage to the trawler? Any evidence of a fire, any reason they might have abandoned ship?"

"No, sir. No damage at all. And anyway, the lifeboats are still aboard."

Then what the hell happened? Where in God's name did they go? How? O'Malley nervously wondered but didn't allow his ap-prehension to affect the sound of his voice. "Understood," he said with authoritative calmness. "The trawler's engines?"

"Shut down, but we got them started again. No problem, Captain."

"Fuel?"

"The tanks are half full."

"What about the shortwave radio?"

"We found it turned off, but it's in working order, sir. If they wanted to, if there was trouble, they could have sent a Mayday alert."

"No one's reported hearing any. Keep checking."

"Aye, aye, Captain."

O'Malley set down the walkie-talkie. Pensive, he stared through the darkness toward the lights on the massive trawler. On occasion, he'd heard stories about vessels found abandoned at sea. The explanations were usually obvious: a rust bucket that an owner had scuttled in order to collect insurance but that had failed to sink as the owner intended, or a yacht that pirates had looted after killing the passengers (raping them as well, if there were females) and throwing the corpses overboard, or a fishing boat that drug smugglers had abandoned because they feared that the Drug Enforcement Agency suspected their cargo and was about to try to capture them.

In previous centuries, O'Malley was aware, a crew would sometimes (though rarely) mutiny, execute their captain, toss him to the sharks, and use lifeboats to escape to a nearby coastline. Again from previous centuries, he knew about ships upon which a plague had broken out, one by one the corpses of victims hurled overboard until the last man alive, suffering from the hideous disease, had managed to complete a diary about the ordeal and then jumped into the ocean, preferring a quick, relatively painless death by drowning instead of a prolonged, agonizing one.

Then, too, O'Malley had heard legends about crewless ghost ships, the *Flying Dutchman,* for example, although in that case the captain was reputed to be still aboard, doomed to drift for all eternity because of a gamble that he'd lost with the Devil.

The most famous abandoned ship was the *Marie Celeste,* a brigantine transporting commercial alcohol from New York to Italy, found crewless between the Azores and Portugal in 1872. But O'Malley had never understood why that ship acquired its mysterious reputation. After all, its sails had been damaged, its cabins soaked with water, its lifeboats missing. Obviously a severe storm had frightened the crew into thinking that the *Marie Celeste* was about to sink. They'd foolishly used the lifeboats to try to escape and been swallowed by the storm-churned sea.

All easily explainable.

But despite O'Malley's familiarity with these accounts, he'd never in all his lengthy, varied experience in the Coast Guard actually ever come across an abandoned vessel. Certainly, he'd seen barges torn apart on reefs because of a storm, but they didn't fit in this category. A ship in calm, open water, drifting without a crew for no apparent reason? O'Malley shook his head. He wasn't superstitious or fanciful. Although he felt a chill, he didn't believe in lost gambles with the Devil or visitors from outer space abducting humans or time warps or the Bermuda Triangle or any other of the ridiculous theories that the supermarket tabloids promoted. Something was terribly wrong here, yes, but its explanation would be logical, and by God, he intended to find out what that explanation was.

He turned to a crewman. "Contact headquarters in Portland. Tell them what we've got here. Ask them to send another cutter. Also ask for assistance from the local police, maybe the DEA and the FBI. Who knows how many other agencies will be involved by the time we sort this out? Also . . . I'm sure headquarters will think of this . . . they'd better notify the *Bronze Bell*'s owner.''

"Right away, Captain."

O'Malley brooded again toward the massive trawler. There were so many details to anticipate. He couldn't leave the *Bronze Bell* with his men on board her, but as soon as the other Coast Guard cutter arrived, either it or the *Sea Wolf* would begin a search for sailors in the water. At dawn, air reconnaissance would join the search. Meanwhile the *Bronze Bell* would be escorted to Portland, where various investigators would be waiting.

The two-way radio crackled. "Still nothing, Captain. I mean we've looked *everywhere,* including the cargo hold. I'll tell you this. They sure had good luck fishing. The hold's almost full."

A thought abruptly occurred to O'Malley. "Almost full? What were they using to fish?"

"This big a catch, they had to use nets, sir."

"Yes, but what *kind* of nets?" O'Malley asked.

"Oh shit, sir, I think I see what you mean. Just a minute."

O'Malley waited. The minute stretched on and on.

"Damn it, you were right, sir. The bastards were using drift nets."

Furious, O'Malley pressed his hands on a console with such force that his knuckles whitened. Drift nets? Sure. The *Bronze Bell* was owned by South Koreans. They, the Taiwanese, and the Japanese were notorious for sending trawlers into the North Atlantic's international waters, casting out drift nets made of nylon mesh that spread for dozens of miles behind each trawler. It had recently been estimated that as many as *thirty thousand miles* of these nets were in use in the North Atlantic, scooping up every living thing, in effect strip-mining the ocean. The nets were intended to be an efficient means of trapping enormous (unconscionable!) amounts of tuna and squid. The effect was to depopulate these species. Worse, the nets also caught dolphins, porpoises, turtles, and whales, creatures that needed to surface periodically in order to breathe but that couldn't when caught in the nets. Eventually, cruelly, they drowned, their carcasses discarded as commercially useless when the nets were reeled in. Thus those species, too, were depopulated.

The bastards! O'Malley thought. The murderous bastards!

He strained to keep rage from his voice as he spoke into the walkie-talkie. "Is the net still in the water?"

"Yes, sir."

"Then turn on the winches. Haul the damned thing in. We'll be taking the *Bronze Bell* to Portland. The weight of the drift net will hold her back."

"I'll give the order, sir."

O'Malley seethed, glowering at the trawler. Shit! *Shit!* Those fucking drift nets. Those irresponsible—

A voice blurted from the walkie-talkie, "Oh, my God, Captain! Jesus! Oh, my—!" The man on the other end sounded as if he might vomit.

"What's the matter? What's wrong?"

"The drift net, we're hauling it in. You can't believe how much fish it—! Christ! And the dolphins! The porpoises! I've never seen so many. Dead! They're all dead! Tangled in the net. A fucking nightmare! The crew!"

"What? Say again! The—?"

"Crew! Twenty! Thirty! We're still counting! Oh, God in heaven! Jesus, Mary, and Joseph! We've found the crew! They were tied to the net! They drowned the same way the dolphins and—"

The next sound from the walkie-talkie was unmistakable: anguished, guttural gagging, the Coast Guard officer throwing up.

8

Brooklyn

The sign on the stake outside St. Thomas More grade school said, CLOSED, NO TRESPASSING, PROPERTY OF F AND S REALTY. Stapled to the sign was a piece of paper, which in legal-looking fine print explained that this area had been rezoned for multiple-family dwellings. Another sign—this one on the school's front door—said, SCHEDULED FOR DEMOLITION, FUTURE SITE OF GRAND VIEW CONDOMINIUMS.

The school, a three-story, drab brick structure, had been built in 1910. Its wiring, plumbing, and heating systems were so in need of expensive repairs that the local diocese, at the limit of its financial resources, had been forced to sell it and arrange for Catholic students in the neighborhood to attend the newer but already crowded St. Andrew's school two miles away. Parents who in their youth had gone to St. Thomas More and had sent their children there mourned its passing, but as the bishop had indicated in his letter—read by the local pastor to his parishioners during Sunday mass—the Church faced a looming monetary crisis. Regrettable sacrifices had to be made, not only here but in almost every diocese across the nation. Prayers and donations were required.

At eight, the smog was already thick, the air sultry, as three cars turned into the teachers' abandoned parking lot beside the school. The cars were dark, four-door, American sedans, each with F AND S REALTY stenciled in yellow on their sides. Two men got out of each car, greeting the others with a nod. In their late thirties to early forties, they wore subdued, light-weight, polyester suits. Five held clipboards, the sixth an oversize metal briefcase. They considered the once-vital school and the plywood that now covered its windows.

"A pity," one man said.

"Well," another man said, "nothing lasts forever."

"Nothing?"

"At least, on earth."

"True," the third man said.

"And you know what the bottom line is," the fourth man said.

The fifth man nodded. "The collection plate."

"Did you bring the key?" the sixth man asked.

The first man patted his suit-coat pocket.

They approached the school's front door, waited while the first man unlocked it, and stepped through its creaky entrance, letting their eyes adjust to the shadows, smelling dust and mold.

The first man shut the door and locked it, the shadows thickening. His voice echoed, emphasizing the building's desolation. "I suppose any room will do."

"It's better on the second floor," the man with the briefcase said. "Less chance of our being overheard in case someone stands outside near a window. I noticed gaps in some of the plywood."

"Agreed," the second man said.

"All the same, we'd better check this floor."

"You're right," the first man said. "Of course."

Now the echo came from their footsteps as they crossed the hallway. While four of the men inspected each classroom, the boys' and girls' rest rooms, a storage room, and the various closets, the fifth man made sure that the back door was locked, and the sixth man checked the basement. Only then did they proceed up the creaky stairs.

Throughout, the first man had the eerie sense that they were intruding, that the spiritual residue of more than eighty years of eager, laughing children had been absorbed by the building, that there were . . . for lack of a better word . . . ghosts here, and that all they wanted was to be left alone to play here one last time, their final summer. Sentimental, he admitted, but in a profession that so often required him to be cynical, he decided that for a few harmless seconds at least, he could indulge himself.

The man was of medium height and weight, with brown hair, hazel eyes that tended to assume the color of the clothes he wore, and unremarkable features, so average that no one ever remembered him. Over many years, he'd trained himself to be a chameleon, and yesterday afternoon he'd followed Tess to LaGuardia Airport.

When he reached the second floor, he squinted higher toward the continuing stairs, then right and left, noticing open-doored classrooms and two drinking fountains that seemed unnaturally low until he recalled that they weren't designed for adults. Shrugging, deferring to the man with the oversize briefcase, he said, "Which room do you like?"

"The one on the left above the parking lot."

"As you wish."

"But not until . . ." The man with the briefcase pointed upward toward the final floor.

"Do you really think it's necessary? The dust on the stairs hasn't been disturbed."

"I was trained to be thorough. Your expertise is surveillance, but mine is . . ."

The first man nodded. "And you do it superbly."

"I accept the compliment." The man's eyes glinted.

"I'll check the upper floor while the others inspect the rooms on *this* floor. In the meantime, since we're under pressure, can you . . . ?"

"Yes, I'll set up my equipment."

Five minutes later, after having inspected the musty upper floor where he found no one, the first man descended to the middle floor and the room on the left above the parking lot. He and his associates had been very careful in selecting this meeting place. It was highly unlikely that their enemy had managed to trace them here. Mostly—he suspected—the man with the briefcase was concerned that despite the abandoned school's locked doors and barricaded windows, a drug addict or else one of the city's innumerable homeless might have discovered a way to gain access and find sanctuary here. Even a drug addict might make sense of their conversation and become an informant.

At the same time, the chameleon reminded himself that the enemy, over many years, had demonstrated remarkable cleverness, extreme survival characteristics, ruthless determination, including the ability to counterattack. No matter how carefully this abandoned school had been chosen, the fact was that the rendezvous site had been used four times already. A pattern had been established, and whenever a pattern occurred, that pattern could be discovered. The man with the briefcase was right. There was no harm in being cautious.

The chameleon noticed two things when he entered the classroom. First, the sixth man, the electronic-security specialist, had opened his oversize briefcase, plugged a monitor into a battery, and was using a metal wand to scan the blackboard, the ceiling, the walls, the floor, and the furniture. Second, the other men—normally so serious and dignified—were seated in cramped positions in miniature table-topped chairs designed for ten-year-olds. The absurd situation reminded the chameleon of scenes from *Gulliver's Travels* and *Alice in Wonderland*.

"It's clean," the sixth man said, replacing his equipment in the briefcase, shutting it, and locking it.

"Then we'll begin." Although the chameleon had been deferential until now, he assumed the place of authority, sitting at the teacher's desk.

As one, each member of the group reached into his suit-coat pocket, removed a ring, and placed it on the middle finger of his left hand. Each ring was identical, handsome, distinctive, a twenty-four-karat band on top of which a large gleaming ruby was embossed with the golden insignia of an intersecting cross and sword.

"May the Lord be with you," the chameleon said.

"And with your spirit," the five men replied.

"*Deo gratias*," all six of them said together, completing the ritual.

The chameleon scanned his fellow hunters. "To begin, I must make a confession."

The group narrowed their eyes, straightening as best they could in the confinement of their diminutive chairs.

"You." The chameleon nodded toward the sixth man, the electronic-security specialist, who unlike the others was somewhat overweight. "Earlier we exchanged compliments about our respective skills. But I'm forced to admit that I've made a mistake in terms of *my* skills, or at least my *team* has made a mistake, and I always take responsibility for the men I've trained."

"What sort of mistake?" The second man tilted his glasses, frowning over them.

"One of the enemy tried to intercept photographs that the woman took in our target's apartment."

The fourth man hunched his broad shoulders. "Perhaps the attempt was an unrelated matter. We've been distracted by false alarms before. How can you be positive that this person was one of the enemy?"

"He had gray eyes," the chameleon said.

"Ah." The third man pursed his thin lips. "In that case . . ."

"Indeed." The fifth man's gaunt cheeks throbbed.

"I entered the photo shop and pretended to be a customer. I stood as close to him as I am now to you," the chameleon said. "I couldn't fail to recognize the characteristics. He might as well have been the target's brother."

"Perhaps he was," the broad-shouldered fourth man said. "I still don't understand. What was your mistake?"

"My responsibility was to follow the woman. My team's responsibility was to pursue and capture the *man*." The chameleon shook his head in distress. "They failed."

"*What?*" The sixth man, the electronic-security specialist, glared. "They saw him leave the shop and . . . !"

"He was brilliant. From reports I was given, he seemed to sense immediately that he was being stalked. He ran. My team gave chase. He darted down alleys. He rushed across streets, veering through traffic. *Still* he was chased. He entered a restaurant."

"And?"

The chameleon raised his hands. "He vanished."

"*How?*"

"If my team had been able to determine that, they certainly would have continued to chase him. I repeat, I accept responsibility for their failure."

"But that does no good," the sixth man continued. "Accept as much blame as you want. The ultimate fact is, the enemy was within your team's grasp, but they didn't succeed."

"Yes." The chameleon lowered his head. "That's the ultimate fact."

"He must have had an escape route planned." The third man pursed his lips again.

"No doubt," the solidly built fourth man said. "They're like ferrets. They can dodge and squirm and find holes where you'd never expect. How else could they have eluded us for so long?"

"That's not the point," the overweight sixth man objected. "Their survival skills are well-known. But *we're* supposed to be better."

"And we are." The second man adjusted his glasses. "Because virtue is on our side. But sometimes it appears that providence tests our determination."

"I don't accept rationalizations. If what you're telling me is that the Lord helps those who help themselves, then we're obviously not trying hard enough!'' The sixth man glowered toward the chameleon. ''Or in this case, *you and your team* aren't trying hard enough. Certainly I've done *my* part. I installed a tap on the woman's phone and on the *policeman's* phone within an hour of your instructions. I also arranged for our people in Washington to be able to monitor calls made from car phones. Every important government executive has one these days, although I don't understand why they use them, given the security risk.''

''What more do you want me to say? I can't change the past. However, I *can* resolve to do better in the future.''

''But this isn't the first time you've made mistakes!'' the sixth man added. ''When you managed to find our target, you should have arranged immediately for his abduction and interrogation!''

''I disagree.'' The chameleon gestured. ''Since the target didn't realize he'd been discovered, I thought it prudent to continue watching him in case he might lead us to *other* targets or . . .''

''But why would he have done such a foolish thing? The man was a fugitive from his group. They wanted him as much as *we* did.''

''Exactly,'' the chameleon said. ''We waited in case his group caught up to him. As a consequence, we'd have had *other* vermin to capture, question, and eliminate.''

''Regardless, the tactic *failed*,'' the sixth man complained. ''His group *did* discover where he was, and instead of being captured, they succeeded in eliminating *him*.''

''It was raining that night. The weather interfered with—''

The sixth man scoffed, ''The weather. *How did the target's fellow vermin catch up to him?*''

The chameleon scowled. ''Probably using the same method *we* did. The target was skilled in hiding. He constructed a new identity for himself. He never stayed longer than six months in any city. He arranged for elaborate smoke screens to conceal where he lived. In theory, he was undetectable. But human nature is imperfect. There were certain things about the man that he couldn't or wouldn't change. Specifically his fascination with video documentaries. That's how we found him the first time in Los Angeles, by checking the video companies. Of course, he'd moved on before we found his employer. But then we picked up his trail once more, the same way, in Chicago. Yet *again* he'd moved on. But finally, after using all the resources at our disposal, we located him at Truth Video in Manhattan. And if *we* could find him that way, I take for granted that the vermin he was running from could."

"Still, that raises another question," the muscular fourth man said. "After they executed the target, appropriately by fire, the same method *we* would have used, why did they also set fire to his apartment, and why did they wait several days before they did it?"

"My surveillance team tells me that the target's hunters never entered his apartment the night they killed him," the chameleon said. "From Friday evening onward, he acted with greater caution, as if he suspected he'd been located. He broke an appointment with the woman, Tess Drake, on Saturday morning. He remained in his apartment all that day. Saturday night, he apparently decided to flee under cover of the storm. My team had concluded that his behavior was too erratic. They planned to grab him while they could, in the middle of the night as he slept. But that plan was interrupted when *other* targets arrived, with the same intention as *our* group. Events occurred quickly. The hunters discovered their quarry when he rushed down the stairs. As we know, the man was in superb physical condition."

"Well, aren't they all?" the second man asked rhetorically.

"But he was also skilled in hand-to-hand combat," the chameleon said. "He fought with his hunters, eluded them, raced from the building, but during the fight, he'd injured his leg and—"

"Yes, yes," the electronics expert said impatiently. "They trapped him and burned him alive before your team could formulate a new plan and if not capture and interrogate, at least exterminate them all. Another nest would have been wiped out."

"You weren't there. Don't make judgments," the chameleon said. "My team was composed of three men, sufficient for their original mission. But the target and his hunters amounted to six. The only equalizer would have been pistols. But in so heavily guarded an area as the mayor's house near Carl Schurz Park, if there'd been shooting, the police would immediately have been put on alert and blockaded the district. My team could not take the risk of being captured and questioned by the authorities."

"*What* risk?" the sixth man growled. "Your men knew the rule. If they were captured, before they could be interrogated, they had an obligation to kill themselves." He tapped his ruby ring and the poison capsule hidden beneath the stone on his and every other ring.

"I wonder," the chameleon said. "In my team's place, would you have been eager to take a chance that you knew would fail, with the certainty that you'd have to kill yourself?"

"You bet your soul, I would."

"No, not *my* soul. *Yours*," the chameleon said. "I doubt you'd have risked being captured. You're a technician, not a combat operative, and your pride makes you want to live too much."

"Maybe you don't hate the vermin as much as *I* do," the sixth man said.

"I doubt that as well."

"You're evading the issue. The fire in the apartment. What about it?"

"My assumption is that the other targets had made such a commotion in the apartment building that they didn't dare go back right away for fear of being found by the police. Also it may be that the targets concluded that the man who called himself Joseph Martin had been so scrupulous about hiding his true nature that he wouldn't leave anything incriminating in his apartment. That's all speculation, but this is not. We know that they decided to watch the woman he'd befriended, in case she behaved in a way that suggested she knew his secret. We, of course, watched the woman because she was the only connection we had with the target. She went to the morgue and managed to identify his body. The next day, the detective from Missing Persons took her to the target's apartment. Immediately afterward, she left a roll of film at a one-hour developing service. It doesn't take a genius to conclude that she must have found something of such interest in the target's apartment that she took photographs there and wanted them developed at once. When one of the target's executioners failed to get the photos, he and the others decided that the apartment now had sufficient priority for them to risk going back. Whatever they found, they needed to destroy it. And fire, of course, not only purifies. It conceals theft."

"But what did they find?" the third man asked.

"My guess?" The chameleon hesitated. "An altar."

The fourth man gasped.

"Probably one of their statues. *That,* above all, they would have to retrieve. Regardless if someone had seen it and taken photographs of it, the revelation wouldn't matter as much as the object itself. The *statue* would be too sacred to them for it to be allowed to fall into unclean hands."

The group squinted in disgust.

"God damn them," the second man said.

"He has," the sixth man said. "But now, after having come so close, we've lost them."

"Not necessarily," the chameleon said.

"Oh?" The fifth man raised his head.

"You've got a new lead?" the fourth man asked.

"They appear to have become fixated on the woman," the chameleon said. "Recent events suggest that they believe she knows too much, especially given the photographs she took and then, of course, her sudden trip to Alexandria, Virginia. As we know from our background check, her father was powerful in the government and had many even *more* powerful associates with whom her mother remains in contact. It would appear that the woman, Tess Drake, is determined to find out why her friend died. It would also appear that our targets are *equally* determined to stop her and conceal all evidence of their existence."

"Wait. A moment ago, you said 'recent events.' " The sixth man straightened. *"What recent events?"*

"Well," the chameleon said. "Yes." He hesitated. "They're the reason I requested this meeting." His eyes and voice became somber. "Last night . . ."

He described what had happened to his counterpart.

"They burned him?" The sixth man turned pale.

"Yes." The chameleon tasted bile as he stood from the dusty teacher's desk. "Our watcher had two men working with him. Both were on foot, one hiding behind the mansion in case the woman went out the back, the other farther along the street, among bushes. The latter man saw a silver Corniche leave the mansion. When the car drove by, he managed to get its license number, eventually using his contacts to find out who owned the car. That's how we know that Brian Hamilton was at the mansion. The latter man also saw the assassin rush toward the watcher's car and shoot him. The next thing, the assassin drove the Taurus away. The watcher's backup man hot-wired a Cadillac on the street and pursued. He found the Taurus burning in a shopping mall's otherwise-empty parking lot. When he realized that there wasn't any way he could help, he left the scene before the police arrived.''

"But if our man was already shot, why did they . . . ?'' The second man's voice cracked.

"Set fire to him?'' The chameleon grimaced. "No doubt, to make an example. To demoralize us.''

"In that case, they failed,'' the third man said with fury. "They'll pay. I'll put them in hell.''

"We *all* will,'' the sixth man said.

"And make them pay for other things as well,'' the chameleon said, his mouth tasting sour.

"You mean there's *more?*'' The fourth man jerked upright, inadvertently banging his knees against the top of the small desk.

"Unfortunately. Last night, at the same time our operative was shot while he watched the mansion . . .''

9

Brian Hamilton set down the cellular telephone in the shadowy backseat of his silver Corniche, frowned, and leaned forward toward his bodyguard-driver. "Steve, you heard?''

The husky former Marine, an expert in reconnaissance, nodded firmly. "That was Eric Chatham. You want me to drive to his home.''

"Exactly. Get me to West Falls Church as soon as possible.''

"I'm already headed toward the freeway.''

With that taken care of, Brian Hamilton slumped back and brooded. The story that Tess had told him . . . and the photographs she'd shown him . . . troubled him greatly. Whoever the man called Joseph Martin had really been, there was something he'd been hiding.

Or running from. Hamilton was sure of that. Yes. Whatever that something might be, it was as terrible as the bloodstained whip in Joseph Martin's closet and the grotesque sculpture that Tess had photographed.

Back at the mansion, Hamilton had described that photograph as weird, but the adjective understated his severe revulsion. The bas-relief statue filled him with disgust.

He bit his lip, with a deepening apprehension that Tess had become involved in something so twisted and dangerous that it might get her killed. Hadn't she said that she feared she was being followed?

Hamilton's jaw muscles hardened. Whatever was going on, he intended to use all his power, all his influence, every IOU at his disposal, to find out what threatened Tess and to make sure it was stopped.

After all, he *owed* her. For several reasons. Not the least of which was that he'd been her father's friend but had followed orders from his superiors and reluctantly sent Remington Drake to Beirut to negotiate a secret arms deal with the Christians against the Moslems. As a consequence, he'd been responsible for her father's abduction by the Moslems, Drake's torture, and eventual brutal death. It wasn't any wonder that Tess hated him. By all means, she had good reason. But if helping her and possibly saving her life would erase that hate, Brian Hamilton had all the motivation he needed, especially since her mother and he had come to an arrangement. After all, he couldn't very well have a stepdaughter who loathed him.

Continuing to brood, he noticed that his bodyguard had reached the freeway and was speeding toward Falls Church, Virginia, ten miles away. In a very few minutes, Brian Hamilton would be able to describe his problem to the director of the FBI and demand that Eric Chatham use the full resources of the Bureau to find out who Joseph Martin had been and who had killed him. As much as Hamilton owed Tess, Eric Chatham owed *him,* and now, by God, it was payback time.

"Sir, we might have a problem," the bodyguard-driver said.

"What problem?" Hamilton straightened.

"It's possible we're being followed."

His stomach suddenly cramping, Hamilton pivoted to stare through the car's back window. "The minivan behind us?"

"Yes, sir. At first, I thought it was just a coincidence. But it's been tailing us since before we left Alexandria."

"Lose it."

"That's what I'm trying to do, sir."

The Corniche sped up.

But so did the minivan.

"Persistent," the driver said.

"I told you to lose it."

"Where, sir? We're on a freeway, if you don't mind my pointing out the obvious. I'm doing *ninety.* And I don't see an exit ramp."

"Wait a minute! It's changing lanes! It looks like it wants to pass us!" Hamilton said.

"Yes, sir. It could be . . . possibly . . . maybe I'm wrong."

The minivan, having veered into the passing lane, increased speed and came abreast of the Corniche. But as Hamilton watched, he felt his heart lurch. On the minivan's passenger side, someone was rolling down a window.

"Look out!" Hamilton's driver blurted.

Too late.

From the open window, someone threw a bottle. The bottle had a rag stuffed into its mouth.

The rag was on fire.

"Jesus!"

The bodyguard swerved toward the freeway's gravel shoulder, frantically reducing speed, but the bottle—which must have been constructed from specially designed, brittle glass—shattered on impact against the Corniche's windshield and spewed blazing gasoline over the car.

Blinded by flames—

—on the hood!—

—and oh, Christ, on the windshield!—

173

—the driver tried desperately to control his steering. In the backseat, Hamilton gaped to the left, horrified to see the van streak sharply toward the Corniche. He felt the van slam brutally against the Corniche's side, slam it again, and *again,* and propel the Corniche off the freeway's shoulder.

Hamilton's stomach dropped. The Corniche, now completely engulfed with flames, crashed through a guardrail, soared through the air, and collided with . . .

Hamilton screamed. He never knew what the car hit. The sudden, shocking force of the crash slammed him forward, catapulting him up, over, and beyond the front seat, walloping his skull against the dashboard.

But what the passengers in the minivan saw with calculated satisfaction was that the Corniche had impacted against a massive steel electrical tower. The collision burst the Corniche's fuel tank. A huge exploding fireball disintegrated the car and spewed pieces of flesh, bone, and metal for fifty yards in every direction, the flames gushing upward for a hundred feet. As the minivan sped onward, disappearing among traffic, its rear window reflected the spectacular pyre in the darkness beside the freeway.

10

The chameleon removed the folded front section of the *New York Times* from beneath a notepad on his clipboard. He held it up so the group could see the headline—"Former Secretary of State Dies in Fiery Freeway Disaster"—then handed the newspaper to the second man. "When you're finished, pass it around."

"I've already read it. I didn't know the connection, but the moment you mentioned Brian Hamilton, I realized what you were getting at."

"Well," the third man said, "*I* didn't have a chance to read the paper this morning. Let me see."

One by one, the somber-faced men read the article.

"Fire," the sixth man said with disgust. "They're so in love with fire." Lips curled, he set down the paper and studied the chameleon. "You seem to have so many answers. What about *this* one. Why did they kill him?"

"I don't have answers exactly. What I do have are calculated assumptions," the chameleon said. "Tess Drake makes a sudden trip to see her mother. When she gets to the mansion in Alexandria, is it a coincidence that the former secretary of state and current main adviser to the President just happens to be waiting there when she arrives? Not likely. I have to conclude that so important a man was summoned by the woman, that Hamilton—a friend of her dead father—was the person she primarily wanted to see and not her mother, that Tess Drake was using her late father's influence to enlist powerful help in discovering who Joseph Martin was and why he was killed."

The third man shrugged. "Assumptions, as you admit. However, I grant that they're logical."

"And I also have to conclude that the enemy followed Tess Drake to the mansion just as our own people did," the chameleon continued. "When the enemy identified Hamilton's Corniche in the driveway and realized what the woman was doing, they must have decided that Hamilton's death was essential to keeping their secret. It's my belief that they wanted to prevent him from telling others what he'd learned and using his connections with the government to enlarge the scope of the investigation."

The fifth man traced his finger along pencil engravings on the desktop of his miniature chair. "Possibly."

"You don't sound convinced."

"Well, your assumptions make sense to a point, but . . . What I have a problem with is . . . If the enemy went to the trouble and took the risk of assassinating Hamilton, they still wouldn't have solved their problem, at least not completely. Their secret would not yet be fully protected. To accomplish that, they'd have to be totally, absolutely thorough, and the most important person to eliminate would be . . ."

The chameleon nodded. "Precisely."

"You're telling me . . . ?"

"Yes."

"Dear God!" the sixth man said.

"My thought, as well. . . . Dear God. . . . Last night . . . shortly after two . . ."

11

Standing rigidly in her bedroom in the mansion in Alexandria, Tess cramped her fingers around the telephone as she listened to Craig's gravelly, urgent voice.

"I want you to promise me," Craig said. "Swear it. *Be careful!*"

"I guarantee," Tess emphasized. "I won't take any chances."

"Keep your word. And promise me this as well. Swear you'll phone me tomorrow as soon as you get copies made of the photographs. Then send them to me by Federal Express as fast as possible."

"I will. I promise," Tess said.

"Look, I don't want to sound like a jealous lover, but I'll feel a whole lot better when you get back here."

"Honestly," Tess said, "I'll be okay. Just because someone torched Joseph's apartment, it's a big leap to thinking I'm in danger."

"Oh, yeah?" Craig raised his voice. "Then what about the guy in the photo shop?"

Tess didn't answer. She reluctantly admitted to herself that she'd been feeling more and more uneasy.

"Okay, what's your mother's address and phone number?" Craig asked, and coughed. "I think it's a good idea . . . I want to be able to reach you if anything *else* happens that you should know about.''

Tess gave him that information.

"Good," Craig said. "I repeat, I wish you'd get back here."

"Look, even if I *were* in Manhattan, what could you do, assuming you're right and I'm in danger? *You can't stay with me all the time.*"

"You never know. It might come to that."

"Hey, don't exaggerate." Tess quivered. "You're scaring me."

"Good. At last. I'm finally getting my point across." The lieutenant's voice dropped, the long-distance static crackling. "And anyway . . ." He sounded nervous. "Would it really be so bad if I were with you all the time?"

"What?" Tess frowned. "I'm not sure what you mean."

"I told you yesterday on the way to Joseph's apartment. This started out as police business. Now it belongs to Homicide, not Missing Persons. But I still want to stay involved. Because of you."

Tess frowned harder.

"No response?" Craig asked.

"I'm trying to sort this out. Are you saying what I *think* you're saying?"

"As far as I'm concerned, this isn't business anymore. I want to get to *know* you."

"But . . ."

"Whatever it is, say it, Tess."

"You're ten years older than me."

"So what? You've got a prejudice? You don't like mature men, *dependable* men, guys like me who've been there and back and around some and don't have any illusions or expectations and don't make problems?"

"It's not exactly that. I mean . . ." Tess squirmed. "It's just . . . Well, I never thought about . . ."

"Well, do me a favor and *give* it some thought. I don't want to be pushy. I know a lot's been happening, not the least of which is you've lost your friend, and I'm sorry for that, and I repeat, I don't want to make problems for you. I'm patient. But hey, I bathe every day."

177

Tess couldn't help it. She laughed.

"Good," Craig said. "I like that. I like to hear you laugh. So think about it, would you? Or at any rate, keep it in the back of your mind? No big deal. No pressure. But maybe . . . damn it, I'm so . . . maybe, when this is over, we can talk about it."

"Sure." Tess swallowed. "If . . . When . . . I promise, when this is over, we'll talk about it."

"That's all I'm asking. You don't sound enthusiastic, but that's okay—I appreciate your patience. This next part, however, *is* business. I don't care how busy you are—just make sure you call me tomorrow when you send me the copies of those photographs."

"Word of honor," Tess said. "Good night."

"Good night," Craig responded. "And by the way, I don't gamble. I seldom drink. And I'm kind to animals, children, the poor, the infirm, not to mention the aged. Think about it." The lieutenant broke the connection.

Tess listened to the emptiness of the long-distance static, breathed out in confusion, trembled, and set the phone on its receptacle.

For several moments, she didn't move.

Oh, Christ!

She hadn't counted on this. She'd been vaguely aware of the lieutenant's attraction to her, but she'd ignored it. There'd been too many other things to concern her.

But now that the subject was in the open, Tess didn't know how to respond. Craig was pleasant enough, and indeed he was good-looking in a rugged sort of way. For sure, he'd taken pains to be kind and helpful. And she'd definitely appreciated his company in trying circumstances.

But did she feel *attracted* to him? Physically? *Sexually?* Certainly it didn't match the powerful, overwhelming identification she'd experienced with Joseph the first time she'd met him.

Tess recalled the theory in *The Dove's Neck Ring* that love at first sight was actually love at *second* sight.

Because the souls of the lovers had known each other in a previous existence and now recognized each other in this reborn earthly form.

Damn it, Tess thought, what am I going to do? I don't want

to embarrass or insult the lieutenant. But after all, Craig *is* older than me. At the same time . . .

. . . Tess paced . . .

. . . I do feel something for him.

And maybe being comfortable with a man is better than suffering a sickening blaze of passion.

She remembered that *The Dove's Neck Ring* had referred to physical—as opposed to spiritual—passion as an infirmity, a type of illness.

What am I going to do?

Tess felt guilty. She'd been distant and perhaps even rude to Craig when he'd raised the subject of his attraction to her at the end of their conversation.

Her guiltiness troubled her. I can't let the subject hang in the air, she thought. Too many other things to worry about. I have to get this settled.

She picked up the phone.

To call the lieutenant.

To explain to him what she'd just been thinking.

To be totally honest and with kindness confess her uncertainty.

But when she held the phone to her ear, she frowned. There wasn't a dial tone.

Impatient, she jabbed down the disconnect button, raised it, and listened again.

Still no dial tone.

More impatient, she tapped the disconnect button several times.

Nothing.

The line was dead.

But the line had been working a minute ago. *Why would—?*

Tess trembled, a chill surging through her. Earlier, she'd felt a chill as well, caused by the mansion's air-conditioning system.

Now the whisper of air from the vent contributed to her chill, but not because the air was cool. Nostrils widening, she stepped toward the vent low on the wall hidden by a chair beside her bureau.

Pulse rushing, she stooped, moved the chair away, and sniffed the stream of air.

A vague acrid smell made her shiver.

Smoke? Is that—?

Her throat felt stung.

It *can't* be smoke!

But the smell intensified, and with the next deep breath that flared her nostrils, she coughed.

Panic squeezed her chest. As she gasped, she straightened in terror, seeing a thin wisp of gray drift out of the vent.

Fire!

For a moment, her body refused to move.

Abruptly a spring seemed to snap within her, and she charged toward the bedside phone to dial 911. Instantly, her stomach dropping deeper, faster, she remembered that the phone had been dead the last time she'd tried it. Frantic, she tried it again. Still no dial tone! Jesus. She grabbed the cotton pullover that she'd taken off earlier and desperately put it back on. Then she clutched *The Dove's Neck Ring* along with the photographs and crammed them into her purse.

With a final look toward the air-conditioning vent from which an increasing wisp of gray drifted out and made her cough harder, she darted toward the bedroom door, yanked it open, and lunged out.

12

The hallway was dark. Someone, presumably the butler, had turned off the lights after Tess and her mother had gone to their rooms. Even the staircase to her left and the vestibule below it were shrouded in darkness. Only the glow from the lamp on her bedside table allowed her to see. She rushed to the right along the murky hallway and reached the door to her mother's room.

Urgent, she shoved it open and groped to flick at the light switch. The overhead chandelier blazed. She stared. Her mother, who lay in a canopied bed similar to Tess's, wore eyeshades, even though the draperies were closed. As a consequence, she didn't respond to the sudden gleaming light.

Tess coughed even harder. *This* room, too, was hazy from smoke wafting out of the air-conditioning vent. "Mother!" She hurried toward the bed. Her mother was snoring. "Mother!" Tess shook her.

"Uh . . ." Her mother turned onto her side.

Tess shook her repeatedly. "Mother! Wake up!"

"Uh . . ." Her mother stopped snoring. "I . . . What . . . ?" Lethargic, she pawed at her eyeshades and clumsily raised them to her forehead, squinting through sleep-puffed eyes. "Tess? Why are you . . . ? What's the . . . ?"

"You have to get out of bed! Hurry!"

"What's that"—her mother coughed—"*haze?* It smells like . . ."

"Smoke! The house is on fire! Hurry, Mother! You have to get out of bed!"

Shock jolted her mother fully awake. *"Fire?"* She fumbled at the sheets and squirmed to raise herself. "Quickly! Call the fire department!"

"I can't!"

"What?"

"I tried! The phone isn't working!" Tess said.

"It's *got* to be working." Her mother reached for the bedside phone.

"No! I'm telling you, Mother! The phone isn't . . . ! Damn it, come on! We have to leave!"

Her mother strained to overcome her grogginess and raise herself. She wore a frilly, rose-colored nightdress. It had bunched around her knees, but as she lurched to her feet, its hem dropped toward her ankles. She pivoted in confusion, mustered strength, and shuffled toward a closet. "Help me get dressed."

"There isn't time!" Tess grabbed her arm. "We have to get out of here!" The room was thick with haze now. Both women coughed. "For God's sake, Mother, let's go!"

With a hand on her mother's back, Tess urged her toward the bedroom's open door.

But only when they reached the shadowy hallway did Tess stiffen with complete understanding. Dread flooded through her.

No! she thought.

First the phone stops working?

Then the mansion's on fire?

It isn't a coincidence! It's not accidental!

They did this!

They think I know too much! They want to kill me!

Craig's right! *Why didn't I listen?*

It was her mother's turn to insist on moving forward. "Hurry!" She shoved at Tess. "What's the matter! Why did you stop?"

Dear God, Tess thought, what if they're in the building?

Smoke detectors wailed. In the bedrooms. In the corridor. In the vestibule, the kitchen, and other locations downstairs. Their combined unnerving shriek made Tess want to clamp her hands across her ears.

But her panicked mind alerted her. No! They wouldn't just start a fire and run! They'd want to make sure I . . . !

What if they're in the house?

They'll try to stop us from getting out! They'll want our deaths to seem like an accident!

But if they have to, if we try to escape . . . !

They'll kill us before the fire does!

"Tess, why are you stopping?" Her mother frowned, at the same time pressing the sleeve of her nightdress against her mouth, breathing stridently through it. "What's *wrong?* The smoke's worse! We'll suffocate if we don't—!"

"Mother?" As Tess's premonition worsened, a fierce, startling thought controlled her. "Whatever happened to father's handgun? Do you still have it?"

"I don't understand. Why would you—?"

Tess whirled toward her mother. "Just pay attention. After father died, did you keep it? *Do you still have his handgun?*"

Her mother coughed. "Why does it matter? We have to—"

"The handgun, Mother! *What did you do with it?*"

"*Nothing.* I left it where he always put it, the same as I left his other things." Even after six years, renewed grief strained her mother's already fear-strained features. "You know I couldn't bring myself to part with anything he owned."

Smoke swirled behind them. To the left, in the vestibule below the staircase, the darkness was interrupted by a flicker as if from a hesitant strobe light.

The fire!

Tess cringed. She gripped her mother's shoulders. "In the other bedroom?"

"Yes. That room's exactly the way it was the day your father said good-bye to me and went to Beirut."

Tess fervently kissed her mother's cheek. "God bless you! Hurry! Follow me!"

"But we need to . . . ! I still don't understand!"

"I don't have time to explain! All you need to understand is I love you, Mother! And I'm trying to save your life!"

"Well!" Her mother strained to breathe. "That's good enough for me."

With a terrified glance toward the flickering flames in the vestibule, Tess jerked her mother's hand and urged her toward the right along the hallway. "Just pray, and do everything I tell you."

She reached a farther door to her right and banged it open. In the darkness, she fumbled along the inside wall to find the light switch.

"Before you . . . There's something I'd better tell you," her mother said.

"Not now!"

But as Tess flicked the switch and the overhead light gleamed, Tess knew what her mother had wanted to explain. She blinked in astonishment.

This bedroom was the one that her father had used when he came home late at night after emergency meetings at the State Department, so he wouldn't disturb Tess's mother when he undressed to go to sleep.

But now the bedroom resembled the delapidated interior of Miss Havisham's house in *Great Expectations*. Six years of dust covered everything, the carpet, the bed, the end tables, the lamps, the phone, the bureau. Cobwebs clung to the corners and dangled from the ceiling, making Tess flinch as if she were about to enter a nest of spiders. The rapid movement of the door she'd shoved open had caused dust to swirl, the cobwebs to sway, creating a haze that was emphasized by the smoke spewing out of the air-conditioning vent.

"Mother!"

"I tried to tell you."

Horrified, Tess rushed ahead, each frantic footstep raising dust. She swung her arms, clearing the cobwebs, repelled by their stickiness.

"I left everything the way it was." Her mother struggled after her, coughing. "The day I learned that your father was dead, I took one final look at this room, closed the door, and never came in here again. I told the servants to keep that door closed."

With increasing revulsion, Tess noticed that even her father's slippers, layered with dust, remained beside the bed. She was too distraught to ask her mother what on earth had made her turn this room not into a shrine but a crypt. But the smoke was denser. All she had time to care about was . . . !

She yanked open the top drawer of a table next to the bed, fearing that her father might have taken his pistol with him when he went to Beirut. But exhaling sharply, she saw that the handgun was where he'd always kept it.

Her father had been an operative in Marine Intelligence when he'd served in Vietnam. That was where he'd met Brian Hamilton, a Marine general supervising "Eye" Corps. After the war, her father had joined the State Department, belonging to its little-known Intelligence division. Later, after Brian Hamilton had retired from the military, he, too, had joined the State Department, in the diplomatic division, eventually convincing Tess's father to switch from Intelligence to diplomacy. But Tess's father had retained his nervous habits from Vietnam. Although he seldom went armed when on an assignment in a potentially dangerous foreign country, he'd made sure to keep a handgun in the house where he could easily get to it in case someone broke in at night.

The weapon was made in Switzerland, a SIG-Sauer 9-mm semiautomatic pistol. A compact, short-barreled handgun, it held an unusually large number of rounds in the magazine, sixteen, and unlike most other pistols, it had a double action, which meant that it didn't need to be cocked to be fired. All you needed to do was pull the trigger.

Tess knew all this because when she was twelve, she'd happened to see her father cleaning the gun and had shown such curiosity that her father had decided she'd better be taught about it so she'd respect it and more important, stay away from it. After all, she'd been a tomboy. She hadn't been repelled by guns the way many girls her age might have been, and she took to target shooting as easily as she'd developed expertise in basketball, track and field, and gymnastics.

Frequently, when her father went to a range to practice his marksmanship, he'd invited her to come along. He'd taught her how to take the weapon apart, clean it, and reassemble it. He'd instructed her in the proper way to aim—both hands on the pistol, both eyes open, both front and rear sights lined up. But the main trick, he'd said, was to focus your vision not on the sights but rather on the target. The sights would seem blurred as a consequence, but that was okay, you got used to it. After all, the target was your objective, and you had to see it clearly. Anytime the sights were in focus but the *target* was blurred, you were aiming wrong.

After an equally thorough explanation of how to load the magazine, insert it securely into the handle, and pull back the slide on top of the pistol so that a round was injected into the firing chamber, her father had finally allowed Tess to fire the weapon.

Don't yank on the trigger. Squeeze it.

She'd felt slightly apprehensive about the recoil, but to her delight, from the first, she'd discovered that the jerk when the gun went off had not been nearly as bad as she'd feared. Indeed she'd *enjoyed* the recoil, the release of power, and the noise of the gun's going off had been muffled by the ear protectors that her father insisted she wear.

Toward the end of her teenage years, she'd been able to place all sixteen rounds in a circle the size of a basketball at a distance of thirty yards, but then, as she'd started college, she'd lost all interest in shooting with the same abruptness that she'd initially been fascinated by it. Perhaps because her father had been away from home so much.

She grabbed the pistol from the drawer and mentally thanked her father for having taught her. He might have saved her life.

She pressed a button on the side and disengaged the magazine from the handle, nodding when she saw that the magazine was loaded. After reinserting the magazine, she pulled back the pistol's slide and let it snap forward, chambering a round. The hammer stayed back. She gently squeezed the trigger and with equal gentleness lowered the hammer so the gun wouldn't go off accidentally. So far, so good.

But it worried her that the pistol hadn't been cleaned and oiled in six years. The slide had felt slightly hesitant when she pulled it back. If her worst fear was justified and she was forced to defend herself, would the gun jam when fired?

Tess didn't dare think about it. "Come on, Mother! Let's go!"

"But you still haven't told me! Why did you want the gun?"

"Insurance."

"What do you *mean?*"

Tess didn't answer but rushed with her mother through the cobwebs toward the open door and the hallway.

Now the flicker of flames downstairs radiated upward and made the hallway seem lit by shimmering candles. Urging her mother, Tess raced to the left toward the top of the staircase, staring nervously downward, pistol ready. But instead of targets, what she saw was a blaze that crackled, growing to a roar in the vestibule. The bottom of the stairs was consumed by flames. Tess felt and stumbled back from the upward rush of heat. There wasn't any way that she and her mother could run through the swelling fire and cross the vestibule to reach the mansion's front door. For certain, her mother didn't have the dexterity to keep up with Tess, and equally for certain, Tess had no intention of getting ahead of her mother.

At the sight of the flames, her mother whimpered.

"The back stairs!" Tess said. "Hurry!"

She guided her mother along the smoke-filled hallway. Coughing, bent low because the air near the floor was less hazy, they came to the stairs that led down to the kitchen.

Here, too, a flicker illuminated the bottom, but at least it was a reflection off a wall. The fire itself wasn't in view.

We might have a chance, Tess thought.

She led the way, descending, telling her mother, "Stay close!"

The smoke alarms kept wailing.

At once a figure appeared at the bottom, charging toward them. Tess aimed the pistol.

A man blurted, "Mrs. Drake?"

"Jonathan!" Tess's mother said.

Nervous, Tess lowered the pistol.

The butler reached them. He wore pajamas. "I was sleeping! The smoke nearly . . . ! If the fire alarms hadn't wakened me . . . !" He had trouble breathing. "I tried to come up the front staircase to warn you, but the vestibule's—!"

"We know," Tess said. "Can we get out through the back?"

"The fire's in the kitchen, but the servants' quarters haven't been touched."

"Yet."

The three of them rushed down the stairs.

"Did you see anyone else inside?" Tess demanded.

"Anyone else?"

"Edna? What about Edna?" Tess's mother sounded hoarse.

"I woke her and told her to leave before I came for you," Jonathan said.

"You didn't see anyone *else?*" Tess repeated urgently.

The butler sounded confused. "Why no, Miss Drake. I don't understand what you mean. Who else would—?"

Tess didn't have time to explain. At the bottom, she squinted to her left toward an open door and the harsh glare of flames in the kitchen.

The heat was so intense that she had to raise an arm to shield her face.

But the heat singed that arm. If the flames reach this hall-way . . . !

Before Tess realized what she was doing, she lunged, grabbed the side of the door, and slammed it shut. Her hand stung.

Nonetheless the pain was worth the risk she'd taken. The door provided a buffer. She clutched her mother and stumbled forward, following Jonathan along a hallway toward the servants' quarters.

Despite the closed kitchen door, this hallway, too, was filled with smoke, a hot wind making the haze swirl. But at least Tess didn't feel scorched. Although she barely saw the doors to the butler's room and the maid's, the closer she came to the exit at the mansion's rear, the more breathable the air became.

She couldn't wait. Any moment now, they'd be outside in the clear, cool night.

But her second fear made Tess falter, trembling. They're probably hiding in the garden, aiming from the shrubs, ready to kill us when we try to leave.

"Tess, you're shaking so much!" her mother said. "Don't worry! We're almost free!"

Free? Tess thought. There's a good chance we're about to be shot!

They reached the back door.

It was open, smoke billowing out as cool air spewed in. Then the smoke dispersed, and as Jonathan hurried forward, Tess saw beyond him—

—twenty feet ahead!—

—in the glow of the flames from the windows!—

—a woman sprawled facedown in the grass. Blood soaked the back of her nightgown.

"Edna," Jonathan gasped.

Tess tried to stop him. "No!"

But Jonathan pried away and raced toward his fellow servant. *"Edna."*

The last word he ever said. Halfway toward her, Jonathan straightened, seemingly jolted by a cattle prod. A *lethal* prod.

Dark fluid erupted from his neck. *More* fluid spurted from his back. Jonathan appeared to be attempting a trick, to grasp his neck, his chest, and his forehead simultaneously.

Not enough hands!

Like a clumsy acrobat, he fell.

Thrashed pathetically.

Quivered.

Lay still.

Tess's mother screamed. Either she didn't understand what had happened, or else she did understand and panic seized her, or perhaps she felt desperate to try to help her servants. For whatever reason, she fought to squeeze beyond Tess and scramble out of the mansion.

Tess clawed to stop her, but the hand that clutched her father's pistol failed to snag on her mother's nightgown. The *other* hand clasped at lacy frills, which snapped from the strain.

Her mother escaped her.

"No!"

Tess gaped as her mother's frail, diet-thinned body didn't heave back like a catapulted acrobat but rather pirouetted, then sank, arms fluttering, like an exhausted ballerina. With blood-spurting holes in her abdomen and chest.

Tess wailed.

In grief.

In horror.

In *rage*.

Bees seemed to buzz around her, walloping the doorframe, slamming against the corridor's walls. Bullets. From silenced hand-guns in the backyard shrubs!

The bullets overcame Tess's shock-induced paralysis. She stumbled backward, pivoted to run, and lurched to a halt at the sight of flames eating through the closed kitchen door.

What am I doing?

I can't run back inside!

I'm trapped!

Too many thoughts sped through her mind. Her mother's death. The gunmen outside. The fire.

Paralysis again controlled her.

I can't stay here!

But I can't go outside!

Think!

The fire kept licking through the kitchen door, brightening the smoke-filled hallway.

The basement. I can get to the basement. The door's in this hallway. I can hide downstairs in a corner. I can use the laundry tub to soak rags and wrap myself in—!

No! That's crazy! I wouldn't have a chance. When the smoke filled the basement, no matter how many wet rags I tried to breathe through, I'd still be suffocated.

And the heat would be unbearable!

And the overhead floor would eventually collapse. I'd be buried by flaming—!

Fear made her tremble so hard that her bladder muscles nearly failed.

But I can't just stand here!

The smoke made her bend over, retching.

At once a new thought gave her frantic hope.

It might not work!

But God help me, it's my only chance!

She held her breath and scurried forward, dodging past the fiery kitchen door. The heat struck her clothes. For a terrifying moment, she was certain that their cotton would burst into flames.

Blinded by the smoke, she reached the stairs, tripped, banged painfully forward, and clambered on her hands and knees up the steps. The heat became mercifully less, although the smoke increased, and when she had to breathe, her lungs rebelled, her chest racked with spasms. Determined, she scrambled faster, harder, and suddenly the steps ended. Pawing at nothing, propelled by her thrusting knees, she arched through the air and sprawled, slamming her chin on the upstairs floor.

Ahead, at the hallway's midpoint, even with the smoke, she had no trouble seeing the flames at the top of the vestibule's staircase. With a roar, they swelled toward the ceiling.

Hurry! The smoke made her eyes weep. It seared her throat.

She struggled to a crouch and darted forward, moaning as she neared the increasing heat, the spreading blaze. The crackling whoosh of the flames became deafening.

She whimpered, seized with terror that she might not be able to reach her destination, that the surge of blistering heat would force her back.

No choice now! She cursed, mustered her resolve, and veered to the left. Chased by a gushing arm of flame, she found her open bedroom door, lurched through it, and slammed the door shut behind her.

By comparison with the furnace of the hallway, the air in her bedroom was wonderfully cool, although thick, acrid smoke continued to sting her eyes. Her exertion forced her to breathe and made her cough so deeply that she spit out phlegm.

She didn't care! She had a chance now!

Move!

The glow of the lamp on her bedside table was useless, so enveloped by haze that it was almost invisible.

That didn't matter! In this familiar bedroom, she didn't *need* to see in order to do what she had to. She lunged past a chair and reached French doors. When she yanked them open, she couldn't believe how delicious the outside air smelled. Flames that shattered windows to her right illuminated the gardens and shrubs below her.

But all Tess paid attention to was the giant oak tree beyond the small balcony outside her room.

That oak tree had been the reason Tess had broken her arm when she was eleven. One Saturday afternoon, after having come home from her gymnastics class, she'd been so excited by her progress on the overhead bar that she'd studied the oak tree from the balcony and wondered how easy it would be to leap toward the nearest branch, then swing toward a farther branch until she reached the trunk and climbed down, hand over hand, to the ground.

Tempted beyond her ability to resist, she'd leapt, grabbed the branch, clung by one hand while she'd stretched her other hand toward the next branch . . . and screamed when she felt her fingers slip . . . then screamed again, even more fiercely, when she'd hit the lawn, her left arm twisted under her. The arm had projected in a wrong—a *horribly* wrong—direction. Until that moment, she'd never known a greater agony.

Her father had burst from the house and rushed to pick her up, then raced to the garage and driven her, speeding through red lights, to the nearest hospital.

Her father.

Dead.

How much she missed him.

And now her mother was dead as well! Tess still couldn't adjust to the sight of the blood from the bullets that had struck her mother's abdomen and chest.

She couldn't believe it had happened.

Dead?

Her mother *couldn't* be dead.

You bastards!

As flames squeezed through the top, bottom, and sides of her bedroom door, Tess crammed the handgun into her burlap purse, tugged its top closed, and wrapped the purse's strap repeatedly around her wrist until there wasn't any slack.

The flames no longer squeezed but *erupted* through the sides, top, and bottom of her door.

No time!

Tess retreated into the smoke of her bedroom. Responding to her years of training, she crouched, braced one foot behind the other, and bent her knees in a sprinter's pose.

She blurted a prayer.

And propelled herself forward.

13

She jumped, felt her sneakers touch the balcony's ornate metal railing, and vaulted outward, hurtling through the air. In the dark, she feared that the past would reoccur, that she'd lose her grasp on the tree limb and plummet toward the lawn.

But she was twenty-eight now. Her tall, lithe body reached the tree much sooner than she expected, her long arms stretching, her firm hands clutching.

The jolt of grabbing the branch swung her down, then up toward another branch. She took advantage of that motion, and as the branch she held began to droop, she hooked her legs around the farther branch and dangled, her hips bent toward the ground, balancing her weight between one branch and the other. The moment the branches stopped bobbing, she groped, hand over hand, shifting her legs, toward where the two branches converged. With an expert twist, she upended herself, facing downward now, and inched along the two branches, finally clutching the trunk where she huddled, supported by stout limbs, concealed by leaves.

Her heart pounded so fiercely that she feared she might become sick.

Had the gunmen seen her leap from the balcony?

Despite the flames that burst from windows near the front of the mansion, she strained to convince herself that *this* area remained in shadow.

The branches had bobbed. True. Yes. She couldn't pretend that they hadn't. But if the gunmen were concentrating on the doors from the mansion, they might not have thought to look toward this side of the house where there weren't any doors.

And in particular, they might not have thought to glance toward the least likely exit, a balcony on the upper floor.

Well, Tess trembled, I'll soon find out.

She yanked open her purse and tugged out her pistol. It gave her great satisfaction to think that the men who'd killed her mother might be killed by the gun her father had trained her to use. Even though it hadn't been cleaned in six years. Even though the spring in its magazine might have been weakened from so many years of having been loaded.

Tess couldn't think about that risk. All she could think about was . . . !

Descending the tree.

Doing her best to escape through a barrier of thick evergreen shrubs toward the darkness of a neighboring mansion.

She climbed down the tree, huddled at the base of its murky trunk, aimed toward the shadowy back of the mansion, saw no one, and bolted toward the shrubs on her right.

A bee seemed to buzz. A bullet splintered the oak.

In midstride, Tess whirled, crouched, and raised her father's pistol.

A lunging target appeared, silhouetted by flames that suddenly gushed at the back of the mansion. A target with a gun! A target who stooped and aimed toward Tess.

The lessons at the shooting range came back to her.

She squeezed the trigger. The pistol roared, its recoil jolting the barrel upward.

Ignore the recoil. Never take your eyes from the target.

She stared at the gunman and realized, heart lurching, that she'd missed!

She dove as the gunman fired. His weapon had a silencer. She didn't hear the spit when the gun discharged, but she definitely heard the bullet whiz over her.

Flat, both hands gripping the pistol, Tess aimed more deliberately, concentrating more fiercely, firing again. The roar made her ears ring.

With an inward scream of triumph, she saw the gunman stagger back and topple. At once her stomach cramped, from tension, from the shock of what she'd just done.

She couldn't allow herself to feel guilty about . . . ! *She had to get away.*

Scrambling upward, consumed by frenzy, she raced toward the shrubs on the right. In the distance, sirens wailed. The fire department. Maybe the police. Someone in a neighboring mansion must have called them! But the sirens were too far away. They wouldn't get here soon enough to help her. Keep running!

Someone shouted from the front of the mansion.

Tess pivoted. A man with a gun darted into view.

Reflexively Tess aimed. She squeezed the trigger. Again. Then again! The first bullet struck the mansion's wall. The second hit a tree behind the gunman.

But the third knocked the gunman backward.

Tess again screamed inwardly with triumph.

Directly, the silent cheer stuck in her throat.

No!

The gunman had managed to stay on his feet. He continued to raise his weapon. Her own gun roaring, Tess fired *again* and slammed the man onto the lawn.

She sprinted past a flower garden, hearing bullets zing from the back of the mansion. They slashed the evergreens she ran toward and made her dive again.

Frantic, she rolled against the bottom of the shrubs, twisted, aimed at a gunman racing in her direction from the back of the house, shot three times, missed, but at least made the gunman scramble behind the cover of a gazebo.

The mansion was completely in flames now. The sirens wailed louder. Closer. As the gunman leaned from the side of the gazebo, aiming, Tess angrily shot yet again.

He spun out of sight.

But not smoothly. Tess tried to assure herself that it was possible she'd hit him, although maybe she'd merely splintered wood near his face.

She couldn't tell. It didn't matter. No time!

She crawled through a narrow gap at the bottom of the shrubs, felt branches scrape her skull, her back, her hips, and charged to her feet the moment she was through the hedge. She ran through the fire-illuminated shadows in the spacious backyard of the neighboring mansion.

Lights were on in the house. She imagined the frightened residents scrambling toward the street in case the fire spread and their own house caught fire.

Despite the roar of the blaze, she heard branches scrape behind her. Whirling, she shot three times toward where the hedge moved, heard a man groan, and urged herself onward through the deepening darkness of the extensive yard.

She veered past trees, lunged through flower gardens, tripped against the low rim of a lily pond, nearly tumbled into the water, but caught her balance and skirted the pond, running faster.

Count how many rounds you've shot, her father had always insisted.

But in her frenzy to escape, Tess had forgotten her father's rule. How many times did I shoot?

She couldn't remember. More than ten, she was sure of that. Perhaps thirteen or . . . The pistol would be almost empty.

Fear chilled her despite the sweat that soaked her clothes and dripped from her face. She had to conserve her ammunition.

Chest heaving, she came to another line of evergreens. In the darkness, she couldn't help spinning to face the blazing mansion a hundred yards away. Flames licked from her bedroom. The violation made her furious. Her past, her youth, were being destroyed. Trembling, she detected no sign of anyone's chasing her and sank to the ground, scurrying beneath the farther shrubs.

In the next mansion's yard, she realized, tense, that she couldn't keep running in this direction. It was too predictable. All her pursuers had to do was hurry along the street in front of the house, get ahead of her, hide, and wait to kill her when she tried to leave the area. Her only hope was that the sirens, now very close, would force her hunters to flee.

But she couldn't count on that. She had to guarantee her protection. *How?*

Breathing rapidly, shaking, confused, afraid, she made an urgent choice and instead of continuing to sprint across this yard, she darted toward its rear. After passing through the darkness between a swimming pool and a tennis court, she found her way blocked by a high stone wall. She glanced around, desperate, in search of a ladder or a tree near the wall, *anything* that would allow her to get over the top.

Nothing.

She retreated toward the swimming pool. Next to a maintenance shed, she found a long metal pole. The pole had a net at one end, obviously used for skimming leaves and other debris from the surface of the water.

Hurry! She pressed the pole against the bottom of the shed, squeezing it, flexing it, twisting. The pole was strong yet pliant. Maybe.

Her temples throbbed from the force of her rapid heartbeat. No choice.

Tess crammed the pistol into her purse, which still hung securely from her waist. With equal speed, she gripped one end of the pole, shifted the other end toward the back of the yard, lifted the pole, and raced toward the wall.

When the far end of the pole was five feet from the wall, she rammed it into the lawn and hurtled upward.

It had been years since she'd practiced this event. In track and field, pole-vaulting had never been her favorite activity. But now she had to pretend she was in the Olympics. As her body arched higher, she felt the pole begin to bend. Its metal creaked. If it snaps . . . !

With a stunning jolt, she slammed against the top of the wall, clawed with one hand, snagged the rim, let go of the pole, fumbled with her other hand, and dangled from the wall, squirming upward.

At the top, hands scraped and bleeding, ignoring the pain, Tess lay flat, then hung from the other side, and dropped toward blackness. She feared she'd hit a bench that might break her ankle.

Or a stake that supported a sapling and might impale her.

Instead her feet struck the soft earth of a garden, and with practiced agility, she bent her knees, tucked her elbows against her sides, then rolled across pliant dirt and cushioning flowers.

In a frenzy, she sprang to her feet, studied the gloom ahead, the vague shadows of trees, the bulky, dark outline of another mansion, drew the pistol from her purse, and ran.

When she'd been ten, her best friend had lived here. They'd often played in this yard, and one of their favorite games had been hide-and-seek.

Tess remembered an afternoon when she'd found so good a hiding place that her friend had finally given up looking.

Now Tess hurried toward that hiding place, hoping that the yard had not been relandscaped. When she heard the trickle of water, she increased speed.

In a corner at the back, she came to boulders that had been piled and cemented together to form a miniature, shoulder-high imitation of a mountain from the top of which water bubbled and streamed down a series of zigzagging crests toward a goldfish pond. A pump in an alcove behind the boulders kept the water circulating.

The alcove had a metal hatch to protect the pump from bad weather. Bushes flanked the boulders. Tess crept through the sharp-edged bushes, knelt at the back, and groped in the darkness, finding the hatch.

She squirmed into the alcove, closing the hatch behind her. In total blackness, with the pump whirring next to her, she sat with her knees bent toward her chest, her arms around her knees, her head stooped. The cramped position made her muscles ache, but at least she could rest and gain time to decide what to do.

Years ago, the reason her friend hadn't been able to find her was that they'd once investigated this alcove, and Tess's friend had been disgusted by the spiderwebs inside. Her friend hadn't thought to look here because her friend would never have chosen to hide here. But Tess had been a tomboy, and spiderwebs had meant nothing compared to winning the game.

Now, feeling spiderwebs against her hair as well as something tiny with many legs skittering across her right hand, making her skin tingle, Tess again ignored what would have nauseated her friend, although she needed all her discipline to repress a shudder. The main thing was that she'd reached safety. In this grown-up, deadly version of hide-and-seek, no stranger could find where she'd hidden, because no stranger could possibly know about this alcove behind the boulders.

Tess winced. Her hands hurt from scratches and burns. Her back stung from when she'd crawled through the shrubs. Her legs, arms, and chin throbbed from the numerous times she'd struck objects or fallen.

But the pain in her body was nothing compared to the pain in her soul. Her mother was *dead!*

No! Tess couldn't believe it. She couldn't adjust to it.

She'd killed at least two men tonight, and she couldn't adjust to that either, no matter how much she'd cursed—and continued to curse—the gunmen who'd killed her mother and no matter how fiercely she'd sworn to get even.

She wanted to vomit.

No! Instead, silently, she wept, hot tears streaming down her cheeks as she trembled in the cool, damp, black confinement of the alcove.

She needed to think.

In time, when she decided the area would be safe, she needed to get away.

But more than anything, she needed to find out who was after her and why they'd turned her life into hell.

And get even. The bitter, angry thought kept coming back. Yes, someone definitely was going to pay.

She fingered her purse. As exhaustion overwhelmed her, she thought of the photographs that her purse contained, and *one* photograph especially, as repulsive as it was confusing. The bas-relief statue. A muscular, long-haired, handsome man straddled a bull and sliced its throat while a dog lunged at the gushing blood, a serpent sped toward a clump of wheat, and a scorpion attacked the bull's genitals.

Insanity!

14

In the dust-laden classroom on the second floor of the abandoned school in Brooklyn, the chameleon completed his report.

The room—shadowy because of the plywood over its windows—was silent for a moment, the chameleon's associates frowning.

"So the woman escaped?" the fourth man finally asked, unconsciously twisting the ruby ring on the middle finger of his left hand, grasping its insignia of an intersecting cross and sword.

The chameleon hesitated. "I believe so. The member of our watcher's team who hid behind the mansion didn't see the woman leap from the balcony to the tree. But he did see her climb down the tree to the lawn. And he definitely saw her shoot two men."

"But where did she get the weapon?" the fifth man asked.

The chameleon shrugged.

"Are you sure the enemy didn't chase the woman and catch her?" the second man asked.

"I can't be certain. The fire department and the police arrived. Their approaching sirens gave the enemy ample warning, time to pick up their dead and flee the area before the authorities arrived."

"I hope that our own operative fled successfully," the third man said.

The chameleon nodded. "More, I believe there's a good chance that the woman is safe."

"But we don't know where she is." The sixth man scowled.

"The enemy doesn't either. If I understand your logic, you counted on using the woman as bait to attract the quarry. But your plan won't work now. We're back to where we started."

"Not necessarily." The chameleon squinted. "At the moment we don't know where the woman is. But we will—and soon."

"How?"

"You put a tap on the woman's phone."

"As you ordered," the electronics expert said.

"And on the policeman's phone. In her place, desperate, confused, afraid, what would *you* do?" the chameleon asked.

"Ah." The sixth man leaned back. "Of course. She'll contact the policeman." With a smile, he added, "So now we concentrate our surveillance on *him.*"

"Eventually he'll lead us to the woman," the chameleon said. "More important, I take for granted that the enemy will be as clever as always. After all, they've had years of practice. Does anyone doubt that their logic will be as calculated as mine, that they'll come to the same conclusion?"

The fifth man traced his finger through the dust on his miniature desk. "They've proven their survival skills. Again and again, they've anticipated our traps."

"But perhaps not this time," the chameleon said. "Wherever the policeman goes, *he'll* be the bait that attracts the quarry. The hunt continues. At the moment, I have a team watching Lieutenant Craig, although their primary purpose, of course, is to watch for the enemy."

"In that case, we'd better join the hunt," the fourth man said.

"Absolutely," the third man said.

The others stood quickly.

The chameleon gestured. "A moment. Before we leave, there's one other matter I need to explain."

They waited.

"As we know, the enemy—the vermin—are increasing their repugnant activities. There's no anticipating the horrors to which they'll descend as a consequence of their hellish errors. At the same time, I grant that in the past week a great many errors—tactical— were committed on our side. Several were my fault. I've readily admitted that. But judgment day is *now*. Recent events prove how unstable the situation has become. I'd hoped that we could accomplish this assignment on our own. I'm no longer certain we can. Pride is not my shortcoming. I don't hesitate to ask for help if I think our mission requires it.''

"Help?" The sixth man furrowed his brow.

"I've contacted our superiors. I've explained the situation. They agree with my assessment and *agree with my request*. At half past noon, a team of specialists will arrive at Kennedy Airport.''

"Specialists?" The sixth man paled.

"That's right. I've sent for a team of enforcers.''

TWO

OUTRAGE AND RETRIBUTION

THE SACRIFICIAL VICTIM

1

Newark, New Jersey

In his ramshackle office in a rusted corrugated-metal building on the fringe of the city's docks, Buster "Right Hook" Buchanan scraped a wooden match across his desk and lit the remnant of a cigar he'd butted out last night before going home. No point in being wasteful. After all, this was a *Cuban* cigar, the last of a box that don Vincenzo—always thoughtful—had sent to him on his birthday two weeks ago.

Good old don Vincenzo. He knew how to make his employees happy. Especially those who worked hard for him, and Buster "Right Hook" Buchanan was as hard a worker as he'd been a tough longshoreman in his youth and then a fierce boxer. A contender. For sure.

On impulse, reminded of his favorite profession, Buster clenched his fists, did a little fancy footwork, jabbed rapidly right and left, then delivered his famous powerful right hook.

Got you! He glared down at his phantom KO'd opponent. But at once the thought of his long-ago glory in the ring made Buster frown. The cheers of the frenzied spectators. The stroking praises of his manager. The different kind of stroking from women, so many women, *gorgeous* women, eager to fuck a celebrity. Buster shook his head. The cheers, the praises, the women . . . Some nights it seemed as if . . . They haunted him.

Buster tried a little more footwork, a little more jabbing, but he was overweight now, twenty years older, and let a fact be a fact, his doctor had warned him to take it easy.

Not that Buster was afraid. Hell, he'd *never* been afraid. He could still drop three guys in a bar fight. *Any*time. Hadn't he done so last night in his neighborhood tavern on the way home from work? Damned right. Nonetheless his impulsive footwork and jabbing, combined with the smoke from the cigar stub in his mouth, made him wheeze. He felt like that one time he'd taken a vacation to Colorado and had never been able to catch his breath in the mountains.

Maybe I ought to give up these cigars. After all, that's what the doctor said.

Shit, no. Life's too short. Hey, what does that frigging doctor know? Was *he* a contender? Sure, it's easy enough for him to give advice. He looks like a kid, for Christ's sake. And that Rolex he wears. He must have been born with a silver spoon in his asshole. He doesn't understand.

Too bad—too *damned* bad—about those last three bouts. Buster had always regretted being forced to take a dive—no, *three* dives—because don Vincenzo had a cousin who was a fighter and who'd been chosen to be the contender that Buster was supposed to be.

Well, that cousin's glass jaw had put the kibash on *his* career, Buster thought with bitter delight. But *my* career had gone in the toilet, and . . .

Never mind. Waving smoke from his face, puffing on the final remnant of his Cuban cigar—at least, don Vincenzo remembered the guys he owed favors—Buster told himself he had work to do. Or else don Vincenzo would be pissed.

Buster savored the final puff from Castro's tobacco and

crunched the last of the butt in an overflowing ashtray. Got to get this frigging place cleaned up sometime, he thought.

But there was work to do, and as Buster scowled at the scratch mark that his match had left on his battered wooden desk, straight across a circular stain made by a beer can, he told himself that a working man needed rewards now and then. Not just cigars, but . . .

Yeah.

Buster groped beneath his desk and grabbed the last can of beer in a hollow-sounding twelve-pack. He popped the tab and took several deep swallows.

Vitamins.

Yeah.

He licked his lips, then reminded himself. Work to do. Any minute, Big Joe and his brother were due to arrive at this warehouse with the truck. The three of them would unload the red plastic containers that, except for their color and what they were made of, resembled the canister of natural gas attached to Buster's outdoor barbecue grill.

Not that Buster liked to barbecue. Although his nagging wife did. What a pain in the ass.

When he, Big Joe, and Big Joe's brother emptied the containers into several large metal bins, they'd close the hatches on the bins to conceal their contents and use a forklift truck to place the bins in a sling, which would hoist them onto a barge. Tonight, the three of them would take a cruise down the Hudson River and across to the tip of Long Island.

And dump the shit they were carrying.

Because their cargo—Buster sipped more beer and shivered— was medical waste.

Used needles.

Contaminated bandages.

Infected blood.

Rotting human tissue.

Well, Buster thought, and guzzled more beer, it's a dirty job—

—he forced himself to chortle—

—but some poor bastard has to do it. Especially for don Vincenzo.

Despite the beer that cleared his head from this morning's hangover, Buster sobered.

Yeah, *especially* for don Vincenzo. Because if you refuse the don, you make him unhappy, and when the don's unhappy, you get your knees broken. And that's only for starters. Fuck the Cuban cigars. When the don's unhappy, he doesn't just have your knees broken. He butchers you.

And anyway, what's the harm in dumping the needles and the bandages into the ocean? Buster asked himself, wishing he'd thought to buy more beer. There's a landfill crisis. That's what I read in the frigging papers. Too much garbage. Not enough space to get rid of all that shit. Too many frigging condominiums. Not enough holes in the ground. And nobody wants—what do they call them?—incinerators to get rid of medical waste. The damned yuppies think they'll get a disease if they breathe the smoke. But don Vincenzo's got the biggest garbage-disposal outfit in eastern New Jersey. So where's he supposed to put all the junk, especially the crap from the hospitals?

The answer was simple.

There's plenty of ocean.

You bet. More than half the world, maybe three-quarters, is frigging water, isn't it? Plenty. I mean *plenty* of room for a few barges of needles and bandages.

Okay, all right, the tide sometimes works against us, Buster thought. Sometimes the shit drifts back toward land. Sometimes the needles and bandages float up on the beaches.

Give me a break. Is that *my* fault? I do my job. I dump the stuff. If the ocean works against me, *I'm* not to blame.

Yeah, he thought.

Sure.

So a few yuppies don't get to swim in the ocean for a couple of days while the junk's cleaned up.

So what?

Let the cleanup squad do its job while I do mine.

A buzzer sounded. Buster set down his beer and straightened. The buzzer was the signal that Big Joe and his brother had backed the truck toward the warehouse and were waiting for Buster to raise the door.

About time. Buster pressed a button. A rumble shook the rickety warehouse as its door rose. Big Joe's truck backed into the warehouse toward the barge containers. Its engine burping, the truck stopped.

Buster jabbed the button that lowered the rumbling door and stalked from his office. "You're late," he growled as the driver's door swung open.

But Big Joe didn't step down.

In his place, a man whom Buster had never met jumped lithely onto the concrete floor.

"Hi." The man, in his thirties, in *great* shape, grinned.

"Who the hell are *you?*"

"I hate to say it, but Big Joe had an accident. Tragic. Terrible."

"*Accident?* What kind of . . . ?"

"Horrible. A fire. His trailer. Died in his sleep."

"My God." Buster wheezed. "But Big Joe's brother . . . ! Where is he? Does he know?"

"In a way."

"That doesn't make sense! Either he does, or he doesn't!"

"Well, he did, that's for sure," the handsome, robust stranger said. "But he doesn't anymore. See, he's dead. Another fire. Awful His house burned down last night."

"*What are you telling me?*"

"You're next."

With a bang, the truck's passenger door jolted open, two men leaping down.

Buster rubbed his eyes. The other men resembled the *first* man.

Trim.

Lithe.

Handsome.

Tawny skin.

Early thirties.

As they neared him, Buster realized that they resembled each other in a *further* way. It had to be a trick of the light. They all seemed to have gray eyes.

"So, Buster, we've got a problem," the first man said.

"Oh, *yeah?*" Buster stepped backward and raised his famous right fist. "*What* problem?"

"The needles. The bandages. The contaminated blood. You're poisoning the ocean."

"Hey, all I'm doing is what don Vincenzo tells me."

"Sure. Well, you don't need to take his orders anymore. Don Vincenzo's dead."

"What?"

"Would you believe it? Amazing. Really. No kidding. Yet another fire."

Buster stumbled farther backward. "What the fuck? Hey, don't come any closer! I'm warning you!"

"Yeah, yeah, yeah." With unbelievable agility, the first man ducked under Buster's jabbing fists, avoided the former contender's famous right hook, and slammed his nose so hard that Buster fell to the floor, seeing double, spewing blood.

"Listen carefully," the man said. "We're not going to burn you."

Sickened by his pain and his doubled vision, Buster wheezed in relief. He had to admit that any of these three men were in better condition than any opponent he'd faced. If they were willing to bargain, maybe he had a chance.

"So you'll let me go?" Buster wished that he'd never met, had never surrendered to don Vincenzo.

"Afraid not," the man said. "Actions have consequences. But flames aren't always the best deterrent. Sometimes the punishment has to fit the crime. A different example is often required. Just a moment before I show you."

The three men put on surgical facemasks, gowns, and rubber gloves.

"Jesus!" Buster said.

"If that's your preference. My companions will now hold you down."

"No!"

"Don't resist. Your death will be more painful."

As Buster squirmed and struggled and screamed, while two men held him down, the other man shoved a handkerchief into Buster's mouth to silence him. Then the man adjusted his rubber gloves and proceeded to unscrew various red plastic containers on the truck, pull out numerous contaminated hypodermic needles, and plunge each of them into various portions of Buster's body.

His arms.

His legs.

His throat.

His groin.

His eyes.

Wherever.

When the three men were finished, after they left the warehouse and the body was finally discovered, the newspapers described the corpse as a pincushion.

Inaccurate. Buster "Right Hook" Buchanan was really a *needle*cushion, and if the thousands of points shoved into every portion of his body hadn't killed him, at least one of the diseases from those many infected needles would eventually have led to his death, that is if his lung cancer from his years of smoking cigars hadn't killed him first.

2

Lieutenant Craig's apartment was a one-room efficiency in the cramped basement of a converted town house on Bleecker Street in lower Manhattan. Once he'd owned a house in Queens, or at least the bank had, but four years ago, his former wife had gained title to the property during their divorce agreement.

Craig dearly wished he was back there. *Not* because of the house. He'd never liked mowing the lawn, shoveling snow, or doing any of the other chores that a house required, although the truth was that his work had kept him so busy he'd seldom been home to do those chores—or to pay enough attention to his wife and two children.

That's what he really missed, not the damned house but his family. Some nights, his heart ached so fiercely that he couldn't sleep, and he lay on his back on his fold-out bed, staring at the ceiling. How he wished to God that he'd tried harder.

But Craig had discovered that marriage and police work seldom mixed. Because being a cop was like having a *second* marriage, and a cop's wife could get as jealous about his work as she could about another woman. So many other guys in his department were divorced as well. The only good thing was that at least Craig's former wife had been generous about his visitation privileges. He did his best to spend time with his son and daughter on weekends, probably more time than when he'd been married, but the trouble was that his children were in their teens now, and being with their father didn't excite them as it had when they were toddlers.

I sure made a mess of things, Craig thought as he entered his shower, closed the door, and turned on the faucets. Hot water stung him. So what am I *thinking?* How come I want to get involved with a woman who's ten years younger than me? Am I nuts? The only reason Tess and I are connected is the trouble she's having. When that gets settled—

—you mean, *if*—

—no, *when*—

—hey, don't get pessimistic—

—she'll want nothing to do with me. She certainly didn't sound enthusiastic about the idea of a friendship, a *close* friendship, when I talked to her on the phone last night.

Craig increased the lancing pulse of hot water, rinsed shampoo from his hair, and shook his head. Hey, what do you expect? She's in mourning. Never mind that she met her friend, whoever Joseph Martin really was, only three times. There's a good chance somebody's following her. She's preoccupied, not to mention scared. Your timing was lousy.

He shut off the water, stepped from the narrow shower stall (there wasn't a bathtub), and toweled himself dry. With the meticulousness of a divorced man who'd come to realize the tremendous amount of maintenance that his former wife had done and he'd never noticed, he used a squeegee to wipe water off the shower stall so there wouldn't be lime stains. He'd already shaved. All he needed to do was comb his hair, slap on some after-shave, dab on a little deodorant (the maintenance never ended), get dressed, and make himself eat breakfast.

In his bedroom—which was also his living room and his kitchen—Craig started to boil water for coffee. By habit, he turned on his radio to catch the news, and on impulse, he picked up the phone. It might not be a smart idea. He'd probably be repeating his mistake. All the same, he felt a compulsion to talk to Tess, to explain that he was sorry for putting pressure on her. He read the note he'd made last night when she'd told him her mother's phone number, and as he pressed buttons on the phone, he vaguely heard the radio announcer describe a new round of mortar battles that had broken out between the Christians and the Moslems in Beirut. Why don't they get their shit together? Craig thought, and listened to the long-distance static.

He heard a buzz.

Another buzz.

And then a female voice, not Tess's, in fact not even a *human* voice but one of those robot-sounding computer simulations.

"The number you have called is not in service."

Not in service? Craig frowned. I must have pressed the wrong buttons.

He studied the note he'd made, wondering if he'd written down the wrong numbers, and tried to phone again.

"The number you have called is not in service."

Jesus, I *did* write down the wrong numbers.

Boiling water made the kettle shriek. Craig turned off the stove, frowned harder as he spooned instant coffee into a cup, then stiffened when the radio announcer said:

". . . completely destroyed a mansion in an exclusive district of Alexandria, Virginia."

Alexandria?

A premonition made Craig lunge toward the radio to increase the volume.

"Three people trying to escape the blaze were shot and killed," the announcer said. "Two servants and Melinda Drake—"

Craig's throat constricted.

"—widow of Remington Drake, former State Department envoy who was tortured to death by Moslem extremists six years ago in Beirut. Authorities have not been able to identify the assailants or determine their motive for the slayings, but fire investigators have concluded that the blaze was due to arson.''

Arson? Two servants? Tess's mother?

But what about—?

Craig grabbed the phone, jabbed the numbers for information, got other numbers, jabbed them, got through to *Alexandria* information, and finally reached the Alexandria . . .

''Police department,'' a gruff man said.

''Homicide.'' Craig struggled to control his breathing.

Click. Buzz. Silence.

Come on! Come . . . !

''Homicide,'' a husky-throated woman said.

''My name is William Craig.'' Another struggle to control his trembling voice. ''I'm a lieutenant in the Missing Persons division of the New York City police department. My badge number is . . . My superior's name is . . . His office phone number is . . . I'm calling from my home. If you want, I'll give you that number while you verify who I am.''

''Before we get complicated, Lieutenant, why don't you catch your breath and tell me what you need?''

''The arson at Melinda Drake's house. The gunshot victims. Did you find another victim? The daughter. *Tess* Drake.''

''No. Only the servants and the . . . What do you know about a daughter, Lieutenant? Why would you think she was at the house? What's your interest in this matter?''

''I . . . It's too complicated. I need to think. I'll call you back.'' Craig slammed down the phone.

Tess was safe!

No.

A sudden, fierce thought made him grip the kitchen counter. What if she didn't escape the fire? What if she died in the house? What if the investigators hadn't found her body yet?

Trembling, Craig yanked open a cupboard and grabbed for the yellow pages, desperate to make a reservation on the soonest flight to Washington National Airport. He'd rent a car there and drive to . . .

His hands faltered. Abruptly he shut the directory.

What the hell good would I do in Alexandria? I'd be useless. All I'd do is end up pacing, watching the investigators search the mansion's wreckage.

But I've got to do *something*.

Think! Hope! All you know for sure is that two servants and Tess's mother were shot while they tried to escape the flames.

But that doesn't mean *Tess* didn't manage to escape.

Please. Oh, Jesus, *please,* let her be all right.

If she escaped . . .

What would she do? Obviously she'd be frightened. She'd hide from whoever had tried to kill her.

And then?

Maybe . . .

Just maybe she'd call me.

Who else can she turn to? Who else does she know she can trust and depend on? I might be the only hope she's got.

3

Afraid, Tess felt naked. Shivering despite the morning's humidity, she rang the mansion's doorbell again. She kept glancing nervously beyond the trees and shrubs in the large front yard toward the hedge-flanked entrance to the driveway. So far she'd been lucky. Since she'd lunged to the porch, no cars had passed along the narrow, quiet street, but if any did, and if the drivers noticed her, and if one of those cars belonged to the men who'd tried to kill her . . .

Hurry. The next time she pressed the doorbell, Tess didn't take her thumb from the button. Another fear made her tremble. What if the mansion wasn't occupied? What if the Caudills had gone to their summer place in Maine? Desperate, she wondered if she ought to break in. No! There'll be burglar alarms!

Her childhood friend had long since moved away, first to college and then with her husband to San Francisco, but the parents still owned this mansion, and during the night, while Tess had hidden in the damp, black, constricting alcove behind the boulders in the backyard fountain, she'd ignored the increasing pain in her cramped muscles and struggled to focus her grief-filled, terror-racked thoughts in an effort to decide what to do next. Although the answer had been obvious, her confusion had been so great that it had taken her until the morning to remember that the people who owned this mansion had once been like a second set of parents to her.

As the skin beneath her thumbnail whitened from the force with which she pressed the doorbell, Tess's hope dwindled, her fear increasing. Please!

Abruptly she breathed as the door was jerked open. A rigid butler scowled, surveying her grimy jeans, torn pullover, soot-covered face, and grungy, spiderweb-tangled hair.

"Mrs. Caudill?" Tess said. "Please! *Is she here?*"

"Mrs. Caudill donates to shelters for the homeless. There are several downtown." The butler began to shut the door.

Tess shoved her hand against the door. "You don't understand!"

"Mrs. Caudill can not be disturbed." The butler straightened and grimaced, his nostrils twitching. Tess realized that her clothes must reek from smoke, sweat, and fear. "I'll be forced to call the police if you don't leave."

"No! Listen to me!" Tess said. She pushed at the door.

The butler resisted.

"My name's Tess Drake! Mrs. Caudill knows me!" Heart pounding, she heard a car approach along the street and squirmed urgently to get through the narrow opening.

The butler struggled to block her way.

"I'm a friend of Mrs. Caudill's daughter!" Tess said, and fought to shoulder the butler aside. "I used to come here often! Mrs. Caudill *knows* me! Tell her it's—"

"Tess?" a puzzled woman said in the background. *"Tess? Is that you?"*

"Mrs. Caudill! Please! Let me in!"

On the street, the car sounded nearer.

"That's fine, Thomas. Open the door," the unseen woman said.

"Very well, madame." The butler glared at Tess. "As you wish."

The car was close to the mansion's driveway as Tess darted through the door. The butler shut it, muffling the sound of the car.

Tess paused and breathed deeply. She clutched her purse—it felt heavy with its added burden of the photographs, the book, and the handgun—and gazed in relief at Mrs. Caudill, who stood in the foyer, near the entrance to the mansion's dining room.

Mrs. Caudill was fifty-five, short, somewhat stout, with pudgy cheeks that were emphasized by the circular rims of her glasses. She wore a brilliantly colored, oriental housecoat and blinked in surprise, apparently not only because of Tess's unexpected arrival but because of her disheveled appearance as well. "Good Lord, Tess! Are you all right?"

"Now I am."

"The fire! Last night, I could see the flames from my bedroom window. The sirens wakened me. Where have you *been?* What *happened* to you?"

Although her legs were stiff, Tess managed to hurry toward her. "Thank God, you're home. Mrs. Caudill, I need help. I'm sorry for barging in like this, but—"

"Help? Why, of course, dear. You know you're always welcome. I remember when you used to come to play with . . ." Mrs. Caudill almost reached to hug Tess but restrained herself when she got a closer look at Tess's filthy clothes and smelled the smoke wafting off her. "Your arms! Look at those bruises! And your hands! *They're blistered. You've been burned.* You need a doctor!"

"No!"

"What?"

"Not a doctor! Not yet! I don't think the burns are serious, Mrs. Caudill. They sting, though. If you've got a first-aid kit . . ."

"Yes. Exactly. And we need to get you cleaned up! Quickly! Upstairs! Thomas!'' Mrs. Caudill spun toward the butler. "I don't recall where . . . The first-aid kit! *Where do we keep it?* Bring it as fast as you can!''

"By all means, madame,'' the butler said dourly.

"This is my daughter's friend! Tess Drake! The fire last night!''

"Yes, madame?''

"That was her *mother's* house!''

"Now I understand, madame,'' the butler said, more dour. "Tess Drake. However, I regret . . . It's no doubt my fault, but madame, she spoke so quickly . . . I apologize. In the haste of the moment, I failed to catch her last name.''

"Thomas, stop bowing. And for the love of the Lord, stop scraping. As my daughter used to say, get with it.''

"Of course, madame.''

Mrs. Caudill grasped the long hem on her colorful, oriental housecoat. With unexpected agility, given the combination of her age and weight, she hurried with Tess up the mansion's front staircase. "But you still haven't told me. Where have you been? What happened to you? Why didn't the *police* . . . ? Or the firemen . . . ? Why didn't they take you to a hospital?''

"It's all a . . .'' Tess rubbed her knotted brow and tried to sound convincing. "All a blur. The smoke alarms woke me. The flames. I remember being trapped. I remember jumping out my bedroom window.''

"Jumping?'' Mrs. Caudill looked aghast.

"But after that . . . ? I don't know. I seem to recall hitting my head. I guess I ran. Evidently I collapsed. The next thing, I woke up in your backyard.''

"How on earth did you—?''

"I have no idea, Mrs. Caudill. I must have been hysterical.''

"No wonder. In your place, I'd have fainted. It must have been horrifying. You've been through a . . . Tess, your mother . . . I hate to . . . Do you realize what happened to your mother?''

Tess halted on the upper landing as grief cramped her throat and sorrow squeezed her chest. Tears blurred her vision and scalded her cheeks. "Yes.'' Her voice cracked. "God help me, *that* part *isn't* a blur.''

"I'm sorry, Tess. I can't express how much I . . . Your mother was a fine, noble woman. The strength she mustered when she learned that your father had been killed. She was remarkable. And now I can't believe that someone shot her. It's all been so shocking. What's this world coming to? I truly can't imagine. I tossed and turned most of the night. You must be devastated."

"Yes, Mrs. Caudill. I feel so . . . 'Devastated' doesn't begin to describe it. Really, thank you. I appreciate your sympathy." Tess pawed at her tears, feeling grit on her cheeks. The tears streaked the soot on her hands.

"No need to thank me. In fact, I'm flattered that you thought to come here. Regina's been away so long. It's been too many years since I've had a chance to mother anybody."

The sound of footsteps made Tess spin.

With a stiff-backed stride, the butler came up the stairs, hands cradling a plastic container with a red cross on its white lid.

"Good. The first-aid kit. Finally," Mrs. Caudill said. "Come on, Tess. Your burns need attention. We're wasting time." The portly woman guided her hurriedly toward a door halfway along the upper hallway. "You remember that this bathroom belonged to Regina?"

"How could I forget? I used it often enough."

Mrs. Caudill smiled. "Yes, the old days." In contrast with her smile, she sounded melancholy. "The good days." She opened the door.

Tess faced a huge, white bathroom with spotless countertops and tiles. The same as she remembered. Reassuringly familiar. In back, a door on the right led to Regina's bedroom. Also in back, on the left, a steam room stood next to a shower stall.

But what Tess noticed most, anticipating, barely able to restrain her eagerness, was the deep, wide tub.

Mrs. Caudill took the first-aid kit from the butler, set it on the marble counter between two sinks, and retreated toward the hallway. "Soak, Tess."

"Don't worry, Mrs. Caudill. I intend to."

"And take as long as you want. In the meantime, I'll sort through some clothes that Regina left behind. As I recall, you and she were almost the same size."

Tess nodded, nostalgic. "Yes, we used to borrow from each other. But Mrs. Caudill, please, nothing fancy. Jeans, if possible. A shirt or a pullover. I'd like to stay casual."

"Still a tomboy?" Mrs. Caudill's eyes twinkled.

"I guess. In a way. Dresses make me uncomfortable."

"As long as I've known you, they always did. Well, I'll do what I can. Now get in that tub and *soak*. And while I think of it. I'd better phone the police. They'll want to—"

"No, Mrs. Caudill!" Surprised by her outburst, Tess felt as if snakes writhed in her stomach.

"I beg your pardon?" Mrs. Caudill's brow furrowed. "I don't understand. What's the matter? The police must be told. They need to talk with you. You might know something that will help them find the monsters who set fire to your mother's house and killed—"

"No! Not yet!" Tess tried to restrain her panic.

"I *still* don't understand." Mrs. Caudill deepened the wrinkles on her forehead. "You're confusing me."

"I'm not ready. I feel so . . . If you call the police, they'll hurry to get here. But I don't think I'm strong enough to answer their questions right away. I need to clear my head. I need to . . . My mother. I doubt I can talk about what happened just yet. I'd probably . . ." Tears trickled down her cheeks. "I wouldn't be able to control myself."

Mrs. Caudill debated, allowing her brow to slacken. "Of course. How foolish of me. I wasn't thinking. You're still in shock. But you realize you'll have to talk to the police eventually. It'll be a strain, but it has to be done."

"I know, Mrs. Caudill. Later, after I get cleaned up and feel rested, I'll call them myself. Soon. I promise."

"By all means. First things first. And the *first* thing is, get into that tub while I try to find you some clothes." Despite her reassurance, Mrs. Caudill continued to look confused as she backed toward the hallway and shut the bathroom door.

Or maybe her expression was one of pity. Tess couldn't tell as she found herself alone in the bathroom.

Reflexively, she locked the door. Her emotions in turmoil, she quickly undressed and threw her torn, dirty, smoke-reeking clothes into a corner. Even her socks and underwear stank of smoke. At once she opened the hot-water faucet on the tub, shut the drain, and poured in fragrant bath salts. As soon as steam began to rise, she adjusted the cold-water faucet, used a finger to judge the temperature of the water, and climbed into its wonderfully soothing warmth.

Briefly the blisters on her arms and hands stung. Then the pain went away, and she settled back, enjoying the heat rising deliciously past her hips, her groin, her stomach, her breasts. Only when the water came close to the overflow drain did she reluctantly grope forward to shut off the taps. Her cramped muscles gradually relaxed.

But she didn't feel contented. As she stared at the soot that clung to the soap bubbles bobbing on the water, she asked herself, frowning, why was I so insistent? Why didn't I want Mrs. Caudill to phone the police?

Dear God, my mother was killed. Two servants were killed. I was almost killed. For sure, whoever set fire to the house won't give up. They'll keep hunting me. Whatever their reason, it's serious enough that they're prepared to go to any lengths to get at me.

Why? Is it something to do with the photographs that man tried to steal from me?

What did I see in Joseph's apartment that they don't want me to know about and presumably anyone else to know about?

Tess shuddered at the memory of the bas-relief statue on Joseph's bookcase. Grotesque. Repulsive.

What did that statue mean? What kind of sick mind could possibly have designed it? And why was Joseph attracted to it? What did it say about his mind? Clearly he hadn't been the good-natured, gentle man that he seemed, not if he had a habit of whipping himself until he bled and then going to sleep with that thing brooding down at him from the bookcase. And now, Tess reminded herself, Joseph's apartment had been burned, the sculpture had been stolen, and the only evidence of its existence was the photograph in her bulging purse.

She trembled so forcefully that the soot-filmed bubbles on the water rippled. The first thing I should have done when I got inside this house was call the police. I need help!

So why don't I want Mrs. Caudill to phone them?

The answer came with startling urgency. Because I don't want *anyone to know where I am.* Whoever's hunting me will make the assumption that I'll get in touch with the police.

So they're probably monitoring police communications. If I phone the police, word will get out. The killers will scramble to get here *before* the police. And this time . . .

Tess shuddered.

They're so determined I don't think they'd fail. They'd kill *all* of us.

The butler.

Mrs. Caudill.

Me.

Tess imagined Mrs. Caudill screaming as blood spurted from bullet holes in her body.

No! I can't have their deaths on my conscience! And I can't depend on the police to protect me. I need time to think. I *have* to keep hiding. Until I'm absolutely sure I'm safe! What am I going to do?

4

With greater anxiety, Craig paced his one-room apartment. In the background, he barely heard the swelling voices of an opera, Puccini's *Turandot,* that by habit he played when he was nervous.

Phone, Tess! Please! If you're all right, for the love of God, *phone!*

But the longer he waited, the more despondent he became. Something was very wrong.

He frowned at his watch and realized that he should have been at the office an hour ago. Immediately, in midstride he froze, struck by a sudden thought. The office? Maybe Tess figures that's where I am. Maybe that's where she'll try to get in touch with me.

If she tries to get in touch with me.

If she wasn't killed in the fire and her body hasn't been found yet.

No, don't think like that! She's all right! She's *got* to be all right!

Craig grabbed the phone and pressed the numbers for his office. Impatient, he heard a buzz.

Another buzz.

"Missing Persons," a raspy voice said.

"Tony, it's Bill. I—"

"Finally. Where the hell have you been? We've got problems here. Luigi called in sick. The phones keep ringing. We've got eight new cases, and the captain's grumbling about everybody goofing off."

"I promise, Tony, I'll be there soon. Listen, have I had any messages?"

"Plenty."

Craig's heartbeat sped. "Is there anything from Tess Drake?"

"Just a minute. I'll check. But . . . Who's that woman shrieking in the background? Opera? Since when did you become Italian?"

"The messages, Tony. Check the *messages*."

"Yeah, okay, here, I've got them. Give me a chance to . . . Bailey. Hopkins. Nope. Nothing from any Tess Drake."

Craig slumped against the kitchen counter.

"Speaking of messages, the captain got a call a while ago from the police in Alexandria, Virginia. They claim you phoned them. Something about a fire. They say you sounded a little strange. What's going on?"

"I'll explain when I get to the office. Tony, this is important. If Tess Drake calls for me, make sure you get a number where I can reach her."

Craig hung up the phone. While Pavarotti's rich voice soared toward the peak of an aria, Craig stared at the kitchen counter. With a curse, he roused himself into motion, turned on the answering machine, and shut off the stereo. Compelled, he snapped his holstered revolver to his belt, put on his suit coat, and hurried from his apartment, locking its two dead bolts behind him.

As Craig rushed up the ten steps from his basement apartment and emerged on the noisy street, the morning smog irritated his throat and made him cough again. Near a row of garbage cans, he stopped at the curb, didn't see a taxi, hunched his shoulders in frustration, and broke into an awkward jog toward Seventh Avenue. The sudden effort made him breathe heavily.

Tess is right, he thought. I let myself get out of shape. I need to start exercising.

Tess. The urgent thought of her triggered a flood of adrenaline through his body. Sweating, he jogged faster, desperate to find a taxi.

5

Behind him, near Craig's apartment on Bleecker Street, two nondescript men bent down from the curb to examine the engine of a disabled car. When they noticed Craig start to jog toward Seventh Avenue, they slammed down the engine's hood, scrambled into the small Japanese vehicle, made a tight U-turn, and hurried to follow him.

Farther down the street, inside a van whose sides were marked with perfect copies of telephone-company insignia, a somber man picked up a cellular phone while his equally somber partner adjusted dials on a monitor and continued to listen to earphones.

The first man, aware that cellular broadcasts were capable of being monitored, spoke indirectly.

"Our friend has left the ballpark. A few teammates are going with him. . . . The *opposite* team? It seems they're not ready to play. At least, we haven't seen them. But our catcher is worried about his girlfriend's health. He hoped she'd phone him at the clubhouse. She didn't. He believes she might call him at his office. Meanwhile we've got some time, provided the opposite team doesn't arrive. So we'll do our catcher a favor and hang around the club-house, just in case his girlfriend finally does call and wants to leave a message. I take for granted that someone will be at his office? . . . Good. After all, if his girlfriend needs help, I'd hate for our catcher to be alone.''

6

Appallingly, the water in the tub was so filmed with soot that Tess had to drain it, rinse the tub, and refill it. Even after her second bath, she still didn't feel clean and finally had to use the shower, washing her tangled hair three times.

She couldn't find a blow dryer, so she simply combed her hair, which thank God was short and easy to manage, and which now was finally blond again, not blackened with ashes.

She used the first-aid kit to put antibiotic cream on her burns. They didn't seem deep, although clear liquid seeped from them and they'd begun stinging again. She was tempted to bandage them, but she'd read somewhere that it was important for air to get at burns as long as they weren't serious, and she hoped these weren't. At the moment, though, her burns and bruises were the least of her problems.

Mrs. Caudill had knocked on the bathroom door and explained that she'd laid out some clothes in the adjoining bedroom. Tess wrapped a towel around her breasts and hips, then stepped through the door to the right, finding socks, underwear, jeans, and a short-sleeved, burgundy blouse on the bed. She hurried to dress, discarding the bra. It felt good to have clean clothes against clean skin. They fit her almost perfectly. But the tennis shoes that Mrs. Caudill had found were another matter—a half-size too small. Tess had to use the grimy sneakers she'd hoped to discard. Grabbing her burlap purse, which was grimy as well, gave off smoke fumes, and would have to be replaced, she decided she'd better get downstairs before Mrs. Caudill changed her mind about calling the police.

In the foyer, she heard noises from the dining room and entered to find a maid placing a silver tray of toast, jam, bacon, scrambled eggs, and orange juice at the end of the long, oak table. Steam rose from a coffeepot.

Mrs. Caudill had changed from her housecoat to a dress and sat near the end of the table, the *Washington Post* before her. Seeing Tess come in, she smiled, although her eyes were dim with melancholy. "Well, you certainly do look better." With effort, Mrs. Caudill straightened. "I hope you don't mind. I don't know your tastes, but I took the liberty of having Rose-Marie prepare you a breakfast. You must be famished."

The aroma of the food made Tess's stomach growl. She hadn't realized until now how weak she felt from hunger. In place of supper last night, all she'd had to eat was the liver pâté her mother liked.

Her mother. With renewed force, grief swept through her, chilling, numbing. She resisted the tears that came to her eyes, knowing that, given the stress ahead of her, she didn't dare lose control. It seemed impossible . . . She still wasn't able to adjust to . . . had trouble believing . . . refused to admit that her mother was dead.

It couldn't be!

Needing all her discipline, Tess somehow managed to return Mrs. Caudill's smile. "Thank you. You've been too kind."

"Spare me the compliments, Tess. You can thank me by eating everything on your plate. Today will be, excuse my French, an s.o.b. You're going to need all your strength."

"I'm afraid you're right." Tess sat at the table, unfolded her napkin, and with a trembling hand picked up a gleaming silver fork. She amazed herself by how quickly she devoured the meal, even though this was far from her usual breakfast. She'd long ago restricted eggs (too much cholesterol) and bacon (carcinogenic nitrates) from her diet.

As she finished the last of her orange juice, gaining energy from the enormous amount that she'd eaten, Tess impulsively thought to ask, "Where's your husband? At the Justice Department? Up at your summer place in Maine?"

"My husband?" Mrs. Caudill's face turned pale. "You mean you don't know?"

"Know?" Tess set down her glass. "Know what? I'm not sure . . ."

"My husband died three years ago."

"Oh." Tess's voice dropped. Shock rippled through her. She felt paralyzed, uncertain what to do or say next.

Then she *was* certain, and she reached to touch Mrs. Caudill's hand, gently squeezing it. "I'm truly, painfully sorry. I liked him. Very much. He always made me feel welcome."

Mrs. Caudill bit her lip. "Yes." She restrained a sniffle. "He was a decent, loving man."

"If you don't mind . . ."

"What?"

"Talking about it."

"Mind?" Mrs. Caudill shook her head. "Not at all. In fact, in an odd way, it helps me. Go right ahead. I'm a tough old lady."

"What *happened?*"

"A heart attack." Mrs. Caudill sighed. "As much as I did my best, I could never convince him to cut back on his work load. I kept telling him to take more vacations or at least stay away from the office on weekends." Her lips trembled. "Well, I guess he died where he wanted to be. Not at home but at the office."

Death, Tess thought. I'm surrounded by death.

"So I know how you feel, Tess. Lord, I wish I didn't, but I do. My husband. Your mother. We'll miss them. Our lives are less without them." Mrs. Caudill braced her shoulders as if she didn't want to pursue the topic. She nodded glumly toward the *Washington Post* in front of her. "The fire at your house . . . the killings . . . apparently they happened too late last night to be reported in this morning's paper. But perhaps we should turn on the radio. There might be some new information, some further developments you should know about."

With a cringe, Tess recalled the nightmare, the flames, her mother being shot. The thought of hearing it described on the radio appalled her. Nonetheless she was desperate to know if the police had managed to catch the men who'd shot her mother. "Yes. That's a good idea."

"And then of course, now that you're rested, you'll have to phone the police."

"Exactly," Tess lied. "I was just about to do that."

But her attention was directed toward the newspaper in front of Mrs. Caudill. The headline faced away from her. Even so, she managed to decipher what it said and turned cold, stiffening. She gasped, leaned forward to grab the newspaper, and twisted it so the headline glared up at her.

Brian Hamilton Dies in Freeway Accident

"Oh, my God." Bile from her breakfast burned into Tess's throat. *"Brian Hamilton's dead?"* She frantically read the article.

"A van forced his car off the road." Mrs. Caudill sounded depressed. "Either a maniac or a drunken driver."

Tess kept scanning the article. *"Then Brian's car hit an electrical pole? His car exploded?"*

"If he wasn't killed in the crash, the flames would have . . . To think he survived all those years in combat in Vietnam, only to die in a pointless car accident."

"But I just saw him last night!" Tess jerked upright from her chair. "I spoke to him at my mother's house!"

"Yes, I forgot. He and your mother were friends. Because of your father."

"It's not just that. I asked him to do me a favor. I . . ."

"A favor?" Mrs. Caudill asked.

A welter of frightening thoughts collided in Tess's mind. The fire at the mansion. The accident on the freeway. She couldn't believe that the two were coincidental. Whoever had killed her mother had also killed Brian Hamilton! They'd somehow found out that Tess had summoned him! They feared the information that Tess had given him!

They're killing everybody who knows what *I* know! They're killing everyone I come in contact with!

No! Mrs. Caudill! If I don't get out of here, *she'll* be next!

"I have to use your phone." Tess tried desperately not to sound terrified.

"To call the police?"

"Right," Tess said. "The police. It's time. I need to talk to them."

"There's a phone in the hallway. Another one in the kitchen."

Hallway? Kitchen? Which would be more private? A *maid* was in the kitchen.

"The hallway," Tess blurted, and hurried from the dining room.

Her fierce thoughts multiplied. She'd *hated* Brian Hamilton because he'd sent her father to Beirut where he'd been murdered.

But last night she'd made a bargain with the man she hated, and now the man she hated was dead. Because he'd set out to cancel the debt he owed by trying to use all his power to learn everything he could about Joseph Martin.

Death. Everyone I speak to . . .

Not me, though! *I'm* still alive.

And I'll get even!

She reached the phone in the hallway, groped into her purse, fumbled past the handgun, and yanked out the card that Craig had given her.

Craig! *He* was the only person who'd understand. The two of them had been through this nightmare together almost from the start.

But Craig knew what *she* knew. Maybe *he* was in danger. She had to warn him.

Glancing urgently toward his card, she pressed numbers on the phone.

"This is Bill Craig. I'm not home right now, but if you'll leave your name and . . ."

Damn! She'd forgotten the time. He'd be in the office now. She jabbed the disconnect lever and pressed more buttons, this time for . . .

"Missing Persons," a raspy voice said.

"Lieutenant Craig." Tess struggled not to hyperventilate.

"He's out of the office. But if I can be of help. I'm sure—"

Tess slammed down the phone.

No! I need Craig! The only man I can trust is Craig!

"Tess?"

Spinning, Tess faced Mrs. Caudill, who'd nervously emerged from the dining room.

"Did you talk to the—?"

"Police? You bet! They want me downtown right now. I hate to impose, Mrs. Caudill, but if you've got a car I can . . ."

"My home and my cars are yours. Use my *husband's* car. I've kept it licensed and maintained. On the slim chance that I'd ever be brave enough to resist my memories and drive it."

"What kind of car did he . . . ?"

"A Porsche nine-eleven. It's got plenty of . . . what do the kids say? . . . guts."

"Just like your husband, Mrs. Caudill."

"Believe it, Tess. Take the car. Use it. My husband would have liked that. Plenty of guts. Because I've got a feeling that your problems are worse than I imagine. And terrible problems need . . ."

"Guts?" Tess raised her arms. "Your intuition's on target, Mrs. Caudill. I do have problems. Beyond belief. I don't have much time. Not to be rude, but quickly, the keys. Where are the keys?"

7

Maintaining his composure but braced for a confrontation, Vice President Alan Gerrard stepped past the metal detector and the Secret Service guards in the White House corridor, their features remaining stolid as he entered the Oval Office. Since Gerrard had been chosen—to the nation's astonishment—as the President's running mate in the election three years ago, Gerrard had been invited to the Oval Office only eight times. His few visits accounted for his renewed surprise that the office was so much smaller than it looked on television.

Outsiders might have been puzzled by the Vice President's lack of access to the President. But Gerrard understood too well. After all, he'd been chosen as a running mate not because of any skills but merely because of three coincidental, pragmatic, political reasons.

One, he'd been a senator from Florida, and that southern connection balanced the President's *northern* connection as a former senator from Illinois.

Two, Gerrard was forty—fifteen years younger than the President—and Gerrard's handsome, movie-star features made him appealing (so the President's demographic advisers claimed) to young voters, especially women.

Three, and probably most important, Gerrard had a reputation for being compliant, not causing trouble, following the Republican Party line, and hence he wouldn't be a rival to the President, who already anticipated the *next* election and didn't want anyone upstaging his take-charge personality.

But no matter how much the campaigning President's logic had made sense in theory, its practical effects had almost been disastrous. The public, the media, and political analysts had not merely been surprised by the President's choice; they'd been appalled.

"Gerrard knows more about tennis than he does about politics. He's more at home at a country club than he is in the Senate. He's got so much money he thinks everyone drives a Mercedes. He's never made a decision about anything without asking advice from all of his contacts, including his gardener. God gave him great looks, then went for a walk, and forgot to add brains."

And on, and on.

Republican leaders had begged the future president to reconsider his choice for a running mate. Fearful, Gerrard had heard strong rumors that the President had almost relented but had finally concluded that to change his mind would make him look indecisive, a poor way to start an election campaign. So the President had kept Gerrard on the ticket but had distanced himself as much as diplomatically possible from his running mate, sending Gerrard to make speeches in the least important, least populated districts, exiling Gerrard to the boonies, in effect making him disappear from the voters' minds.

Due to several factors—the weak Democratic opposition and the President's strong connection with the previous revered administration—Gerrard's side had won the election, and the President had immediately distanced himself even more from Gerrard, using him as the token White House representative at the blandest of social functions, then sending him on innocuous goodwill missions around the globe. Lately, columnists had taken to calling Gerrard "the invisible man."

At least until four days ago.

Oh, yes, indeed.

Four days ago.

That was when Gerrard had become *very* visible and exercised his limited authority, shocking every political theorist in the country.

As Gerrard shut the door behind him, he noticed that the Oval Office was empty except for the President, Clifford Garth, who sat behind his wide, polished desk in his high-backed, bulletproof chair in front of a bulletproof window that overlooked the White House lawn.

The President was fifty-five, taller than he looked on television, trim from the two miles he swam every day in the pool in the White House basement. He was narrow faced, which sometimes gave his mouth an unfortunate pinched expression. He had authoritative dark eyebrows that contrasted effectively with a distinguished touch of gray in his neatly cut, short hair. His skin was normally tanned, from daily exposure to a sunlamp, but today the President's cheeks were vividly scarlet. His eyes—which as a rule displayed a calm, controlled, reassuring thoughtfulness—bulged and blazed with fierce emotion.

"Yes, Mr. President? You wanted to see me?" Gerrard asked.

"See you? Damned right I want to see you." The President stood with force. "I waited as long as . . . I'd have told you to get here four days ago, but I needed *that* much time to control myself! Never mind the political liability. I didn't want to get arrested."

Gerrard shook his head. "I don't understand. Arrested, sir?"

"For murder." Garth raised a rigid arm and gestured in a frenzy toward the ceiling, moving his index finger from left to right. "Imagine the headline. Imagine my satisfaction. 'President loses his mind, attacks Vice President, throws the bastard across the desk in the Oval Office, and strangles the son of a bitch, making his tongue stick out.' You dumb . . . ! What the hell did you think you were doing? Just for fun, did you decide to pretend you had power? You stupid . . . !''

"Yes, I understand. I assume you're referring to the vote on the Senate's clean-air bill," Gerrard said.

"My God, I'm stunned! I didn't know you had it in you. You've suddenly become a genius. You read my mind, Gerrard. You're *right* that's what I'm referring to. The Senate's clean-air bill!''

"Mr. President, if we can discuss this calmly . . .''

"*Calmly?* This is as calm as I get when I'm . . . In case you've had a memory lapse, I'll remind you! *I'm* the president. Not you! Now I haven't found out—yet!—how the opposition managed to sway enough of our senators to vote against us, but I guarantee— you can bet your future and your *children's* future—I will! But what gives me a shrieking headache . . .'' The President shuddered. "What I *haven't* found out . . . and what keeps me awake all night . . . and what makes me want to drive a pen through your heart . . . is why *you* turned against me! I almost dumped you three years ago. You ought to be grateful. I gave you a cushy job. No responsibilities! Just coast and go to banquets, try not to get too drunk, and when your Barbie-doll wife's not around, you've got the chance to screw any Republican groupie who's got big enough tits and knows how to keep her mouth shut. So why didn't *you* know enough to keep *your* mouth shut? For God's sake, Gerrard, the vote on the clean-air bill was tied! Since you've gone simple on me, I'll remind you. The vice president's job is to break the tie, which means he votes for administration policy. But you voted against me! You broke the tie in the opposition's favor!''

"If you'll just listen for a moment, Mr. President."

"*Listen?*'' Garth shuddered to the point of apoplexy. "*Listen? I* don't listen. *You* do. *You're* the assistant. *I'm* the boss. And what *I* say goes. Except that *you* don't seem to get the message!''

"The clean-air bill's a good one," Gerrard said calmly. "The atmosphere's polluted. It's poisoning our lungs. The latest report gives us forty years before the planet's doomed.''

"Hey, I'll be dead by then! What do *I* care? You want to talk about doomed? *You're* doomed. Come election time, you're out, pal! I need a VP who's smart enough to cooperate, which God help me I thought you were. But all of a sudden . . . and I don't understand this . . . you've got a mind of your own.''

"I voted according to my conscience,'' Gerrard said.

"Conscience? Give me a break.''

"In my opinion, the bill ought to go further. This year, *every day,* in New York harbor alone, we've had an oil spill. Not to mention along every coast. Alaska. Oregon. California. New Jersey. Texas. My home state of Florida. Never mind the oil spills. Never mind the raw sewage in the rivers and harbors. Never mind the herbicides and pesticides in the drinking water or the leaks from nuclear plants. Let's just concentrate on the air. It's terrible. Government has to take control.''

"Gerrard, pay attention to realities. Our administration has to protect the industries that employ our voters, keep our economy stable, and pay taxes—admittedly not as much as they could, but let's not forget those industries contribute to our dwindling balance of trade with foreign nations. The bottom line is, Gerrard—''

"Let me guess. When the crisis gets bad enough, we'll somehow deal with it.''

The President raised his jaw. "Well, what a surprise. You finally got the idea.''

"The problem is . . . ,'' Gerrard said. "What you don't seem to grasp . . .''

"Hey, I grasp everything.''

"The crisis is *now.* If we wait any longer, we can't—''

"You've forgotten American know-how. You've forgotten World War Two. American enterprise has shown, *repeatedly,* that it can solve every problem.''

"Yes, but . . .''

"What?''

"That was then. This is now. And we're not as enterprising as the Japanese.''

"Good Lord, I hope you haven't told that to the press.''

"And reunited Germany will be even *more* enterprising," Gerrard said. "But I don't believe that *they'll* save the planet any more than *we* will. Greed, Mr. President. Greed's always the answer. It always wins out. Until we all tremble and wheeze to death."

"You sound like a damned radical from Berkeley in the sixties."

"Okay," Gerrard said, "I admit that stringent controls on air pollution will affect virtually every American industry. The costs to contain the pollution—sulfur dioxide, chlorofluorocarbons, cancer-causing industrial emissions, carbon dioxide from automobile exhaust—I could go on, but I don't want to bore you—the expenses will be enormous."

"Finally. Gerrard, I'm really surprised. You've grasped the point. Sulfur dioxide, which causes acid rain, comes from coal-burning power plants. So if we outlaw coal in those plants, we put hundreds of thousands of miners out of work. Chlorofluorocarbons, which deplete the ozone layer, are a by-product of the cooling systems in refrigerators and air conditioners. But there's no alternative technology. So what do we do? Put those industries out of work? Do you honestly believe that any American would agree to do without an air conditioner? Automobile emissions contribute to global warming. Right. But if we force the car companies to reduce those emissions, it'll cost them billions to improve their engines. They'll have to charge more for the cars. People won't be able to afford them, and Detroit'll go out of business. Don't get me wrong, Gerrard. I worry about the lousy air. Believe me. After all, I have to breathe the damned stuff. So does my wife. My children. My *grand*children. But you want to know what also worries me, *really* worries me? The faltering economy . . . the negative balance of trade . . . the growing national debt . . . the Mideast crisis . . . *they* give me panic attacks! So I don't care about forty years from now. I have to concentrate on controlling this month! This year! And you're not with the program, Gerrard. So let me inform you of what's going to happen. If the House agrees with the Senate and the clean-air bill shows up on my desk, I'm going to veto it."

"Veto?"

"Good for you. You're paying attention. Now do your best to stay alert. When the Senate reconsiders the bill, *this* time you'll

235

urge them to vote against it. Open your ears and listen. *Against*. Is that clear enough?''

"*Very* clear.''

"Then don't screw up again!''

Gerrard seethed, although outwardly he tried to seem humble. "Of course, Mr. President. Your logic is clear. And indeed I understand your motives. After all, business is what this government considers most important.''

"You bet your ass. Business is what keeps this country going. Never forget it.''

"Believe me, Mr. President. I don't intend to.''

8

Three minutes later, after the President finished cursing Gerrard, his parents, his wife, his movie-star good looks, and even his tennis abilities, Gerrard was finally allowed to leave the Oval Office.

Again, the Secret Service guards kept a stolid expression, not simply because of professional detachment but as well because they sensed the political weather and realized that Gerrard now had even less importance than when he'd entered the President's office.

Or so Gerrard concluded as he pulled a handkerchief from his suit-coat pocket and wiped his apparently clammy brow, walking with equally apparent uncertain steps along the White House corridor.

Presidential aides turned away, attempting to conceal their embarrassment for him but clearly showing their relief that *they* weren't considered expendable.

Gerrard didn't care. He had no pride. What he *did* have was a mission, and it struck him as ironic that the President's last insult—about his tennis abilities—related directly to Gerrard's next appointment, a tennis match at an extremely private Washington club. He took an elevator down to the White House garage and was driven in his limousine—with two cars containing Secret Service agents, one before and one behind him—to a fashionable suburb. There, he entered a low, sprawling, glass-and-glinting-metal building that had won an architectural award three years ago. Even from the front, the *pock-pock-pock* of volleyed tennis balls was audible. Gerrard's driver and his Secret Service guards remained outside, as he instructed. They kept a discreet watch on the parking lot and the entrance to the building, although they didn't maintain a maximum level of vigilance. After all, who'd consider Gerrard a sufficiently important target to want to harm him?

In the tennis club's luxurious locker room, he changed from his suit to a fashionable athletic top and designer shorts. His four-hundred-dollar tennis shoes were Italian, their leather hand-stitched, a gift from a diplomat on one of Gerrard's so frequent goodwill missions. His custom-made racket, constructed from space-age materials and worth two thousand dollars, had been a present from his wife. He grabbed a monogrammed towel, checked a mirror to make sure his movie-star hair was perfectly in place, then strolled from the rear of the club and squinted in the smoggy sunlight, facing eight chain-link-fenced courts, seven of which were occupied. In the eighth, a lean, tanned, distinguished-looking man of forty, dressed in tennis clothes, was waiting for him.

Gerrard stepped through the court's open gate, closed it, and shook hands with the man. "How are you, Ken?"

"Troubled. And you, Alan?"

"The same. I just had what the columnists would call a chewing-out from the President." Gerrard massaged his right eye.

"Anything you couldn't handle?"

"As far as my ego goes, no big deal. But strategically . . . ? I'll tell you about it later. I mean, we're supposed to be here to play tennis, after all, and to tell the truth, I need to get rid of some stress." Again, Gerrard massaged his right eye.

"What's wrong with—?"

"Nothing important. The smog's so gritty it irritates my eyes. If the itch gets any worse, I'll have a doctor give me some ointment."

"But you're sure it won't interfere with your game? I've been looking forward to beating you today. The thing is, I'd prefer to do it on even terms," Ken said.

"No matter. On even terms or not, you'd still have trouble beating me."

"Okay, then, challenge accepted. Serve." With a smile, Ken walked to the opposite end of the court.

Ken's last name was Madden, and he was the deputy director of covert operations for the Central Intelligence Agency. He and Gerrard had gone to Yale together, had both belonged to its influential, secret society of Skull and Bones as well as Yale's tennis club, and had kept in touch over the years. Their friendship was long and well-established. No political commentators gave it much attention. Once a week, since the present administration had come into power, the two former fraternity members had made a habit of this game, at least when Gerrard was in town and not exiled by the President on yet another international goodwill mission. The critical factor was that playing tennis was exactly what the media and the public expected Gerrard to be doing, and in so exclusive a setting where reporters and minor diplomats were refused admission, the weekly match—like so much about Gerrard—had become invisible.

As a rule, Gerrard's and Madden's skills were equal, their matches won by a very close margin. If Madden was victorious one week, Gerrard would be victorious the next. But today, despite Gerrard's confident challenge, the irritation in his right eye did impair his ability. He lost the first set, managed with difficulty to win the second, but didn't have a chance in the third. That was all they had time for.

Gerrard bent over, breathing heavily, surprised by his exhaustion. The smog, he thought. The damned smog. "Sorry." He reached the net, shook hands with Madden, and toweled his sweaty face. "I apologize for the clumsy match. I'll try hard to be more challenging *next* week." As he had repeatedly, he rubbed his right, weeping eye.

"Yeah, since we started, that eye's gotten worse. It's red now. You'd better do something about it."

"Maybe if I rinsed it with water."

"Why not?" Madden shrugged. "Give it a try. At least the

club's got a reverse-osmosis purification system. Otherwise the chemicals in the water would make your eye even worse.''

They walked toward the side of the court while in the background other players continued their matches.

"So tell me," Madden said. They stood with their backs to the clubhouse, taking care to block their conversation in case they were being monitored by directional microphones. "Tell me about the President."

"He plans to veto the clean-air bill."

Madden shook his head. "Dear Lord. The stubborn fool."

"I guarantee I gave him my best arguments," Gerrard said. "But he just wouldn't budge. According to him, when the problem gets bad enough, American businesses will suddenly come up with a miracle cure."

"What a joke. I didn't realize the President had a sense of humor, even if it *is* unintentional," Madden said. "When the problem gets bad enough? Doesn't he realize that the problem's bad enough already?"

"To him, it's like the mounting budget deficit. Let the *next* generation take care of it. Right now, he says his primary obligation is to hold the country together." Gerrard toweled more sweat from his face.

Madden sighed. "Well, it's not as if we didn't expect him to react that way. But we had to do the right thing. We had to give him the chance."

Despondent, Gerrard draped his towel around his neck. "However, it gets worse."

"*Oh?*"

"The President feels betrayed. He's confused. In a panic. He can't comprehend how the opposition swayed so many Republican senators to switch party allegiance and vote for the bill. He's so furious about their defection that he claims he's doing his damnedest, using all his investigators, to find out what made them do it."

"We expected that as well. Political reflex," Madden said. "But I can't imagine many senators confessing they were blackmailed. Because, after all, the next obvious question would be *why* were they being blackmailed, and I don't believe a senator would be stupid enough to destroy his or her career by confessing bribes, kickbacks, cocaine addiction, adultery, and a few other, even more serious matters our people discovered. Insider stock trading. Hit-and-run manslaughter while intoxicated. One case of incest. No, those senators will keep their mouths shut. They're experienced. Better yet, God bless them . . . at the same time *damn* them . . . they're practical. It's a pity we couldn't find *more* senators with something to hide. But on balance, it kind of gives me faith in the system. Not everybody's got a deep, dark secret. Even so, if we *had* been able to scare just a few more senators, the vote would have been in our favor. And *you* wouldn't have had to compromise your position and break the tie by voting against the administration.''

Gerrard shrugged. ''No problem. I can tolerate the President's contempt. What *is* a problem is that after he vetoes the bill, and after he sends it back to the Senate, we'll have to put pressure on more senators to gain the two-thirds vote we need to override his veto.''

''Well . . .'' Madden glanced around, assessing the security of their position. ''We've got the power. We've got the influence. All the same, the vote'll be close. In the meantime, when you continue not to cooperate with the President's policy . . .''

''Yes, that worries me,'' Gerrard said. ''The President might restrict my activities even more. He might put me on ice until he can choose another vice president when the next election comes up. But it's vital that I keep going on those goodwill missions. I have to keep coordinating our efforts.''

Madden stared down at the concrete surface of the tennis court. ''Yes, it's vital.'' He straightened. ''Regrettably, he leaves us no choice. But the group knew—and they *agreed*—that we'd have to do it sooner or later.''

''And now,'' Gerrard said, ''it'll have to be sooner.''

''Without question. The President showed the nation . . . not to mention the *world* . . . how brave he was when he went to that antidrug conference in Colombia last year. Cynical journalists were taking bets on when and how the cocaine lords would have him assassinated. But the President survived . . . I consider it miraculous . . . and now he's overconfident. Next week, he's flying to Peru for yet *another* drug-control conference. I'm not clairvoyant, but I think that this one time I can definitely predict the future. The President won't be coming back. Alive, at least. A week from tomorrow, we'll have a new president. A more enlightened one.''

"I hope I'm worthy of the responsibility," Gerrard said.

"Well, as you're aware from your frequent goodwill trips, you'll have a great deal of help from our counterparts."

"Yes, by sending me on those trips, the President was his own worst enemy."

Madden stared again toward the concrete surface of the tennis court.

"Something else?"

"Unfortunately." Madden frowned.

"What's *wrong?*"

"We may have a security breach," Madden said.

Despite his tan, Gerrard paled. "What kind? How serious? Why didn't you tell me before? We might have to postpone—"

"I don't think that'll be necessary. Not yet, although if we have to, we will postpone next week's plan, of course. I didn't want to trouble you until now, because I thought the matter had been taken care of. However, it wasn't. You need to be informed in case you can use your authority to help us."

"What *kind* of security breach?" Gerrard insisted.

"I told you last week that our search team had finally found the defector."

"I remember," Gerrard said impatiently. "And I also remember that you assured me he'd been eliminated in the appropriate manner."

"He was."

"Then—?"

"The defector met a woman," Madden said. "The friendship was brief and recent, to all appearance casual. Our search team didn't consider it important until the woman showed unusual interest in the defector after his death. She went to the police and somehow managed to identify the charred body. With information she supplied, an NYPD Missing Persons detective was able to locate the defector's apartment and take the woman there. As soon as she left the apartment, she delivered photographs to a shop that specializes in quick development. Naturally the surveillance team wondered what was in the photos. They attempted but weren't able to obtain them. Curious, they decided to search the defector's apartment.''

"You mean they hadn't already?" Gerrard flinched.

"They admit the mistake. In their defense, the defector had assumed such deep cover that it didn't seem likely he'd risk keeping anything from his former life.''

"You're saying he *did?*"

"In his bedroom." Madden's jaw hardened. "The surveillance team found an altar.''

Gerrard gasped.

"They destroyed it," Madden said. "More important, they took the statue.''

"But that still leaves the woman and the photographs.''

"Correct. Last night, a team tried to solve that problem.''

"Tried?''

"They failed. In the meantime, she'd spoken with Brian Hamilton and—''

"Hamilton? What's *he* got to do with—? He died in a freeway accident last night!''

"His connection with the woman? I haven't told you the worst part. The woman's name. Theresa Drake.''

"Tess? Not—''

"Remington Drake's daughter. She went to Alexandria last evening to use her late father's influence with the government in an effort to learn about the defector. At her request, Brian Hamilton was on his way to the FBI director. But our team managed to stop him.''

"We killed Brian Hamilton?" Gerrard jerked his head back.

"And the team did its best to kill the woman as well. The fire at her mother's house. Perhaps you heard about it. Tess Drake escaped. We don't know where she is, but there's no doubt that she threatens us. We're using every resource to find and stop her. That's why I'm briefing you. Granted, you have plenty to be concerned about as it is, but you did know her father.''

"Yes. In fact, I knew him well.''

"Then it's possible she'll try to contact you and ask for help.''

"Ah," Gerrard said. "Now I understand.''

"It might not come to that. We have a plan that we think might lead us to the woman."

"How?"

"It involves the detective she went to for help. There isn't time to explain." Madden looked around, noticing a team of players waiting to take their turn on the court. "We've been here too long. We need to leave before we attract attention. Assuming an emergency doesn't prevent it, I'll see you here next week."

"God bless."

"And God bless you. By all means, let me know at once if the woman . . ."

Gerrard nodded somberly.

So did Madden. They left the court, assumed their public personalities, made a few pleasant comments to the waiting players, and entered the back of the clubhouse.

"Your eye looks worse," Madden said.

"Yes, I'd better do something about it." Gerrard stepped into the shower area, relieved to find that the room was empty. He approached a mirror, studied his bloodshot eye, and tenderly removed a contact lens, preparing to rinse the eye with water. To all appearances, his irises were a photogenic blue, but without the contact lens—which he needed not to correct his vision but because the lens's blue provided a disguise—the color of Gerrard's right iris now was gray.

9

"A woman phoned for me, but you didn't get her number?" Craig glared at Tony in the Missing Persons office at One Police Plaza. He was out of breath from having rushed into the building. "I told you . . . !"

"Hey, she hung up before I could ask. I couldn't even get her name. For all you know, she might not be Tess Drake."

" 'Might not' isn't good enough! I have to know!"

"Do me a favor, will you? Stop shouting. It gives me a head-ache. And why don't you just tell me what's going on?"

A gravelly voice interrupted, "Good idea. That's what *I'd* like to know."

They swung toward the open door to a private office where Captain Mallory, a bulky man in his forties, peered angrily over glasses pushed low on his nose. He had his jacket off, his shirtsleeves rolled up. "The last I heard, you worked in this department." He stalked toward Craig. "So I'd appreciate it, and I'm sure the chief, the mayor, and the taxpayers would appreciate it, if you showed up on time." Mallory's voice became more crusty. "In fact if you showed up at all. For a couple of days this week, I haven't had the faintest idea in hell *what* you've been doing or *where* you've been! What's this about the Alexandria police department? Their Homicide division called to find out if someone was impersonating a New York City detective. You! Last night, they had several murders down there. Rich. A high-society district. *What do you know about them?"*

Craig swallowed, stared, and slowly sank toward a chair. Despite his cough, he murmured, "I wish I hadn't given up smoking."

"It wouldn't matter. You can't smoke here anyhow. I'm wait-ing, Craig. *What's going on?"*

Craig hesitated. "On Tuesday . . ." He struggled to order his thoughts. "A woman came to see me . . ."

For the next ten minutes, Craig explained: about the morgue, Carl Schurz Park, Joseph Martin's apartment. He concluded with Tess's sudden trip to Alexandria and the news he'd heard on the radio.

Captain Mallory made a sour face. "Correct me if I'm wrong. The sign on the door says Missing Persons, right? As soon as the corpse was identified, it wasn't our responsibility anymore. The job belonged to Homicide. So why the hell were you still involved?"

"I did turn it over to Homicide," Craig said. "I kept them informed."

"You haven't answered my question! *Why were you still—"*

"Because of the woman." Craig felt his cheeks turn red. His voice dropped.

"What about her?" Mallory insisted.

"She got to me."

"What are you saying?"

"It's personal."

"Not anymore! As far as I'm concerned, this is official!"

"I didn't want to stop seeing her."

"You're telling me you fell in love with her?"

"I . . . Yeah, I guess that's what happened. That's right. Yeah, I fell in love with her.

"And all this happened since Tuesday? Jesus, she sure must be good-looking." Mallory raised his hands in exasperation. "Craig, when you were at the police academy, do you remember one of the rules your instructors kept pounding into your brain? Don't get involved with the customers! It always leads to a foul-up. It causes mistakes. It gets very messy!"

"Hey, you think I had a choice? It's not like I told myself, why don't I do something stupid and fall in love with this woman? It happened all of a sudden! I couldn't help what I was feeling!"

Mallory slumped against a desk and shook his head. "Brother, brother, brother. Okay. So we've got a problem. Fine." He straightened. "So we'll fix it. The first thing is, you phone Alexandria Homicide and tell them everything you know."

Craig stared. "No, I don't think so."

"What?"

"I'm not sure getting in touch with them is a good idea. Not yet, at least."

"I gave you an order!"

"Look, if she's alive . . . and Tony took a call a while ago that makes me think she is . . . she's on the run. She's being hunted. If we tell Alexandria Homicide and they start looking for her, whoever wants to kill her will monitor the police radios. The moment they find out where she is, they'll do their damnedest to get to her before the squad cars do."

"Stop thinking like her boyfriend, Craig, and act like a cop. She needs protection, for God's sake!"

"I *am* thinking like a cop. You know as well as I do! No

matter how hard the Alexandria police try, they can't guarantee her safety anymore than *we* could. If someone wants to kill you bad enough . . . and what happened last night proves how determined these people are . . . nothing can stop them.''

"But you think *you* can stop them,'' Mallory said.

"What I think I can do is bring her in quietly, safely.''

"John Wayne to the rescue.''

"Give me a break,'' Craig said. "Whatever's going on, it's not like anything I've ever come across. These people are vicious. They're organized. They're determined. And they love to play with fire. I don't know *why* they want to kill her . . . maybe something they're afraid she knows . . . but they've proven they'll take down as many people as they have to in order to get at her. The moment she comes out of hiding, if she asks the Alexandria police for help and word gets around, which it's bound to, she's dead. I think Tess has figured that much already. It explains why she decided to avoid the police.''

"You're theorizing.''

"No. Otherwise, Alexandria Homicide wouldn't have called you, wondering what *I* know that *they* don't know.''

"Okay.'' Mallory debated. "That makes sense. But you've still got to talk to them. This isn't just a matter of one department cooperating with another. You've got to explain what you think's going on. Otherwise you're concealing information about multiple felonies, and you know what happens to people who do that. You're not a bad guy, all things considered, but that doesn't mean I like you enough to visit you in prison. Pick up that phone.''

"No. Wait. Please. Just give me a few more minutes.''

"What are you hoping? That she'll call *you?*''

"Right. Then maybe I *will* have something to tell the Alexandria police. She trusts me. So maybe we can figure out a way to bring her in safely.''

The phone rang on Tony's desk. Before Craig could stand and get to it, Tony picked it up.

"Missing Persons . . . Just a minute.'' Tony extended the phone toward Craig.

"It's *her?*'' Craig asked.

"No. Alexandria Homicide.''

Craig froze.

At once another phone rang, and this time Captain Mallory picked it up. "Missing Persons. . . . Yeah, you bet. Right away."

Craig glanced from one phone to the other in bewilderment.

"Better take it," Mallory said. "It's a woman, and the way she says your name, it's like she's in trouble and she needs help from God."

Craig lunged for the phone.

10

"Tess, is that you?"

At the sound of Craig's voice, Tess felt her knees weaken. *Jesus. At last!*

After having nervously backed the sleek, black Porsche 911 from the spacious garage next to Mrs. Caudill's mansion, she'd felt naked with fear. Her right hand had trembled as she'd changed gears, driving from the secluded, expensive neighborhood.

She'd passed few cars, but that had only made those few cars more suspicious. There was too great a chance that the killers would have left a sentry in the area. Repeatedly she'd checked her rearview mirror. No one seemed to be following her. But when she left the exclusive neighborhood and increased speed onto a crowded four-lane thoroughfare next to which laundries, quick-food restaurants, and video stores blighted the area, she realized that in the dense traffic she wouldn't be able to tell if a car pursued her.

Worse, her own car—costly and ostentatious—was a liability. In her youth, she'd overheard her father's conversations on the telephone. *Just make sure,* he once had said. *Whatever car they use, it can't be fancy. It has to blend.*

Well, this car certainly didn't blend. Passing drivers in non-luxurious vehicles assessed the Porsche with envy.

Damn, she thought, and clutched the purse beside her—the pistol within it—for reassurance. When she saw the telephone booth at the edge of the crowded parking lot of a shopping mall, she braked to a stop beside the booth, hurried from the car, fumbled a credit card from her wallet, grabbed the receiver, and again phoned Craig's office.

"Yes," she breathed. "It's me. I tried to call you earlier."

"I thought that might have been you. Thank God, you're alive. I was so afraid . . ."

"They burned . . . They killed my *mother*."

"I know, Tess. I'm sorry. You must be . . . When I see you, I'll try to . . . I can't make the pain go away, but I'll do my best to share it. What's important now is that *you* weren't killed as well."

"Not *yet!* But they'll keep hunting me! I'm terrified that I'm being followed. What am I going to do? Whoever's after me will watch the local police station. I can't go there, and if I phone the police, I'm afraid the killers will tune in to police broadcasts. I need help!"

"Listen. Don't panic, Tess. I promise. I'll make sure you're protected. Where *are* you? I hear traffic in the background."

"I don't . . . I . . . On the outskirts of Alexandria. I'm in a phone booth near a shopping mall."

"Christ, you can't stay there." Craig coughed. "Is there any place you can hide until I get to Alexandria?"

She trembled and tried to think.

"Tess?"

"I can't involve my former friends. *They* might get killed. I thought of a movie theater, but with so many people around, in the dark, I wouldn't feel safe. Maybe the library. Maybe a museum. But they're so public I wouldn't feel safe there either."

"Just a minute. I have to put you on hold. Don't hang up. I'll be right back."

"No, wait!"

"Tess, it's important. Stay right there."

She heard a click. Then the line was silent, except for the long-distance static.

Her hands shook.

Hurry! Please!

Furtive, she stared around at the crowded parking lot, at ominous strangers getting out of cars.

Two men stood next to a van and squinted in her direction.

Tess shoved her hand in her purse, grasping the pistol.

The two men rounded the van, about to flank her, but unexpectedly changed direction and walked toward the shopping mall.

Tess exhaled, realizing that they'd simply been admiring the Porsche.

Craig, hurry!

At once his voice was back on the line. *"Tess?"*

"What have you been doing?" Her voice quavered.

"Look, I'm sorry. I didn't think that would take so long. I needed some information. I'll be on a Trump shuttle that's supposed to land at Washington National Airport at two oh seven. How did you get to that shopping mall? Have you got a car?"

"Yes."

"What kind? I need to recognize it."

"A Porsche nine-eleven. Black."

"I have to give you credit. Even if you're scared, you travel in class."

"Craig, spare me the humor."

"I'm only trying to keep up your spirits. Okay, if it's business you want, pay attention. There's a Marriott hotel in Crystal City near the airport. As soon as I arrive, I'll grab a taxi and watch for your car at the hotel's entrance. At the latest, I ought to be there by two-thirty."

"But that'll be three hours from now!"

"I've already figured that. Drive to Washington. Take a tour of the Capitol Building. With so many guards there, no one would dare try to get at you. Just be careful when you leave and return to your car."

"Be careful? Since last night, being careful is *all* I've been trying to do."

"Well, try even *harder*. And in the meantime, I'll contact the Alexandria police. I'll tell them what's going on."

"No! If this gets on their radio . . . !"

"Tess, you've got to trust me. I'll talk to their chief. I'll make sure he keeps a lid on this. I won't tell him where you are or where we're going to meet. All I want is to organize a team to take you to a place that's secure."

"There *isn't* such a place!"

"Believe me, there is. A house. A hotel room. A farm. Whatever, wherever, I guarantee you'll be smothered with guards. Just keep control! Please. A few more hours, and this'll be *over*."

"No! You're wrong!"

"I don't . . ."

"They'll *always* be waiting. They'll *never* give up. This won't ever end!"

"It will if we can find out why they want to kill you. Once their secret's out—whatever it is—they won't have a reason to stop you from talking."

"If we can find out what they're so afraid I know. If. If! *If!"*

"I'm telling you, keep control."

"But it doesn't stop just with me!" Tess said. "I'm not the only one in danger!"

"I don't understand. Nobody else is—"

"Wrong! Don't forget! Craig, you were *with* me. You heard me talk about Joseph. You went with me to Joseph's apartment. You saw what was in his *bedroom*. If the killers followed both of us, to protect their secret they might come after *you!"*

Craig didn't answer for a moment. "So let the sons of bitches try." He coughed again. "The Marriott near the airport. Two-thirty. Drive past it until you see me. I'll recognize your car."

"You make me feel . . ."

"This isn't the time to be evasive."

"Confident. I'll be as clever as my father. I'll be there."

11

She hung up the phone, studied the strangers in the parking lot, felt vulnerable, and hurried to get into the Porsche.

Drive to Washington, Craig had said. Take a tour of the Capitol Building. But the idea of being in so public a place, even in the presence of guards, made her nervous. There *had* to be a less dangerous alternative.

As she drove from the shopping mall, Tess checked her rear-view mirror to see if she was being followed. Several cars left behind her. With a deep breath, she again touched her purse, feeling the reassuring bulk of the pistol inside.

Abruptly the pistol made her recall the men she'd killed last night, and the memory sickened her. But anger and fear were stronger. She hadn't counted how many times she'd fired. In this morning's confusion, she'd failed to remove the pistol's magazine to see how many rounds were left. Her father would definitely not have approved. The gun might be empty, for all she knew.

I've got to be able to defend myself!

A quick glance toward the side of the road made her notice a cluster of stores. One store in particular caught her attention.

She steered sharply toward it, parked in front, and hurriedly entered the building, slowing when she closed the door, doing her best to look calm.

"Yes, ma'am?" the muscular, sporting-goods clerk asked. Behind the counter, he cast his eyes up and down, assessing her face and figure, smiling—almost leering—with approval. "How can I help you?"

"I need two boxes of ammunition for a SIG-Sauer nine-millimeter pistol."

"You must have plans for some heavy shooting." He made the remark sound suggestive.

"The instructor in my target-practice course insists that we buy our own ammunition."

"Well, I can promise, if you were in *my* class, I'd give you the ammunition and the lessons for free." The clerk raised his eyebrows.

"In that case, I guess it's too bad you're not in my class," Tess said.

The clerk was too absorbed by her braless breasts beneath her thin blouse to detect her muted irony.

While he turned his back to get the two boxes of ammunition, Tess reached in her purse to pull out her wallet, taking care that the clerk wouldn't see the handgun.

In the process, her fingers brushed the packet of photographs. As if she'd been jolted by an exposed electrical wire, she remembered that Craig had insisted last night that she have copies made and sent by Federal Express to his office. But everything was different now. She didn't have *time* to obey Craig's orders, and for damned sure, she wouldn't feel safe waiting for the copies to be developed. She had to keep moving!

"Would you mind? Have you got an envelope?" she asked the clerk. "Can I buy a stamp from you? I'd really appreciate it."

"For such a pretty lady, why not?"

"Thanks. I'll make a point of coming back."

"Believe me, you'd be welcome. There's a range past that door. We could do some, what you might call, *private* shooting."

Tess struggled to tolerate his banter, her mind in turmoil. "And I bet your aim's on target."

"Never had complaints."

Give me a break! Tess inwardly screamed. She managed not to cringe, paid for the ammunition, then took the envelope and the stamp. The negatives! she thought. I'll mail Craig the negatives. At least *they'll* be protected.

At once the thought of the photographs—and the vivid recollection of the grotesque sculpture in Joseph's bedroom—made Tess's stomach burn with the forceful realization of where she had to go next.

It certainly wasn't the Capitol Building.

12

Craig slammed down the phone.

Captain Mallory, startled by the furious determination on Craig's face, jerked up his arms. "Well, now I've heard everything. A lieutenant giving orders to a police chief."

"Hey, it worked, didn't it? The Alexandria department's co-operating."

"If you want to call it that. Even over here, I heard him shouting. When he gets his hands on you . . ."

"Tell me about it. What did you expect? I didn't have a choice. I couldn't . . . I didn't *dare* . . . give him specifics about my rendezvous with Tess. The killers are too well organized. If even *one* patrol car talks about the Marriott hotel on its radio and if their transmissions are being monitored, Tess'll be shot when she arrives."

"But apparently you got the Alexandria chief to prepare a safe house. I have to admit I'm impressed. There's just one problem, Craig."

"*Only* one? I see so many, I—"

"Yeah, a problem. I haven't given you permission to leave. *You* don't run this division. You're *way* beyond your authority."

"I told you, I'm going!"

"Even if I suspend you?"

"Do what you have to. Fire me for all I care!"

"You stubborn . . . !"

"I don't have time to argue. All I *do* have time for is to grab a taxi and get to LaGuardia before that plane takes off!"

"In noon-hour traffic? Lots of luck finding a cab."

"Then I'll take a patrol car!"

"No!"

"*What?*"

"Wrong! *You* won't take a patrol car."

"Don't get in my—"

"Tony will. He'll drive you to the airport."

Craig blinked in surprise. "Did you just say . . . ?"

"Get moving, Craig. Watch your ass. And if the Alexandria chief gives you trouble, tell him to phone me."

"I can't believe . . . I don't know how to . . ."

"Thank me? By getting back here alive. By doing some work for a change. Tony, if traffic's really lousy, use the siren."

13

As the patrol car squealed from One Police Plaza, two men watched intensely from a perfect duplicate of a telephone-company van parked down the street. Each had a ring in his pocket, a gleaming ruby overlaid with a golden insignia of an intersecting sword and cross.

In the van's front seat, the first man—a stern surveillance expert—compared the blurred, passing faces in the cruiser to a photograph in his hand. "I think it's him!"

"You *think?* We have to be *sure.*" In the back, the second man continued to monitor earphones.

"I *am* sure."

"But you said you *think,* and that's not good enough. I wish we'd been able to put a tap on the phones in the Missing Persons office. Wait. I'm getting something." The second man adjusted his earphones. "My, my. The police dispatcher's telling all patrol cars to run interference and make sure *that* cruiser . . . its numbers match . . . reaches LaGuardia in time for a one-o'clock Trump shuttle to Washington National Airport."

"Is that good enough for you?"

"Yeah," the technician said. "Definitely good enough. Make the call."

The man in the front seat picked up a cellular phone and pressed numbers. "The catcher has left the plate. We think he's so upset about his girlfriend's health that he needs to see her in the Washington ballpark." He gave the details of the flight.

On the phone, the chameleon's voice responded. "But what about the opposition?"

"So far no show. Maybe they don't want to play right now."

"Not possible. Not when we're in the finals. You can bet their team's in the area. Keep checking for talent scouts. *We'll* check the Washington ballpark. But don't forget. The opposite team has a habit of showing up when we least expect them."

14

Heart pounding, Tess scrambled into the Porsche outside the sporting-goods shop and peered urgently around, afraid that a car would suddenly park beside her, that men would lunge out, shooting. She yanked the handgun from her purse, maintaining sufficient presence of mind to keep the weapon low, out of sight from anyone outside the car. Frantic, she pressed the button that released the pistol's magazine and discovered that there were only two rounds left in the magazine, plus one in the firing chamber.

Jesus. Quickly she jerked the cardboard lid off one of the boxes of ammunition she'd bought and shoved fourteen more rounds into the magazine, filling it. In theory, the weapon held only sixteen rounds, but with the round that was already in the firing chamber ("one up the spout," her father had liked to call it), the handgun's capacity now was seventeen.

The moment Tess slid the magazine back into the pistol's

handle, snapping it into place, she felt as if a tight band around her chest had been relaxed. At least now she'd be able to defend herself. She hoped.

I have to get out of here.

She crammed the handgun into her purse, shoved the boxes of ammunition under the driver's seat, twisted the ignition key, stomped the accelerator, and urged the Porsche into a break in traffic on the busy thoroughfare.

The envelope! While in the sporting-goods store, Tess had printed an address on the envelope, licked the stamp that the clerk had sold her, and stuck the stamp onto the envelope. Now, as she drove, she fumbled with one hand to remove the packet of photographs from her purse, open the flap, and slide the negatives into the envelope.

Ahead, to the right. Tess felt her breathing quicken when she saw a post-office truck at a dropbox outside a minimall. She swerved off the road, braked quickly beside the truck, licked and sealed the envelope, then leaned out the Porsche's window, handing the envelope to the mailman as he carried a bulging bag from the dropbox toward the truck.

"Late delivery." Tess managed a smile. "I hope you don't mind."

"Makes no difference to me. Love your car."

"Thanks."

"How does it handle?"

"Watch." Tess rammed the gearshift into first, tromped the gas pedal, and squealed away.

But she wasn't showing off. If anyone was following her, she wanted to get away from the postman as fast as possible. She hoped desperately that no one had seen her hand over the envelope. Too many deaths already. Too much grief. She prayed that she hadn't put the *postman's* life in danger as well.

Back on the road, veering in and out of traffic, trying to make it difficult for anyone to keep up with her, Tess drove as quickly as she dared without the risk of being stopped by the police for violating the speed limit.

Her destination was Washington, as Craig had advised.

But not the Capitol Building. No way! Not anymore!

She had a better idea. Not a safer one. But it was definitely more important.

More critical.

The statue. That grotesque, repulsive statue. Her life was threatened because she knew about the damned thing. She had to find out what it meant, and there was only one person she could think of who might be able to tell her.

15

Slumped in the backseat of his limousine, en route from the tennis club to his office, the Vice President brooded about the woman whom the deputy director for CIA covert operations had warned him about.

Tess Drake?

Why did it have to be her who threatened him?

During his friendship with her late father, Alan Gerrard had frequently met Tess when she was a teenaged, gangly, sensuous tomboy. Her lean, athletic body, combined with her trim, perky breasts and short, blond, saucy hair, had appealed to him.

Not in a sexual way, of course. Not at all. Despite the President's assumption that Gerrard, like many politicians, took advantage of fund-raisers to have sex with politically important groupies, the truth was that Gerrard, through stern discipline, had trained himself to repress his sexual urges.

Gerrard was married. Yes. And his wife was beautiful, photogenic, often featured in the top magazines. But his wife upheld his pure, rigid values, and during their twenty-year marriage, in the thousands of nights that they'd shared the same bed—as companions, as helpmates, as *soul* mates—they'd engaged in sex a total of only three times, and during those three ritualistic occasions, they'd permitted themselves to experience the base pleasures of the flesh strictly for the purpose of producing children.

No, Gerrard's attraction to Tess had not at all been carnal. On the contrary, he'd merely admired her as a fine example of a blossoming, healthy, young woman, a perfect example of the human species, and now it deeply troubled him that she, of all people, given her biological perfection, had become a threat and would have to be killed. His distress did not prevent him, however, from dearly hoping that Tess would be silenced as immediately as could be arranged.

In the backseat, the phone buzzed. Gerrard straightened and hurriedly picked up the phone. Only a few people had this number, and no one called it unless the matter was important.

Perhaps the message related to Tess. Perhaps she'd already been found and silenced.

"One moment, sir," a woman's voice said. "The President is calling."

Gerrard subdued his disappointment.

With amazing promptness, Clifford Garth's voice growled, "Pack your bags. You're taking another trip."

Gerrard made a pretense of sighing as he replied to the man whose funeral he'd attend as the newly appointed president ten days from now. "What is it this time? A fund-raiser in Idaho? Any excuse to get me out of town?"

"No. Overseas. Spain's president just died from a heart attack. I've already sent my condolences. You'll be our official representative at the funeral."

Funerals, Gerrard thought. Apparently I'll be going to a lot of them. He regretted the deaths, no matter how much they were necessary.

"If that's what you want."

"Right. You just keep thinking like that," Garth growled. "You do everything I want, and we might even get along. I doubt it, though."

With an expletive, the President broke the connection.

Pensive, Gerrard set down the cellular phone. He wasn't totally surprised by the news of the Spanish president's death. The media had reported that the man's health had not been good lately. However, to be sure, the Spanish president's dwindling condition had been encouraged, and in that respect, the only true surprise was that the politician's death had occurred much sooner than the schedule Gerrard had been told about indicated.

Spain. The country was fascinating. Like England, it had a parliamentary monarchy. If the king died, his oldest child would take his place, and his next oldest child after that, or perhaps his wife or his nearest cousin or . . . There was no way to control the succession. But the Spanish parliament was another matter. Its president, chosen by the Congress of Deputies, could be eliminated and replaced by another official. And that official, carefully placed, elected by the pressure of blackmailing various members of the Spanish Congress of Deputies, would be sympathetic to Gerrard's concerns. After all, they were relatives, admittedly distant, but neither time nor separation could mute their bond. Each of them, and many others who shared Gerrard's spirit and mission, would soon fulfill their common destiny.

Spain. How appropriate, Gerrard thought.

16

Eric Chatham, director of the FBI, walked somberly up a slope past brilliant white tombstones in Arlington National Cemetery. Trim, in his forties, his face lined with weariness from the responsibilities of his profession, he turned to study the cluster of smog-veiled trees at the bottom of the hill. In the distance, even more veiled with smog, the white marble obelisk of the Washington Monument towered. Chatham tried to remember the last time he'd seen the Monument totally unobscured. With concern, he watched a car stop on a lane a distance from where his own was parked. Kenneth Madden, deputy director of covert operations for the CIA, got out of the car's backseat, left his bodyguards, and proceeded up the hill to join him.

The two men assessed each other. Although in theory the FBI and the CIA had different mandates and jurisdictions, in practice those mandates and jurisdictions often blurred, sometimes making the two organizations rivals. For Madden to visit Chatham at his office, or vice versa, would have been sufficiently unusual that reporters might have taken notice. Similarly they couldn't have met at a restaurant or a comparable public place, where their joint presence would not only have attracted attention but their conversation could easily have been overheard. A phone call was the simplest solution, and indeed Madden *had* called, but only to explain that he had something delicate to discuss and they ought to do it in person. Arlington Cemetery had been acceptable. Few people would notice them there.

"Thanks for agreeing to meet me on such short notice," Madden said. "Especially during lunch hour."

Chatham shrugged. "It's hardly a sacrifice. I don't have much of an appetite today."

"I know what you mean. My own stomach's sour."

"Because of what happened to Brian Hamilton?"

Madden nodded mournfully. "It was quite a shock." He surveyed the gravestones. "I realized only after we agreed to meet here that we'll be back on Monday for the funeral."

"I wasn't aware that you and Brian were close," Chatham said.

"Not as close as the two of you, but I thought of him as a friend. At least as much as most people in this town can be a friend to anyone else. We sometimes worked together in matters related to the National Security Council."

The deputy director of CIA covert operations didn't elaborate, and the FBI director knew that it would be a breach of professional ethics for him to do so.

"What did you want to see me about?" Chatham asked.

Madden hesitated. "Another tragedy occurred last night. The fire and the deaths at Melinda Drake's house."

Chatham inwardly stiffened but showed no reaction. "Yes. The widow of Remington Drake. I agree. Another tragedy."

"I tried to phone Melinda Drake's daughter in New York. To express my condolences. I couldn't reach her. But the editor at the magazine where she works told me that Theresa—Tess—decided to fly down and visit her mother in Alexandria last night. I'm afraid that whoever set fire to the house and killed her mother—I can't imagine why—may have tried to kill Tess as well. But so far, the fire investigators haven't found her body in the wreckage. That makes me suspect that Tess escaped. If so, she's apparently in hiding, too afraid to surface."

"Perhaps," the FBI director said. "The assumption's reasonable. But what's your interest in this matter? Do you *know* Tess? Did you know her father?"

Madden shook his head. "Tess? Not at all. But her father? By all means. In the old days, I often briefed him on hazardous conditions in various countries where he was going to negotiate for the State Department. And when he died . . . the way he died . . . the way those bastards tortured him . . . well, I wish he'd been one of my operatives. I despise what happened to him, but God bless him, he didn't talk. He was a *hero,* and his daughter—for his sake—deserves the full protection of the government."

The FBI director squinted. "Protection of . . . ? Be specific."

"I got a call this morning." Madden gestured. "From Alan Gerrard. Hey, whatever your opinion of the Vice President, I listen—and you would, too—when he gives an order. He and Remington Drake were as close as you are—*were*—to Brian Hamilton. Gerrard wants every pertinent government agency to do what they can to help her. That means you and me. The Bureau and the Agency."

"I have trouble with . . . This is a domestic issue," Chatham said. "It doesn't come under your jurisdiction."

"No argument. I'm just telling you what the Vice President said, and in fact, that's why I'm here. Because this *is* a domestic issue. At least so far as I can tell, although the Agency's checking further. I don't want to cause more rivalry between us. The ball's in your court. What the Vice President would appreciate is for you to make a call to the Alexandria police. If Tess Drake surfaces and gets in touch with them, the VP would be grateful—he emphasized that word—*grateful*—if you instructed the local police to turn the matter over to you and then to contact the Vice President's office as well as mine, just in case in the meantime we *do* discover that this is more than a domestic matter.''

Chatham scowled, assessing the deputy director from the CIA. He wasn't used to sharing information with the Agency.

At the same time, his friendship with Brian Hamilton insisted. He was sorely determined to find out if the death of his friend had truly been an accident.

''He phoned me last night,'' Chatham said.

''Who?''

''Brian. He. insisted on coming to my home. I expected him around eleven o'clock. He told me he needed a personal favor. He said it related to Remington Drake, his widow, and his daughter.''

Madden, who seemed to have a perpetual tan, turned gray. ''You're telling me that *Brian's* death and what happened at Melinda Drake's house . . . !''

''Might be related? I don't know. But I certainly intend to find out. Tell the Vice President I'll cooperate. I'll talk to the Alexandria police chief. I'll make arrangements to take over and relay information.''

''I guarantee the Vice President will appreciate—''

''Appreciate? Fuck him. I don't care what he appreciates! All I care about is Brian, Remington Drake's widow, and his daughter.''

''So do I, Eric. So do I. But since Brian's dead . . . and Remington Drake's wife . . . we have to concentrate on the living. On Tess. For our friends, we need to do our best to protect her.''

Chatham grimaced. ''Lord help me.''

''What's wrong?''

''You have my word,'' Chatham said. ''But I have to tell you, I don't like working this close with the Agency.''

''Relax. It's one time only. And the goal's worth the compromise.''

''That's exactly what we've got. A compromise. One time only.''

''For now. *This* time,'' Madden said, extending his hand.

Chatham hesitated. Reluctantly, he shook with him. ''I'll be in touch.''

"And I know you'll do your usual best."

Tense, they separated, each passing brilliant-white gravestones down the slope toward his car.

After Madden nodded to his bodyguards and his chauffeur, he paused, turned, and stared back toward the cemetery. Although his group had a primary plan for finding Tess Drake, Madden's experience in CIA covert operations had taught him always to have a backup plan, and now that plan, too, was in motion.

He came close to smiling.

But triumph fought with melancholy. Madden regretted that Brian Hamilton would be buried here on Monday. A necessary sacrifice.

Even so, he didn't regret at all that ten days from now there'd be another funeral here—for the President.

And that Alan Gerrard would assume control.

17

Trembling, Tess braked the Porsche to a stop outside a well-maintained Victorian house near Georgetown, grabbed her purse with its reassuring pistol, and hurried up the steps to the wide porch, pressing the doorbell.

No one answered.

She rang the bell again.

Still no answer.

Nervous, she wasn't surprised. At least, not exactly. The man who lived here, her former art professor at Georgetown University, was renowned for spending his summer vacation in his backyard, tending, caring for, *whispering* to, his magnificent collection of lilies.

But that had been in the old days, Tess remembered with painful nostalgia. After all, she hadn't seen her beloved professor since she'd graduated six years ago.

Professor Harding had been old even then. Perhaps he'd retired. Or perhaps he'd gone to Europe to study the art he so worshiped and the enthusiasm for which he so ably communicated in his courses.

All Tess knew was that he'd treated his students as if they were part of his family. He'd welcomed them to his home. At sunset, amid the glorious lilies in his garden, he'd offered them sherry, but not too much—he didn't want to cloud their judgment—and described the glories of Velázquez, Goya, and Picasso.

Spanish. Professor Harding had always been partial to the genius of Spanish art. The only competition for Harding's admiration had been . . .

Tess stepped from the porch and rounded the side of the house, proceeding toward the backyard. After so many years, she hadn't remembered Professor Harding's phone number, and in any case, she'd felt too panicked, too exposed, too threatened, to stop at a phone booth and get his number from information. Needing somewhere to go, she'd decided to come here directly and take the chance he was home. There was no alternative. She had to know.

But as she reached the backyard, her immediate fears were subdued. She felt a warm flush of love surge through her chest at the sight of Professor Harding—much *older*—distressingly infirm— as he straightened painfully from examining a waist-high lily stalk.

The backyard was glorious with the flowers. Everywhere, except for a maze of narrow paths that allowed visitors to stroll in admiration, the garden was filled with abundant, myriad, trumpet-shaped, resplendent, many-colored tributes to God's generosity.

Tess faltered amid the beauty. She clutched her purse and the weight of its pistol, reminding herself of how far she'd come, not necessarily forward, since leaving Georgetown University. How she wished she was back there.

Professor Harding turned and noticed her. "Yes?" Trembling, he fought to maintain his balance. "You've come to see my . . . ?"

"Flowers. As usual, they're wonderful!"

"You're very kind." Professor Harding used a cane and hobbled toward her. "To my regret, there once was a time . . ."

"Your regret?"

"The poisonous air. The equally poisonous rain. Eight years ago . . ."

"I was here," Tess said. "I remember."

"The lilies were . . ." Professor Harding, wrinkled, alarmingly aged, sank toward a redwood bench. His white hair was thin and wispy, his skin slack, dark with liver spots. "What you see is *nothing*. A mockery. There once was a time, when nature was in control . . . The lilies used to be so . . ." He stared toward his cane and trembled. "Next year . . ." He trembled increasingly. "I won't subject them to this poison. Next year, I'll let them rest in peace. But their bulbs will be safely stored. And perhaps one day grow flowers again. If the planet is ever purified."

Tess glanced defensively backward, clutching the outline of her handgun in her purse, then approaching.

"But do I know you?" Professor Harding asked. He steadied his wire-rimmed glasses and squinted in concentration. "Why, it's Tess. Can it actually be *you?* Of course. Tess Drake."

Tess smiled, her tear ducts aching. "I'm so pleased you haven't forgotten."

"How could I possibly forget? Your beauty filled my classroom."

Tess blushed. "Now you're the one who's being kind." She sat beside him on the redwood bench and gently hugged him.

"In fact, if I'm not mistaken, you were in *many* of my classes. Each year, you took a course." The professor's voice sounded like wind through dead leaves.

"I loved hearing you talk about art."

"Ah, but more important, you loved the art itself. It showed in your eyes." Professor Harding squinted harder, as if at something far away. "Mind you, in honesty, you weren't my *best* student. . . ."

"Mostly Bs, I'm afraid."

"But by all means, you were certainly my most *enthusiastic* student." The professor's thin, wrinkled lips formed a smile of affection. "And it's so good of you to come back. You know, many

265

students promised they would—after they graduated and all.'' His smile faded. ''But as I learned to expect . . .''

''Yes?''

''They never did.''

Tess felt a tightness in her throat. ''Well, here I am. Late, I regret.''

''As you always came late for class.'' The old man chuckled. ''Just a few minutes. I wasn't distracted. But it seems you couldn't resist a grand entrance.''

Tess echoed the old man's chuckle. ''Really, I wasn't trying to make a grand entrance. It's just that I couldn't manage to get out of bed on time.''

''Well, my dear, when you're my age, you'll find that you wake up at dawn.'' The professor's frail voice faded. ''And often earlier. *Much* earlier.''

He cleared his throat.

Their conversation faltered.

Even so, Tess found that the silence was comfortable.

Soothing.

She admired the lilies.

How I wish I could stay here forever, she thought. How I wish that my world wasn't falling to pieces.

''Professor, can we talk about art for a while?''

''My pleasure. As you're aware, apart from my lilies, I've always enjoyed a discussion . . .''

''About a bas-relief statue? I'd like to show you a picture of it.'' Apprehensive, Tess withdrew the packet of photographs from her purse, taking care to conceal the handgun.

''But why . . . ? You're so somber.'' Professor Harding narrowed his white, sparse eyebrows. ''Have you lost your enthusiasm for the subject?''

''Not for the subject,'' Tess said. ''But as far as *this* goes . . .'' She showed him the photograph of the statue. *''This* is another matter.''

Professor Harding scowled, creating more wrinkles on his forehead. He pushed up his glasses, then raised the photograph toward them. ''Yes, I can see why you're disturbed.''

He shifted the picture forward, then backward, and with each motion shook his head. "Such a brutal image. And the style. So rough. So crude. It's certainly not something I care for. Certainly not Velázquez."

"But what can you tell me about it?" Tess held her breath.

"I'm sorry, Tess. You'll have to be more specific. What exactly do you need to know? What's your interest in this? Where did you find it?"

Tess debated how much to tell him. The less the old man knew, the better. If the killers found out that she'd come here, ignorance and infirmity might be the difference that saved Professor Harding's life. "A friend of mine had it in his bedroom."

"That doesn't say much for his taste. His bedroom? This doesn't belong even in a toolshed."

"I agree. But have you any idea who might have sculpted it? Or *why?* Or what it *means?* Are there any sculptors you know or you've heard of who might have done it?"

"Dear me, no. I can see why you're confused. You think this sculpture might relate to a contemporary school of . . . I don't know what I'd call them . . . neoprimitives or avant-garde classicists."

"Professor, forgive me. I'm still not a very good student. What you just said . . . You've lost me."

"I'll try to be more enlightening. This photograph. It's difficult to tell from the image, but the sculpture seems to be in perfect condition. Distinct lines. No missing sections. No chips. No cracks. No sign of weathering."

"I still don't . . ."

"Pay attention. Pretend you're taking notes."

"Believe me, I'm *trying.*"

"The object, its craft, its execution, are recent. Very distinct. But the image itself is . . ." Professor Harding hesitated. "Old. Very old. This is a copy, Tess, of a sculpture from as long ago as . . . oh, I'd guess . . . two thousand years."

"Two thousand years?" Tess gaped.

"An approximation. It's not my specialty, I'm sorry to say. Anything before the 1600s is outside my expertise."

Tess slumped. "Then there's no way you can help me understand what it means?"

"Did I say that? *Please.* I merely admitted my own limitations. What you need is a classical scholar with training in archaeology."

Tess glanced at her watch. Half past twelve. Craig would be at LaGuardia by now. He'd soon be flying to Washington. She had to meet him at two-thirty. Time. She didn't have much time!

"A classical scholar with . . . ?" Tess breathed. *"Where on earth am I going to find . . . ?"*

"Young lady, I'm disappointed. Have you forgotten the marvelous woman I'm married to? *She's* the brains of the family. Not me. And until five years ago, she belonged to the Classics Department at Georgetown University. Come." Professor Harding leaned on his cane and stood from the redwood bench. He wavered for a moment. "Priscilla's been taking a nap. But it's time I woke her.

It really isn't good if she misses lunch. Her diabetes, you know. Perhaps you'd care for a bite to eat.''

"Professor, I don't mean to be rude. I'm really not hungry, and please—oh, God, I hate this—I'm in a hurry. This is important. Terribly urgent. I need to know about that statue.''

"Well." Professor Harding studied her. "How mysterious you make it seem. Good. I can use some stimulation.'' The old man shuffled unsteadily along a path, the fragrance of his lilies tainted by smog. "But if it's *that* urgent, if you don't mind the familiarity, you'd better put your arm around me so I can walk a little faster. I confess I'm curious. So let's wake Priscilla and stimulate *her*. Let's find out what that odious image means.''

18

Kennedy International Airport

The Pan Am 747 from Paris arrived on time at 12:25. Among the four hundred and fifty passengers, six men—who'd sat separately in business class—were careful to leave the jet at intervals, and with equal care took different taxis into New York. They were all well-built, in their thirties. Each wore a nondescript suit and carried a briefcase as well as an underseat bag. None had checked luggage. Their features were common, ordinary, average.

Their only other shared characteristic was that while they'd been pleasant to the flight attendants, their polite remarks had seemed to require effort, as if each man had urgent business that preoccupied him. Their eyes communicated the gravity of their concerns: distant, pensive, cold.

In Manhattan, at diverse locations, each man got out of his taxi, walked several blocks, took a subway at random, got off a few stops later, hired another taxi, and arrived several minutes apart on avenues west of the Museum of Natural History. After assessing the traffic, parked cars, and pedestrians in the neighborhood, each approached a brownstone on West Eighty-fifth Street and rang the doorbell.

A matronly woman opened the door, blocking the narrow entrance. "I don't believe we've met."

"May the Lord be with you."

"And with your spirit."

"*Deo gratias.*"

"Indeed." The woman waited. "However, a sign is required."

"Absolutely. I'd feel threatened if you didn't ask."

The last man to arrive reached into his suit-coat pocket and showed her a ring. The ring had a gleaming ruby. The impressive stone was embossed with the golden insignia of an intersecting cross and sword.

"*Deo gratias,*" the woman repeated.

Only then did the woman open the door all the way, stepping backward, bowing her head, respectfully allowing the visitor to enter.

In an alcove to the left of the door, a grim, intense man in a Kevlar bullet-resistant vest lowered an Uzi submachine gun equipped with a silencer.

The woman closed the door. "Did you have a good flight?"

"It didn't crash."

"The others arrived not long ago."

The visitor merely nodded, then followed the woman up narrow stairs to the second floor. He entered a bedroom, where the five other members of his team had already changed into unobtrusive clothes and now were taking apart and reassembling pistols laid out on the bed.

The weapons, Austrian Glock-17 9-mm semiautomatics, were made of sturdy polymer plastic, their only metal the steel of the barrel and the firing mechanism. Lightweight, dependable, their main advantage was that metal detectors often failed to register them, and when disassembled, the pistols frequently weren't noticed on airport X-ray machines.

"Your street clothes are in the bureau," the woman said.

"Thank you, sister."

"Your flight was long. You must be tired."

"Not at all."

"Hungry?"

"Hardly. My purpose gives me energy."

"I'll be downstairs if you need anything. You *will* have to hurry, however. The schedule has been increased. You have tickets for a three-o'clock flight to Washington National Airport. The bait is in motion."

"I'm pleased to hear that, sister. And the enemy? Have the vermin taken the bait?"

"Not yet."

"They will, however." His voice became an ominous whisper. "I have no doubt. Thank you." He guided her from the bedroom. "Thank you, sister. Thank you." He shut the door.

The matronly woman gripped the banister, proceeded hesitantly down the stairs, then paused before the guard at the entrance. "They make me shiver."

"Yes," the haggard man with the Uzi said. "Once before, I worked with enforcers. For a day afterward, my marrow still felt frozen."

19

Tess waited, squirming impatiently on a chair at Professor Harding's kitchen table. The spacious room, in the back of the Victorian house, was clean and uncluttered, painted blue. A large window provided a magnificent panorama of the thousands of glorious, many-colored lilies, but she was too preoccupied to pay attention to them. Some time ago—too long—Professor Harding had left her here while he'd gone upstairs to wake his wife.

Tess kept glancing nervously toward her watch. It was five after one. She fidgeted. Unable to control her anxiety, she stood and paced, locked the back door, abruptly sat down again, and continued fidgeting.

Hurry! Craig's plane would be in the air by now. He expected her at the Marriott hotel near Washington National Airport in less than ninety minutes.

I won't be able to stay here much longer!

But I can't just *leave*.

I've got to *know!*

At once she exhaled, hearing muffled footsteps on a staircase at the front of the house.

The next thing, she heard murmured voices. The footsteps shuffled along a corridor, approaching the kitchen.

Tess bolted to her feet as Professor Harding escorted his wife into view.

But at the sight of the woman, Tess felt her stomach turn cold. No!

So much time! I've wasted so much . . . !

Priscilla Harding looked even more infirm than her husband. She was tiny, thin, and stoop-shouldered. Her wispy white hair was mussed from her nap, her face wrinkled, pale, and slack. Like her husband, she needed a cane. They clung to each other.

"Professor," Tess said, trying not to insult their dignity by revealing her alarm. "If only you'd told me. I'd have been more than happy to go upstairs with you and help bring your wife downstairs."

"No need." The old man smiled. "Priscilla and I have managed to get along without help for several years. You wouldn't want to spoil us, would you? However, I appreciate your consideration."

"Here, let me . . ." Tess hurried around the table, gently gripped Priscilla Harding, and helped her to sit.

"Good," the professor said, breathing with difficulty. "Our little exercise is over. How do you feel, Priscilla?"

The woman didn't answer.

Tess was alarmed by the lack of vitality in her eyes.

My God, she isn't alert enough to . . .

She can't *possibly* answer my questions!

Professor Harding seemed to read Tess's mind. "Don't worry.

My wife's merely groggy from her nap. It takes Priscilla a while to regain her energy. But she'll be fine as soon as . . ."

The old man opened the refrigerator's gleaming door and took out a syringe. After swabbing his wife's arm with rubbing alcohol, he injected her with what Tess assumed was insulin, given the professor's earlier remarks about his wife's diabetes.

"There," the professor said.

He returned to the refrigerator and removed a plate of fruit, cheese, and meat that was covered with plastic wrap.

"I hope you're hungry, my dear." He set the plate on the table, took off the plastic wrap, then shifted unsteadily toward a counter to slice some French bread. "I suggest you start with those sections of orange. You need to maintain your—"

"Blood sugar?" Priscilla Harding's voice was thick tongued, surprisingly deep. "I'm sick of . . ."

"Yes. That's right. You're sick. But in a few moments, after you've had something to eat, you'll feel much better. By the way, that navel orange is excellent. I recommend you try it."

With a weary glance toward her husband, Priscilla Harding obeyed, her arthritis-gnarled fingers raising a slice of the orange to her mouth. As she chewed methodically, she shifted her gaze, puzzled now, toward Tess.

Again Professor Harding seemed to read her thoughts. "Forgive my rudeness, dear. This attractive young woman is a former student of mine, but of course her beauty can never compare to yours."

"You bullshitter."

"My dear. Tsk, tsk. And in front of company."

Priscilla Harding scrunched her wrinkled eyes in amusement.

"Her name is Tess Drake," the professor said, "and she has a favor to ask. She needs to make use of your scholarly abilities."

Priscilla Harding's eyes rose, much less vapid. "My scholarly . . . ?"

"Yes, it's a bit of a mystery we hope you can solve," the professor said. "I tried to assist my former student, but I'm afraid her questions are beyond me. They're not at all related to my field of expertise."

Her eyes gaining brightness, Priscilla ate another section of orange.

"The sliced beef is very good. Try it," the professor said.

"What kind of favor?" Priscilla asked, and continued eating, her eyes even more alert. "What sort of questions?"

"She'd like you to examine a photograph. The photograph shows . . . or so I believe . . . a modern reproduction of an ancient bas-relief statue. A rather brutal one, I should add. So prepare yourself. But when you feel your strength coming back, if you'd . . ."

"Richard, the older you get, the more you avoid the point. A photograph? A modern replica of an ancient sculpture? Sounds fascinating. By all means, I'll be happy to look at it."

Tess felt tense from the pressure of speeding time. "Mrs. Harding, thank you."

"Please, there's no need to be formal. I'm Priscilla." She munched on a piece of bread, wiped her hands on a napkin, and reached toward Tess. "The photograph?"

Tess took it from her purse and slid it across the table.

Mrs. Harding pulled glasses from a pocket in her dress and put them on, peering down at the photograph.

She kept chewing the bread.

Stopped chewing.

And swallowed hard. Her jaws assumed a grim expression.

She didn't speak for several moments.

What is it? Tess thought.

Hurry!

Priscilla nodded grimly. "I've seen something like this, a very similar image, several times before."

Muscles rigid, Tess leaned forward. "But why do you look so troubled? The knife, the blood, the serpent, the dog. I know they're repulsive but . . ."

"And the scorpion. Don't forget the scorpion," Priscilla said. "Attacking the testicles of the dying bull. And don't forget the flame bearers, flanking the victim, one torch pointing upward, the other down." The old woman shook her wrinkled face. "And the raven."

"I thought it was an owl."

"My God, no. An owl? Don't be absurd. It's a raven."

"But what do they *mean?*" Tess feared her control was about to collapse.

Priscilla trembled. Ignoring Tess, she directed her attention toward her husband. "Richard, do you remember our summer in Spain in '73?"

"Of course," the professor said with fondness. "Our twenty-fifth anniversary."

"Now don't get maudlin on me, Richard. The nature of that occasion—however much I enjoyed it—is irrelevant. What *is*, what's important, is that while you stayed in Madrid and haunted the Prado museum—"

"Yes, Velázquez, Goya, and—"

"But not Picasso. I don't believe Picasso's *Guernica* was exhibited then."

"Please," Tess leaned farther forward, her voice urgent. "The statue."

"I'd seen the Prado many times," Priscilla said. "And I'm a classicist, not an art historian. So I sent Richard on his merry way while I went on my own way. After all, I like to believe I'm a liberated woman."

"You are, dear. How often you've proven that." The professor shrugged with good nature and nibbled on some cheese.

"So I went to ancient Spanish sites whose artifacts intrigued me." Priscilla's eyes became misted with favorite memories. "Mérida. Pamplona."

"Pamplona? Isn't that where Hemingway . . . ?"

"With apologies, Tess, pretend you're in my husband's classroom. Be polite, and don't interrupt."

"I'm sorry, Mrs. . . ."

"And don't make polite noises. I told you I'm not 'Mrs.' Not when you're my guest." Priscilla concentrated. "How I loved those . . . In ruins outside each village, I found etchings, engravings, and in a small museum outside Pamplona, I found a statue like *this*. Weathered. Broken. Not clean with perfect engravings. Not distinct in its outline. But it was the same as this photograph. And later, in my fascinating travels, while I waited for Richard to exhaust his compulsion for Velázquez and Goya . . . Apparently I'm like Richard. I'm so old I fail to get to the point."

"But what did you find?" Tess tried not to raise her voice.

"More statues." Priscilla shrugged. "Further engravings."

"Of?"

"The same image as *this*. Not frequent. *In situ,* they were always hidden. Always in caves or grottoes."

"Images of—?"

"Mithras."

Tess jerked her head up. "What or who the hell is . . . ?"

"Mithras?" Priscilla mustered energy. "Are you religious, Tess?"

"Sort of. I was raised a Roman Catholic. In my youth, I believed. In college, I lapsed. But lately . . . ? Yes, I suppose you could say I'm religious."

"Roman Catholic? Ah." Priscilla bit her lip, her tone despondent. "Then I'm afraid your religion has . . ."

"What?"

"Competition."

"What are you talking about?"

"Ancient competition. Stronger than you can imagine. It comes from the start of everything, the origins of civilization, the roots of history."

"What the hell . . . ?"

"Yes, hell." Priscilla's face drooped, at once haggard again. *"Heaven and hell.* That's what Mithras is all about."

"Look, I can't take much more of this," Tess said. "You don't know what I've been through. My mother's dead! People are dying all around me! I'm supposed to be at National Airport to meet someone in an hour. And I'm scared. No, that's an understatement. I'm *terrified.*"

"About Mithras? I sympathize." Priscilla clutched Tess's hand. "If this photograph . . . if this statue's related to your problems . . . you have reason to be terrified."

"Why?"

"Mithras," Priscilla said, "is the oldest god I know of, and his counterpart's the most evil and unforgiving."

"This is . . ." Tess shuddered. *"Crazy.* What are you . . . ?" She clenched her fists, her fingernails gouging her palms.

"Talking about?" Priscilla stood with difficulty. "Stop glancing at your watch. There's a great deal to teach you . . . and warn you about . . . and prayers to be said."

A SERPENT,
A SCORPION,
AND A DOG

1

Western Germany, south of Cologne, the Rhine

Headlights glimmered through fog along a seldom-traveled lane. Years earlier, between the Great Wars, it had often been used by fishermen who'd laid their bicycles behind bushes, removed tackle kits from baskets on the front of their bikes, assembled fishing rods, and followed well-worn paths down the thickly treed slope to favorite spots on the river. Children once had scampered along the bank. On warm summer days, mothers had spread blankets on sweet, lush grass and opened picnic baskets, the aroma of sausage, cheese, and freshly baked bread drifting out. Bottles of wine had cooled in shallows.

But that had been long ago, and in Germany, while at the same time in Washington Tess listened with horror to what Professor Harding's wife explained to her; this wasn't day, and even if it had been, no one came to fish here anymore. Few people came here for any reason and certainly not to picnic, for the stench from the river would have fouled the aroma of freshly baked bread, and the poison

277

in the water had long since been absorbed into the soil, blighting the grass and trees, and the sludge that choked the current had long since killed the fish.

On *this* evening, however, the passengers in the car that jolted along the lane did think about picnics and fishing, although their thoughts were bitter, making the men frown with anger at glimpses of leafless trees and stunted bushes in the fog.

All except *one* passenger, who frowned for another reason.

Indeed he trembled. "You won't get away with this! My guests are expecting me! I'll be missed!"

"You're referring to the reception at your estate?" the driver asked, then shrugged. "Well, your guests will just have to do without you, Herr Schmidt."

"Yes," another man said. "Too bad. They'll simply have to wait."

"And wait. And wait," a third man said.

"What do you want from me?" the silver-haired, lean-faced, tuxedo-clad man demanded. "Ransom? If *that's* what you want, what are we doing *here?* Let me use a phone! I'll arrange—! My assistant will deliver any amount you demand! No police!"

"Of course not, Herr Schmidt. I can guarantee," the driver said. "Later maybe, but not for now. There'll be no police."

"What are you talking about?"

"Justice," a man with a pistol said.

The pistol was wedged against the silver-haired man's neck.

"Examples," another man said. "Here." From the backseat, he leaned forward, telling the driver, "When I was a child, *this* was my favorite path. The river was so . . . ! How I *loved* this place. Now look at it! Look at how *ugly* it's become! Here! Yes, stop right *here.*"

"Why not?" The driver shrugged again. "It's as good a place as any."

"For *what?*" Schmidt demanded, voice trembling.

"I already told you," the man with the pistol said. "Justice."

The driver stopped among skeletal bushes at the side of the lane, dead branches snapping. He turned off the headlights and stepped from the car while his companions opened other doors and dragged Schmidt, struggling, into the fog-shrouded wasteland. The sleeve of his tuxedo tore on a barkless tree limb.

"Ah, too bad," the man with the gun said. "What a terrible shame."

"Yes, a pity," the driver said.

They reached a bluff and forced Schmidt down the sterile slope. At once, the sickening fumes from the river enveloped them, making them cough. In terror, Schmidt resisted so fiercely that the men were forced to drag him downward, his patent-leather shoes scraping over rocks. Where the zigzagging, barely detectable path became steep, one of the men used a shielded flashlight to guide their way.

At the oppressive grassless bottom, the light revealed the foam along the river's edge, the slime on the water, and the sludge that thickened the current. The area smelled like a cesspool, for sewage, too, fouled the water.

"What a damnable . . . ! I used to be able to swim here!" the man with the gun said. "And the fish . . . the fish tasted so pure and delicious. Their meat was so white, so flaky, at the same time solid. The way my mother dipped them in milk. She used to cover them with biscuit crumbs, and—"

"Fish?" Schmidt whimpered. "What are you *talking* about? *Fish?* Why does that—? For God's sake, if your purpose was to scare me, you've succeeded! I admit it! I'm terrified!" His control collapsing, the silver-haired prisoner began to sob. "How much do you want? *Anything!* Please! I swear on my mother's grave, I'll pay you anything!"

"Yes," the driver said. "That's right. Anything. You'll pay."

"Name it! Just tell me how much! It's yours! *Mein Gott,* how *much!*"

"You still don't understand how much you must pay," another man said. *"You did this."*

"Did . . . ? *What* did I . . . ?"

"This." With disgust, the fourth man gestured toward the noxious desecration of the river. *"You.* Not alone! But you share the responsibility!"

"With?" Schmidt voided his bowels.

"With the other greedy industrialists who demanded profits,

no matter the cost to nature. Billionaires who wouldn't miss the comparative few millions it would have taken to keep the river pure and the sky free of poison.''

"Millions?" Schmidt shook his head, frenzied. "But my board of directors, my shareholders, would have . . . !''

"Millions? Yes! But only at the start!'' the man with the gun corrected. "A onetime-only expense. But that was years behind us. *Now* the cost would be greater. Much, much greater. And the river's so poisoned, so dead, that it might take decades before it's revived, if ever, if the dead can *ever* be brought back to life.''

Scowling, the man with the flashlight stepped closer. "Pay attention, Herr Schmidt. We didn't choose this place merely because we used to love to come here when we were children. Not at all. We chose it because . . .'' The grim man gestured. Even in the fog, the lights that silhouetted the numerous huge factories upriver were gloomily visible. Indeed the fog was not completely natural. Smoke containing toxic pollutants added to it. Nearby, a drainage pipe from one of the factories spewed nostril-flaring chemicals into the water. The foam accumulated.

"We chose this site because we wanted you to witness your crimes,'' the driver said.

"Sins," the man with the gun corrected.

"Sins?" Schmidt cowered. "You're all lunatics! You're—!''

"And sins must be punished,'' the man with the flashlight said. "As you indicated, you're eager to pay.''

"And *will* pay,'' the fourth man said.

Schmidt pressed his hands together. "I'm begging you.'' He sank to his knees. "I promise. I swear. My engineers will redesign the waste system in my factories. The cost doesn't matter. I'll stop the chemicals from reaching the river. I'll speak to the other manufacturers in the area. I'll convince them to prevent the discharge from—''

"Too late,'' the man with the gun said.

"—from pouring into the river.'' Schmidt sobbed. "I'll do anything if you'll just—''

"Too *late,"* the man with the gun repeated. "An *example* has to be made.''

"Many examples,'' the man with the flashlight said.

"Justice," the driver said.

"I'm thirsty," the fourth man said. "The walk down that slope made my mouth dry."

"Mine, too," the man with the gun said.

"And Herr Schmidt, I imagine that *your* mouth feels especially dry. From *fear*. I believe you deserve a drink."

The fourth man removed a plastic container from a knapsack on his shoulder. Repelled but determined, contracting his chest, visibly holding his breath, he stooped toward the noxious fumes that rose from the water's edge and scooped foam, slime, sludge, and sewage into the container.

Schmidt screamed. "No! I can't drink from . . . ! Don't make me swallow . . . ! That stuff'll kill . . . !"

The man with the flashlight nodded. "Kill you? Indeed. As it killed the fish. As it killed the river. As it killed the trees and the bushes and the grass. As it's slowly killing the people in the cities who depend on the river for water, however much the cities try to purify that water."

"Regrettably, an example has to be made," the man with the gun said, "*Many* examples. If it's any consolation, take heart. You won't be alone. I promise. Soon many of your fellow sinners will join you. Many lessons need to be taught. Until the *ultimate* lesson is finally learned. Before it's too late. That is, if it's not too late already."

The man with the container of sludge pressed it against Schmidt's mouth.

Schmidt wailed, then clamped his lips tightly together, jerking his face away.

"Now, now," the man with the container said. "You must take your medicine."

The other men held him firmly.

"Accept your fate," the man with the flashlight said. "Taste the product of your success."

Schmidt struggled, desperate, yanking his arms, straining to escape the rigid hands of his captors.

"Destiny, *mein Herr*. We must all confront it." The man with the container raised it again toward Schmidt's clamped jaws.

Again Schmidt jerked his face away.

"Well," the man with the flashlight said, disappointed. "That leaves us no choice." With relentless strength, he tugged Schmidt downward. The other men helped him, using their knees along with their hands to force Schmidt onto his back, straining to keep their prisoner's thrashing face pointed toward the murky, fog-and-smoke-clogged sky.

The man with the container knelt and pressed a nerve behind Schmidt's ear.

Schmidt screamed reflexively.

At once, another man rammed a funnel into Schmidt's mouth, clamped it firmly between his lips, watched the container being raised toward the funnel, and nodded as foam, slime, sludge, and sewage were poured down Schmidt's throat.

"Perhaps, in one of your future lives, you'll be more responsible," the man said. "That is, if we're successful, if anyone has a *chance* for a future life."

Later . . .

After the corpse was discovered and the autopsy was performed . . .

The medical examiner debated about the primary cause of death. In theory, Schmidt had drowned.

But the chemicals that filled his stomach and swelled his lungs were so toxic that, before he drowned, his vital organs might easily have failed from instant shock.

2

Craig, you were with *me. You heard me talk about Joseph! You saw what was in his* bedroom. *If the killers followed* both *of us, to protect their secret they might come after* you!

Remembering Tess's warning when she'd phoned him at One

Police Plaza, Craig squirmed against his seat belt and directed his troubled eyes toward the smog beyond the window of the Trump Shuttle 727 about to land at Washington National Airport.

Come after *me?* he thought.

Until Tess had mentioned it, that possibility hadn't occurred to him. He recalled—and had meant—what he'd replied. Let the sons of bitches try. The truth was, he would welcome a confrontation. Anything to stop the madness. Anything to save—!

Keep running, Tess! he thought. Be clever. Don't take chances. *Soon. I'll be there soon!*

Prior to leaving One Police Plaza, he'd phoned the security personnel at LaGuardia's Trump Shuttle terminal to alert them that he was a police officer who'd be bringing credentials, that he'd be prepared to fill out all the forms and comply with all the complex procedures, including an interview with the pilot, that allowed him to carry his handgun aboard this plane. On the way to the airport, he and Tony had done their best to make sure they weren't being followed, although in the chaos of noon-hour traffic that was almost impossible.

Now, concealing his gesture from the passenger next to him, Craig kept his right hand beneath his suit coat, his fingers clutched around the .38-caliber, Smith & Wesson revolver's handle. Not that it mattered. If there *was* trouble, it certainly wouldn't happen during the flight. Certainly not shooting. Too dangerous. The bullets would rupture the fuselage and depressurize the cabin, at the risk of causing the jet to crash. All the same, the feel of the weapon gave him confidence.

As casually as his nerves would allow, Craig glanced around. No passenger seemed to care about him.

Good, he thought. Just keep control. He strained to reassure himself. You've taken every precaution you could think of. You're in the flow now. You're committed. You've got to go with whatever happens!

Still, he hadn't noticed the gray-eyed man ten seats behind him, who appeared to nap, thus hiding the color of his eyes, and who, under various names, had bought a ticket for every Trump Shuttle flight from LaGuardia to Washington National Airport since the woman had disappeared last night.

Not that the gray-eyed man had intended to use all the tickets. Instead he'd waited, unobtrusively watching the terminal's entrance, in case the woman's detective-friend arrived. One of his counterparts had kept a similar watch at the Pan Am shuttle terminal.

About to give up hope, abruptly seeing his target get out of a police car, the gray-eyed man—pulse speeding—had strolled inside the terminal, passed through the security checkpoint, presented the ticket for his flight, and boarded the jet before the detective did. In that way, he followed the detective paradoxically from in front and almost surely prevented the target from suspecting he had company.

Yes, the woman had escaped last night. But thanks to the onboard phone, which the gray-eyed man had asked a flight attendant to bring to him, he'd been able, using guarded expressions, to alert additional members of his team that the detective was en route to Washington National Airport, presumably to rendezvous with the quarry.

The woman.

She was dangerous. She knew too much.

So—it had to be assumed—did the determined detective, who showed far too great an interest in the woman.

When the two came together, they would both be silenced, the photographs would be destroyed, and the covenant would at last again be protected.

3

"Evil," Priscilla Harding said.

The stark word caught Tess's attention.

She, Priscilla, and Professor Harding had moved from the kitchen to a downstairs study in the Victorian house near Georgetown in Washington. Now that Priscilla's insulin had taken effect and her blood sugar was stabilized by the lunch she'd eaten, the elderly woman seemed ten years younger. Her eyes looked vital. She spoke with strength, although her cadence was slow and deliberate, as if by habit she used the lecture style she'd perfected during her many years as a professor.

But Tess didn't have *time* for a lecture. She needed to know about the statue right *now*. Hurry! She had to meet *Craig*.

Priscilla noticed her impatience and sighed. "Stop looking at your watch. Sit down, Tess, and listen carefully. This isn't something I can condense, and if you're in as much trouble as you described, your life might very well depend on an absolute understanding of what I'm about to tell you."

Tess hesitated. Suddenly tired, she obeyed, sinking toward a leather chair. "I apologize. I know you're trying to help. I'll do my best to . . . If this is complicated, I'd better not . . . In fact, I don't dare try to rush you. Tell it *your* way."

Nonetheless Tess felt her muscles ache from tension as she watched Priscilla take several thick books from a shelf and place them on a desk.

" 'Evil,' " Tess said. "You mentioned 'evil.' "

Priscilla nodded. "Evil is the central dilemma in Christian theology."

"I'm afraid I . . . What does that have to do with . . . ?"

"Think about it. How do you reconcile the existence of evil with the traditional concept of a benign, all-loving, Christian God?"

Tess frowned in rigid confusion. "Really, I still don't understand."

Priscilla raised an arthritis-swollen, wrinkled hand. "Just listen. We know that evil exists. We encounter it every day. We hear about it on the radio. On television. We read about it in the newspapers. Moral evil in the form of crime, cruelty, and corruption. Physical evil in the form of disease. Cancer. Muscular dystrophy. Multiple sclerosis." Priscilla's voice dropped. "Diabetes."

She hesitated, then sat despondently behind the desk.

Brooding, Priscilla continued, "Of course, some deny the existence of, even the *concept* of, evil. They claim that crime is merely the result of poverty, inadequate parental guidance, or lack of education, et cetera. They place both the causes and the blame on society, or in the case of someone so repugnant as a serial killer, they attribute the killer's violence to insanity. They also refuse to consider that diseases have theological implications. To them, cancer is a biological accident or the consequence of substances in the environment.''

"But they're not wrong," Tess said. "I work for a magazine that tries to protect the environment. Carcinogenic substances are all around us.''

"Absolutely," Professor Harding said. "The poisons are evident. My lilies struggle to blossom. They're not half as brilliant as they used to be.''

"Richard, if you wouldn't mind . . .'' Priscilla tapped her gnarled fingers on the desk. "I'm suddenly terribly thirsty. I'd appreciate very much if you went to the kitchen and brewed us some tea.''

"Why, of course.'' Professor Harding grasped his cane. "Any special preference?''

"Whatever you choose, I'm sure will be fine.''

"In that case, I think Lemon Lift, dear.''

"Excellent.''

As Professor Harding hobbled from the study, Priscilla narrowed her wrinkle-rimmed eyes toward Tess. Alone, the two women faced each other.

"Carcinogenic substances and so-called biological accidents are exactly my point," Priscilla said. "Physical evil. Theological evil.''

Tess shook her head. "But how can cancer have anything to do with theology?''

"Pay attention. According to Christianity, a generous, loving God made the universe.''

"That's right," Tess said.

"So what kind of God would add crime and cancer to that universe? The existence of those evils makes the traditional Christian God seem not at all benign. In fact, it makes Him seem cruel. Perverse. Inconsistent. That's why the Devil was invented.''

Devil? Tess thought. What the . . . ? This is getting . . .

"Lucifer," Priscilla said. "The topmost angel in heaven. The superstar of God's deputies. But the Light Bearer, as he's sometimes called, wasn't satisfied with being a deputy. No, that powerful angel wanted even *more* power. He wanted *God's* power. He thought he could compete. But when he tried, God pushed him down—oh, so far down—to the depths, to the newly created fires of hell. And God changed his name from Lucifer to Satan, and Satan in his fury vowed to corrupt God's perfect universe, to introduce evil into the world.''

''But *that* part of Christianity always seemed to me a myth,'' Tess said.

''To *you*. However, the majority of Christians, especially fundamentalists, believe and base their lives on that conception. God and the fallen angel. Satan is a convenient explanation for the spreading evil around us.''

''You sound like the nun who gave me catechism lessons every Sunday after mass.''

''Do I?'' Priscilla wrinkled her already wrinkled brow. ''Well, I'm about to teach you a *different* catechism. And it might undermine your faith. As well, I regret to say, it might terrify you.''

Tess straightened, her muscles cramping as she listened with greater tension.

''The trouble with using Satan as an explanation for the existence of evil,'' Priscilla said, ''is that God can still be accused of perversity. Because God *tolerates* Satan's evil. Because He *allows* Satan to oppress us with crime and disease.''

Tess shook her head once again. ''The nun who taught me catechism used to say that God decided to condone Satan's evil rather than destroy him—in order to test us. If we overcome the temptation of evil and accept the hardship of disease, we can gain a higher place in heaven.''

''Now, Tess, really. Do you honestly believe that?''

''Well . . . Maybe not. But at least, it's what I was taught.''

''And this is what *I* was taught.'' Priscilla's tone became bitter. ''Richard and I had a son. Jeremy. Our only child. When he was ten, he died—in excruciating pain—from bone cancer. Thirty years later, I still wake from nightmares of how much he suffered. That sweet, dear, perfect boy never harmed anyone. He didn't have the faintest idea of what sin was.'' Priscilla's eyes misted. ''Nonetheless, God allowed that vicious disease to torture my son. If Satan is responsible for evil, *God* is responsible for Satan and ultimately for what happened to Jeremy. I still blame God for what happened to my . . .'' The mist in Priscilla's eyes faded, replaced by a hard determination. "So I come back to the question I asked you earlier. How can a benign, all-loving God permit evil? The Christian attempt to provide an answer, by inventing a fallen angel, is not at all satisfactory.''

Priscilla scowled, then continued, "However, there *is* another myth that provides a more logical explanation for the existence of evil. Thousands of years before Christ, our ancestors believed in *two* gods, a good one and a bad one, coequal, both of them fighting for control of the universe. That version of Satan wasn't a fallen angel but rather a divinity. The virtuous god was independent from and hence couldn't be held responsible for the evil god and the viciousness that the evil god inflicted on us. The earliest evidence we have for this belief comes from the fourth millennium B.C. in ancient Iraq, specifically in the valley between the Tigris and Euphrates Rivers. That's where tradition tells us the Garden of Eden was supposed to have existed.''

"The serpent in the garden,'' Tess said.

"Exactly. But that serpent wasn't a fallen angel. He was a symbol of an evil god in combat with a virtuous one.''

Tess couldn't help staring toward a clock on the wall. Craig. He'd be landing at Washington National Airport soon. He expected her to *meet* him!

"Don't look at the clock, Tess. Look at me. Keep paying attention.'' Priscilla braced her shoulders with professional sternness. "The concept of opposite but equally powerful gods spread throughout the Mideast. By the time it showed up in ancient Iran, around one thousand B.C., the virtuous god had a name. Mithras.''

Tess jerked straighter. *"Mithras?* You mentioned him before.''

"Yes. The figure in the bas-relief sculpture,'' Priscilla said. "Now do you understand why I had to go into so much detail? The figure killing the bull is not a man. He's a god. Various later religions, Zoroastrianism and Manichaeism, also used the concept of equal, competing good and evil gods. But essentially those gods are versions of Mithras and his evil counterpart. We're talking old, Tess. Very old. That's what I meant when I said that Mithras comes from the roots of history. He's the most ancient notion of a god we have any specific knowledge of, and it's only by chance that . . .''

Professor Harding interrupted, supporting himself with his cane while he wheeled in a cart upon which a teapot, cups, and a plate of biscuits were arranged.

"Thank you, Richard."

"I'm pleased to help, dear."

"It's only by chance that *what?*" Tess asked, impatient for Priscilla to continue.

"Milk, dear?" Professor Harding asked.

"Just a little."

Tess became more impatient, barely able to restrain herself from telling Priscilla to hurry.

While Professor Harding poured the tea, Priscilla pensively opened one of the books she'd set on the desk, leafed through it, and found the page she wanted. "Let me describe a religion to you. When you enter its church, you dip your hand in a holy-water basin and make the sign of the cross. On the altar, you see a representation of the physical form of your God. During the service, you receive a communion of bread and wine. You believe in baptism, confirmation, salvation through good works, and life after death. The physical form of your deity has his birthday on December twenty-fifth, and his rebirth occurs during the Easter season."

Professor Harding wrapped each steaming teacup with a napkin and handed them to Priscilla and Tess. "Catholicism," he said.

"Yes, that would be the logical assumption, Richard. However, with apologies, you're wrong." Priscilla kept staring at Tess. "It's Mithraism."

"What?" Tess set down the teacup and blinked in surprise. "But how can there be so many parallels? You said that Mithraism came *long* before Christianity."

"Think about it." Priscilla lowered and peered over her glasses. "I'm sure the answer will occur to you."

"The only explanation I can . . . It doesn't seem possible. Christianity *borrowed* from Mithraism?"

"So it appears," Priscilla said. "For the first three centuries after Christ, while Christianity struggled to survive, Mithraism was a major force in the Roman Empire. Several Roman emperors not only endorsed it but were members. Mithras is sometimes called the sun god, and because of him, Sunday assumed sacred importance for the Romans and eventually for Western culture. Mithras is often pictured with a sun behind his head, and that sun became the halo around the heads of major figures in Christian art. The cross, by the way, is an ancient symbol that represents the sun. Thus believers in Mithras made the sign of the cross when they entered their church to worship the sun god.''

Priscilla turned the book and slid it toward Tess. ''Here's a photograph of an ancient bas-relief depicting a Mithraic communion service. Notice that the pieces of communion bread have a cross etched into them.''

''*Before* Christianity?'' Tess felt off-balance. ''But this is . . . All my religious training, everything I took for granted about Catholicism . . . I feel like I'm sinking.''

''I warned you.'' Priscilla raised her swollen fingers. ''I told you that what I had to say might undermine your faith. I tried to prepare you when I said it might be terrifying. In more ways than one. But I'll get to that.''

Professor Harding sipped from his teacup, sighed in appreciation of the taste, swallowed with pleasure, and interrupted. ''My dear . . .''

''Yes, Richard?''

''When I came in, you said it was only by chance that . . . *What* was only by chance?''

''That's what *I* want to know,'' Tess said.

''I meant . . .'' Priscilla narrowed her gaze. ''It was only by chance that Mithraism didn't assume the dominance in Western culture that Christianity now has. As I mentioned, in the first three centuries after Christ, several Roman emperors pledged themselves to Mithras. But all of that changed with Constantine. In the year 312, just before Constantine was about to send his army against his major enemy in the famous battle at the Milvian Bridge, Constantine had what he later described as a vision.''

''Vision?''

''Perhaps it's another myth. Constantine peered toward the sky and claimed that he saw a cross of light imposed on the sun. He interpreted this as a message from God and ordered his soldiers to paint similar crosses on their shields. They entered and *won* the battle—under the sign of the cross. Considering that the cross is an ancient symbol for the sun and that Mithraism favored that symbol as a reference to its sun god, historians aren't clear why Constantine seemed arbitrarily to decide that *this* cross referred to the crucifix, the cross upon which Christ had died.'' Priscilla settled back. ''In any event, Constantine converted to Christianity and eventually made it the primary Roman religion. Christians, who until then had been tolerated at best—when not spurned or thrown to the lions— were quick to take advantage of their sudden influence. Their urgent priority was to stamp out the sect that rivaled them. Mithraic chapels were sought out and destroyed. Mithraic priests were killed, their corpses chained to their altars . . . to so desecrate the Mithraic chapels that they'd never be used again. The balance of history tilted, and Mithraism abruptly declined. Persecuted as heretics, its few remaining followers went into hiding. In small groups, they performed their rites in secret. But no matter how stringently they were hunted, they managed to survive. In fact, to this day, Mithraism is practiced in India.''

Priscilla sipped her tea, gaining strength. ''But in Europe, the last vestige of Mithraism was eradicated during the Middle Ages. In the thirteenth century, the concept of two opposing, equal gods—one good and one evil—surfaced again in a town in south- western France called Albi. The Catholic Church referred to the name of the town and declared that this unexpected reappearance of Mithraism was the Albigensian heresy. After all, there could only be *one* God. The papally authorized crusaders, thousands of them, converged on southwestern France and massacred anyone—multi- tudes!—whom they suspected of being a heretic. Eventually they forced the supposed disbelievers onto a mountain fortress. Montsé- gur. There, the crusaders waited until the heretics surrendered due to starvation and thirst. The crusaders then herded the heretics into a wooden stockade, set fire to it, and watched while the heretics burned. That was the last time, more than seven hundred years ago, that a version of Mithraism raised its head in the Western world.''

"But you don't look convinced," Tess said.

"Well." Priscilla debated. "A rumor persists that the night before the massacre, a small group of determined heretics used ropes to descend from the mountain fortress, taking with them a mysterious treasure. I've sometimes wondered if pockets of the heretics might have survived, remaining in hiding to the present day. And the photograph of that sculpture makes me suspect I'm right. It's not as if you can walk into an art gallery that specializes in ancient artifacts and simply buy one of these objects off the shelf. If any were available, the price would be outrageous because, as I told you, most of the bas-relief statues were destroyed after Constantine converted to Christianity. The few that survived are museum pieces. The best two I know of are in the Louvre and in the British National Museum."

"But you saw similar statues in Spain in 1973," Tess said.

"Yes, weathered engravings in grottoes outside Mérida. And a badly broken bas-relief in a small museum outside Pamplona. Then, to my great surprise, a few sculptures hidden in isolated caves in the area. That's what made me wonder if the heresy continued to survive. Surely the local villagers had explored those caves and knew about the statues. They'd been left there, hidden, for a reason, I thought, and I took care to leave them exactly where I'd found them, out of respect, not to mention fear. After all, I didn't want to anger the local villagers by stealing a sacred part of their tradition, and I did have the sense I was being watched as I left the caves."

"You never told me that, dear," Professor Harding said.

"Well, I haven't always told you everything, Richard. I didn't want to concern you. I've had many adventures on my determined solitary journeys, and if you'd known, you might have tried to stop me from going on other journeys. But that's a separate matter. My point is, Tess, your photograph doesn't show an *ancient* statue. It's a painstaking *modern* recreation. In marble. Someone went to a great deal of trouble and expense to have it made. The question is, *why?*"

"And," Tess insisted, "what does it mean? Why would the ancients have considered it religious? Why is Mithras slicing the throat of the bull?"

4

Washington National Airport

Craig waited tensely for the jet to reach the docking platform. He unsnapped his seat belt and lunged to his feet the instant the seat-belt warning light was extinguished. In a rush, he squirmed past other passengers in the aisle, anxious to leave the plane.

Past the exit gate, he hurried through the crowded terminal, checking warily around him, apprehensive about anyone who might show an interest in him. Outside the terminal, he fidgeted, forced to stand in a line with other travelers wanting taxis. Finally it was Craig's turn. As an empty cab stopped at the curb, he scrambled into the back, telling the driver, "The Marriott hotel in Crystal City." Sweating, Craig glanced repeatedly at his watch.

The taxi arrived at the hotel slightly ahead of schedule, two twenty-five, about when Craig had predicted to Tess that he'd reach the rendezvous site.

A uniformed doorman approached Craig while he paid the driver and the taxi pulled away. The doorman seemed puzzled that Craig had no luggage. "Are you checking in, sir?"

"No. I'm expecting someone."

The doorman frowned and stepped backward. "Yes. Very good, sir."

Craig nervously scanned the busy highway, watching for a black Porsche 911. The car wouldn't be hard to recognize. Anytime now, Tess would steer off the highway and stop before him. Craig would dart into the passenger seat. They'd speed away.

Sure. Anytime now.

Craig coughed from the smog and began to pace. He glanced at his watch.

Two-thirty.

Two thirty-five.

Two-*forty*.

She must be having problems with traffic.

Any minute now, I'll see her.

As solemn men with rings in their pockets watched from a replica of a UPS truck in a parking lot across the street . . .

As gray-eyed men stared with vicious resolve from the window of a restaurant farther along the street . . .

Craig's muscles hardened.

Two forty-five.

He breathed heavily.

Tess!

For God's sake, what happened? Where the hell *are* you?

5

"You said you saw the sculpture in a bedroom of a friend?" Priscilla asked.

Tess hesitated, again unsure how much to reveal for fear that the Hardings would be in danger if the people hunting her found out that she'd come here. "Yes, the statue was on a bookshelf."

"From the rigid expression on your face, it's obvious something else troubles you."

Tess made her decision. Urgency compelled her. She had to know. "The bedroom . . ."

"What about it?"

". . . looked strange."

Priscilla leaned suddenly forward. "How?"

"There weren't any lamps. The overhead bulb didn't work. The floor was covered with candles. And next to the statue, on each side, there were *other* candles."

"Candles? Of course. And one pointed upward, the other downward?" Priscilla asked at once.

Tess jerked her head back in surprise. "Yes. How did you know?"

"The photograph of the sculpture. The torchbearers flanking Mithras. One torch is raised, the other inverted. Tess, I very much suspect that what you saw was a makeshift version of a Mithraic altar. What *else* haven't you told me?"

With a shiver, Tess relented completely, prepared to tell Priscilla everything. Rapidly she explained, from the start, a week ago Wednesday—could it have been only that recently?—the first time she'd met Joseph. The gold Cross pen she'd dropped in the elevator.

Joseph had studied the pen and murmured its name almost with reverence.

Gold Cross.

Tess now knew what those words had meant to Joseph.

The symbol for the sun god.

6

Near Washington National Airport, the smog became thicker. In the replica of the UPS truck that stood in a parking lot across from the Marriott hotel, a man with a ring in his pocket spoke into a phone equipped with a scrambler to prevent anyone from overhearing his conversation. "No, he just keeps pacing in front of the hotel. Every thirty seconds, he checks his watch. It's obvious he's waiting for someone. This *has* to be the rendezvous site. Anytime now, the woman ought to arrive."

A voice on the other end of the line said, "But you're sure he doesn't know you followed him from the airport?"

"As certain as I *can* be," the man in the truck said. "The moment the target left the plane and got into a taxi, one of my operatives used a portable phone to warn me. We were parked at the exit from the airport. When we saw the cab that the bait had hired, we pulled out ahead of him. He went directly to the hotel. We parked across the street.''

''And the *enemy?*'' the voice on the other end demanded. ''Have you seen any evidence of the vermin?''

''Not yet. But we have to assume that they followed the detective just as *we* did. If the woman's as great a danger to them as we suspect they fear, he's the only way for them to locate her.''

''Keep watching! Keep searching for them!''

''We're trying. I've got another team patrolling the highway. But this area's extremely congested. Unless you get up close to the vermin and happen to notice the color of their eyes . . . We won't know for certain until the enemy makes its move. Wait a . . . Hold it!''

''What?'' the voice on the other end said fiercely.

''Something's happening! In front of the hotel. I don't understand! The bait just—!''

7

Craig kept pacing. With greater tension, he suddenly noticed movement to his right and spun, apprehensive, his hand beneath his suit coat, grasping his revolver. He relaxed only slightly when he saw that the movement was the hotel's thin-lipped doorman walking toward him, frowning harder.

Don't tell me he's going to insist I check in or stop loitering outside the hotel! Craig quickly removed his hand from his weapon and reached toward a pocket inside his suit coat, ready to pull out his police ID, anything to appease the doorman.

But what the doorman said was so unexpected that Craig restrained his gesture, paralyzed with bewilderment.

"Is your name Craig, sir?"

Craig felt a chill. "Yes. *But how did you know that?*"

"Sir, the clerk at the check-in desk just received a phone call. From a woman who, to say the least, is upset. She demanded that someone hurry outside and see if a man was waiting. She said if the man's name was Craig, she had to talk to him at once."

Tess, Craig thought. It had to be! What had happened? What was wrong?

"The phone!" Craig said. "Where is it? Is she still on the line?" He hurried toward the hotel's entrance.

"Yes, sir," the doorman said, following briskly, troubled. "She insisted that we not hang up."

Craig pushed open the hotel's front door, lunging in. His eyes struggled to adjust to the shadows after the smoggy sunlight. The check-in desk was directly across from him. Hurrying toward it, Craig fumbled in one of his trouser pockets, pulled out a ten-dollar bill, and handed it to the doorman.

"Thank you, sir. I appreciate your—"

"Don't go far. I might need your help. I've got more money."

Craig reached the desk "My name is Craig. There's a call for—"

"Definitely." A clerk straightened, picking up a phone, extending it across the counter.

"Tess?" Craig's hand cramped around the phone as he pressed it against his ear. "Where *are* you? What *happened?*"

"Thank God, you waited," she said.

Craig exhaled at the sound of her voice.

"I was worried," she said, "that you might have—"

"Left? No way! I promised I'd wait. Answer my question. What *happened?*"

"Don't worry. I'm safe. At least, as safe as I *can* be until you get here."

"Where?"

"Craig, I think I've found out what's been happening, and it makes me even more terrified. I don't have time to explain, and this isn't something we can talk about on the phone. Write down this address."

Distraught, Craig glanced toward the counter, grabbed a pen and a pad, and frantically printed the information she gave him.

"It's important," Tess said. "Get here as fast as you can."

"Count on it." Craig tore off the sheet of paper, shoved the phone toward the clerk, and blurted, "Thank you."

In distress, he spun toward the doorman, thrusting twenty dollars at him. "Get me a taxi. *Now.*"

8

In the parking lot across the street from the hotel, the solemn man with a ring in his pocket straightened behind the steering wheel in the replica of the UPS truck.

Again he spoke into the cellular phone. "The bait! I see him! The detective! He's outside the hotel again. He's getting into a taxi!"

On the other end of the phone, the chameleon responded with equal intensity. "Follow him! Alert the other unit! Remain in contact. A team of enforcers is en route from LaGuardia!"

The man behind the steering wheel felt his stomach cramp as he set down the phone.

Enforcers?

He hadn't been told that this mission was considered so desperate. He had the unnerving sense that events were out of control, that brutal forces were converging, that a terrible, ultimate battle was about to begin.

Obeying instructions, he used a two-way radio to alert his other team, then twisted the ignition key, heard the engine rumble, and glanced toward the rear of the truck. There, five men waited, their expressions strained, ignoring him, rechecking their handguns.

The driver, breathing rapidly, stomped the accelerator and sped from the parking lot in pursuit of the taxi.

9

In the Marriott's lobby, a well-built, tanned, expensively dressed man in his thirties stepped through the entrance and approached the check-in desk, carrying a briefcase.

"Excuse me." His manner was deferential toward the clerk, his voice smooth but sounding concerned. "I wonder if you could help me. I had an appointment to meet a man here, but traffic delayed me. Unfortunately, I don't see him anywhere. He must have become impatient and left. I wonder if . . . Is it possible? Did he leave a message. His name was Craig."

"As a matter of fact, sir, a man by that name *was* here, and indeed he was waiting for someone," the clerk said. "A minute ago, he received a phone call and left."

The well-built man looked disappointed. "My boss . to put it mildly . . . won't be happy. My promotion's at stake. I had important contracts for Mr. Craig to sign. I don't suppose you know where he went."

"I regret to say no, sir. Mr. Craig wrote directions on that pad and tore off the sheet of paper. But he didn't mention where he was going."

"On that pad, you say?"

"That's correct, sir."

The well-built man studied the indentations that Craig's strong printing had made on the page beneath the one he'd torn off. "Did you happen to overhear the name of the person he spoke to?"

"A woman. Her name was Tess, sir."

"Of course. Well, I thank you for your trouble," the man said, giving the clerk twenty dollars.

"That's really not necessary, sir."

"Ah, but it is." The well-built man tore off the next sheet on the pad, feeling the indentations of Craig's printing. "If you don't mind."

"Not at all, sir."

"Very good."

As the well-built man walked briskly from the lobby, the clerk glanced with satisfaction at the twenty-dollar bill and thought with interest that in all his years of greeting guests, it was seldom that he'd met anyone who had gray eyes.

10

In a rush, Tess reentered the study. "Thanks for letting me use the phone."

"No need to thank us," Professor Harding said. "The main thing is, did you manage to contact the man you were supposed to meet?"

Tess nodded forcefully. "He'll be here as quickly as he can. I'll feel a *lot* better when he is. In the meantime . . ." She spun toward Priscilla. "The statue. You were about to explain what it meant. Keep talking. Why is Mithras slicing the neck of the bull?"

Priscilla shoved her glasses higher onto her nose and studied the photograph. "I can understand why you're mystified. Like most depictions of rites sacred to various religions, this object appears incomprehensible. Imagine an aborigine who's spent all his life on a small Pacific island, totally isolated, with no experience of Western customs. Imagine if he were brought to America and taken to a Catholic church. Then imagine his reaction when he saw what hung behind the altar. The statue of Christ on the cross, hands and feet pierced by nails, head crowned with thorns, side slit open, would be an absolute, horrifying mystery."

"Wait," Tess said. "After everything we've discussed, you're telling me you *don't* know what the statue means?"

"On the contrary, I *do* know what it means," Priscilla said. "What I'm getting at is that without a knowledge of the traditions and symbols of an unfamiliar religion, you can't appreciate why a particular image is important to that religion. But the moment the symbols are given meaning, the image becomes perfectly clear. To me, this statue is as easy to interpret as an image of Christ's crucifixion. Lean closer toward the photograph. Examine the details I point out. I suspect that soon you'll realize how simple they are to interpret."

"Simple?" Tess shook her head. "I really have trouble believing that."

"Just try to be patient." Priscilla placed her right index finger on the photograph. "Why don't we start with the bull? Notice that the marble of the statue is white. The *bull* is white," Priscilla said. "After his death, he'll become the moon. Logically, you might

301

expect that the bull would become the sun, given that Mithras is the sun god. But there's a deeper logic. The moon is a version of the sun at night. It illuminates the darkness, and in this case, it represents the god of light in conflict with the opposite god, the evil god, the god of darkness.''

"Okay," Tess said, "I see that logic. But what I don't is . . . Why does the bull have to *die?*''

"Did you ever read Joseph Campbell? *The Masks of God: Primitive Mythology?*''

"In college.''

"Then you ought to know that in almost every religion there's a sacrificial victim. Sometimes the god is the victim. In Christianity, for example, Jesus dies to redeem the world. But often the victim is a substitute for the god. Among the Aztecs and Mayans, they frequently chose a maiden, who gave up her life as a surrogate for, a sacrifice to, the god. The most common method was to cut out her heart.''

Tess winced.

Priscilla continued, "In the case of Mithras, the bull dies not only to become the moon but to give life to the earth. The ritual execution probably happened during the vernal equinox . . . the arrival of spring . . . to regenerate the world. It's a traditionally sanctified time of the year. Most Christians don't know it, but that's the reason Easter is so important in their religion. When Christ leaves the tomb just as the earth comes back to life. And Mithras, too, came back to life in the spring.''

Tess struggled to concentrate, her forehead aching with intense frustration.

"Regeneration," Priscilla said. "Out of death comes life. That's why Mithras slices the throat of the bull. There has to be blood. A great deal of blood. The blood cascades toward the ground. It nourishes the soil. You can see grain sprouting from the ground near the bull's front knee. Many ancient religions required blood— sometimes human, sometimes animal—to be sprinkled on the fields before the crops were planted.''

"But that's repulsive.''

"Not if you believed. It's no more repulsive than the impli- cations of communion in the Catholic Church, swallowing bread and wine that symbolize the body and blood of Christ to regenerate your soul.''

"Okay,'' Tess said. "Point granted, although I never thought about it that way before. But what about the dog in the statue? Why is the dog lunging toward the blood? And why is the serpent—?''

With a tingle that swept from her feet to her head, Tess abruptly realized. Dear Lord, Priscilla had been right. Everything was suddenly, vividly clear. "The dog and the serpent!''

"What about them? Can you tell me?'' Priscilla's eyes gleamed.

"They represent evil! The dog is trying to stop the blood from reaching the ground and fertilizing the soil! The serpent wants to destroy the wheat! And the scorpion's evil, too! It's attacking the bull's testicles, the source of the bull's virility!''

"Excellent. I'm proud of you, Tess. Keep going. Can you tell me about the torchbearers?''

"The flame pointing upward signifies Mithras. The flame pointing downward represents his evil competition.''

"You must have been a brilliant student.''

"Not according to your husband,'' Tess said.

Professor Harding set down his teacup. "What I said was, you weren't my *best* student. But you were bright enough and certainly enthusiastic.''

"Right now, 'enthusiastic' doesn't describe what I'm feeling. I'm grieving for my mother. I'm desperate. I'm scared. The raven, Priscilla. Tell me about the raven.''

"Yes.'' Priscilla sighed. "The raven. On the left, from above the upraised torch, on the side of good, he watches the sacrifice. You have to understand. Mithraism had seven stages of membership, from beginners to priests. And the first stage was called the raven. As it happens, the raven was also the sacred bird in their religion. It was a messenger sent from heaven, ordered to witness the ritual sacrifice, to observe the renewal of the world, the death of the bull, the blood cascading toward the earth, the return of spring, the fertilization of the soil.''

"Now I understand too well.'' Tess quivered. "It's what I've devoted my life to. Mithras wants to save the planet, and his evil counterpart wants to destroy it.''

11

Lima, Peru

Charles Gordon, a short, frail importer-exporter, slumped behind his desk. Although his office window overlooked the Rímac River, he ignored the dismal view and did his best to concentrate on a catalogue of the various American products that he'd tried, with little success, to sell to local merchants. His gaudy bow tie and ill-fitting suit had attracted smirks from the local population when he'd rented this office a month ago, but his clothes were now an accepted, tired joke that made him in effect invisible.

Bored, his only consolation was that Lima was only seven miles from the Pacific. This close to the sea, the temperature was moderate, the drab city far enough from the towering mountains to the east that the air was breathable. No high-altitude wheezing for him. In that respect, this assignment wasn't bad. Except that the operative who called himself Charles Gordon got tired of the charade involved in pretending to conduct a profit-earning business.

He had a business, all right.

But it wasn't import-export.

No, his business was death, and profit, in the normal sense of the word, had never been his motive.

As the brochure in his hands drooped, the trilling bell on his fax machine made him jerk upright. He quickly stood, crossed toward a table on his left, and watched a page unroll from the fax machine.

The message was from the Philadelphia office of his American supplier, notifying him that a shipment of laptop computers would soon be arriving. The message gave the quantity, the price, and the date of shipment.

Well, finally, Charles Gordon thought.

It didn't trouble him that so sensitive a message had been sent via his easily accessed telephone line. After all, his American supplier was, to all appearances, a legitimate corporation, and the laptop computers would arrive as promised. Even if someone suspected that the message was in code, no one could decipher its true meaning—because the code had been chosen arbitrarily. Kenneth Madden, the CIA's deputy director of covert operations, had explained it to Gordon the evening before the operative had flown to Peru.

The date of the shipment had nothing to do with the date of the mission. The quantity and the price of the laptop computers were irrelevant. What the message referred to was President Garth's imminent trip to Peru for a drug-control conference. The president's intention was to attempt to convince the Peruvian government to pay subsidies to farmers who switched to less lucrative crops than the easy-to-grow coca plants that local drug lords, among the world's major suppliers, needed to make cocaine.

But the President would never reach the conference.

12

Tess hesitated. In the study in the Victorian mansion near Georgetown, a memory nagged at her subconsciousness. In a flash, it surfaced. "But what about the treasure?"

Priscilla frowned, puzzled by Tess's abrupt change of topic.

"Before I used the phone, you mentioned a mysterious treasure," Tess said. "In southwestern France, in the thirteenth century."

"Ah." Priscilla nodded. "Yes. When the Catholic crusaders killed tens of thousands of heretics to eradicate a new version of Mithraism."

"You called it Albigensianism," Tess said. "The last stronghold of the heretics was a mountain fortress."

"Montségur." Priscilla squinted.

"And you said that the night before the final massacre"—Tess trembled—"a small group of heretics used ropes to descend from the mountain, taking with them a mysterious treasure."

"A rumor. A persistent legend, although as I mentioned, it could have some basis in fact. Since Mithraism survives in India, it might have survived in Europe as well. A small group conducting its rites in secret. To avoid the Inquisition."

"*If so*"—Tess raised her voice in frustration—"*what would the treasure have been?*"

Priscilla shrugged. "The obvious answer is wealth of some sort. Gold. Precious gems. Indeed, as recently as the Second World War, the Nazis believed that such a treasure existed and was hidden in the area near Montségur. Hitler sent an archaeologist, a team of engineers, and an SS unit to search for it in the numerous caves in the region. Evidence of their excavations can still be found. However, the treasure was not. At least, no one ever indicated that a treasure had been discovered, and surely, given something so dramatic, word would have spread. Then, too, another theory is that the treasure was the Holy Grail, the chalice from Christ's Last Supper. And still another theory claims that the treasure was a person, that Christ—contrary to tradition—married and had a son, a descendant of whom was the leader of the Albigensians. Those latter theories were made popular in a book called *Holy Blood, Holy Grail*. But those latter theories are nonsense, of course. Because the Albigensians had only a superficial resemblance to Catholics. They descended from a tradition much older than Christianity, one that happened to use rituals similar to those of Christianity, but that in fact was based on the theology—opposing good and evil gods— of Mithraism. The heretics would have had no respect for the so-called Holy Grail, and they wouldn't have cared if Christ had a son who established a bloodline. No," Priscilla said, "whatever the treasure, assuming it even existed, it more than likely was the obvious: wealth."

Tess breathed with excitement, although her excitement was tinged with fear. "I disagree."

Priscilla adjusted her glasses, confused. "Oh?"

"I think there *was* a treasure. Not wealth. At least not in the ordinary sense, although it definitely was mysterious."

Professor Harding leaned forward, propping his hands on his cane. "I confess you've made me curious. What are you suggesting?"

Tess rubbed her forehead. "If the heretics feared that their religion was about to be destroyed, if a small group managed to escape"—she darted her eyes toward Priscilla, then Professor Harding—"what's the one thing those heretics would have considered so important that they wouldn't have dared to leave without it?"

Professor Harding frowned. "I still don't follow."

Priscilla's eyes, however, gleamed with fascination.

"The treasure without which the heretics had no meaning," Tess said. "Something so valuable that they couldn't allow it to be destroyed and equally important, *desecrated*. Something mysterious in the deepest sense of the word. Something so . . ."

"Sacred," Priscilla blurted. "Absolutely."

"You understand?"

"Yes!" Priscilla gestured emphatically toward the photograph. "The image of Mithras that stood on their altar! When Constantine converted to Christianity, the Christians destroyed the Mithraic chapels. For all the heretics at Montségur knew, the sculpture *they* possessed might have been the only one in existence. If they left it behind, when the crusaders found it—"

Tess anticipated, "The crusaders would have smashed it to pieces. The heretics *had* to protect the statue in order to protect their religion." In imitation of Priscilla's earlier gesture, Tess jabbed a finger at the photograph. "That statue. There's no weathering on its marble. No cracks. It's in perfect condition. A pristine replication of an ancient model. To borrow your words, someone went to a great deal of trouble and expense to reproduce that statue. Why? It makes no sense unless . . . I think I know the answer. It terrifies me. God, I think that statue's a copy of the one from Montségur, but I don't think it's the *only* copy, and I *don't* think . . ." Tess stared at Priscilla. "We've been talking around this possibility all afternoon, so why don't I say it outright? My friend *believed* in

Mithraism. There are others who believe as he did. *They're* the ones who killed my mother, who killed Brian Hamilton, and who tried to kill me. To stop anyone from knowing about their existence."

"Fire," Priscilla interrupted.

"What about it?" Tess struggled to control her shaking.

"You said your friend was killed with fire."

"And then his apartment was set on fire, and my mother's house was set on fire, and Brian Hamilton died in flames in a freeway accident. Why is fire so—?"

"It purifies. It symbolizes divine energy. Out of the ashes comes life. Rebirth. Fire was sacred to Mithraism. The sun god. When the torch is held upward, it signifies good."

"But how can all of this killing be good?"

Priscilla suddenly looked aged again. "I'm afraid there are two things I haven't told you about Mithraism."

Apprehensive, Tess waited, trembling.

"First," Priscilla said, "followers of Mithras, particularly those in the Albigensian sect, the ones at Montségur, believed in reincarnation. To them, death was not an ultimate end but merely a beginning of another life, until finally—after many lives—their being was perfected and they went to heaven. In that respect, they believed in the theories of Plato."

Tess remembered that *The Collected Dialogues of Plato* was one of the book's in Joseph's bedroom. "Keep going."

"The point is," Priscilla said, "a follower of Mithras was able to kill without guilt because he believed that he wasn't ending someone's life but merely transforming it."

Tess was appalled. "You said there were *two* things. What's the . . . ?"

"Second, followers of Mithras were used to killing. They were *trained* to kill. Don't forget the statue. The knife. The blood. Roman soldiers converted *en masse.* Mithraism was a warrior cult. By definition. In their souls, they believed that they were engaged in a cosmic struggle of good against evil."

"The bastards," Tess said. "To defeat what they thought was evil, they'd do anything!"

"I'm afraid that's true."

"They'd kill *anyone,* including my mother!" Tess raged. "The sons of . . . ! When I get the chance—and I'm sure I will because I'm sure they'll come for me again—they'll learn the *hard* way about the difference between good and evil!"

13

As the taxi rounded a corner and proceeded along a street of well-maintained, century-old houses near Georgetown, Craig stiffened in the backseat, seeing a black Porsche 911 parked ahead at the curb. Abruptly he leaned forward, pointing urgently. "There," he told the driver. "Where that sports car . . ."

"Yeah." The driver scanned the numbers on houses. "That's the address you want, all right."

Craig glanced behind him, checking yet again to make sure he hadn't been followed. There wasn't much traffic. A few cars passed through an intersection back there. A UPS truck turned at the corner but headed in the opposite direction from where the taxi had gone. Halfway down the other block, the truck stopped. A uniformed driver got out, carrying a box toward a house.

Craig had seen several UPS trucks on his way here. They were as commonplace as Federal Express and post office trucks. He had no way to tell if that particular truck had been tailing him. Indeed, contrary to popular misconception, Craig knew that unless you had a team using various cars to help you, or unless your opponent was clumsy, it was almost impossible to spot motorized surveillance, especially if your enemy also had a team and alternated vehicles.

Well, Craig thought with growing unease as the taxi stopped behind the Porsche, I've done what I could. I can't keep cruising around the city. I've got to make a choice. I've got to commit. Tess is waiting for me. She needs my help.

Nervous, Craig paid the driver and left the taxi. While it drove away, he studied the Victorian house, saw colorful, high-stalked flowers along the side, and wondered what on earth Tess was doing here. In a rush, he approached the front steps.

14

"Sorry. Wrong address," the solemn man with a ring in his pocket told the woman whose doorbell he'd just pressed. "My mistake. This package belongs down the block."

The woman had curlers in her hair and looked annoyed that she'd been interrupted. Inside the house, a TV game-show host announced outstanding prizes, his audience applauding.

"Really, my apologies," the man said. He wore the brown uniform of a UPS delivery man. When he turned to carry the package back to his truck, he heard the woman slam the door behind him.

At the truck, he climbed behind the steering wheel and turned to the five men in back. They had their handguns ready and ignored him, their concentration focused toward the rear window and the taxi pulling away from the Porsche parked in front of a house in the middle of the next block. The tall, rugged detective stood on the sidewalk for a moment, then disappeared past trees and bushes, approaching the house.

"Well, this might be another false rendezvous, but it's my guess that the bait led us to the quarry," the solemn man said, and closed his door. "Now all we have to do is wait for the vermin."

"Assuming they followed him as well. But we didn't see any sign of them," one of the men in the back said.

"Just as *we* were careful and hope that *they* didn't see any sign of *us*," the man in front said. "We know, however, that their only chance to find the woman is to follow the detective."

In back, someone murmured, "I'll feel more confident when our other unit shows up."

The man in front nodded. "And even *more* confident when the enforcers arrive. I called our man at the airport. He'll instruct them where we've gone."

Another man in back asked, "How long will they take to—"

"Their plane lands in half an hour," the man in front said. "Figure another twenty minutes after that. We've got a car waiting to bring the enforcers."

"In which case, we just have to hope that the vermin don't make their move before . . . Wait a moment. I see a car."

The gunmen stared out the rear window.

"It isn't our other unit," one of them breathed.

The man in front concentrated. Through the rear window, he saw a blue Toyota round the corner, approaching. A thirtyish man drove, an attractive woman beside him.

"Do you think it might be—?"

"They probably live in the neighborhood. But if they *are* the vermin, they've made a mistake." The man in front drew his pistol. "Six against two. They're outnumbered."

The car passed the truck's back window, no longer in sight. As the solemn man turned toward his sideview mirror to watch the car continue forward, he flinched.

The woman hurled a canister through his open window.

The canister hissed.

The car kept driving down the street.

"No!" the solemn man screamed.

At once he shuddered and slumped. Invisible nerve gas filled the truck. The men behind him scrambled to open the back door.

Too late. As the gas touched their skin, they convulsed, voided their bowels, vomited, and lay still.

15

———

"But what about the photograph of the books?" Tess demanded. "Do their titles mean anything?"

Priscilla removed a magnifying glass from a drawer in the desk and held it over the photograph. *"Eleanor of Aquitaine . . . The Art of Courtly Love . . ."*

"The one in Spanish means *The Dove's Neck Ring,"* Tess said.

"I know. It's another treatise on courtly love. Eleventh century as I recall."

Tess blinked in surprise. "You can't imagine the trouble I went through to learn that, and you just . . ."

"Hey, it's my specialty, remember?" Priscilla's wrinkled lips formed a modest smile. "These titles are all related. It's just like with the sculpture. Once you understand the background, everything's clear. Eleanor was the Queen of France during the century before the fall of Montségur. Aquitaine, where Eleanor came from, was in southwestern France. She established—and her daughter, Marie de France, continued to maintain—a royal court in that region."

Tess nodded, having learned that much when she'd read the introduction to *The Dove's Neck Ring* the previous night at her mother's home, just before the fire had . . . !

With a shudder, grieving, she forced herself not to interrupt.

"Southwestern France," Priscilla emphasized. "Where Mithraism resurfaced, in the form of the Albigensian heresy, shortly after Eleanor's death. Eleanor encouraged the notion of courtly love, a strict set of rules that idealized the relationship between men and women. Physical union wasn't permitted until after a stringent code of overly polite behavior was obeyed. The Albigensians adapted courtly love for their own purposes. To them, after all, the good that Mithras fought for was spiritual. The evil of the opposing god

was physical, belonging to the world and the flesh. For example, Albigensians were vegetarians, allowing only the purest of foods to enter their bodies.''

"My *friend* was a vegetarian.'' Tess felt startled.

"Of course. And I imagine he didn't drink alcohol.''

"Right,'' Tess said.

"And he exercised rigorously.''

"Yes!''

"He needed to deny and control his flesh,'' Priscilla said. "It's what I'd expect from someone who believed in Mithras. But the Albigensians also believed that sex was impure, that carnal desires were one of the ways that the evil god tempted them. So they abstained, except for rare occasions, allowing intercourse only for the exclusive purpose of conceiving children. A necessary, grudging surrender to the flesh. Otherwise their community would have dwindled and died. With that rare exception, in the place of sexual relations, they substituted highly formal, immensely polite *social* relations that they borrowed from the concept of courtly love.''

"My friend insisted that we could never be lovers, never have sex,'' Tess said. "He claimed he had certain obligations he had to follow. The most we could ever have was what he called a platonic relationship.''

"Of course.'' Priscilla shrugged. "Plato. Another of the books on the shelf in this photograph. According to Plato, the physical world is insubstantial. A higher level should be our goal. You see how it all comes together?''

"But what about . . . ?''

The doorbell rang. Tess had become so absorbed by the conversation that the sudden disturbance made her flinch. At once she realized.

It must be—

Priscilla jerked up her head, anticipating. "I imagine that's your other friend. The one you phoned from here a while ago. The man who expected you to meet him near the airport.''

Tess stared toward the exit from the study. "God, I hope. Priscilla . . . Professor Harding . . . I have to explain. My friend's a . . .''

"No need to explain," Professor Harding said. "Any friend of yours is welcome here."

"But you have to understand! He's not just a *friend*. He's—"

Again the doorbell rang.

"—a policeman. A detective from New York's Missing Persons." Tess reached inside her canvas purse. "But maybe I'm wrong. Maybe it's someone else. What if it's—?" She withdrew the handgun from the purse.

Priscilla and Professor Harding blanched at the sight of it.

Grasping the trigger, Tess ordered, "Hide in that closet. Don't make a sound. If it's *them* and they kill me, if they come in here and take the photographs, they might be satisfied. They might not search the house! They might not find—!"

The doorbell rang a third time.

"I shouldn't have come here! I hope I haven't—!" Tess couldn't wait any longer. "Pray!"

She lunged from the study, assumed the stance her father had taught her, aimed her handgun down the hallway toward the front door, and said a silent prayer of thanks when she saw Craig's tense, confused face through the window in the door.

As he pressed the bell yet again, Tess hurried along the hallway, yanked the door open, and tugged him inside, thrusting her arms around him. "I've never been so glad to see anyone in my life."

With her left hand, she slammed the door shut behind them, leaned past him to lock it, and hugged him even harder.

"Ouch!" Craig said. "I hope that pistol isn't cocked! You're pressing its handle against my back!"

"Oh." Tess lowered the pistol. "I'm sorry! I didn't mean to—"

Wary, Craig glanced at the pistol. "Good, it *isn't* cocked. Where did you *get* that? Do you know how to use it?"

"Yes. A *very* long story. Craig, I've learned so much! I've got so much to tell you!"

"And I want to hear it, believe me." Craig hugged her in return. "I've been so worried about you. I—"

Tess felt Craig's reassuring arms around her. She felt her breasts against his chest, her nipples unexpectedly tingling. The warmth surging through her was equally unexpected. Responding to an irresistible impulse, she kissed him. In the midst of fear, the pleasure she received from Craig's embrace was like . . .

She'd been meant to be in his arms . . .

Craig's lips against hers . . .

Hers against his . . .

From the moment they'd met.

Abruptly Tess felt suffocated. Pushing away, sliding her hands from Craig's back, around his broad shoulders, toward his firm chest, she peered upward, straining to catch her breath. She studied his strong-boned, hard-edged features, which suddenly struck her as being handsome, and told herself, screw love at *first* sight. *Second* sight is better. It gives you a chance to think, to get your priorities straight. Passion is fine. But devotion and understanding are better.

This man—whatever mistakes he made in his marriage—never mind what happened before I met him—is decent and kind. He cares for me. He's willing to risk his life to help me.

He doesn't just love me.

He *likes* me.

Someone discreetly cleared a throat behind them.

Turning, Tess saw Priscilla and Professor Harding standing self-consciously in the hallway near the door from the study.

"I'm sorry for interrupting," Professor Harding said, "but . . ."

"No need to feel sorry." Tess smiled. "And we don't have to worry."

"I gathered that," Priscilla said, her wrinkled eyes crinkling with amusement, "from the way you greeted him."

Tess blushed. "This is my friend. Lieutenant Craig. His first name's . . . You know," she told Craig, "you never mentioned it to me. But on your answering machine, I heard . . ."

"It's Bill." Craig walked down the hallway, extending his hand. "Bill Craig. If you're friends of Tess . . ."

"Oh, definitely," Tess said.

"Then I'm very pleased to meet you." Craig shook hands with them.

"Mr. and Mrs. Harding," Tess said. "They're both professors."

"Please, Tess, I told you no formalities." Priscilla gave her first name to Craig. "And this is Richard, my husband. And don't you dare refer to either of us as professor."

Craig chuckled. "I can already see that we're going to get along." His expression sobered. "But Priscilla . . . Richard . . . we have things to discuss. *Important* things. And time's against us. So why don't you bring me up to speed? What are you doing here, Tess? What's going on?"

Priscilla gestured. "Come into the study."

"And perhaps you'd like some tea," Professor Harding said.

"Richard, for heaven's sake, the lieutenant came here to help Tess, not to be offered tea."

"Actually I could use a cup," Craig said. "My mouth's dry from being on the plane."

They entered the study.

For the next fifteen minutes, while Craig politely sipped tea, he listened impatiently to what Tess . . . and then Priscilla . . . and on occasion, Richard . . . told him.

When they finished, Craig set down his cup. "If I told this to my captain, he'd think you were, to put it politely, letting your imaginations get carried away. But never mind. *I* believe—because I saw the statue. And Joseph Martin's dead. And Tess, your *mother's* dead." He shook his head in commiseration. "And Brian Hamilton's dead. And *you're* in danger. All because of—"

"Something that happened more than seven hundred years ago," Priscilla said.

"What *else* haven't you talked about?" Craig asked.

"The titles of the books on the shelf in Joseph Martin's bedroom," Priscilla said. "Before you rang the doorbell, I was about to explain that *The Consolation of Philosophy,* a sixth-century treatise written by an imprisoned Roman nobleman, describes the wheel of fortune."

Craig shook his head, confused.

"An image for the ups and downs of success and failure. The book analyses and condemns the physical values—wealth, power, and fame—by which people addicted to worldly success are tempted and ultimately disappointed. Because physical values are temporary and insubstantial. It's exactly the type of book that someone who believed in the spiritual values of Mithras would find appealing."

"Okay." Craig frowned. "But why did Joseph Martin keep a copy of the Bible? That doesn't fit. From what you've told me, Mithraism doesn't believe in Christianity."

"True," Priscilla said. "Their theologies are different, but both religions share similar rites, and both reject worldly goals. For Joseph to read the Bible would be comparable to a Christian reading about Zen Buddhism, for example, because its mystical basis was different from but could be applied to his own religion."

"Anyway, Joseph didn't read the *entire* Bible," Tess said. "He ripped out most of the pages, except for the editor's introduction and the sections written by John. I don't understand. Why the preference for John?"

Priscilla raised her shoulders. "Because John's sections in the Bible most closely approximate the teachings of Mithraism. Here." She held her magnifying glass over a photograph that showed a page and a passage that Joseph Martin had underlined in one of John's epistles. " 'Love not the world. If any man love the world, the Father is not in him. For all that is in the world—the lust of the flesh, the lust of the eyes, and the pride of the world—is not of the Father but is of the world. And the world passeth away, and the lust of it, but he that doeth the will of God abideth forever.' Does that sound familiar?"

Tess nodded soberly. "Take away the reference to the Father, substitute Mithras, and it matches everything you've told me."

"But there's something *I* don't understand," Craig said. "Why the *Scofield* edition of the Bible? Is *that* significant?"

"Oh, very much," Priscilla said. "When Ronald Reagan was president, most of America's foreign policy was based on Scofield's interpretation of the Bible." She studied another photograph. "Here's an underlined section from Scofield's introduction. 'The Bible documents the beginning of human history and its end.' " Priscilla glanced up. "The climax of the Bible, John's Book of Revelation, describes the end of the world. Ronald Reagan believed that the end—the Apocalypse—was about to occur, that a cosmic battle between good and evil, God and Satan, was about to take place. Remember all that business about the Soviets being the evil empire? Reagan also believed that in the cosmic battle, goodness would triumph. I suspect that's why he encouraged confrontation with the Soviets, to begin Armageddon, with the total confidence that the United States—in his opinion, the only good—would triumph.''

''Madness,'' Craig said.

''But also very much like Mithraism, provided you think of Satan as an evil god and not a fallen angel,'' Priscilla said. ''In that respect, it's not at all surprising that Joseph Martin kept an abbreviated version of this Bible near his bedside.''

''Keep going,'' Craig said. ''The other books I saw on Joseph Martin's shelf. *The Millennium. The Last Days of the Planet Earth.*''

Priscilla set down the magnifying glass. ''Obviously, Joseph Martin was obsessed by the impending year two thousand. Each millennium is a traditional time of crisis, every thousand years a time of fear, an apprehension that the world will disintegrate.''

''And this time,'' Professor Harding said, ''given the poisons that wither my lilies, the prediction might not be wrong. *The Last Days of the Planet Earth?* I thank the Lord I'll be dead before that happens.''

''Richard, if you die before me, I'll never forgive you,'' Priscilla said.

Craig, despite his distress, couldn't help smiling. ''I wish my former marriage had been as good as yours.''

''We survive,'' Priscilla said.

''Yes,'' Craig said. ''Survival.'' He put his hand on Tess's shoulder.

Electricity jumped, making her tingle.

Craig stood. ''I'd better phone the Alexandria police chief. He and I will get you to a safe house, Tess. Richard and Priscilla, you'll be out of this. In no danger.''

''I hope,'' Tess said.

''The nearest phone is in the kitchen.'' Professor Harding pointed. ''To the left. Down the hallway.''

With fondness, Tess watched Craig start to leave.

But at once Craig hesitated and swung back, frowning. ''There's one thing I still don't understand. Nothing you've said explains it. I'm really bugged by . . . Tess, if Joseph Martin believed in Mithras, and if the people trying to kill you believe in Mithras, why did they kill *him?*''

The study became silent. No one was able to answer.

Craig frowned harder. "I mean, it just doesn't make sense. Why did they turn against one of their own?" Shaking his head in confusion, he continued from the study.

Yes, Tess thought. Why did they hunt Joseph down and set fire to him? Troubled by the question, she watched Craig enter the hallway.

16

And abruptly she frowned even harder than Craig had.

Because Craig didn't pivot to the left toward the phone in the kitchen, as he'd been told.

Instead he paused, glanced sharply to the right, and dove to the floor, at the same time drawing his revolver.

No! Tess thought.

With a cringe, she heard two muffled spits, then the ear-stunning roar of Craig's revolver. Once! Twice!

Priscilla screamed.

Craig surged from the floor, scrambling down the corridor to his right.

Despite the ringing in her ears, Tess heard a man groaning. Paralysis seized her. Biting her lip, she forced herself into action, grabbed her pistol, and lunged toward the hallway. The stench of cordite assaulted her nostrils. Spinning, using the doorjamb for cover, aiming to the right, she saw two men sprawled on the floor in the hallway. Craig kicked pistols from their hands, leapt over their bodies, and slammed the front door shut, locking it, crouching below the door's window.

But I shut and locked that door after Craig arrived! Tess thought. How did—?

One of the men kept groaning. With a sudden gagging sound, he trembled and no longer moved. A pool of blood widened on the hardwood floor around both men. Stunned, Tess gaped at the crimson stain on each man's chest, where Craig's bullets had struck them.

Adrenaline scalded through her. Even so, Tess felt cold. She stared past the corpses toward their pistols, more appalled, noting that the weapons were equipped with silencers.

"Get down!" Craig ordered, checking to make sure that the men were dead.

Tess hurriedly obeyed. "How did they—?"

"Picked the lock!" Craig said. "They must have listened outside the study window! They knew where we were! They decided to take the chance that we wouldn't hear them sneak inside!" Staying low, he risked furtive glances through the door's window, tensely darting his gaze this way and that, scanning the porch. "I don't see any other—"

"The back door!" Tess said. In a rush, she turned, charging down the hallway toward the kitchen.

"Be careful!" Craig warned.

She barely heard him, too preoccupied by an urgent fear.

The hallway became a blur.

But the moment Tess entered the kitchen, she saw with appalling clarity.

Outside, on the back porch, a man smashed his gloved fist through the kitchen door's window.

Tess heard shards of glass fall, crashing into smaller pieces on the floor. At the same instant, the man thrust his hand through the jagged hole in the window, groping for the lock.

Tess raised her pistol and fired.

The man's right eye exploded.

Tess didn't have time to react to the horror.

Too much! Because behind the falling man, *another* man raised a pistol with a silencer.

Tess was far beyond conscious decisions. Automatically, she pulled the trigger again. Her ears rang as she shot the man in the forehead. In a spray of blood, the man arched up, then down, disappearing, his no-longer-visible body thumping heavily on the back porch.

"Tess!" Craig yelled from the front of the house. *"Are you—?"*

"All right! Yes! I'm all right!" Tess ducked behind the kitchen table, aiming toward the back door. "God held me, I just shot two men!"

"Don't think about it! Remember, they wanted to shoot *you!*"

"Hey, I'm too scared to think! All I want to do is stay alive!"

"Grab the phone! Dial nine one one!"

Tess scuttled backward, aiming her pistol toward the back door. She yanked the kitchen phone off the hook beside the refrigerator and urgently pressed numbers, listening.

"Craig, the phone's dead!"

Priscilla screamed again.

"Stay low, Priscilla! Don't go near the windows!" Craig yelled.

"My husband!"

"What about him?"

"I think he's having a heart attack!"

"Get him down on the floor! Open his collar!" Tess shouted.

Another assassin appeared at the kitchen window.

Tess aimed and shot. The bullet plowed up his nostrils. His face erupted.

Tess bent over, vomiting.

"Tess!" Craig roared.

She fought to speak. "I'm all right! Keep watching the front!"

Priscilla screamed again. "Richard isn't breathing!"

"Tess!" Craig ordered. "Get back to the hallway! Watch the front and rear while I—"

"Yes! Take care of Richard!"

Tess retreated, hunkering midway along the corridor, jerking her gaze toward each door, pistol clenched, while she felt Craig lunge past her and into the study. Still sick, wiping vomit from her lips, she heard Craig press Richard's chest and breathe forcefully into his mouth, again, then again, administering CPR.

"I can feel his heartbeat!" Craig said. "He's breathing!"

"He needs oxygen! A doctor!" Tess kept staring back and forth toward each door.

"Priscilla, your face is gray! Lie down here beside your husband! *Tess, any sign of—?"*

"No! Maybe we got them all!"

"We don't dare count on that! *Priscilla, is there another entrance to the house?"*

Priscilla murmured, "Through the basement."

"Where's the inside basement door?"

"The kitchen." Priscilla sounded weaker.

"Tess!" Craig ordered.

But Tess was already on her way, darting toward the kitchen. Behind her, she heard Craig enter the hallway, watching the front.

As she reached the kitchen, Tess heard something else, however, and the sound made her spine freeze. Footsteps beyond a door to her right. She whirled to face it, saw the doorknob turning, and fired at the door. Wood splintered. She fired again and heard a moan, a body tumbling down the stairs.

She didn't know how many others might be in the basement. If there were several and they rushed through the door in a group, she might not be able to shoot all of them before one of them shot *her.*

The basement door was next to the stove. With strength that came from years of daily workouts, her energy intensified by fear, she shoved against the side of the stove and propped it against the basement door.

"The neighbors, Craig! They must have heard the shots! They'll call the police! All we have to do is wait and hope the police can get here before—"

Craig didn't answer.

"What's wrong?"

"You don't want to know!" Craig said.

"Tell me!"

"These big old Victorian houses were built so solidly . . . The walls are so thick . . . From outside, the shots might be too muffled for anyone to hear from another house. Besides, we can't take for granted that the neighbors are even home. And the hedge on each side conceals the gunmen!"

Tess felt sick again. "You're right, I wish I didn't know!" She kept her weapon aimed toward the back door.

In contrast with last night, *this* time she'd counted how many times she'd pulled the trigger. Five. That left twelve rounds in her pistol. If the gunmen rushed the house, she might have enough to kill them all.

But how many more could there be? Six were already dead. Surely just a few, if any, were left. All the same, she desperately wished that she'd thought to dump extra rounds into her purse, that she hadn't shoved the two boxes of ammunition under the front seat of the Porsche.

"Craig, you shot twice! Your revolver holds six! Have you got any other—?"

Yet again Craig didn't answer.

Oh, Jesus, Tess thought. He's got only four rounds left, and my bullets don't fit his revolver.

"I picked up the two pistols from the men on the floor at the front. I still don't see any *other* men. Maybe you're right! Maybe we got them all!" Craig said.

"Last night, they burned my mother's house, hoping the fire would get me. And if it didn't, they planned to shoot me when I hurried outside!" Tess said. "*This* time, why didn't they—?"

"Late afternoon, the smoke would be so obvious that a neighbor or a passing driver would call the fire department! Besides, since you got away from them last night, I think this time they want to make sure they finish the job, face-to-face, no doubts! And they want to make sure they get the photographs!"

"I mailed your office the negatives!"

"Good! Priscilla, how's Richard?"

Tess heard her murmur. "His eyes are open. He's breathing. But . . ." Priscilla whimpered.

"What?"

"He can't . . . Richard can't seem to talk."

Tess cringed. A stroke? No! Please, not . . . ! I shouldn't have come here. I shouldn't have put them in danger. "Priscilla, I'm sorry! I—"

"*You* didn't do this. The men who want to kill you did."

"Still no sign of them in front!" Craig said.

"Nothing back here!" Tess crouched behind the kitchen table.

"I'm soon going to need my insulin," Priscilla said.

"I'll get it for you!" Tess kept low, watching the back door while she inched toward the refrigerator. "Craig, what if—? Suppose we *didn't* get them all!" When she opened the refrigerator, with a quick glance she saw a row of loaded syringes and grabbed one. "Suppose a few of them are still outside!" She closed the refrigerator. "Suppose they're afraid that a neighbor *did* hear the shots. They can't wait around. But they'll want to make sure I'm—!" She backed nervously toward the corridor, her left hand cradling the syringe. "They might get desperate enough to try what they did last—"

17

"Night," she began to say, but flinched as an object smashed through the big kitchen window, glass flying.

The object was metal.

A canister.

It banged on the floor.

A grenade?

A gas bomb?

Tess had no way of knowing.

All she did know was that the thing was rolling toward her. She couldn't get away in time! She had to—!

She dropped the syringe, barely hearing it shatter as she lunged toward the kitchen table and heaved it over so its top landed on the canister.

At the same time, her heart pounding, the canister blasted apart, flames whooshing sideways from beneath the tabletop.

A *fire* bomb.

"Craig!"

He didn't respond.

"Craig!"

In the front of the hallway, glass fractured.

"Craig!"

"They're—!"

Something exploded. Flames reflected down the corridor.

"Priscilla, a fire extinguisher!" Craig yelled. *Have you got a—"*

"In the pantry." Priscilla's voice shook. "Next to the refrigerator."

"I'm getting it!" Tess scrambled past the fridge and yanked open a door.

Next to shelves of boxes and cans, the fire extinguisher was mounted to a clamp on a wall. She rammed her pistol under her belt, grabbed the fire extinguisher with one hand, released the clamp with the other, then pulled out the pin that secured the extinguisher's lever, and spun toward the flames gushing from beneath and eating through the overturned table.

Desperate, she aimed the extinguisher's nozzle, pressed the level down, and spewed a thick white spray toward the blaze.

Foam gushed over the table, over the flames.

Coughing from smoke, Tess inwardly shouted in triumph as the flames diminished.

But another canister crashed through the window. As it landed, *before* it erupted, Tess tried to smother it with a dense pile of foam.

Whump! The canister blew apart, chunks of metal bursting through the foam. Tess kept aiming the nozzle, spraying the flames, which struggled, dying.

"Tess!" Craig yelled from the front. "I need that extinguisher!"

Trembling, she glared at the kitchen window, saw no one, and darted into the hallway, stunned, unable to see the front door because of the spreading blaze. In a frenzy, she pressed the extinguisher's lever again, spraying foam toward the flames.

Craig didn't try to take the extinguisher from her, realizing she had control. "Someone has to check the back!" he blurted. "I'll trade places!" He was gone.

Tess kept spraying.

The flames diminished.

Then the *foam* diminished.

Abruptly it stopped.

We've got to get out of here! Tess thought. Throwing down the empty extinguisher, she ran toward the study.

On the floor, Professor Harding blinked with a look of helplessness. Beside him, Priscilla quivered, her face gray, terrified.

Tess tried not to show her own fear. "Can you walk, Priscilla? Can you reach the hallway?"

"Do I have a choice?"

Their next target might be this study, Tess kept thinking. If they throw a fire bomb through the study's window . . . !

She scooped up the photographs, crammed them into her purse, slung the purse across her shoulder, and bent toward Professor Harding.

He lay on a carpet. Grabbing its end, she tugged both it and the limp weight of Professor Harding across the floor into the hallway, joining Priscilla, who sagged against a wall.

At the front of the hallway, the flames spread, their roar increasing.

Crash! A canister hurtled through the study window. Fire gushed over the desk, the chairs, the floor.

"Let's go, Priscilla!" Tess gripped the carpet, dragging Professor Harding toward the kitchen.

Another canister must have landed there. To the left of the refrigerator, the room was ablaze.

Craig wheezed, enveloped with smoke, his revolver aimed toward the kitchen door. "They'll be waiting for us!" He fought to breathe.

"The paths in the garden!" Tess said. "If we can get there, the flowers are tall enough to hide us!"

"But what about Priscilla and Richard? How are we going to—?"

Tess whirled toward Priscilla, realizing that the aged woman wasn't strong enough to drag her husband to safety. The flames became more powerful. Tess winced from the heat. "Craig, you'll have to go ahead!"

"But I can't leave you!"

"We'll die if we stay here! There isn't another—! Go! I'll be right behind you! Reach the garden, then cover me!"

Craig hesitated.

The flames roared toward them, singeing.

"Open the door!" Tess said.

Craig stared, then nodded. With fierce resolve, he jerked the door open and raced outside.

For a fraction of an instant, Tess's mind played a trick. The afternoon changed to night. This house became her mother's house.

It was happening again! They'll kill us the same as they killed my—!

No! I've got to—!

Tess clutched the carpet, rushing backward from the kitchen, dragging Professor Harding through the door into the haze-choked sunlight. Priscilla did her best to hurry and follow.

Tess heard a shot. Ignoring it, she tugged Professor Harding across the back porch, bump, bump, down the steps, feeling the jolts to his body, wincing in sympathy.

Another shot. Tess released the carpet and spun, her pistol drawn, searching for a target.

Craig had reached the paths in the garden. He crouched behind a section of scarlet lilies, hardly visible, shooting toward the left of the house.

But *behind* Craig, rising from a path beyond a farther section of lilies, a gunman appeared, aiming toward Craig.

Tess fired. The gunman jerked.

Tess fired again. The gunman toppled backward, arms splayed, crashing among the flowers, lily stalks snapping.

"Priscilla, lie down! Hug the grass!" Tess ordered.

At once she whirled, saw a target at the *right* corner of the house, shot, missed! Shot again. And blood flew from his throat.

Sweating, breathing hard, Tess hunkered, pivoting to the left, then again to the right, searching for other targets.

Apart from the crackle of the blaze in the house, the backyard became eerily silent.

"Hurry, Priscilla! Follow me!"

Again Tess tugged at the carpet, at Professor Harding, hurrying backward toward Craig, toward the paths among the flowers.

She feared that any second a bullet would blow her head apart. Breathing harsher, deeper, she reached a path, kept tugging, yanked Professor Harding behind a section of flowers, and gasped when she saw that Priscilla was only halfway across the lawn.

A man appeared at the right of the house.

Tess aimed.

The man ducked behind the corner.

"Craig!" Tess yelled.

"I see him!"

"Cover me!"

Tess bolted forward, reached Priscilla, picked her up, grasping her shoulders, the back of her knees, and ran, bent over, collapsing behind the flowers, their fragrance in contrast with the stench of her fear.

Immediately she knelt, risked exposing her face, and aimed toward the left side of the house.

The lilies gave no protection from bullets, she knew.

But at least they obscured her from a killer's aim.

Sweat rolled off her brow. Her eyes stung. Her chest heaved.

She hurriedly squinted behind her in case another gunman was hidden among the flowers.

The man at the side of the house. Where the hell had he gone?

"Craig! *Do you see him?*"

"No!" Craig kept aiming.

Tess noticed that he'd dropped his revolver, which he must have emptied, and now held one of the pistols that he'd picked up inside the house.

Behind her, flowers whispered.

Again Tess whirled, squinting, her weapon ready.

Not quickly enough.

A man's arm thrust from the lilies, the rest of him hidden. His powerful thumb pressed a nerve at the back of her neck.

Agony!

Paralysis!

Wanting to scream, unable to, helpless, Tess watched her gun fall. Equally helpless, she felt the man squirm soundlessly from the flowers and press his weight over her onto the path. His thumb kept pressing the nerve on her neck.

With his other hand, he raised a silenced pistol and aimed toward Craig in the next row among the flowers.

Tess tried again to scream.

Impossible.

"Lieutenant!" The man dove as Craig whirled and fired.

"Lieutenant!" the man repeated. "I'm going to show my head! I'm going to use your friend as a shield. If you're foolish enough to think that you can kill me, if you aim at me, I'll kill her."

"Then I'll kill *you!*" Craig said.

"But your friend is more important. Pay attention, Lieutenant. Think."

The only noise was the crackle of flames from the house.

"Lieutenant," the man commanded, his grip still paralyzing Tess, his weight still upon her. "You're about to see the head of your friend."

Furious, Tess felt the man twist his grip on her neck and force her to raise her head while he kept his own head behind hers.

Craig made a tentative motion with his pistol.

"Lieutenant, don't do it," the man said, calmly aiming his weapon. "You're compromised. You can't possibly hit me. I don't intend to kill either of you. I assure you I'm a friend. But if you persist and attack me, I'll do what's necessary. Listen to reason. My team just saved your life."

"What are you talking about?"

"We shot the remaining attackers. There isn't time to explain. I need your help."

In the distance, sirens wailed.

"The authorities are on their way," the man said, maintaining his calm, although his tone was paradoxically emphatic. "We have to get out of here. I could have killed you. I didn't. That's a sign of good faith. Here's another sign of good faith." The man shoved his pistol beneath his belt. He released his thumb from the nerve on Tess's throat.

The sirens wailed closer.

Abruptly Tess found she could move. Angry, she squirmed beneath the man's weight.

He stood.

She rolled away, her throat in pain, and fought to recontrol her muscles, lurching clumsily to her knees.

"I apologize," the man said.

In the background, flames roared in the house. Smoke spewed.

"Who *are* you?" Tess rubbed her throat.

The man wore a dark sport coat and slacks. He was in his early forties, solidly built, his hair a neutral brown, his face undistinctive, not handsome, not repulsive, the sort of common face she would never notice in a crowd.

"Your savior. Be grateful. And I repeat, I don't have time to explain. Those sirens. Will you cooperate?"

Tess darted an uncertain glance toward Craig.

"Sure." Craig stared. "Provided you give me your weapon."

The stranger exhaled. "If that's what it takes." He removed his pistol from his belt, engaged its safety mechanism, and extended it to Craig, who shoved it into a pocket of his suit coat.

Craig lowered his own weapon.

"Good. Very good," the stranger said. "Hurry." He gestured, and almost by magic, equally neutral-faced, solidly built men emerged from the flowers and the side of the house, holding weapons.

"There's a van in front," The stranger cocked his head, assessing the intensity of the sirens. "Let's go."

"Priscilla and Professor Harding," Tess said.

"We'll take them with us, of course."

Again the stranger gestured. Two men raced from the flowers, lifting Priscilla and Professor Harding.

"She needs insulin," Tess said, "and her husband may have had a stroke."

"It'll all be taken care of. You have my word." The stranger pressed a hand against Tess's back. "Move."

As the sirens wailed closer, the group surged toward the right of the house.

Smoke wafted out of the study's window, obscuring Tess's gaze.

Then the smoke cleared, and she saw two bodies. She flinched and stared away, the front yard before her, trees and shrubs, a van looming.

"The Porsche!" Tess said. "I got it from a friend! She can't be involved!"

"Give me the key!"

Tess groped in her purse and threw it.

The stranger caught the key, tossed it to another man, and ordered him, "Follow us!"

Tess and Craig scrambled into the van. Other men hurried inside with Priscilla and Richard, slamming the van's side hatch shut. A driver stomped the accelerator, squealing away from the curb.

Behind the van, the Porsche sped to follow. The two vehicles rounded a corner, disappearing from the street, just as Tess, bewildered, heard the approaching sirens wail toward the burning house, nearing it from a different direction.

"So, all right," Craig said, hoarse. "You claim you saved our lives. So we got away. So what do you want from us?"

The stranger peered backward from the passenger seat. "Very simple." He scowled. "Your help. To eliminate the vermin."

"What?"

"This isn't the time or place to discuss it," the stranger said. "Arrangements have to be made. Your friends need medical attention, and several of our associates have been—"

"Hold it," Tess said, glancing toward the rear window. "We're being followed. Behind the Porsche."

"That UPS truck and the gray sedan?" The stranger nodded. "They belong—or used to belong—to several of our associates. The vermin executed those two squads before attacking the house."

"Executed?" Craig demanded.

The stranger ignored the interruption. "We found the vehicles, the corpses inside them, a block apart as we arrived. The evidence indicates that nerve gas was used. Members of my own team now drive those vehicles. Security and honor insist. We must not abandon our dead. The corpses of our brave departed require the proper rites, honorable burial in consecrated ground. *Requiem aeternam dona eis, Domine.*"

331

"Et lux perpetua luceat eis," the other men added, somber, reverential.

Tess shook her head, confused, astonished. At first, she thought she was hearing gibberish. Then, abruptly, the realization startling her, she blurted, "You're *praying? In Latin?"*

The stranger squinted. "Do you understand what it means?"

"No." Tess fought to speak. "I'm a Catholic, but . . ."

The stranger sighed. "Of course. You wouldn't be able to translate. You're too young to know what the mass sounded like before Vatican Two ordered it changed from Latin into the vernacular. 'Grant them eternal rest, Lord, and let perpetual light shine upon them.' It's from the mass for the dead."

Even more startled, Tess suddenly realized something else. "My God, whatever you are, you're also . . . !"

"Also what?" The stranger studied her.

"Priests!"

"Well," the stranger said, "that gives us something *else* to discuss."

18

The grimy-windowed rectory, behind a boarded-up Gothic church on the outskirts of Washington, had a weed-grown parking lot. The UPS truck and the gray sedan had long since veered away. Only the van and the Porsche remained.

As the stranger stepped from the van, joining Tess and Craig, who left by the side hatch, he explained, "This is one of many churches that the Vatican's dwindling finances have forced the Curia to sell. Not to worry. We're safe here. Did you notice the sign in front?"

"F and S Realty," Tess said.

"You're very observant. It's our own corporation. We're negotiating the sale ourselves. Eliminating the middle man, so to speak."

"Unless it's a middle *woman*," Tess said.

"By all means," the stranger said. "I did not intend to be sexist. For now, however, we still control this church and the rectory. The neighbors will assume you're potential buyers. No one who lives in this area will bother us."

"Except . . . Unless . . ." Tess glanced around nervously.

"You mean, the vermin? None of your attackers survived to follow. The others don't know about this place. I repeat, we're safe here."

"You keep calling them 'vermin,' " Craig said.

"A precise description."

"Where did the UPS truck and the gray sedan go?" Tess asked.

"I assumed you understood from my earlier remarks. Our departed associates require a mass for the dead. It's being arranged."

"And burial in consecrated ground," Tess said.

"Yes. For the good of their souls. . . . The Porsche. Where does it belong?"

Tess gave the address. So much had happened, she felt as if days instead of hours had passed since she'd left the comfort of Mrs. Caudill's home. "I'd be grateful if the authorities couldn't trace the car to her."

"I guarantee that," the stranger said. "As long as you remember what you just promised."

"Promised?"

"That you'll be grateful."

Tess squirmed.

The stranger approached and spoke to the Porsche's driver. With a nod, the man backed the sports car expertly from the lot and drove away.

"And," Tess said, "my friends."

"Richard? Priscilla? Like you, Tess, I'm concerned about them," the stranger said.

"You know my *name*?"

"More than that. I know virtually *everything* about you. Including your relationship with Lieutenant Craig. My briefing was thorough. The men in the van have paramedical training. They're monitoring the heartbeat and respiration of your friends. Richard and Priscilla are stable. But they do need further help. So my driver and a paramedic will deliver them to a doctor at a private clinic that we control. The authorities won't be able to question your friends until the doctor, who works for us, has taught them how and what to answer. In the meantime, Priscilla and Richard will be well taken care of.''

''Thank you.'' Tess breathed.

''I don't need thanks. What I insist on is what you promised—gratitude,'' the stranger said. He motioned toward the driver in the van, who steered from the lot and headed toward the clinic.

''Gratitude?'' Craig rested his hand on the stranger's weapon, which he'd shoved in a pocket of his suit coat.

Three of the neutral-faced men gripped pistols and flanked him.

''Yes,'' Craig said. ''Of course. By all means. What am I thinking of? Gratitude!''

''So why don't we go inside the rectory,'' the stranger said, ''and discuss how glad you are to be alive? And discuss our mutual problem? And discuss the vermin?''

''The vermin.'' Tess jerked up her arms, assaulted by insanity. ''You bet. The vermin. We certainly have to discuss the—''

''You're verging on lack of control,'' the stranger said. ''I urge you, don't lose it.''

''Listen, I've kept control through hell,'' Tess said. ''I've seen my mother die. I've been chased and shot at. I've shot in return. I've killed. Do you honestly think that you and these three men scare me? I'm an expert in keeping control, no matter how terrified I . . . !''

''Tess, I say it again—you don't need to be afraid. We're here to help you, not *threaten* you. As long as Lieutenant Craig keeps his hand away from the weapon I graciously surrendered to him.''

''Well, your generosity is obviously a problem,'' Craig said. ''Here. Watch my hand. I'll move it slowly. Carefully. Fingertips only. No threat, right? Here. Satisfied? Take it. The way things are, with these men beside and behind me, it's useless to me anyhow.''

Craig handed the weapon to him.

"Dramatic but unnecessary," the stranger said. "Especially since I can see the bulge of another weapon under your belt, concealed by your suit coat. No problem. You don't know it, but we're working together."

"Oh, yes, of course," Craig said.

"I understand your skepticism. All right, then," the stranger said. "We'll enter the rectory. We'll exchange opinions. I'll tell you about the vermin, and *you'll* tell me if you're prepared to help."

"What I *need* is help," Tess said.

"Wrong! To save your life, what you *need* to do is cooperate, to help exterminate the vermin."

19

The rectory smelled of must. In the gloomy vestibule, cracked-leather chairs were positioned at random, a dust-covered desk the center of focus. Cob-webbed religious pictures hung on oak-paneled walls in need of polishing.

Tess felt exhausted, the aftereffect of adrenaline. "Before we begin . . ."

"Whatever you need," the stranger said.

"The bathroom."

"Of course. To the right. Down that hallway. The first door on the left. I'm sure you'll want to clean the traces of vomit from your chin and your blouse."

Tess raised a hand, embarrassed.

"No need to be self-conscious. On occasion, during violence, I've vomited as well."

"How encouraging," Tess said grimly. She proceeded toward the rest room, entered weakly, and locked the door. Only as she opened her belt did she notice that unaware, she must have picked up her handgun after the stranger had released his paralyzing grip in the garden.

The weapon nearly fell from her loosened belt. She grabbed it, set it next to her on the sink, pulled down her jeans, and settled onto the seat. Her nostrils quivered. Her urine stank from fear. Disgusted, she rose, rebuckled her pants, and rinsed her face, doing her best to swab the stains from her blouse.

At once, she grabbed the gun. All along, the stranger must have noticed it beneath her belt. He could have taken it anytime.

But he'd let her keep it.

Why?

A sign.

A gesture.

Of cooperation.

Of reassurance.

All right, she thought, and zipped up her jeans, returning the gun beneath her belt. I'm getting the message.

Feel safe.

But don't be aggressive.

She flushed the toilet, unlocked the washroom door, and walked with feigned confidence down the hallway toward the vestibule.

20

In the dim light through the murky windows, Tess glanced at Craig, who sat on one of the cracked-leather chairs. He sipped from a glass of water.

So did the other men. Several bottles and glasses had been placed on the desk.

When the stranger handed her a glass, Tess suddenly realized how dry and thick her tongue felt. She hurriedly drank, barely tasting the cool, pure liquid. She couldn't remember when she'd been this thirsty.

She grabbed a bottle, refilled the glass, and drained it. Drops of water clung to her lips.

When she reached to refill the glass yet again, the stranger gently put a hand on her arm. "No. Too much at once might make you sick."

Tess studied him, then nodded.

"Sit," the stranger added. "Try to relax."

"Come on. Relax? You've got to be kidding." All the same, Tess moved a chair next to Craig. Its brittle leather creaked when she slumped upon it.

"So." The stranger raised his eyebrows. "Is there anything else you need? Are we ready now for our talk?"

"I'm definitely ready for answers." Craig straightened, rigid. "Who the hell are you? What's this all about? What's going on?"

The stranger considered him. His brooding silence lengthened. At last he sighed. "I can't answer *your* questions until you answer mine."

"Then we're *not* ready for a talk," Craig said. "I ran out of patience quite a while ago. I—"

"Please," the stranger said. "Indulge me." He directed his eyes toward Tess. "How much have you discovered about the vermin? Do you understand why they want to kill you?"

Tess frowned. "The way you say that . . . Your tone. It doesn't sound as if you're puzzled. It's as if you already know the answers but wonder if *I* know."

The stranger cocked his head. "Impressive. To repeat my earlier compliment, you're very observant. But what *I* know isn't the issue. Tell me. *How much have you discovered?*"

Tess pivoted toward Craig, who debated, then shrugged.

"It's a standoff," Craig said. "Go ahead. Tell him. Maybe he'll answer *our* questions."

"Or maybe if I do, they'll kill us."

"No, Tess," the stranger said. "Whatever happens, we are *not* your enemy. On the contrary." He reached inside a pocket of his jacket and placed a ring on his finger.

The other men followed his example.

Their rings were dramatic. Each had a glinting golden band, a shimmering ruby embossed with a golden intersecting cross and sword.

"Few outsiders have seen these rings," the stranger said. "We show them as a sign of respect, of trust, of obligation."

"A cross and a sword?"

The stranger lowered his gaze toward the ring. "An appropriate symbol. Religion and retribution. Tell me, Tess, and I'll tell you. *Why do the vermin want to kill you?*"

"Because of . . ." Confused, frightened, Tess opened her mouth.

Hesitated.

Then confessed. Unburdened. Revealed.

Throughout, she glanced at Craig, who pretended to listen, his shoulders braced, while he checked the exits, never interrupting.

Mithras. Montségur. The treasure. Joseph's bedroom. The bas-relief statue. A war between a good god and an evil one.

Exhausted, Tess slumped back, the cracked-leather chair sagging beneath her. "They want to stop me from telling others what I know, from showing the photographs."

"Yes." The stranger caressed the cross and the sword on his ring. "The photographs. Let me see them."

Tess fumbled in her purse and handed them over.

The stranger's face became rigid with hate when he examined them. "It's what we suspected. A damnable altar."

Craig scowled. "So Tess was right. All of this was pointless. You haven't heard anything you didn't already know."

"On the contrary, I've learned a great deal." The stranger passed the photographs to his companions, who studied them with equal loathing. "I've learned that you know so much I can't, as I'd hoped, deceive you with half-truths. I won't be able to use you without providing a fuller explanation than I'd planned." He brooded. "It presents a problem."

"How?"

"I need you, but I can't trust you. I can't depend on your silence. Just as the vermin are determined to protect *their* secrets, so we guard ours. How can I be sure that you'll stay quiet about what I tell you?"

"Yes, it's a problem," Craig said. "Apparently you'll just have to trust us anyhow."

"Lieutenant, I'm not a fool. The moment you're free, you'll report everything you've heard to your superiors. It might be better if I released both of you right now. True, you've seen the rings. However, they tell you nothing."

"Let us go? Then you meant what you said?" Craig shook his head, puzzled. "You don't intend to harm us?"

"After saving your lives?" the stranger asked rhetorically. "I've already shown my commitment to your safety. There's the door. It isn't locked. You're free to leave. By all means, do so."

"But," Tess said, "if you let us go, we'll be back where we started."

"Exactly," the stranger said. "The vermin will continue to hunt you, and without our help, I fear that the next time they'll succeed in killing you. A pity."

Craig's voice became husky. "What kind of mind game are you playing?"

"I need reassurance. Do you love this woman?"

Craig answered without hesitation. "Yes."

It made Tess proud.

"And are you willing to admit," the stranger continued, "despite your best efforts, there's a good chance she'll die without our help? At the very least, that you and she will be forced to keep hiding, constantly afraid that the vermin are about to attack again?"

Craig didn't respond.

"Answer me!" the stranger said. "Are you willing to condemn the woman you love to an uncertain future, cringing at the slightest sound, always terrified?"

"Damn it, obviously I want to protect her!"

"Then give me your word! On the soul of the woman you love, swear to me that you'll never repeat a word I say to you!"

"So it's *that* way." Craig glared.

"Yes, Lieutenant, *that* way. The *only* way. Do I need to add that if you break your vow and tell the authorities, this woman will never trust you again?"

Craig kept glaring.

"And do I need to add something else?" the stranger asked.

"If you break your vow, the vermin won't be the only group that hunts her. *We* will. I myself would kill her to punish you if you betrayed us."

"You son of a bitch."

"Yes, yes, vulgarity vents emotion. But it settles nothing. You're avoiding my demand. Are you willing to swear? For the woman you love, are you prepared to make a solemn pledge of silence?"

Craig's cheek muscles rippled.

Tess couldn't restrain herself. "Craig, tell him what he wants!" She swung toward the stranger. "You have *my* word. I won't repeat anything you say."

"But what about *you*, Lieutenant?"

Craig clenched his fists. His shoulders seemed to broaden. Slowly he swallowed. "All right." He exhaled forcefully. "You've got it. Nothing means more to me than keeping Tess alive. I don't want *another* group trying to kill her. I give you my word. I won't betray you. But I have to tell you, I hate like hell to be threatened."

"Well, that's the point. A vow means nothing unless a threat is attached to its violation. Actually two points."

"Oh? What's the second one?"

"You already mentioned it. What we're here to discuss . . . Hell."

21

Tess blinked. A sharp pain attacked her forehead. "I don't understand."

"Hell," the stranger emphasized. "Where the vermin belong. Where we've devoted ourselves to send them."

"I still don't . . ." Abruptly Tess dreaded what the stranger was going to tell her. She braced herself for another assault on her sanity. "Why do you keep calling them vermin?"

"No other word applies. They breed like rats. They infest like lice. They're vile, contemptible, destructive, loathsome, morally filthy, worse than plague-ridden fleas, spreading their evil, vicious, repugnant heresy."

The litany of hate jolted Tess's mind. She lurched back in her chair, as if she'd been pushed. "It's time. You promised to explain. Keep *your* word. Who *are* you? In the van, I said I thought you were priests, but . . ."

"Yes. Priests. But *more* than priests. Our mandate makes us unique. We're enforcers."

"What?"

The stranger nodded, his eyes gleaming.

Tess struggled to ask him, *"For . . . ?"*

"The Inquisition."

Tess had trouble making her throat work. Her consciousness swirled. *"What are you talking about?* That's crazy! The Inquisition ended in the Middle Ages!"

"No," the stranger said. "That's not correct. The Inquisition *began* in the Middle Ages. But it persisted for several hundred years. In fact, it wasn't officially dissolved until 1834."

Tess winced. She couldn't adjust to the realization that so cruel an institution—the relentless, widespread persecution of anyone who didn't follow strict doctrine—had survived until so recently. Its victims had been tortured, urged to recant their heresy, and if they refused, burned at the stake.

Flames! she thought.

Everything led back to flames!

The stake of the Inquisition! The torch of Mithras!

But there was more. Tess wasn't prepared as the neutral-faced stranger, his eyes gleaming brighter, continued.

"You'll note I used the word 'officially,' " he said. "In truth, the Inquisition did not end. *Un*officially, amid the greatest secrecy, it remained in action. Because its necessary work had not yet been completed. Because the vermin had not yet been eradicated."

"You're telling us"—Craig sounded appalled—"that a core of inquisitors followed secret instructions from the Church and persisted in hunting down anyone who strayed from orthodox Catholicism?''

"No, Lieutenant, that's *not* what I'm telling you."

"Then . . . ?''

"The Church was firm in its order to disband the Inquisition. No secret instructions were given. But secrecy was followed nonetheless, on the part of inquisitors who felt that their crucial mission could not in conscience be interrupted. Before they died, they trained others to take up the mission, and *they* in turn trained others. An unbroken chain, until *we* now train others but more important, fight the enemy.''

Tess slumped. "Too much." She fought to retain her sanity. "Too damned much. Just because your victims don't go to mass on Sunday?''

"Don't trivialize! It makes no difference to me who goes to mass on Sunday. Anyone who worships God, the *one* God, in his or her own way, is not my concern. But those who believe in an *evil* god in combat with the true good Lord are by definition as evil as the god they hate. Mithraism.'' The stranger almost spat. "Albigensians. Dualists. The survivors of Montségur. *They* are my enemy. They managed to escape. They took their statue with them. They hid. They festered. They spread. And now they're out of control, or to be exact, about to *assume* control. They killed your friend. They killed your mother! They want to kill *you!* I won't rest until I destroy them!''

"Okay, just a minute. Calm down," Craig said. "Back up. What do you mean they're about to assume control?''

"After they escaped from Montségur, the small group of heretics fled from southwestern France, trying to put as much distance as possible between them and their hunters. They headed farther south into Spain, where they sought refuge in an isolated mountain valley, the range that we now call the Picos de Europa. There, they determined to replenish their cult, to learn Spain's language and customs, to try to blend, which they did successfully, practicing their contemptible rites in secret. For more than two hundred years, they flourished, eventually sending contingents to other sections of Spain. After all, in case their central nest was discovered, the other nests would still have a chance to preserve their repulsive beliefs.''

"Pamplona and Mérida," Tess said.

The stranger's gaze intensified. "Why do you mention those areas?"

"Priscilla. The woman your men took to the clinic. *She* told me," Tess said. "In fact, almost everything I know about Mithraism comes from her. She used to be a professor. She's an expert in—"

"Answer my question. What do you know about those areas?"

"On a research trip, Priscilla saw Mithraic statues in caves near those cities."

"Truly, I never expected . . . You've told me something I *didn't* know. We've been trying to find the central nest. Now you've pointed me toward possible other nests."

"Answer *my* question," Craig said. "What do you mean they're about to assume control?"

"After two hundred years, the heretics felt secure. But then in 1478, the Spanish Inquisition began. Earlier there'd been purges throughout various other countries in Europe, but the *Spanish* Inquisition was by far the most extreme. Enforcers hunted heretics everywhere. No village was too small to avoid a purifier's attention. But the vermin—resourceful, resilient—fled again. To northern Africa, specifically Morocco. Taking utmost precautions, they came together for a critical secret meeting in which they decided that in order to protect their religion, they needed to *counter*attack, to rely on every devious means possible to guarantee their survival. The final decision was to train representatives to leave the nest, conceal their true identity, and seek power, to embed themselves within society and gain sufficient political influence to stop the persecution. To infest! As you might expect, their initial efforts were minor. But since the 1400s, the heretics have spread, multiplied, and infiltrated every important institution in Europe and America. They've risen to the highest levels of government. It was due to their influence that the Inquisition was finally dissolved. And now the crisis is universal. They're about to assume complete control, to impose their vicious errors upon the world."

"Obviously you're exaggerating," Craig said.

"Hardly. It's impossible to exaggerate the extremes to which they've gone. The vermin are convinced that the evil god is destroying the planet. They feel an urgency as the year 2000 looms.

The millennium and all it implies. Crisis. Apocalypse. Not satisfied with manipulating governments, they've organized their own Inquisition. They've sent assassins to eliminate anyone they feel is dominated by the evil god. You must have noticed the pattern. The killings. Everywhere. In Australia. Hong Kong. Brazil. Germany. Kenya. The North Atlantic. America. Industrialists. Developers. Corporate managers. Drift-net fishermen. Ivory hunters. The captain of the oil tanker that polluted and nearly destroyed the Great Barrier Reef. The vermin are executing anyone they blame for the greed, negligence, and poisons that threaten the planet.''

''My God,'' Tess said, ''you're talking about the article I've been working on! Radical environmentalists attacking . . . !''

''No, not environmentalists. And when you speak of God, which God do you mean? I hope not a good god at war with an evil god,'' the stranger said.

''I don't *care* about that! The fact is, the planet *is* in danger! It has to be saved!''

''A commendable notion,'' the stranger said. ''However, if you believe in the one true God as *I* do, then you have to trust that God. *He* knows better than *we* do. If the planet dies, it's His will. It's part of His grand design. A punishment because of our sins. If we don't correct our ways, we'll be destroyed. But the vermin, the heretics, believe they obey a different god. A god that is nonexistent. Their heresy challenges the true God's plan. And for *that*, they'll suffer in hell.''

''Don't you realize?''

''What?''

''You're as fanatical as *they* are!''

The stranger's calm reaction surprised her. ''The situation demands fanaticism. After all, a determined enemy requires an even more determined opponent.''

''That's not what I meant. One god. Two gods. You think *you're* right. They believe *they're* right. The world's collapsing, and you're fighting each other about *theology?* If anything, I empathize with the other side. At least, they're working to save the planet.''

''But they're also trying to kill you,'' the stranger said. ''And they've succeeded in killing many others. Do you condone political assassination? Do you approve of the murders of industrialists, financiers, and—''

''Your goal is to execute the heretics. Nothing would please you more. Killing. That's what you're about. How can you blame *them* for doing the same thing *you* do?''

''There's a difference,'' the stranger said. ''I'm engaged in a war. But I kill combatants, not civilians. In contrast, *they* kill without discrimination. They destroy the innocent as well as the guilty. Your mother. Her only fault was that she happened to be present when they tried to kill *you*. For your mother's sake, I would have expected you to want revenge.''

''Yes, I do want someone to pay, but . . . Oh, Lord, help me. I'm so confused.''

''You're not alone,'' the stranger said. ''To kill contradicts my very purpose as a priest. And yet . . .'' He lowered his gaze. ''I pledged myself to protect the faith.''

The vestibule became silent.

Craig took advantage of the pause. ''I've got a lot more questions.''

''Yes. By all means.'' The stranger slowly raised his head.

''You said that the heretics hurried from Spain when the Inquisition came too close.''

''Correct.''

''Then they went to Morocco.''

''Yes.''

''Which explains Joseph Martin's fascination with *The Dove's Neck Ring,* a treatise on courtly love, written by a Moor who emigrated to Spain.''

The stranger nodded.

''That also explains why Joseph Martin looked vaguely Spanish. Swarthy. Dark haired. With Latin features as opposed to French. Does that mean the heretics not only blended with but bred with the local population?''

''Yes,'' the stranger said. ''At the start, the group was so small that the vermin needed to replenish their gene pool. They converted their spouses to Mithraism and swore them to secrecy.'' The stranger gestured. ''But you didn't mention one more detail about their features. In some descendants of the vermin, there's an unusual gene that makes their eyes gray. It's one of the few means we have to identify them.''

"Gray." With a pang of grief, Tess vividly remembered the compelling color of Joseph's eyes. Their intensity. Their charisma.

"But if the Inquisition came so dangerously close that the heretics abandoned Spain," Craig asked, "why do you think that the central nest is still in . . . ?''

"Spain? Although the heretics came from France, they eventually considered Spain their homeland. We believe they returned. We've searched. But we haven't been able to find that nest.''

"*Another* question. And this one really bothers me," Craig said.

The stranger motioned for Craig to continue.

"If Joseph Martin believed in Mithras, why did his fellow believers turn against him?" Craig asked. "Why did they hunt him down and set fire to him in Carl Schurz Park? It doesn't make sense for them to turn against one of their own.''

"Ah, yes, Joseph Martin. Interesting. He'd have made an excellent informant," the stranger said.

Tess felt a tremor of confusion. "Informant? What do you—?''

"As my associates continued searching, they discovered something totally unexpected," the stranger said. *"One* of the heretics had bolted from the ranks. The deserter was appalled that his group was engaged in massive killing. He fled, determined to practice his religion in private. Cautious, he assumed many false identities, moving from city to city, aware that his former brethren would now consider him a security risk. After all, he knew too much, and if he revealed what he knew, he might have directed *us* toward his brethren. Obviously, from the heretics' viewpoint, the man who eventually called himself Joseph Martin had to be killed. So while *we* tried to find him, his brethren did the same. Los Angeles. Chicago. New York. We followed his trail. We found him. But my associates waited too long. They hoped that the vermin who tracked him would also arrive. My associates wanted many targets. Unfortunately, their plan didn't work, and Joseph Martin was killed.''

"Not just killed. He was *burned!''* Tess said.

"Of course. Why does that surprise you? Remember the torch

of Mithras. The god of the sun. Of fire. That's why the vermin are so devoted to killing with flames.''

"Don't sound so righteous. They're not alone in that. Didn't the Inquisition *also* kill with flames?'' Tess demanded.

"True. There is, however, a distinction.''

"Tell me about it!''

"Their fire, like the phoenix rising, sends their victims to another life, or so they believe. To them, death doesn't always lead to heaven or hell but rather to another stage in existence, a rebirth, a further chance for salvation. Reincarnation. One of the reasons they want the world to survive. So they can be reborn,'' the stranger said. "But *our* fire punishes, nullifies, and purifies, reducing sin to ashes. Moreover, it gives the vermin a foretaste of the ravaging flames of hell.''

"Yes. That's what this conversation keeps coming back to. Hell.'' Tess grimaced.

"Not only that.''

"What?''

"We have to go back to something else.''

"What?'' Tess repeated.

"Just as I'm confident that you intend to keep your promise of silence, so I kept *my* promise. I've told you what I know. Now I repeat. I ask what I did at the start. Will you cooperate? To save your life, are you prepared to help us exterminate the vermin?''

"Save my life? Exterminate the . . . ? I don't see how the two are related.''

"It's really quite simple.''

"Not to me, it isn't.''

"To prevent you from revealing information about them, the vermin will continue to hunt you. The only way to stop them is for you to help us complete our mission.''

"And how am I supposed to do that?''

The stranger's gaze intensified. "By presenting yourself as bait.''

22

Again Tess flinched, the pain in her forehead sharper. "But that means nothing's changed. I'll still be in danger!"

"I guarantee we'll protect you," the stranger said.

"That's bullshit," Craig said. "You know you can't possibly guarantee that. The minute Tess shows herself, the minute the killers find out where she is, they'll organize an attack. They've proven how determined they are. The only defense I can think of is to get Tess to a safe house and surround it with policemen."

"But how long will they stay there?" The stranger shook his head. "They can't keep guard forever. It's too expensive. Eventually they'll be needed elsewhere. For that matter, how long will they manage to remain alert? After a few days, if nothing happens, it's human nature for a sentry to lose his edge, to start to get bored. And that's when—"

"Wait. I know how to save myself!" Tess interrupted.

"Oh?" The stranger sounded skeptical.

"There's an easy solution!"

"Really?" Now the stranger sounded perplexed. "If so, I haven't thought of it."

"All I have to do is tell everyone I meet. The police. Reporters. Television crews. Whoever. I mean *everyone*. About what's happened. About Joseph. About my mother. About the heretics and why they want to kill me. If their motive is to shut me up, after I've finished talking, they won't have a *reason* to shut me up. Because I'll have already told what they *didn't* want me to say! Don't worry. I promised. I'll leave you out of this. But your enemy—!"

"And yours," the stranger said.

"Right," Tess agreed, "and *mine*. The bastards who killed my mother won't have a reason to keep hunting me. They'll be exposed. *They'll* be hunted. They'll have to go into hiding!"

"Tess"—the stranger bowed his head in despair—"you still haven't understood."

"But the logic's so convincing!"

"No," the stranger said. "In the first place, the vermin would want to get even. They'd do their best to kill you on principle, to punish you for the trouble you caused. In the second place, do you realize how outrageous you'd sound? The police, the reporters, the television crews, they'd think you were deluded. In the third place, the information you'd reveal wouldn't make a difference. Suppose—against all odds—that the authorities managed to repress their doubts and actually, amazingly, believed you. What then? If *we*, with centuries of experience in hunting the vermin, still haven't tracked down and killed every one of them, what chance do you think the police would have? You've missed the point. Oh, yes, indeed. I'm very much afraid that you've missed the essential point."

"Which is?" Tess demanded, furious.

"You."

"What's so special about . . . ?"

"You, Tess. Think about who you are! Think about your background! Think about your dead father!"

"What does he have to do with—?"

"Influence, Tess. I'm talking about *influence*. Suppose you did tell policemen, reporters, and . . . No matter. Whoever. When they didn't believe you, *what* would you do? Give up? Say, 'I did my best,' and hide in fear that you'd still be attacked?"

"Of course not!"

"I ask you again! What would you *do*?"

"Keep trying. Keep struggling to avenge my mother's death and Joseph's death."

"Exactly," the stranger said. "You'd use your influence. You'd demand that the friends of your dead, martyred father pay their debts of gratitude. You'd *insist*—at the highest levels of government—that those friends of your father cooperate. And they would, Tess. I believe they would. To satisfy you. To ease their guilty consciences for having sent your father to his death in Beirut for the sake of an illegal arms deal that would have tilted the balance in the Lebanese civil war and given the Christians power over the

Moslems. But I told you—and I remind you—that the vermin have risen to the highest levels of government. We don't know who they are. We haven't been able to identify them. But believe this. Count on it. Your survival depends on it. As you keep insisting, you'll eventually encounter your enemy. You won't know it. You won't be able to identify *them*. But *they'll* know *you*. And they'll do their best to have you executed before you accidentally expose their network and possibly *them*.''

Tess shuddered. "It never occurred to me. I never thought . . .''

"I hate to say this,'' Craig murmured. "He's right.''

"Of course,'' the stranger said. "So now you have your choices. Leave. Keep your pledge of silence, except for what you already know about the vermin. Or cooperate with us. Follow my directions. Help us discover the vermin at the highest level. Then permit us to do our duty and—''

"Killing. I'm so sick of killing.''

"I guarantee you wouldn't like the alternative,'' the stranger said. "The options are before you. Think carefully. Consider your future. Then make your choice.''

"There *isn't* a choice.''

"Be specific,'' the stranger said.

"The way you put it, I'm forced to do what you want.''

"Exactly.''

"But are you certain I'll be protected?''

"On my honor,'' the stranger said.

"I certainly hope you value your honor.''

"More than the vermin, Tess. And remember, we have an advantage.''

"*What?*''

"The one true Lord is on our side.''

"I wish I shared your confidence.''

Tess spun, an abrupt sound jolting her nerves, the rectory's door being opened.

But a man who'd been standing guard didn't seem concerned.

Another enforcer entered, the man who'd driven the Porsche back to Mrs. Caudill. "Nice old lady,'' he said. "She even told her butler to drive me back to Washington. I got out fifteen blocks from here so he wouldn't know about the rectory.'' He handed a paper bag to Tess. "Before I returned the car, I searched it, in case you left anything that might attract suspicion. I found these under the Porsche's front seat."

Despondent, Tess peered inside the bag, although she knew what she'd find—the two boxes of ammunition.

"Thanks." Her shoulders sagged. "The way things are going . . ." Her voice cracked in despair. "It looks like I'll be needing these."

JUDGMENT DAY

1

Two cars pulled up outside. The engines stopped. Doors were opened, then shut.

On edge, Tess warily studied the guard at the entrance to the rectory, who peered through its window, held his weapon at his side, and didn't seem concerned.

Footsteps approached. A moment later, four neutral-faced, trim, lithe men came into the vestibule. Two of the men Tess recognized, the driver and the paramedic who'd taken Priscilla and Professor Harding to the clinic.

The other two men she hadn't seen before. Presumably one had driven the UPS truck, the other the gray sedan, following, then veering from the row of vehicles as the group neared the rectory.

"You disposed of the truck and the car?" the stranger asked.

The latter two men nodded.

"In a parking lot at a shopping mall," one of them said. "Counterfeit license plates. Fake registration. No fingerprints. We even left the keys. With luck, both vehicles will soon be stolen."

"Good. And surveillance? I take for granted—"

"We detected none. Our substitute car hadn't been tampered with. A clean exchange."

"And what about . . . ?"

"The funeral of our associates? It's being arranged. I regret, however, that we won't be able to attend."

"As do I. But our prayers go with them." The stranger lowered his head. After a solemn, brief silence, he made the sign of the cross, exhaled, then turned to the driver and paramedic from the van. "I'm sure Tess will want to know."

"You bet I want to know. The clinic. What did the doctor say about Priscilla and Professor Harding?"

The first man made a reassuring gesture. "The woman was given insulin. After she ate, she became alert."

"And Professor Harding?"

The second man frowned. "The diagnosis is a minor stroke. He's been given medication. Before we left, he managed to speak."

"What did he . . . ?"

"Three words. To his wife. With effort."

"And what were . . . ?"

" 'I love you.' "

Tess felt her throat cramp. "My fault. It's all my . . ."

"No," the stranger said. "It's the *vermin's* fault."

"You can't know how much I want to believe that. But if I hadn't gone to them for information, Professor Harding wouldn't have . . ." Tess glared. "That's what it keeps coming down to, doesn't it? Fewer and *fewer* choices. Then only one. To cooperate."

"The force of circumstance," the stranger said. "And now, I'm afraid, it's time." He gestured toward a phone on the dust-covered desk. "Begin. Call your father's contacts. Demand their assistance. Tell them how helpless you are. Make them feel guilty because of their responsibility for your father's death. Among those who respond, at least *one* of them will be—"

The man who'd driven Priscilla to the clinic interrupted, "This might be important. In the van coming back, we monitored the news on the radio. The fire and the corpses at the house in Washington are being linked to last night's fire, the identical tactics, the similar massacre in Alexandria. The police are—"

The stranger bristled. "I don't *care* about the police. The phone. Tess. Pick up the phone. Call your—"

"Not just yet," Craig said. "I promised the police chief in Alexandria that I'd keep in touch."

"That promise will have to wait."

"Wrong. If I don't phone to reassure him, my career is finished. I could go to prison for failing to cooperate in a felony investigation. That's assuming I manage to stay alive, of course. I mean, why be optimistic? But I *like* my work. I'd *like* to keep doing it. However, there's one thing I *don't* like—not knowing the name of someone I talk to."

"My name? A mere formality. It isn't important."

"To me, it is."

"Then call me . . ." The stranger hesitated. "Yes. Call me Father Baldwin."

"Are you sure you don't want to make it 'Father Smith' or 'Father Jones'?"

"I believe 'Father Baldwin' will do."

"But it's not quite appropriate. Am I wrong, or do I sense a vague European accent? French perhaps?"

"Lieutenant, you finally asked one question too many. Pick up the phone. Reassure the Alexandria police chief, if that's what you feel is necessary for Tess to conduct her mission. Simply tell him you haven't been able to contact her yet. There's no need to worry about the call's being traced. A black box routes the transmission through London and Johannesburg."

"Thorough. I'm impressed."

"We try. But then, after all, we've had hundreds of years of practice."

"It shows." Craig pulled a slip of paper from a pocket of his rumpled suit coat. He studied a number he'd written on the paper, picked up the phone, and dialed.

At the same time, Father Baldwin pressed a button that activated a microphone, allowing everyone to monitor the call. Tess listened to static, to the click of long-distance relay switches, then a buzz as the call arrived in Alexandria.

Another buzz.

A man's voice answered, "Chief Farley's office."

"This is Lieutenant Craig from Missing Persons at NYPD. I believe he's expecting my call."

"Damned right he is. Hang on."

Click. More static.

Craig had been put on hold. He glanced at the man who called himself Father Baldwin. Then he reached to put his arm around Tess. "I know it's tough, babe. Just stay calm."

"If anyone else had called me that . . ." Tess said.

"It's what my father called my mother."

"In that case, it sounds wonderful."

Click.

"Chief Farley here. Where the hell have you been? I expected you to phone—"

"I know. A couple of hours ago. The trouble is, I haven't been able to find—"

"Theresa Drake. She's not my problem anymore. My men are still trying to make sense of what happened at her mother's house last night. The Washington police had a similar attack in their jurisdiction this afternoon. They want to know if the two are connected. But what *I* want to know is how the hell did the FBI get involved?"

"What?"

"They weren't invited, and I can't think of a reason why Melinda Drake's murder should be their business."

At the mention of her mother, Tess winced.

"The *FBI?*" Craig said.

"Eric Chatham—the Bureau's director himself—got in touch with me shortly after noon. He wants to talk to Theresa Drake. National security. Top priority. Confidential. Blah, blah, blah. Hey, I'm good at my job, and when an outsider tries to tell me how to . . . Never mind. I explained my arrangement with you. Now it's out of my hands. I have orders—high-level *government* orders—to instruct you to forget about bringing Theresa Drake to me and instead to phone Chatham. Three times this afternoon, he called to find out if I'd heard from you, to remind me to tell you to contact him at once. Immediately. Craig, what in Christ's name is going on?"

"Chief, I swear I wish I knew."

"Then, you'd damned well better find out. As Chatham says, *now*. The last thing I need is trouble from the FBI."

"I hear you."

"Well, while you're at it, hear *this*, Craig. Someday, you and I will meet, and you'd better be prepared to explain. Take my word, you don't want me pissed off at you. Because I'm a vindictive son of a bitch, and I'll make sure your captain's pissed off at you as well."

"I repeat, I hear you."

"What a surprise. Someone's actually taking orders from me instead of *giving* them to me. Phone Chatham. Here's his private number."

Craig wrote it down.

"Get that bureaucrat off my tail," Farley said. "So I can do my job. So I can find out who murdered Melinda Drake."

"I promise. It'll be taken care of." Troubled, Craig set down the phone.

"So," Father Baldwin said, "it's already started."

Tess frowned in amazement. "You think *Eric Chatham's* part of the group that's trying to kill me?"

"Possibly. I told you they'd risen to top positions. But this might be coincidental," Father Baldwin said. "Did Chatham know your father?"

"Very well."

"Then he might be acting out of loyalty, to try to protect you."

Tess raised her hands, intensely frustrated. "There's just one problem with that logic."

"Oh?" Father Baldwin waited.

"Only the enemy knew I was at my mother's house last night."

"Not true. There was Brian Hamilton, and of course, my associates."

"But Brian Hamilton's dead!" Tess said. "My point hasn't changed. The Alexandria police chief learned I was being hunted because Craig told him. But how did *Chatham* find out?"

Father Baldwin's eyes blazed. "You're suggesting he received his information from the men who attacked your mother's house and failed to capture you?"

"It certainly makes sense to me," Craig said.

"Perhaps." Father Baldwin shook his head. "But what troubles me is that the connection's so obvious. Since 1244 and the vermins' escape from Montségur, the heretics have survived because of their talent for hiding. Over the centuries, they've greatly improved their ability to deceive. If Chatham *is* an enemy, would he take the risk, would he violate his training and draw suspicion to himself by acting so directly?"

"If he and his group felt desperate enough." Tess pivoted toward a religious painting, then whirled back toward Father Baldwin. "By calling Chief Farley and insisting that the FBI take over, Chatham has already accomplished part of their goal. They want to kill me because of the photographs and what I know. But this way, I still haven't been able to tell the authorities."

Father Baldwin didn't answer for a moment. "You may be right. But there's only one way to learn."

Tess breathed. "Yes. To call him." Apprehensive, she reached for the sheet of paper upon which Craig had written Chatham's phone number.

"Wait," Father Baldwin said.

"A minute ago, you were urging me to . . ."

"The situation's changed. Now that we've isolated a possible target, I need to teach you how to react to what Chatham tells you. Meanwhile, other arrangements have to be made. They're mundane but necessary."

"What do you mean?"

"It's after seven."

"So what?"

"You have to eat."

"Forget it. Food's the last thing I'm interested in. I probably couldn't keep it down."

"But you're useless to me if you're exhausted. My informants tell me you don't eat meat. Would fish be acceptable?"

Tess felt intimidated by Father Baldwin's intimate knowledge of her habits. She felt indignant. But the priest's forceful tone had its effect.

"If you're that determined," Tess said, "go ahead, although I don't know why my permission matters. You'll do it anyhow. Sure. Yeah, fish will be fine."

"And Lieutenant, what about you?"

"A week ago, I'd have ordered steak and fries," Craig said. "But now, after having met Tess . . . Whatever she recommends to eat is good enough for me."

"I'll also need your clothing sizes," Father Baldwin said. "What you're wearing is torn and reeks of smoke. Since you'll soon be out in public, to avoid attracting attention you'll have to put on fresh clothes."

"For the second time today," Tess murmured, and discovered she was trembling.

2

Eric Chatham stood at the bottom of the steps that led to the Lincoln Memorial, its massive statue and white marble columns glowing eerily in the darkness. This section of the circular street around the memorial was closed to traffic, but to his right, headlights of vehicles approached along Daniel French Drive to stop at a parking lot, visitors getting out to stroll around and enter the memorial. Chatham studied those cars and visitors, waiting for a man to walk toward him and mention that he'd come from Tess Drake.

The night was warm. All the same, Chatham's stomach felt crammed with jagged chunks of ice. He brooded, unable to subdue his misgivings. It wasn't just that he'd agreed, against all his instincts, to meet in this unorthodox, potentially dangerous way. It was also that this was the second such unorthodox meeting he'd had today, the first during noon hour at Arlington National Cemetery with Kenneth Madden, the CIA's deputy director of covert operations. The meetings were related, and Chatham was more convinced that something disastrous was about to happen. He thought of Melinda Drake's murder and corrected himself. No, not about to happen.

Now. His years of experience as the Bureau's director told him that whatever was wrong had already begun and might even be out of control.

Tess was frightened, that much was certain. When she'd called him two hours ago, he'd been alarmed by her trembling voice, her desperate tone. Before he had a chance to explain why he needed to talk to her, she'd interrupted, claiming that she knew who'd killed her mother, that she had important information about the murder, but that she couldn't reveal it over the phone. She had to tell him about—to let him *see*—the evidence in person.

"Then come to my office . . . No," Chatham had said, "it's more private at my home."

"But I can't trust either place!"

"Forgive me, Tess, but don't you think you're taking precautions to an extreme?"

"After everything I've been through? Eric, you have no idea. In *my* position, you'd be. . . !"

"Okay. Calm down. If you believe you're in that much danger, I'll arrange for special agents to guard my house."

"No! The meeting has to be on my conditions. If you were truly a friend of my father, you'll do your best to help me stay alive!"

Chatham had hesitated. "Yes. For your father. Anything."

"Some friends of mine will pick you up and bring you to where I feel safe."

"Agreed."

"You'll come alone," Tess had said.

"I don't like that, but again, all right." Chatham's forehead had suddenly throbbed.

"It has to be that way, so my friends can make sure you're not followed. The people who want to kill me might be watching you."

"Again, you're being extreme."

"No, Eric, practical! If I'm not careful, they'll use you to find me. It doesn't matter who you are. The heretics have proven how determined they are to stop me."

"Heretics?" The word had frozen Chatham's spine. "What are you talking about?"

"You mean you pretend . . . You're claiming you really don't *know?*"

"If I *did*, would I . . . ?"

"Be there. I'm begging you! Please!" Tess had named the specifics of the rendezvous. "I'll be waiting for my friends to bring you to where I'm hiding."

Now, in the darkness, Chatham glanced nervously at the luminous dial on his watch. Eleven-ten. Amid tourists at the base of the dramatically lit columns and statue of the Lincoln Memorial, he felt chilled in his short-sleeved cotton sweater, despite the night's warmth. After all, the rendezvous was supposed to have occurred ten minutes ago, and although the man who'd been sent to take him to Tess was probably scouting the area to make sure that Chatham had come alone and hadn't been followed by Tess's enemies, the FBI director couldn't help feeling exposed among the numerous passing tourists, any one of whom might be a threat.

Keep control, he told himself. You'll soon be as paranoid as Tess sounded.

Soon be? I already am. I wish I hadn't—

A man stopped beside him and took a photograph of the memorial. He had an average build, nondescript face, and neutral clothes. "It probably won't turn out." The man shook his head. "I brought the wrong speed of film."

"You never know. You might get lucky," Chatham said, tensing.

"Tess Drake," the man said, taking another picture up the stairs toward Lincoln's statue beyond the spotlit looming pillars. "You came alone?"

"As I promised."

"Not to doubt your word, but I checked to make sure."

Chatham shrugged. "I assumed."

"In that case, are you ready to take a ride?"

"Anything to find out what's going on. Let's do it." Chatham turned impatiently to the left toward the murky, tree-enclosed parking lot at the end of Daniel French Drive.

"No, we go *this* way." The neutral-faced man with the camera jerked his head in the opposite direction. "On your right."

Chatham scowled. *"Right?* But . . ."" Turning his nervous eyes in that direction, he saw a waist-high metal barricade that prevented cars from driving around the memorial.

Beyond the barricade, numerous headlights flashed by. Chatham heard the din of speeding cars swarming loudly across Arlington Memorial Bridge to veer farther left, away from the Lincoln Memorial onto Twenty-third Street.

"Yeah, I know," the man with the camera said. "There's no parking lot over there. Not to worry. Everything's been taken care of." He reached inside a leather camera case strapped to his waist and removed a cellular telephone.

Quickly tapping numbers, he listened, then spoke as quickly. "All clear. We're ready. Two minutes? Good. That's about how long it'll take us."

The man placed the telephone back in his camera case. "Would you care for a stroll, Mr. Chatham?" Not waiting for an answer, the man touched Chatham's arm and guided him toward the right, toward the metal barricade.

They skirted it, passing trees whose lush boughs obscured the stars and whose thick trunks flanked an unused, weed-grown section of road.

"If you're wondering," the man said, "I'm not alone. My companions are watching in case anyone's foolish enough to try to come after us."

Nervous, Chatham managed to say, "The Bureau's training team at Quantico might benefit by taking lessons from you."

The man with the camera—which wasn't a camera at all but somehow a weapon, perhaps a hidden gun, Chatham suspected—merely gestured with his free hand. "We'd never agree to do it, but a compliment is always appreciated."

"What *I'd* appreciate is to know what on earth is—"

"Soon, Mr. Chatham. Soon."

They approached the lights and the noise of the off-bridge traffic on the busy thoroughfare. Beyond the trees, on the gravel shoulder, the average-looking man paused, blocking Chatham's way, and in the glare of passing headlights, Chatham realized that the man's ordinary-seeming build was actually sinewy and lithe. Feeling the exhaust-laden wind from the rushing traffic, Chatham concluded that this man was probably more in condition than even the best of his bodyguards.

"So now . . . ?" Chatham asked.

"We wait. But not for long. You heard me say 'two minutes.' I misjudged, however. We're ahead of schedule." The escort pointed.

A van sped off the Arlington Memorial Bridge, veered from the myriad glinting headlights, and stopped at the gravel shoulder. A side hatch slid quickly open.

"After you," the neutral-faced man indicated.

Chatham clambered in, uneasy.

Other neutral-faced men nodded in greeting, their attempt at reassurance negated by their weapons.

As Chatham sat between two of them—no choice, the only place available—his escort followed, hunkered on the floor, and slammed the hatch shut. The van's engine roared. The vehicle skidded from the shoulder, gaining traction, squealing back into traffic.

In the passenger seat in front, a man spoke into a cellular phone. "He wasn't followed? Good. You know where to meet us." He set down the phone and turned. "Welcome, Mr. Chatham. Thanks for cooperating."

"But was all of this really necessary?"

The stranger merely stared at him, as if the answer were self-evident.

"Who *are* you?" Chatham asked.

"Tess explained that earlier. We're friends."

"I'll believe that when I see her. How soon will it be until we get to where she is?"

The man in front looked amused. "Sooner than you think."

Chatham frowned, not understanding.

At once, surprised, he did understand when he heard a familiar voice.

"I'm right behind you, Eric."

Chatham spun, his surprise increasing.

Tess, who'd been crouched out of sight in the rear compartment, rose to sit on a wooden crate. A burly, rugged-faced man in a dark-blue sportshirt, its cuffs folded up, appeared beside her.

Tess grinned, although to Chatham the expression seemed forced, and that made him nervous.

"It's been a long time. Good to see you, Eric."

Chatham scowled, ignoring the pleasantry. "But I thought . . . On the phone, you said that these men would take me to where you were hiding."

"I'm sorry I had to mislead you. In case your phone was tapped and you were under surveillance at the memorial. The way we arranged your pickup, we don't think this van can be followed. But if it is, the enemy will think it's leading them to me. They won't suspect I'm inside. They won't attack it."

"Attack it? And you thought my phone might be tapped?" Chatham shook his head, baffled. "My phone's checked every morning. Who could possibly tap it, or for that matter, who'd dare to take the risk of attacking this van while I was in it?"

"The heretics."

Again, that disturbing word.

"They didn't hesitate to kill Brian Hamilton," Tess said.

Chatham was too shocked to answer.

"*He* was important. So why would they hesitate to kill the director of the FBI? To get at me," Tess said, "to achieve their goal, to stop me from revealing their secret, they'll do anything."

"What are you talking about? Secrets? Heretics?"

Tess handed him several photographs and a penlight.

More baffled, Chatham used the light to examine the photographs, all the while conscious that the neutral-faced men watched him intensely.

One of the images made Chatham grimace. "A man on a bull, slicing its throat?"

"It's a sculpture."

"Where did—?"

"You've never seen anything like it before?" Tess asked.

"No! Of course, not! My God, I'd certainly remember something this grotesque."

The neutral-faced men kept staring at him.

"Tess, I showed good faith. I came alone. I did everything you asked. Now, for heaven's sake, tell me what this is all about."

The man in front interrupted. "How did you know that Tess

and Lieutenant Craig were supposed to contact the Alexandria police?''

''I didn't,'' Chatham said.

''That doesn't make sense,'' Chatham heard behind him.

Chatham whirled reflexively to face the rugged-looking man next to Tess.

''You phoned Chief Farley,'' the man said. ''Why?''

Chatham felt disoriented, having glanced forward, then back, from the neutral-faced man in front to the rugged-faced man in the rear. ''Are *you* Lieutenant Craig?''

''Answer my question.'' The burly man's voice was gravelly. ''If you didn't know that Tess and I were supposed to contact Chief Farley, why did you phone him?''

''Because I promised I would.''

Tess leaned suddenly near, her strong fingers clutching Chatham's arm. ''Promised who?''

''Kenneth Madden.''

''*Madden?*'' The man in front spoke abruptly. ''From the CIA?''

Chatham spun in the forward direction, his mind reeling, even more disoriented. ''Yes, the deputy director of covert operations.''

''What's *he* got to do with—? Why would Madden ask you to phone the Alexandria police?''

''Because the CIA doesn't have domestic jurisdiction. It was easier and it raised fewer questions if the Bureau got in touch with the local police.''

''*Why?*'' the rugged man next to Tess demanded.

''It comes down to pride. The local police don't like us to get involved if the crime's not the kind that automatically makes it our business. But the Alexandria police would have liked it even less if the *CIA* had tried to get involved. That for sure would have caused hard feelings, not to mention a lot of angry phone calls. The point is''—Chatham jerked his gaze from the rugged man in back toward Tess beside him—''you don't understand how much your father's friends are concerned about you. They're shocked about your mother's death. They're afraid that *you're* in danger. So they used the system. They asked me to contact the Alexandria police, the logical law-enforcement officials you'd ask for protection. But your father's friends want to give you greater protection.''

''By 'friends,' you mean the CIA and Kenneth Madden.'' From the front seat, the neutral-faced man's stern voice made Chatham whirl again.

''That's right,'' Chatham said. ''For Tess. For the sake of her father's memory. But what you *still* don't understand is that the urge to protect her goes far beyond the Bureau and the Agency. Much, much higher.''

''Where?''

''To the White House.''

Tess spoke, and Chatham whirled yet again.

''You're telling me''—Tess squeezed Chatham's arm more severely—''that the President himself knows I'm in danger and wants to protect me?''

''No. The *Vice* President.''

''Alan Gerrard?'' The burly man next to Tess looked puzzled.

''Hey, I know what the columnists write about him,'' Chatham said. ''But at least he cares. He told Madden to get in touch with me, and Madden in turn asked *me* to phone Chief Farley. I'm never happy working with the Agency. Their mandate is foreign, ours is here at home, and it's important to keep those jurisdictions separate. But when I get an order from the Vice President, as long as I'm not being asked to break the law, I do my best to comply. The basic message is, I'm supposed to have Tess call Madden.''

''And Madden claims he'll protect her?'' the man in front asked.

''No, Madden's just a relay. It's the *Vice President* who wants to protect her. And that means, I assume, that he intends to use the Secret Service.''

Tess shook her head. ''Why would he take such an interest in me?''

''I told you, because of your father. Like so many government officials, Gerrard felt close to your father, and Gerrard wants the government to pay back its debt to your father—for his bravery and his refusal to talk under torture—by making sure that you're protected.''

As the van crossed back toward Virginia, its occupants silently considered what Chatham had just explained. Headlights flashed past in the opposite lanes.

Chatham broke the silence. "Who are these heretics you keep mentioning?"

Tess glanced toward the man in front, her eyebrows raised as if asking permission.

The man nodded. "You know the limitations."

Tess sighed. "Eric, I hope you've got an open mind."

"After several years as the Bureau's director, not much surprises me anymore. Go ahead. Try me."

"In 1244 . . ."

It took a half hour. Chatham listened, astonished, never interrupting. In the end, he once more used the penlight to study the photograph of the bas-relief statue. "And that's all of it. There's nothing more."

"Not quite," the man in the front said. "But it's all you need to know."

"I assume the rest of it concerns *you* and your involvement in this," Chatham said.

"Don't assume anything. What you already know is enough to put you in danger. Further knowledge would put you at an even greater risk. What do you intend to do?"

"To be honest, if I hadn't seen these photographs . . . if Tess herself hadn't been the one who told me about this . . ."

"It's true, Eric. Every word of it." Tess stared emphatically into his eyes.

"But something this outrageous . . . Obviously I have to verify it."

"Then you'll begin an investigation?"

"Absolutely."

"I hope, discreetly," the man in front said. "Do it yourself. Trust no one. The vermin hide where you least suspect them. Remember what happened to Brian Hamilton. If you're not cautious, you'll be their next victim."

"Give me credit. I wasn't always a bureaucrat," Chatham said proudly. "For thirteen years, before I became an executive, I was a damned fine agent. I haven't forgotten how to conduct an investigation without drawing attention to myself.''

"Then do it," the man in front said. "Prove how skilled you are.''

"How can I get in touch with you? How do I report what I've learned?''

"No problem. *We'll* get in touch with *you.*''

"And expertly, I'm sure. But I don't know why I should trust you,'' Chatham said.

"Because of Remington Drake, Melinda Drake, Brian Hamilton, and Tess.''

"By all means, because of Tess, because of the living.''

"We'll need Madden's phone number.''

"Here. This card has his private number." Chatham frowned. "But I still can't adjust to the implications. If you're right, if this isn't a delusion, then Madden and Gerrard, the CIA's covert-op deputy director and the President's next-in-line, might be part of this.''

"As I told you, the vermin hide where you least suspect them.'' The man in front glanced through the windshield. "Ah, I see that our timing is perfect. The minute we complete our business, we arrive outside your home. By the way, your car has been moved from the parking lot at the Lincoln Memorial. You'll find it outside your garage.''

"And I'll take a guess that the man who delivered it resembled me.''

"Precisely. He strolled toward the back of your house and disappeared.''

"I wish you worked for me,'' Chatham said.

"Be satisfied we're working *with* you.''

As the van stopped, the man who'd escorted Chatham from the Lincoln Memorial slid open the side hatch, got out, and gestured for the Bureau's director to leave.

"Well, I can't say I've enjoyed the ride,'' Chatham said, "but it certainly has been informative, no matter how disturbing it was.''

"What we hoped you'd feel is not so much disturbed as . . .'' The man in front hesitated.

"Frightened?"

"Yes."

"Then," Chatham said, "you've definitely achieved your intention."

3

As the van pulled away from the shadowy curb, as Tess, Craig, and the members of Father Baldwin's team watched Chatham walk past his car in the driveway and enter his large, attractive house, Father Baldwin asked, "Is he one of them?"

"That's hard to know," Craig said. "I looked at him closely. He doesn't have gray eyes."

"That means nothing," Father Baldwin said. "Only *some* of the vermin retain that characteristic. What's more, they sometimes use tinted contact lenses to disguise the color of their irises."

"I watched Chatham closely as well," Tess said. "He responded the way he should have to what I told him. He was believable."

"Of course," Father Baldwin said. "A true professional is *always* believable. I take that for granted. So I don't know whether to trust him. That's why, in his absence, his phone has been tapped, his home has been bugged, and so has his office. He brags that his security measures are checked every morning, but his precautions are hardly adequate against our own techniques. From this moment, every word that he says will be monitored. He'll be followed by the finest surveillance. And if he makes the wrong phone call, if he sees the wrong person, if he says the wrong words, we'll know that he's one of the vermin."

"But I don't think he is," Tess said.

"That remains to be determined," Father Baldwin said. "What

also remains to be determined is the status of Kenneth Madden and Alan Gerrard. We keep moving upward. Perhaps those next-to-the-highest officials in the CIA and the White House are as well-intentioned as you want to believe that Chatham is. But the vermin give off an odor, and my nostrils feel assaulted. The odor is very strong. Make the call.''

"To Madden?''

"Yes. Follow the schedule you were given. Proceed up the bureaucratic levels. We'll find the vermin eventually.''

"All I want is to stay alive,'' Tess said. "I'm not sure I want to keep taking the risk of . . .''

"Remember, they'll kill you unless you give us the chance to exterminate *them*.''

"But if I make the call and I go through the CIA, through Madden and then to the executive branch to Gerrard, I'll still be in danger,'' Tess said.

"Craig and I will be with you, though,'' Father Baldwin said. "And keep in mind, the shoes that both of you were given have homing devices in the heels along with microphones. My operatives will always know where you are and whether you're in danger.''

"Small comfort if I'm being killed while your men try to get to me.''

"Tess, without us, your death is certain. *With* us, you and Lieutenant Craig will have a chance to enjoy the rest of your lives together.''

"That's good enough for me,'' Craig said. "Come on, Tess. We can't give up. As long as we're being hunted, let's fight the bastards, and if we fail, at least we'll have done our best. There's no other choice.''

"But I'm so scared.''

"I know. For what it's worth, so am I.''

Craig hugged her.

"Make that phone call,'' Father Baldwin said. "To Madden. And after that, to . . .''

4

Andrews Air Force Base

One A.M. Nearly blinded by spotlights, Tess and Craig stopped their hastily rented car at the heavily guarded entrance to the tall, chain-link, barbed-wire-topped fence of the military airport.

A broad-shouldered, wary sentry responded immediately, not needing to check the list of names on his clipboard when Tess and Craig identified themselves. "By all means, you're expected. ID," he demanded, adding with stern courtesy, "please."

Tess and Craig showed their driver's licenses.

The sentry examined the documents, compared their faces with the photographs on the licenses, and gave them directions toward the base's VIP wing.

While Tess drove beneath the entrance's rising barrier, she and Craig heard the roar of a jet taking off beyond rows of institutional-looking buildings from which other spotlights blazed.

"Father Baldwin lied," Tess said. "He promised he'd be with us."

"What option did he have?" Craig spread his hands. "Baldwin couldn't come with us, not when Madden told you to meet the Vice President here at Andrews. You and I have worked together long enough that I won't attract suspicion. But if we bring a stranger, an unexpected third party, it'll look like a setup. We couldn't explain Father Baldwin's presence. He'd never survive a background check. And if Gerrard *is* your enemy, we'd make him realize we suspect him. We'd be placing ourselves in a trap."

"You're telling me we're *not* in a trap?" Tess drove nervously toward the impressive floodlit VIP building. "Father Baldwin's men can't possibly get inside this base if we need help."

"With so many sentries around, nothing's going to happen. Not here, at least. Not now."

"You *trust* those sentries?"

"They work for the Air Force, not for Gerrard himself. They can't all be enemies."

"But what about later?" Tess shuddered. "What are we doing here? Why did Madden tell us to come to this airport? Suppose Gerrard tells us to get on a jet?"

Craig thought about it. "We don't know for sure that Gerrard wants to kill you. Or Madden either. All we're doing is following the sequence we were given. Chatham to Madden to—"

"Gerrard. They sound like a fucking baseball team."

"Just keep control," Craig said.

"Hey, I'm not used to risking my life the way *you* are."

"Used to risking my life? When I started out, in a squad car patrolling the Bronx, I *never* got used to it. And even in Missing Persons, I *still* haven't. Every day I wake up, knowing that any door I knock on might have a maniac with a gun behind it."

"Well, we have plenty of guns around us now."

Tess stopped the rented Plymouth before palm-raised sentries next to the VIP building.

"Names, please," one of them said.

Tess and Craig repeated the ritual.

"Identification."

Again they obeyed.

"Get out of the car, please."

The sentries used portable metal detectors to scan them. When one of the detectors wailed, a sentry stared aggressively toward Craig.

"I'm a New York City police officer," Craig said. "I'm carrying my service revolver."

"Not anymore." The sentry tugged the revolver from the holster on Craig's belt.

Tess, who didn't have a permit to carry a handgun, had reluctantly left her pistol with Father Baldwin. She felt helpless, vulnerable.

Distracted by the search, she hadn't noticed a man in an expensive, well-tailored suit walk toward her, appearing as if from nowhere. He was tall, pleasantly featured, in his thirties, with short brown hair, cheery eyes, and an engaging smile. "Ms. Drake, Lieutenant Craig, welcome." He shook hands with them. "I'm

Hugh Kelly, the Vice President's assistant. You arrived just in time. The Vice President's looking forward to seeing you.''

Kelly's reassuring manner made Tess feel somewhat at ease. After the chaos she'd been through, he seemed so normal, so sane, that she began to wonder if she was wrong to suspect that Gerrard was a threat. At the same time, Kelly's remark about "just in time" puzzled her.

"Please, come with me," he said.

Tess expected that he'd lead them into the VIP building. Instead he guided them onto the tarmac, and after a brief walk, Tess peered ahead toward floodlights and something that abruptly made her falter.

"My God," she said.

"Impressive, isn't it?" Kelly said. "It's been on order since 1986. The delays have been a headache, the cost overruns a political embarrassment, from two hundred and sixty-five million to six hundred and fifty million, but finally here she is, and I have to say, in spite of everything, the wait was worth it."

What Tess stared at, overwhelmed, was an aircraft six stories high and so long it would have dwarfed a football field—the hugest 747 she'd ever seen, its lines (including the bulge above its nose) incredibly sleek, exuding power, a large American flag painted on its rudder, the words UNITED STATES OF AMERICA stenciled boldly along its side, its color predominantly white with highlights of red and blue.

"I've never seen . . ." Tess felt so awestruck that she couldn't speak for a moment. "Even when my father was alive, I never saw . . . On television, yes, in newspapers and magazines. But never in person. Up close like this . . . it's hard to believe. It takes my breath away." She spoke with reverence. "Air Force One."

"Actually Air Force Two," Kelly said, "but you really can't tell them apart. Of course, the pictures you saw were of the old one. The seven oh seven. It had to be retired because that model was being phased out, and spare parts were hard to find. It was an awfully fine aircraft. I was sorry to see it go. But that plane can't possibly compare to this new one and its counterpart. Boeing outdid itself. This is truly one of the finest passenger jets in the world, perhaps *the* finest. You'll see what I mean when you board her.''

"Board?" Craig asked in surprise.

"You mean you weren't told?" Kelly sounded equally surprised.

"Our only instructions were to come to Andrews Air Force Base as soon as possible."

"I wondered why you hadn't brought luggage. Don't worry. You won't have to rough it. We've got plenty of overnight kits—toothbrushes, shampoo, razors." Kelly glanced politely toward Tess. "More personal items. And a bathtub-shower. Whatever you need."

"But . . ." Tess hesitated, aware of the miniature radio transmitter built into her shoe, conscious that Father Baldwin would be listening, that *he'd* be as anxious to know the answer to her question as she was. "Where are we going?"

"Spain."

The word made Tess feel light-headed.

Spain. Where Father Baldwin had said that the heretics, fleeing France, had found a new home after the attack on Montségur in 1244.

Spain! Did that mean Gerrard *was* her enemy?

Or was her destination merely a coincidence?

Tess felt frozen. At once, regaining control of her muscles, she braced herself. All of her instincts made her want to turn and run.

But to where?

And *how?* The sentries would stop her. She'd never be able to get off the base.

She fidgeted.

"Is something wrong?" Kelly asked.

"No." Tess tried to recover, to seem natural. "I'm just surprised is all. Everything's happening so fast. Two hours ago, I didn't expect to be coming *here*, and now you tell me I'm flying to Spain."

"I understand what you mean about feeling surprised," Kelly said. "Until just after midnight, I wasn't aware we'd be having visitors." He checked his gold Rolex watch. "We'd better hurry. In ten minutes, we're scheduled to be airborne."

Tess pivoted toward Craig, keeping her face calm but knowing that her eyes revealed her panic.

Craig squeezed her hand, his eyes communicating, we're stuck. We've got to go through with this.

Kelly gestured, leading them onward toward the brightly lit jet.

They reached a tall boarding ramp on wheels.

Tess climbed, counting twenty-six steps, and entered an open hatch behind a massive swept-back wing.

Once inside, sickened by her speeding pulse, she realized that there was no turning back.

Behind, below her, on the tarmac, Air Force personnel pulled away the boarding platform. Inside the jet, a uniformed flight attendant shut the hatch and secured it.

She was trapped on Air Force Two.

5

As she studied her surroundings, Tess noticed that the cabin's width was emphasized by its reduced length. Ahead and behind, bulkheads with doors restricted the space. The seats—she counted seventy—resembled first-class airline accommodations, except that they were even larger, more comfortable looking, and the aisles seemed wider than usual. Numerous phones were attached to the fore and aft bulkheads.

This must be where the press and the president's—in this case, the *vice* president's—team stayed, Tess thought, although she was puzzled that the cabin was empty, except for the uniformed flight attendant.

"We'll be taking off soon," the attendant said, "but I think you have time to enjoy a glass of champagne."

"Mineral water will be fine," Tess said.

"Same for me," Craig said.

"What are you serving?" Kelly asked the attendant.

"Dom Pérignon."

"I'll have some."

"Very good, sir."

"In the meantime," Kelly said, "I'd better tell the Vice President that his guests have arrived." He walked toward the front of the cabin, knocked on the door, and waited.

A discreet pause later, he knocked again.

The door opened.

"Sir, they're here," Kelly said.

"Excellent," a sonorous voice said. The door swung quickly farther open.

Alan Gerrard stepped through.

Although Tess had seen Gerrard often at receptions at her parents' home, and sometimes at less formal get-togethers, she hadn't met him since he'd become vice president.

As he approached her, smiling, he looked the same—movie-star handsome, with a perfect tan, glinting teeth, photogenic features, and magnificent hair. The only difference was that six years had made him look more responsible, more wise, more seasoned, despite his reputation for caring more about tennis than he did about politics.

No matter. Regardless of her suspicions about him, Tess couldn't help responding to his aura of achievement. The vice president. In her mind, the words had magic. She almost surrendered to his influence.

But didn't.

She had to keep reminding herself that he was very possibly her enemy.

Gerrard wore casual but impressive clothes—hand-sewn loafers, finely pressed linen slacks, a custom-made Sea Island cotton shirt, greens and browns. Coming nearer, he held out his arms. "Tess." He embraced her, kissing her cheek with affection, reassurance, and sorrow.

"Your mother." He shook his head. "She's a great loss to everyone, to every politician, including me, who ever enjoyed her gracious hospitality. But most of all, she's a loss to you. She'll be a legend of strength, of generosity, in this jaded community that needs every example of excellence they can possibly find to show them the proper way.''

Tess stepped back, rubbing her tear-stinging eyes. She resolved that the best, least suspicious, most natural thing to do was to treat him the way she had before her father died. ''Thanks, Alan, but don't you think the rhetoric's a little extreme? You're not campaigning, after all. Your sympathy is appreciated. Really. But a simple, straightforward 'I'm sorry' will do.''

Gerrard studied her, evidently not used to irreverence. At once, his eyes twinkled—blue, Tess noticed, although the one on the right looked irritated, streaked with red. ''Good. I'm glad to see you're keeping up your spirits,'' he said. ''Still as feisty as the last time I saw you.''

''I guess I can't help it. I got it from my parents.''

''And God bless both of them. They're sorely missed. Lieutenant Craig, I understand you've been a tremendous help to Tess in her danger and her grief. You're welcome here.''

''Thank you.''

The uniformed attendant brought glasses of mineral water to Tess and Craig, Dom Pérignon for Kelly.

Gerrard seemed slightly self-conscious while they sipped. ''Well''—he rubbed his hands together—''before I explain, before we strap on our seat belts for takeoff, why don't I show you the rest of the plane? I'm very proud of it.''

Tess desperately didn't care, but she acquiesced. ''Lead the way, Alan.''

She hoped that her voice didn't tremble.

''It'll be a pleasure and a privilege.''

With gracious movements, Gerrard proceeded toward the forward bulkhead and revealed his quarters. Tess, in spite of her fear, was amazed by the luxurious accommodations: electric window curtains, a lavatory, a shower-tub, a vanity, closets, twin beds, a television system capable of receiving eight channels simultaneously including images from on-board remote-control cameras so Gerrard could assess waiting crowds before he left the aircraft . . . and two unusual hooks on the bedroom ceiling.

Tess pointed toward them, confused.

"Those. Yes, those. They sometimes keep me awake at night," Gerrard said. "Their implication. I don't like to think about them. They're hooks for intravenous lines in case I'm—to put it delicately—injured. This jet also has a minihospital." He paused, somber. "And a place for a coffin. But"—his expression brightened—"let's not be morbid. There's a great deal more for you to see."

He escorted them back through the central cabin toward the rear bulkhead's door, and beyond it, Tess became even more impressed.

She'd wondered why the seats in the central cabin weren't occupied. Now she understood. In a conference room that looked as if it belonged in a Fortune 500 corporation's headquarters, a dozen men sat in high-backed, upholstered chairs along a large rectangular table.

Secret Service agents, Gerrard explained. They were double-checking their tactics to protect him when he arrived in Spain. Phones and computers allowed them to coordinate their plans with the Spanish equivalent of the Secret Service.

Spain. Again the word sent tremors through Tess. She struggled urgently not to show her fear.

In a farther room, she saw another dozen men, vice-presidential aides using more phones and computers as well as printers and copying machines to polish speeches, verify itineraries, and prepare news releases. TV monitors flanked one bulkhead.

Leaving his aides to their work, Gerrard took Tess, Craig, and Kelly back to the central cabin. "There's more. *Much* more," he said. "A pressroom, although on this trip I'm not allowing reporters. Two galleys with gourmet cooks who can serve us trout almondine or anything else we want. Enough food for a week. A missile-avoidance system. Special shielding to protect the jet's controls from electromagnetic bursts from nuclear explosions. Eighty-five telephones. Fifty-seven antennas. A six-channel stereo system. Two hundred and thirty-eight miles of wiring. A crew of twenty-three. Their quarters are above us. Here, I know that Tess doesn't smoke, and Lieutenant Craig, my researchers tell me you wisely gave it up, although I can still hear the congestion in your lungs, but as souvenirs, why don't you take these?"

Tess grasped and stared down at a packet of matches. They were labeled ABOARD AIR FORCE TWO. As well, she received napkins, memo pads, and playing cards with the same inscription.

"I don't know what to say." Craig shook his head with apparent gratitude. "I'm honored. I've never been much for collecting souvenirs, but I'll treasure these." He pocketed the objects.

The next instant, he abruptly swung his attention toward the increasing shriek of the jet's four engines.

"It seems that we're about ready," Gerrard said.

A servant took their glasses.

"Your attention, please," a voice said through the intercom. "We're cleared for takeoff. All passengers be seated."

Ten seconds later, the Secret Service agents as well as Gerrard's aides came through the aft door, chose seats, and buckled themselves securely.

Tess and Craig did the same.

"I usually stay in my cabin during takeoff, but with the two of you on board, it's a special occasion. If you'll allow me . . ." Gerrard took a seat beside them. As a flight attendant explained the exits and the escape procedures for this Boeing 747, the Vice President leaned toward Tess.

"Obviously you're curious," he said. "Why did I send for you? You must be wondering, why are you here, en route to Spain?"

Tess resisted the drop in her stomach as Air Force Two moved smoothly across the tarmac toward the takeoff strip. She knew that the jet's special shielding prevented Father Baldwin from hearing the transmission from the miniature radio built into the heel of one of her shoes. All the same, she had to know.

"That's right, Alan. What are we doing here?"

The jet reached the runway, its four engines gaining power, roaring now instead of shrieking, propelling the aircraft with such force that Tess was shoved back against her seat.

At once the nose tilted toward the sky. Now the pressure Tess felt was downward again as the 747 gained altitude. At the same time, from beneath the fuselage, she heard a whir and thump as the wheels retracted into the wings and undercarriage. Craig had the window seat, but Tess was able, by leaning across him, to peer out. Amazingly soon, the lights of Andrews Air Force Base became glowing specks far below. Cities blazed to the right and left. Then the night enveloped the aircraft.

"The reason *I'm* here," Gerrard said, "the reason I'm flying to Spain, is that the Spanish president died this morning. A heart attack. A tragic loss not only to Spain but the European Economic Community. I'm being sent as America's official representative at the funeral. But you and Lieutenant Craig are here because I can't think of any place safer for you than aboard this plane. If Air Force Two can survive a nuclear war, the two of you certainly don't need to worry about being attacked while you're with me. All these Secret Service agents—I've instructed them to make sure you're not harmed. Until we sort out this mess, your protection is guaranteed."

The logic was attractive. If Tess hadn't felt ambivalent toward Gerrard, if she hadn't been worried that he was an enemy, her fears would have been subdued. In theory, in the present circumstances, she was absolutely protected, as safe as possible.

"Since your mother's home was attacked last night," Gerrard said, "I've had my investigators working overtime. I've learned about the death of your friend in Manhattan last Saturday night. Burned." He shook his head, appalled. "I've also learned that you and Lieutenant Craig have been trying to determine why he was killed."

Tess debated, then nodded in agreement.

Gerrard continued, "You flew to Washington to see your mother in Alexandria yesterday evening, which makes me suspect that you planned to use your father's contacts to help you investigate, and which in turn also makes me suspect that the attack on your mother's house and the attack on your friend are related, that *you're* the common denominator. More, I believe that Brian Hamilton's death has something to do with this. My investigators found out from his secretary that you called Brian at his office yesterday and that he missed a reception for the Soviet ambassador last night so he could visit your mother—translation, to visit *you*. After you spoke with Brian, he was killed in a freeway accident while en route to see the FBI director. I know that Brian phoned from his car and asked for that appointment because the FBI director told Kenneth Madden at Arlington Cemetery this afternoon, and Madden later told *me*. Finally an attack similar to the one at your mother's house occurred in Washington this afternoon. The owners of the house are missing, but one of them, Professor Richard Harding, taught you art history at Georgetown University. Again you're the common denominator. The coincidence troubles me. Were you *there*, Tess? No, don't look away. This is too important. Tell me. Be honest. *Were* you at Professor Harding's home this afternoon?''

Tess slowly, reluctantly, nodded again, inwardly flinching at the memory of the nightmare.

''The pattern is obvious. Tess, to be blunt, who's so desperate to kill you and in the process to kill the people you've recently contacted? *Why?* It almost makes me nervous to be in touch with you myself.'' Gerrard's latter remark was obviously somewhat exaggerated, given the presence of the Secret Service. No matter. The Vice President continued to look intense.

''Your investigators are very thorough, Alan.''

''That's why they work for me. They're the best.''

''Then maybe they've figured out why I'm in danger.''

''No. Otherwise I wouldn't be asking *you*. Is it the heretics? Do *they* want to kill you?''

Tess felt her cheeks turn pale. ''The heretics . . . ?''

She hadn't expected . . .

She couldn't believe . . .

Straining to keep her breathing steady, she managed only to stare.

''Your friend who was burned in Manhattan? My investigators conducted an in-depth background check. *He* was a heretic,'' Gerrard said. ''We've known about them for some time. At first, there were merely rumors. International gossip. But then a pattern began to be evident. Unusual diplomatic decisions. Puzzling changes in the policies of foreign nations, especially in Europe. Assassinations. Unexpected deaths of foreign diplomats, perhaps even the death of the Spanish president. Something—we don't know what—is happening. Blackmail. Extortion. Votes are controlled. Politicians are subjected to irresistible pressure. Major industries are afraid because several top executives have been murdered. It's not the Soviets. That system's collapsing. It's something else. A *new* threat looms now that the Cold War seems to be over. All because of a group of fanatics who somehow survived from the Middle Ages and decided to preserve their religious theories by disguising themselves and burrowing into the mainstream of international corporations and major governments. We have trouble identifying the heretics—they've had centuries of practice in hiding—but we recognize their trail, and we know that they're determined to destroy both democracy and capitalism. They might be a greater threat than the Soviets—who I still think are raising a smoke screen and trying to conceal their true aggressive intentions—ever were.''

"The evil empire,'' Tess said. ''The Reagan administration was obsessed with that idea. Don't tell me *this* administration also believes that the Soviets—''

"To hell with the Soviets. For all I know, I'm wrong to think they're trying to deceive us. It could be that the heretics have taken charge over there and are responsible for the downfall of the Communist Party. What I'm talking about is—''

With a mighty thrust, then a slight change of tone from the engines, Air Force Two stopped rising, settled, and maintained a level altitude.

The seat-belt light was extinguished.

From a microphone, a voice said, ''All passengers are free to move throughout the aircraft. In case of turbulence—of which you'll have ample warning—return to your seats and refasten your belts.''

In an instant, the Secret Service agents, followed by the Vice President's aides, exited hastily through the rear door to continue their duties.

Gerrard leaned sideways. ''Tess, what I'm asking is, do you believe that the heretics are the people who want to kill you? Because of your friendship with one of them? Because they're afraid you've learned too much about them?''

Tess fought to conceal her shock. She hadn't known what to expect when Gerrard brought Craig and her aboard Air Force Two. For certain, she'd never expected that Gerrard himself would raise the subject of the heretics. What the Vice President had just told her about them—the extent of their conspiracy—was more than she already knew. Maybe she was wrong about him. Did it make sense for him to be so open, to reveal so much, if he was one of them?

Or was he using candor to gain her confidence, to mute her suspicions?

In a quandary, Tess decided that she couldn't pretend to be ignorant. She had to follow his lead. "As near as I can figure, Alan, the answer is yes. But the truth is, although I stumbled across them, I hardly know anything about them." She reached in her purse and showed him the photograph of the statue. "This is the only evidence I have. I found the statue in my friend's bedroom, but later it was stolen. The reason I went to see Professor Harding was that I hoped he could tell me what it meant."

"And did he?"

"His wife did. The man on the bull is a god named Mithras. The serpent, the dog, and the scorpion represent his evil counterpart. They're trying to stop the blood from reaching the ground, the wheat from growing, the bull from being fertile. That information—and the fact that the heretics survived a purge in the Middle Ages and then infiltrated various governments to stop the purge—is all I know."

Gerrard squinted. "Then it's *who* you are, not what you know, that they believe threatens them. They're afraid you'll use your influence with your father's friends, including me, to expose them. The terrible irony is that their killings have been needless, that their desperate efforts are wasted since we already know a great deal more than *you* do about them. Your mother and Brian Hamilton didn't have to die. What a waste. I'm so sorry, Tess."

Tess's throat ached again from grief.

At the same time, she retained sufficient presence of mind to wonder why—if the inner circle of the government knew about the heretics—Eric Chatham had claimed to be ignorant about them.

Surely the director of the FBI would have a major role in investigating them. Had Chatham been so suspicious of Father Baldwin's group that he'd decided to pretend he knew nothing about the heretics?

As she considered the possibilities, uncertainty made her dizzy. What appeared to be sincerity might be deception, and apparent deception might very well be sincerity.

Her consciousness felt clouded. Her sense of reality was threatened.

Gerrard distracted her by clasping her hand. "I promise you

this. I'll use all my power to make them pay for what they did to your mother.''

"Thank you, Alan. If only this nightmare would end.''

"That's another promise. I'll do my best to see that it does end.''

The cabin became still, except for the slight vibration caused by the engines.

Gerrard glanced beyond Tess, his attention devoted to Craig. "Lieutenant, my investigators tell me that you're fond of opera.''

"True.'' Craig frowned.

"No need to be puzzled. My staff is thorough, as I explained.''

"But what does opera have to do with . . . ?''

"If you'll reach in the seat pocket before you . . .''

Craig searched and found a set of earphones.

"Put them on,'' Gerrard said. "Insert their extension into the console beside you. Turn the dial to channel five. You'll hear what I believe is the greatest opera of all—Verdi's *Otello*.''

"Verdi's good, but I've always preferred Puccini.''

"I wasn't told that. I'm sorry—on this flight, all the operas we have are by Verdi, Mozart, and Wagner.''

"Verdi will do just fine.'' Craig coughed. "The thing is, while I listen . . . ?''

"Tess and I will take other seats. We haven't seen each other in too many years. We have memories to share, private matters to discuss.''

Craig straightened nervously.

"Executive privilege,'' Gerrard said. "Enjoy the opera. Tess?'' He stood.

"It's late.'' She stood as well. "Madrid's a long way. You'll be exhausted if you don't get some sleep, Alan. And I'm *already* exhausted. No offense. I'll want to lean against Craig's shoulder soon and doze off.''

"I'll be waiting,'' Craig said.

"We won't be long,'' Gerrard said. "It's just a little story I want to tell her.''

"I hope it's as fascinating as the opera,'' Craig said.

"More so,'' Gerrard said.

"Well, she can't ask for better than that." Craig put on his earphones.

Knowing the tension that Craig fought not to reveal, Tess allowed Gerrard to guide her toward one of many empty seats in the rear of the cabin.

"And now?"

"Actually I have *two* stories," Gerrard said. "One's about vinegar. The other's about frogs."

"Vinegar? Frogs? You're confusing me, Alan."

"You'll understand when I finish."

6

"To begin," Gerrard said as they buckled their seat belts, "I'm told that since I last saw you, since you graduated from college, you've become an environmentalist, not just in your attitudes but as your profession. You're a staff writer for *Earth Mother Magazine.*"

"That's right," Tess said.

"I confess I haven't read the magazine, but my investigators searched through several back issues. They tell me your articles are very informative, the writing quite accomplished. They particularly mentioned how impressed they were with an essay you'd written on the alarmingly rapid disappearance of wetlands and the rare species that inhabit them. What struck my investigators was that it wasn't a topic they would have expected to find interesting, but you made it so and indeed convinced them of how important those wetlands are. The photographs that accompanied the article—taken by you—were exceptional, they said, and made them realize how beautiful the rare insects, birds, and fish that inhabit those wetlands are, what a loss to the planet they'd be. To the world's ecology."

"Thank them for the compliment," Tess said. "Now if they'd

just follow through and donate to organizations devoted to preserving those wetlands.''

"As a matter of fact, they did.''

Tess felt gratified. "Please, thank them twice.''

"I will. Now here's the point. Even though I haven't read *Earth Mother Magazine*, I'm an environmentalist as well. You may have read about the controversy I caused when I voted against the President to break the tie on the Senate's rigid clean-air bill.''

"I did,'' Tess said, "and I have to say I was impressed. You did the right thing.''

"The President has a different opinion. You wouldn't want to have been in the Oval Office when he chewed me out for being disloyal. What he doesn't know is that in matters about the environment I'll *continue* to be disloyal, even if it means he chooses someone else as a running mate in the next election. There comes a time when you have to take a stand, no matter the personal cost.''

Tess felt her suspicions dwindling. Despite her fear, Gerrard had begun to win her respect. "He'd be making a mistake if he dumped you.''

"Write him a letter. Tell him so.'' Gerrard chuckled. A few moments later, he sobered. "Because you're an expert in these matters, maybe you know this story, but I'll tell it to you anyhow.''

He was interrupted. A voice asked, "Sir, would you care for a drink?''

Gerrard glanced up. A flight attendant stood beside him. "The usual. Orange juice.''

"Sounds good to me,'' Tess said.

As the flight attendant departed, Gerrard said, "There's a man I heard about who lives in Iowa. A farmer. His name's Ben Gould. He's a member of the National Audubon Society. He's also an amateur climatologist. Near his barn, he's got a shed with a rain gauge, barometer, wind indicator, and various other weather-analysis instruments. Two summers ago, after an extended period of drought that just about killed his corn and soybeans, his farm was blessed with several days of heavy rain. Or at least Gould *thought* his farm had been blessed. He put on rubber boots and slogged through mud to his weather shack. His rain gauge was almost full. He poured its contents into a sterile container, carried the container into his shack, and dumped the liquid into an instrument that analyses the chemical contents of water. This instrument was computerized. Red numbers glowed on a console. Two point five.''

The flight attendant handed Tess and Gerrard glasses of orange juice along with napkins.

They nodded their thanks.

"Two point five," Gerrard repeated. "What those numbers represented was the pH of the rain, the level of acid. The rule is, the lower the number, the higher the acid. Pure rainwater registers at five point three. But *two point five?* Gould was shocked. He told himself that there had to be a mistake, so he double-checked his readings, using rain from another gauge. But the instrument's console showed the same numbers. Two point five. That's the acid level of *vinegar*. Gould suddenly realized why his crops looked stunted. Vinegar? That's what you put on a *salad*. Not on your crops. It could rain every week, and Gould's crops would *still* look stunted. In a panic, he examined his wind charts. Global warming and its erratic effects had caused the jet stream to veer unusually southward. Into New Mexico. Then across Iowa. New Mexico's copper smelters are notorious for spewing outrageous amounts of sulfur fumes into the atmosphere. Those sulfur fumes, as you know, produce acid rain. And acid rain, in never before such intense concentration, was poisoning Gould's land.''

Pausing, Gerrard sipped his orange juice. "Anyway, that's my story about vinegar. I wish I could say it had a climax, a happy ending, but the fact is, Gould's crops are still being poisoned, and there won't be a happy ending until we have legislation that forces those copper smelters and other heavy industries to clean up their act. Not just legislation in America, but worldwide. In Germany and Czechoslovakia, for example, there are thousands of square kilometers of woodland that have been totally destroyed and blackened by acid rain.''

Tess nodded. "I know about those sections of Germany and Czechoslovakia, but your story about Iowa is new to me.''

"Then write an article on it. Maybe it'll do some good, get people thinking, motivated enough to write to their congressional representative, demanding controls.''

"I will," Tess said. "Poisoned forests don't seem to bother

people unless they see the devastation. But a personal story, like Gould's, might make the crisis vivid.''

"And while you're at it, write the other story I'm about to tell you, the one about the frogs.'' Gerrard drained his glass of orange juice and set it down. "The main character in this one is a biologist named Ralph McQueen. His specialty is amphibians, and each year he likes to make a field trip into the Sierra Nevadas. A decade ago, he checked thirty-eight lakes and found them teeming with yellow-legged frogs. Last summer when he went back, he couldn't believe what he found or rather *didn't* find. The frogs had vanished from all but one of those lakes. In shock, he tried to discover why they'd vanished. His best guess was that some kind of deadly virus had wiped out almost the entire local population. But when he went to a herpetology convention in Brussels last fall, his shock became greater. It turns out that the Sierra Nevadas aren't the only area where frogs are disappearing. From colleagues, he learned that the same thing was happening all over the United States and indeed all over the world—in Costa Rica, Japan, Europe, Australia, Africa, Indonesia, Malaysia, South America, everywhere. The frogs are dying, and no one's quite sure why. Acid rain, pesticides, water pollution, *air* pollution, global warming, too many ultraviolet rays caused by the hole in the ozone layer. Maybe all of those. It's hard to say. But the interesting thing about frogs is that they don't have scales to protect them, and they breathe through their skin, which is very sensitive. That makes them extremely vulnerable to damaging changes in the environment. It used to be that coal miners took a caged canary into the shaft they were working on. If odorless poisonous gases built up, they'd know because the canary, so small, would die first. The miners would have a chance to run from the shaft.''

Gerrard furrowed his brow. "Possibly the frogs are canaries for the planet. Their massive extinction might be a warning that something's very wrong. What's more, their extinction could have disastrous effects on the world's ecology. The frogs eat huge amounts of insects. Without them, flies and mosquitoes—to name just a few—will breed out of control. At the same time, larger life-forms such as birds and animals depend on the frogs for food. Without the frogs, those other life-forms will die.

"Frogs.'' Gerrard shook his head. "So seemingly trivial. So

formerly common. So much a part of nature that we hardly noticed them. I suppose a lot of people could care less if they're dying, but what those people don't realize is that the frogs are an environmental cornerstone, and without them . . .'' Gerrard's voice dropped, his tone despondent. "Write it, Tess. An epitaph for the frogs, for the songs they no longer sing. A warning to everyone who still hasn't realized how endangered the world has become."

"I will. I promise."

Gerrard clasped her hand once more. "I told you those stories not just because we share the same concerns or because the stories relate to your work. I had another motive, one that involves the heretics."

Startled by the mention of the word, Tess came to greater attention.

"What I didn't indicate earlier," Gerrard said, "is that as much as we can determine, the heretics' conspiracy to terrorize corporations and infiltrate governments, to assassinate politicians and replace them with the heretics' own representatives, to blackmail other politicians in order to control their votes on environmental legislation, is due to the heretics' fear about the safety of the world. The photograph you showed me symbolizes their motive." Gerrard gestured as if tracing an invisible image. "A good god trying to fertilize the earth. An evil god trying to stop it. The heretics believe that the evil god has assumed control and is using every effort to destroy the planet." Again Gerrard frowned. "I'm sure you can understand the heretics' point of view. The evidence of the planet's destruction is all around us. Their intentions are the same as yours and mine, although their methods, of course, are repugnant. But a part of me, I confess, sympathizes. If a person gets frightened enough, if legitimate methods don't work, sometimes desperate measures are required. I don't approve, but I do identify with their desperation, the same desperation that forced me to vote against the President and for the Senate's clean-air bill. What I'm getting at is that good and evil aren't always as easily distinguishable as they might seem. If the heretics manage to save the planet, perhaps in the long run their methods are justified. I really don't know. I'm a politician, not an expert in ethics. But I'll tell you this. There are times when I hesitate, when I question how much force we should use to hunt them. If my children live to have grandchildren and those grandchildren breathe clean air, drink pure water, eat uncontaminated food, and flourish, maybe the heretics will have been right. I just don't know.''

He studied Tess, waiting for her reaction.

Tess took a while to answer, mustering, organizing, her thoughts. "I understand what you mean, Alan. Like you, a part of me identifies with the heretics or at least with their motives. Irresponsible corporations ought to be made accountable. Indifferent politicians ought to be removed from government. There's a global crisis, and it has to be faced, to be dealt with and solved. But *murder*, Alan? Extortion? Lives ruined? Families in grief? I've never supported capital punishment, although I did feel the urge to strangle the captain of the Pacific-Rim oil tanker who allowed his alcoholism to impair his judgment and capsize his tanker so its cargo polluted the Great Barrier Reef. But I've never met that captain. I don't *know* him. I don't know his virtues and his strengths, so it's easy enough for me to hate him from a distance. This much I *do* know. My friend who was burned in New York—*he* didn't agree with extortion and murder. And Brian Hamilton never did anything to endanger the environment. And my mother, God bless her soul, was just a simpleminded, heartsick, pampered, pathetic socialite who never did anything to harm *anyone*. In spite of her failings, I loved her. Deeply. When the heretics murdered her—I can still see the blood flying out of her—just so they could try to get at me, when they did that, they made this very personal. Capital punishment? No, I don't believe in it. But revenge, Alan? After what I've been through, after the horror of the past few days, I'd like nothing better than to hunt them down and pay them back. Didn't you promise me that earlier? To help me pay them back?''

Gerrard nodded.

"So what it comes down to, Alan, is that I don't care if the heretics share my commitment to save the world. They're bastards. They're evil—in fact more evil than the evil god they believe they're fighting. They're twisted sons of bitches, and I'll do everything I can to put them in hell, which is where they belong and less than what they deserve. Maybe this planet *isn't* worth protecting if good gets confused with murder, and my mother dies because of that.''

Gerrard stared, then sighed. "Of course. That's exactly what I anticipated you to say. By all means, I agree. I was just pointing out the moral complexities." He glanced at his watch. "It's late." He stood. "I'm pleased that we had this talk, but tomorrow, I have obligations to face. If you'll excuse me . . ."

"Yes, we're both exhausted. But before you leave," Tess said, "your personal assistant mentioned something about toothbrushes, an overnight kit, a shower-tub, a place to . . . I'm afraid I have to pee."

Gerrard blushed. "Our flight attendant will take care of everything you need."

"Thanks, Alan. And it is good to see you again."

"You're the most welcome guest I've had on Air Force Two."

Tess waited until Gerrard disappeared through the forward door into his private cabin. Then she spoke to the flight attendant, who escorted her toward a bathroom in the rear of the plane. Ten minutes later, she reentered the central cabin, buckled her seat belt, and nestled next to Craig.

He was still awake. Removing his earphones, from which Tess heard muted opera, Craig asked, "How did it go?"

"Confusing. Complicated. Disturbing. But I'm too tired to . . . I'll tell you later." With her head against Craig's shoulder, Tess closed her eyes and quickly fell asleep, only to wake several times, shuddering from premonitions.

7

The flight to Spain took five hours, but with the added five hours in time-zone changes, it was just before eleven A.M. when the jet reached Madrid.

Peering down at the airport, Tess was struck by how hazy the air looked. For a moment, she didn't understand why the smog should be worse here than in New York. Then she remembered that in Europe, most cars weren't equipped with emission controls, and that Spain, like the rest of the continent, still hadn't converted to the widespread use of unleaded gas. The dirtier leaded gas was fouling the sky. She instantly remembered something else—Gerrard's insistence last night on the need for international standards to protect the environment.

As the massive 747 touched down with remarkable smoothness, she noticed the airport's terminal to her right, but Air Force Two did not approach it, instead proceeded to a remote section of the tarmac, and came to a stop, the shriek of its engines dying.

Several cars rapidly flanked it, armed men scrambling out to position themselves with their backs to the jet, their assault rifles aimed outward to guard it. At the same time, a black limousine with a diplomatic flag mounted and fluttering on the side of its hood cruised toward a boarding platform that an airport crew rolled against one of the plane's forward hatches.

The occupants of the central cabin burst into motion. Unbuckling their seat belts, Secret Service agents hurried to enter the forward compartment while the Vice President's aides speedily returned to their office in the rear.

Tess and Craig crossed to the left of the plane. Curious, they peered out a window from which they saw a uniformed chauffeur open a back door on the limousine. Two distinguished-looking, gray-haired, diplomatically dressed men got out, shook hands with Gerrard's assistant, Hugh Kelly, exchanged remarks with him, braced their shoulders, and climbed the boarding steps to enter the Vice President's quarters.

"And *now* what?" Craig wondered. Earlier, after a breakfast of fresh fruit and then smoked salmon on a whole-wheat bagel that Tess had recommended, he'd brushed his teeth, washed his face, and shaved. Even so, although he'd slept a few hours, the long flight in combination with jet lag had wearied him. He glanced down at his rumpled clothes. "Not exactly presentable. I hope we have a chance to buy something a little more formal so we don't look conspicuous, given the company we're keeping."

Tess squinted down at her own rumpled blouse and jeans,

nodding in agreement. Mostly what she wished she had was a change of underclothes. "I've got a suspicion that when you travel with the Vice President, what you ask for, someone delivers."

She flinched, an unexpected noise making her turn toward the forward bulkhead. The door to the Vice President's cabin swung open.

Alan Gerrard appeared, wearing an immaculate gray suit, striped tie, and white shirt. His black shoes had been polished to a gleam.

"So," Gerrard said. "I hope you slept well." He rubbed his hands together with enthusiasm. "Are we ready?"

"To do what?" Tess asked.

"To get on another plane."

Tess couldn't help feeling surprised. "The funeral isn't here in Madrid? The president of Spain . . ." She frowned in confusion. "I assumed he'd be buried with full state honors in the nation's capital."

"Well, you're right. The funeral *will* be in Madrid. But it isn't scheduled until two days from now," Gerrard said. "I have several important diplomats to see before then, but I told the Spanish government not to tell the press that I'd be arriving today. There's something I need to do before I begin my duties. In fact, one of the diplomats I need to see, a friend from my former trips here, isn't in town. There's a strong chance that Spain's Congress of Deputies will soon elect him as the country's new president. So we're going to board a smaller, less conspicuous plane and visit his estate. Don't look so hesitant. His home is a showplace. His hospitality is lavish. You'll enjoy yourselves. Really. With my friend's guards as well as my Secret Service agents, you'll still be well protected."

It sounded reasonable, Tess tried to assure herself. But her heart cramped as if ice surrounded it. Bewildered, uneasy, she overcame her hesitation and followed Gerrard into his cabin. Craig put an arm around her while they waited for the Vice President and the two diplomats to descend the stairs to the tarmac. Below, guards surrounded the group as the three men stood near the limousine and shook hands.

Gerrard turned and motioned for Tess and Craig to come down. "The plane's just over there."

At the bottom, Tess stared toward her right. She didn't know about planes, certainly not enough to be able to identify a model or its manufacturer. All she understood was that this one was smaller than she expected, streamlined, a two-engine, executive jet.

"But isn't it dangerous for you to travel in something so . . . ?"

"Unprotected?" Gerrard said. "You mean because it doesn't have special shielding and all kinds of sophisticated communication equipment?" He shook his head, his blue eyes twinkling with amusement. The one on the right looked less irritated. "I'm sure you're aware of what the political columnists say about me. I'm inconsequential. In their opinion, who'd want to kill me?"

"But a terrorist might not care about what the columnists say. You *are* the vice president of the United States."

"Not to worry," Gerrard said. "I've made this side trip before. And as far as security's concerned, only a *very* few trusted officials know that I arrived one day earlier than I was expected. I guarantee we're safe."

Unable to resist Gerrard's hand on her arm—especially in the crowded presence of the numerous stern-eyed guards—Tess allowed herself to be escorted toward the few steps that led upward through the open hatch into the plane.

She felt assaulted by claustrophobia, seeing only a narrow aisle with a row of single seats on each side. Seized by alarm, she realized that with the pilot, the copilot, Gerrard, Hugh Kelly, Craig, and herself, there was room for only five Secret Service agents to join them. Her premonition increased as the security around her began to *decrease*.

Inwardly she winced from the clunking sound the hatch made when the copilot shut and locked it.

Again, as she had when she'd entered Air Force Two, she felt trapped. But more so. It took all her discipline to keep her fingers from trembling when she fastened her seat belt.

Opposite Gerrard, she snuck a nervous glance back to her right, toward Craig, who sat *behind* Gerrard.

Craig winked, and that made all the difference.

Tess smiled in return and realized how much she'd become attracted to him. Whatever was going to happen, no matter the risk, regardless of the possible imminent danger, she and Craig were in this together, and what they felt for each other was great enough that they could survive and defeat any enemy. They *had* to.

Please, God, help us, she prayed. Please, help Father Baldwin. Did he manage to follow us to Madrid? Will he be able to receive the signals from the microphone and the homing device built into my shoes and follow us to wherever we're being taken?

The pilot was given clearance for takeoff. Two minutes later, the jet streaked through the smog toward the sky.

Tess felt more helpless.

Trying to seem relaxed, she made herself peer out the window. As the jet reached its cruising altitude, she saw a vast arid plain below her and occasional slopes that rose to low, flat plateaus, the soil of which had the tint of copper.

"Where are we headed?" She hoped she sounded casual.

"Toward Spain's northern coast," Gerrard said. "A district called Vizcaya. We'll land in Bilbao."

"Bilbao?" She strained to make conversation, hoping that Father Baldwin was listening. "Wasn't there a song about . . . ?"

" 'That Old Bilbao Moon'? Yes, but the song goes back quite a while. I'm surprised you know it. I'm not sure that this Bilbao is the one in the song."

"Is it far?"

"Just an hour." Gerrard shrugged. "Time enough for a nap."

Craig leaned forward. "Why didn't the President himself come for the funeral?"

"Normally he would have." Gerrard turned. "There'll be many European heads of state here, a chance for an unofficial summit. But his schedule's too complicated. He'll soon be leaving on a trip that he planned long ago and he can't postpone—to Peru, for a major drug-control conference similar to the one he went to in Colombia last year. You feel nervous, so imagine how *he* feels with all those drug lords determined to assassinate him. That's why he can't postpone the trip. The President refuses to make it seem as if the drug lords scared him off. His bravery's remarkable. No matter how much he and I don't get along, I hope to heaven that nothing happens to him.''

They settled back as the jet sped onward. Tess closed her eyes and despite her uneasiness, tried to nap. If her premonitions were justified, she knew she'd be needing all her strength.

8

The bump of the wheels' touching down awakened her. Tess rubbed her sleep-swollen eyes and peered outside. Compared to the airport in Madrid, Bilbao's was small, its air less hazy. Perhaps a breeze from the nearby ocean dispersed the exhaust fumes of cars, she thought. Again they avoided the terminal and stopped at a remote section of the tarmac.

Outside, Gerrard spoke as enthusiastically as he had when they'd left Madrid. ''Are you ready for another flight?''

''*Another?* But I thought our destination was Bilbao.'' Tess continued to hope that Father Baldwin was listening.

''Just so we could change to another aircraft. We'll be heading east now, past Pamplona.''

Tess repressed a cringe, remembering that Pamplona was close to where Priscilla Harding had said that she'd found images of Mithras hidden in caves.

Tess sweated, wanting to run, but again Secret Service agents flanked her.

''My friend's estate doesn't have a landing strip,'' Gerrard explained, ''so now we'll be using *this*.'' He pointed.

The sight of the helicopter made Tess feel light-headed. Powerless, weak-kneed, disturbed by her lack of control, she was led aboard, and now with increasing panic, she discovered that there was space enough only for a pilot, Gerrard, Hugh Kelly, Craig, herself, and *two* Secret Service agents. Her protection kept dwindling, her isolation increasing. No matter the confidence that her attraction to Craig had earlier inspired in her, she suddenly felt doomed.

The helicopter's blades whined, turning, spinning, increasing speed until their sound was a whump-whump-whumping roar. With a mighty surge, the helicopter lifted straight up, and Tess, who directed a despairing glance toward Craig, noticed that his expression was equally intense.

He didn't wink this time, and she didn't smile in return. What she did was swallow something hot and bitter.

She forced herself to pay attention to her surroundings, knowing that every detail was important and that she had to regain her discipline.

Study the landscape, her mind insisted. If you get in trouble, you'd better know where you are.

In contrast with the arid, flat, middle portion of Spain, this area along the country's northern coast was lush and hilly. The valleys below her were occupied by farms in which stoop-shouldered men and women wielded scythes to cut tall grass. The men wore trousers, long-sleeved shirts, and wide-brimmed hats. The women had long dresses and handkerchiefs tied around their heads. The absence of motorized farm machinery, combined with the slate roofs and stone walls of the buildings, made Tess feel as if she were experiencing a time warp, that she was witnessing a scene from a previous century.

But those impressions were fleeting—brief, ineffectual attempts to distract herself from her terror.

"That's Pamplona past those hills on the right," Gerrard said matter-of-factly. "You can just make out a few tops of buildings. Northeast of us is the French-Spanish border. We're now in a district called Navarra, and those mountains ahead are the Spanish Pyrenees."

Tess wondered fearfully how close the helicopter was to the Pyrenees in France, to the burned-out ruins of the heretic stronghold on Montségur, to the site of the slaughter that the European crusaders had inflicted and from where more than seven hundred years ago, after a group of determined heretics had escaped with their precious statue, this insanity had begun.

The mountains were spectacular: high, rugged, limestone cliffs, their deep gorges churning with narrow, swift rivers, their slopes thick with pines and beeches.

The helicopter thundered nearer. The peaks seemed to grow, their outcrops more jagged, their steep drops more wild. How high must they be? Tess wondered. At least seven thousand feet, she concluded—not as tall as the ranges she was familiar with, those in Switzerland and Colorado where her father had sometimes taken her to ski. But these had sharper inclines that made them seem taller, and their ravines were more forbidding. Rugged, she'd thought earlier. Wild. The words gained emphasis as she stared at a rapidly looming gorge, feeling dizzy as she lowered her gaze.

Below, amid tangled woods, a narrow dirt road wound past random gigantic boulders, entering the gorge. Abruptly she glanced up and stiffened as the helicopter also entered the gorge, the whump-whump-whump of the rotors intensified by their deafening echo off the craggy wall of rock on each side, the passage so seemingly narrow that she feared the blades would collide with an outcrop.

At once, the gorge ended. She exhaled, relieved, then exhaled again when the helicopter began to descend. A small valley appeared. Dense forest encircled grassland, and at the center, surrounded by a maze of fenced enclosures, small buildings flanked a commanding structure toward which the helicopter quickly dipped.

The structure had stone walls and a slate roof, the same as the farmhouses that Tess had seen in the fields near Pamplona. But that was the only similarity. Because those farmhouses had been small and modest. But what she stared at now, her uneasiness aggravated by the increasing downward tilt and thrust of the helicopter, was so wide and tall, so impressive . . .

"It's a castle," Gerrard explained. "Not the kind you see in England or in France or for that matter, anywhere else in Europe. This is a *Spanish* castle. In the south, they used a Moorish design, but this is a type that's common in the north. It doesn't have the turrets, the parapets, the moat, and the drawbridge that you'd expect.

It's more like a cross between a manor house and a fortress. The stone and the slate are barriers against an attack by fire. The only exterior wood is—''

"At the windows." Tess strained to make herself heard above the roar of the sharply descending helicopter. "Shutters. Even from here, they look thick."

Gerrard nodded. "And inside each room, there's a set of doors. Equally thick. A farther barrier to keep flames from reaching inside. But in theory, no one could torch the shutters because as we get closer, you'll see narrow slits in the five-foot-thick stone walls. An outside archer couldn't cross the open area around the castle to shoot flaming arrows without being hit by archers *within* the castle, and those defending archers, concealed behind those narrow slits, were impossible targets."

As the helicopter slanted lower, approaching a landing pad, Tess noticed animals in the fields, horses in some while in others there were . . . "Your friend's a rancher?" she asked.

Gerrard looked puzzled. Then the wrinkles in his forehead relaxed. "Ah, I understand. You think those are cattle. They're not. They're bulls. My friend breeds them as a hobby. Some of them will be used next month in the famous bullfight festival of San Fermin in Pamplona. I'm sure you've read descriptions of it, the skyrocket each morning, the frantic bulls being forced to run through the streets, the villagers testing their bravery by trying to race ahead of the frightened herd, some of the young men falling, being trampled and often gored. Eight days and nights of parties. Eight afternoons of ritualized death."

Tess indeed had read about it, and now that she was close enough, she was able to distinguish the characteristics of the animals, their muscular flanks, their broad humped backs, their long curved horns projecting from thickly boned foreheads.

Bulls.

They were so much a part of Spain's culture that Tess didn't make the further connection right away. But then she suddenly noticed one particular bull that had been separated from the others. Magnificent, it grazed alone in a field, and any doubts Tess had about whether Gerrard could be trusted, any lingering hopes that Gerrard was not her enemy, were instantly dispelled. Her mind envisioned the photograph in her purse, the image of Mithras slicing the throat of a bull. A white bull. Just like the bull that grazed alone in the field. A bull that was white.

The last of her ambivalence about Gerrard was resolved. Terror possessed her, made all the worse because as her heart pounded and her breathing quickened, she didn't dare let Gerrard notice her abrupt panicked understanding. It was clear now. Absolutely certain. Except for Craig, everyone in this helicopter was a threat, including the two Secret Service agents—she had to assume—because Gerrard must have had a reason to choose these two agents from all the others. She cursed herself for having allowed herself to be swayed last night by Gerrard's charisma and the environmental concerns that they shared. She shouldn't have permitted herself to be tempted to believe that he meant her no harm. She should never have spoken so vehemently against the heretics when he tried to convince her that the heretics' motives possibly justified desperate measures, that the moral issues were complicated. Gerrard had been trying to make a bargain with her, to test and perhaps convert her, but she'd been so emotionally involved in the conversation that she hadn't grasped its true purpose. His attempt to appeal to her logic having failed, he now had only one remaining course of action—to kill her.

Her terror increasing, Tess felt her stomach heave as the helicopter set down, the wind from its rotors bending grass. The roar of the engines diminished to a whine and finally silence. Gerrard escorted Tess outside. Hugh Kelly and the two Secret Service agents stayed near Craig.

What do they think we're going to do? Tess thought. Run?

To where? We'd never reach the trees. The time to run or at least to back off was when we were still at Andrews Air Force Base.

But the plan to determine if Gerrard was one of the heretics had seemed so necessary that she'd obeyed Father Baldwin's instructions, and now it was too late to try to get away from Gerrard. She and Craig were stuck here, and their single chance was to try to make a deal.

Tess mentally shook her head. No, there was another chance—that Father Baldwin and his men would manage to follow the signal from the homing device in her shoe and find her. Again she prayed.

Pay attention, she told herself. Concentrate. Be aware of every-thing.

The air smelled sweet. She savored the fragrance of meadow grass and mountain flowers. As well, the air was amazingly clear, the sky an impressive pure blue. She couldn't remember the last time she hadn't breathed smog. But these impressions were fleeting. What she noticed most was that this circular valley was enclosed by peaks, with only one entrance, the gorge through which the helicopter had approached.

We're trapped, she thought in dismay. All the same, she refused to give up hope. Damn it, there must be *something* that Craig and I can do to protect ourselves.

At once Gerrard spoke. "My friend has been waiting. He's eager to meet you."

Tess swung. A half dozen laborers had been leaning against a wooden fence, examining a group of bulls. Now one of them stepped away and quickly reached the helicopter. He wore dusty boots and sweat-stained work clothes, a red bandanna around his neck. But no matter his common outfit, his bearing was unmistakably aris-tocratic. A tall man, heavy but in no way fat. His arms, legs, shoulders, and chest looked solid, well-exercised. His face was rectangular, tawny, with the texture of leather, strong more than handsome, his broad forehead reminding Tess of the bulls. She judged him to be in his late forties and shifted her gaze to his thick, dark, sheeny hair. His eyes—they were brown, Tess made a point of noticing—glinted when he reached his visitors. His smile gleamed.

"*Señor Gerrard! Buenas tardes! Mucho gusto! Como esta usted?*"

"*Muy bien. Gracias,*" Gerrard said. "*Y usted?*"

"*Excelente!*"

The two men embraced, slapping each other's back.

When they separated, the stranger abruptly changed to English, his voice deep and resonant, a politician's voice. "You've stayed away much too long. You know you're always welcome here."

"I'll try to visit more often," Gerrard said.

"I look forward to it." The stranger ignored the two Secret

Service agents and faced Hugh Kelly. Smiling warmly, he shook his hand. "It's a pleasure to see you again, Señor Kelly."

"The pleasure is mine."

"*Bueno. Bueno.* And Alan, these are your friends?"

"Forgive me for being rude," Gerrard said. "Tess, Lieutenant Craig, this is José Fulano. He has a title and a formal version of his name that's extremely long, but when we're not at the conference table, we like to keep things unofficial. I phoned José while we flew to Madrid and told him you'd be coming here with me."

Fulano shook their hands with delight. "To borrow your American expression, any friends of Alan are friends of mine. You're very welcome. My home is at your disposal. *Mi casa, su casa.* Whatever you need, please don't hesitate to ask."

Sure, Tess thought. What do I need? Like, how the hell do I get out of here? But she pretended not to be terrified and gave him her most pleasant smile. "We appreciate your hospitality, Señor Fulano."

"Please, I'm José."

"Your home is magnificent," Craig said. "I've never seen a more beautiful setting."

Fulano turned and joined them in their admiration of his property. "I spend too much time in Madrid. If I were sane, I'd never leave here." He sighed. "But as Alan understands too well, the pressures of responsibility don't give us much time to enjoy the truly important things, the beauties of life." Fulano glanced at Tess. "When Alan phoned me from Air Force Two, he explained that you're an environmentalist. You'll be pleased to learn that there isn't any pollution here."

"I realized that when we got off the helicopter. I feel like I'm breathing pure oxygen."

Fulano smiled. "You must be exhausted from your journey. You'll want to rest, to bathe. I'll show you to your rooms. I'm sure you'd also appreciate a change of clothes."

"Thank you," Tess said.

"*De nada.*" Fulano guided them proudly past an outbuilding toward the castle.

A cobblestone road, bordered by grass, led toward it. Close, the building looked less tall than from the air, perhaps six stories, but its width and depth remained considerable. The rocks that made up its walls were huge. Most of the shutters were open, revealing tall, spacious windows. On the upper floors, each window had a balcony with pots of colorful blooming flowers and a wrought-iron railing, the bars of which were bent into ornate shapes. Two thick stone slabs formed steps toward a huge, arched, double door made of rich, dark wood.

Fulano pushed one heavy side open and gestured for Tess and Craig to enter ahead of him. More fearful, Tess complied, but not before she noticed armed sentries at each corner of the building. Although they pretended to study the road and the fields, what they really cared about, with surreptitious glances, was she and Craig.

The moment Tess crossed the threshold, her first impression was of sweat cooling on her brow. Evidently the temperature outside had been warmer than she'd realized. The stone of both the walls and the floor made the interior at least ten degrees lower.

Her second impression was of shadows. After the bright sun, she needed several moments for her eyes to adjust. A long, sturdy, antique, wooden table occupied the middle of the entry room. Complex tapestries depicting woodlands and mountains hung on two walls. Another tapestry portrayed a bullfight, the matador thrusting his sword. An ancient suit of armor stood in the far left corner.

The ceiling amazed her: dark, polished, foot-square beams joined perfectly, anchored into the stone walls, supported by pillars and occasional transverse beams. She'd never been in a building that felt more solid.

"This way," Fulano said graciously. He led them across the room, up three more slabs of cool stone, turned left in a muffled corridor, and walked with them up a staircase that was made from the same thick beams that formed the ceiling. The echo of their footsteps was absorbed by the substantial wood and stone below and around them.

The second level was equally amazing, a high, large, open area with a floor and ceiling of massive beams and another long, sturdy, antique table. More tapestries. Wooden, thronelike chairs along the walls. Between each chair, a door.

"This is *your* room," Fulano told Tess, "and this is yours," he said to Craig.

The doors were widely separated.

"Fine," Craig said. "But not to be indelicate, Tess and I are . . ."

"Yes?" Fulano asked, puzzled.

"Together."

"You're telling me that you've. . . ?" Fulano raised his eyebrows.

"Reached an arrangement."

"Yes," Fulano said. "By all means. Forgive my manners. This room," he told Craig and Tess, "is yours. You've had a long journey. You'll no doubt want to rest. But at eight o'clock, please join us in the dining room. It's down the staircase, then left along the corridor. We have a surprise for you."

"I'm eager to see it. We'll clean up and join you at eight," Craig said.

"Bueno."

9

Tess and Craig entered the room, which was lofty and wide, with antique Spanish cabinets, open doors at the window, and an oversize bed. Its tall headboard matched the rich, dark beams of the floor and ceiling.

Craig locked the door.

Tess gripped his arms. "Thank God, you—"

Craig forcefully put a finger on her lips. "I bet the view from this room is magnificent. Those flowers. Did you notice them on the balcony? Why don't we take a look?"

It wasn't as if she had a choice. Craig's hand pressed against her back and urged her toward the balcony.

Past the open doors, leaning against the wrought-iron railing, they had a view of the cobblestone road and the outbuildings, beyond which there were fields—bulls in some, horses in others—then the forest, then the towering mountains. A scented breeze widened Tess's nostrils, but that pleasure was irrelevant.

"I'm sure the room is bugged," Craig murmured. "But I don't think the microphones can hear us on the balcony. Did you notice the sentries?"

"Yes."

"The white bull?"

"Especially."

"We're screwed," Craig said. "Father Baldwin's plan is a disaster."

"Maybe not. He could still—"

"You're dreaming," Craig said. "We're on our own. I don't understand why Gerrard and Fulano haven't killed us yet, but from now on, we forget about Father Baldwin and depend on ourselves."

"Gerrard and Fulano must have a reason for letting us live."

"So far."

With a tremble, Tess agreed. "So far. Something else is going on. Maybe the surprise Fulano mentioned."

"Whatever it is, it's not in our favor."

"So what do we do?" Tess asked. "Try to run?"

"With those sentries? God damn that Father Baldwin," Craig said. "He didn't want to help us. He *used* us. We'd have been safer if we'd never listened to him."

"That's yesterday. We have to deal with *now.*"

"All right," Craig said. "For the moment, we have to go with the flow. When it's dark, maybe we'll find a chance to escape. Through the woods. Into the mountains. At night, when everyone's asleep, I think we can climb down from this balcony. If anyone tries to stop us, I'll do my best to distract them. In that case, you go on without me."

"No way," Tess said. "It's both of us or neither."

"Tess . . ." Craig gently gripped her cheeks, lowered his mouth, and kissed her. "They'll hunt us. There's no point in *both*

404

of us dying. If it comes to a choice, I'd rather that *you* escaped instead of me.''

She kissed him gently in return. ''You weren't exaggerating when you told Fulano that we'd reached an arrangement. We've just never really discussed it. I want to spend the rest of my life with you.''

She tugged his arm.

Craig resisted. ''What are you. . . ?''

''Going back inside. And from now on, we talk like lovers, or else the people listening to the microphones will be suspicious. In Washington, you called me 'babe.' You said that was what your father called your mother. Well, babe, let's complete what we planned to start. If we're going to die, let's . . .'' She suddenly hugged him, sobbing. ''This is all the time we have. Gerrard and Fulano expect us at eight. Let's *use* that time. I very much want a bath, and I *very* much want you to join me.''

She began to unbutton his shirt. She kissed his nipples, her warm tears trickling down his chest.

''You're sure?'' Craig asked.

''I don't plan to die without making love to you. Touch my breasts. Oh, Jesus, Craig, I'm so scared.''

''I know. I'm frightened, too.''

''I don't want to die. I . . . Yes! That feels so good. I'm so scared, Craig! Lower. Touch me lower.''

Tess had mentioned taking a bath together. Now they headed in that direction, pausing frequently to kiss, to remove each other's top, but they never got past the bed. Unsteady, light headed from passion, Tess tumpled with Craig across it, pressing her body onto him. Their kisses became more urgent, their hands more insistent. Moaning, squirming, they continued to undress each other, Tess pulling down his zipper, Craig undoing her belt.

She reached through the open zipper, finding Craig's swollen penis. As she pulled it free, Craig arched his back, shuddered, and cupped her breasts, their nipples rising, hardening. She kicked off her jeans, Craig licking her breasts, then her stomach, shifting lower, pulling down her underwear, kissing her thighs. She yanked off the last of his clothes and twisted, turning, Craig now on top of her, both of them pressing against each other, exploring every portion of each other's skin. Their tongues met, thrusting. She tasted him, her vagina tingling, warm and wet with greater arousal. She thrust her tongue deeper into his mouth, wanting to enter him, to be one with him, and when Craig finally entered *her*, Tess didn't care about the microphones, the strangers listening. She wailed in hot flooding ecstasy. It went on and on, one climax after another, and as Craig's penis lengthened unbelievably, his semen erupting within her, she wailed again, this time in unison with him. They lay back, their bodies filmed with sweat.

She struggled to catch her breath. Her heartbeat thundered, then gradually stopped racing. Neither spoke for several minutes.

They kissed again, this time slowly, tenderly. Craig gently stroked her breasts. Fifteen minutes later, they amazed each other by making love a second time. At last, in exhaustion, their apprehension returning, they did what they'd planned at the start. In a tub that was unexpectedly large, they shared a warm, soothing bath.

10

The time they'd been given was gone.

"Are you ready?" Craig asked.

"No. But if you can think of an alternative, I'd like to hear it."

"I'm sorry. I can't."

"Then let's do this with style."

"I love you."

"And I love . . . Kiss me. Yes, that's so much better."

When Tess and Craig unlocked and opened the door, they found the two Secret Service agents seated across from them, watching, waiting. Without a word, the agents followed them downstairs, to the left along the muffled corridor, and into a spacious dining room.

There, Gerrard and Fulano sat at another antique table. When they smiled and stood in greeting, Tess noticed that Fulano had changed from his work clothes into slacks and a sport coat.

She and Craig had received fresh clothes as well, a servant having arrived ten minutes before they were expected to leave their room. Craig's outfit was similar to Fulano's.

Her own, however, had not been to her liking. Granted, the garments were attractive: a blue scarf, a matching silk blouse, a red cotton skirt, and soft leather sandals that fit as comfortably as slippers.

But Tess had never liked wearing skirts, especially not this one, which came down to her ankles, interfering with her stride, and the sandals meant that she'd been forced to take off her sneakers and more important the homing device in one of the heels. She'd put the sneakers into her ample burlap purse, but she couldn't help suspecting that the outfit Fulano had chosen for her was intended to make it difficult for her to take the opportunity, when night came, of running with Craig toward the forest and attempting to escape across the mountains. Again she felt vulnerable, helpless.

"You look lovely, Tess," Fulano said.

"*Gracias,*" she told him, trying to look modest.

Fulano laughed. "You're learning Spanish."

"I'm afraid it's the only word I know. But really, thank you. These clothes fit me perfectly. They're gorgeous."

"My pleasure."

The doors to the windows of the dining room had been opened. The lowering sun tinted the room with crimson.

"I'm sure you're curious about the surprise I mentioned," Fulano said.

"It sounds like a birthday party. I've always been fond of surprises." As she smoothed her skirt and sat at the table, controlling her fear, Tess noticed that the two Secret Service agents positioned themselves near the door through which she and Craig had entered. She also noticed that outside the windows, armed guards patrolled a stone patio.

Gerrard and Fulano sat when Craig did.

"A brief explanation," Gerrard said. "I get the impression that neither of you has been to Spain before."

"Regrettably, now that I've seen it," Craig said.

"One of the first things you have to understand," Gerrard said, "is that the Spanish have a daily schedule that's pleasantly different from what we're used to in America. They work from nine till one. Then they take a long break for lunch and what I'm sure you know is called a *siesta.*" He shrugged. "They relax. Nap. Make love. Whatever. Then they come back to work at four and stop around seven, after which they greet their neighbors, eat, drink, and discuss the day's activities. What they eat is really a snack, because their main meal occurs very late compared to American customs. Around ten. The snacks they eat earlier are called *tapas,* and those snacks are one of the many glories of Spanish culture. The surprise we referred to is that you're about to experience *tapas.*"

Confused because she expected a confrontation, Tess watched Fulano tap his knuckles on the table. At once, three servants appeared, carrying trays from which they set down numerous dishes.

Not having eaten in a while, Tess couldn't help salivating from the aroma of the food on the ornate plates. It wasn't just that she was hungry. She knew she had to eat as much as she could in order to muster her strength in case she and Craig managed to find a chance to escape.

"First," Gerrard said, "calamari. Are you familiar with—?"

"They're deep-fried squid. Delicious."

"Good," Fulano said. "And these are olives, and these are sardines. Not what you're used to in America. They're fresh and beyond compare."

"And these," Gerrard said, "are delicious pieces of deep-fried chicken. And *these* are shrimp, and of course there's bread, and deep-fried potatoes with mayonnaise, and—"

"Enough!" Craig chuckled, although Tess knew that his enthusiasm was forced. "If this is what you call a snack, I can't imagine what the main meal could possibly be."

"You'll be amazed," Fulano said.

"I bet."

Beyond the windows, Tess continued to notice the sentries patrolling. She quickly pretended to pay attention to the row of various foods. "That stack of plates. How do we . . . ?"

"One type of food to each plate," Gerrard said. "It's important to separate each taste."

"Then let's get to it. I'm starved."

There wasn't any red meat, she noticed, a significant omission given the dietary beliefs of the heretics. With pretended delight, she spooned olives, calamari, and whatever else appealed to her onto various plates, spreading them in a row before her. The *tapas* indeed were delicious, perfectly prepared, each complementing the other.

"Would you like some vintage wine?" Fulano asked. "Spanish wine is superb. Or perhaps some excellent *cerveza.*"

"Excuse me?" Tess looked confused.

"The Spanish word for 'beer.' "

"Thanks." Craig swallowed hungrily. "But I'd prefer water."

"The same with me," Tess said. "Alcohol and I don't get along. It makes me groggy."

"I have the same reaction. Interesting," Fulano said. He filled her ceramic cup from a pitcher.

Tess didn't drink until Fulano filled his own cup and drank the same water.

"My God, I think I'm full," Craig said.

"Exactly when to stop." Fulano chewed and swallowed an olive, placing its pit at the side of his plate. "Remember, the main course is later."

"And now we have another surprise." Gerrard touched a napkin to his mouth.

Here it comes, Tess thought. The condemned have had their final meal.

"Oh?" Craig lowered his fork. "Another? This valley. This castle. These *tapas*. We've been surprised several times already. And now you're telling us there's more?"

"Something truly special. Extremely unusual. It happens only one time each year," Fulano said. "But it does require another helicopter ride to see what I mean. I'm sure you're still tired from your trip, but I promise you won't be disappointed. Indeed you'll find it remarkable."

"In that case, being tired doesn't matter. Let's go." Craig stood.

Uncertain about Craig's strategy, Tess followed his example. The Secret Service agents stood as well.

With another rap of his knuckles on the table, Fulano summoned his servants. While they gathered the remnants of the *tapas*, Fulano pointed Tess and Craig toward the corridor that led outside.

Five minutes later, as the sun touched the rim of the mountains, its glow more crimson, they reached the helicopter. When Tess climbed inside, carefully watched, she felt troubled that she hadn't seen Gerrard's assistant, Hugh Kelly, since they'd arrived.

Where *was* he? Why hadn't he joined them?

She had almost no time to analyze the possibilities. A minute later, as if on an urgent schedule, the helicopter lifted off, veered upward, and sped toward the northern mountains. The sun was now behind the peaks, its bloodred glow reflecting off a purple sky.

Her stomach already tense despite the energy-renewing meal, Tess clutched her tight, crisscrossing shoulder belt and expected that at any time the two Secret Service agents would grab her, unbuckle her restraints, and throw her, twisting and turning, into the valley.

Instead everyone stayed in position, the helicopter rising higher, nearing the shadowy mountains.

"Alan tells me that you've been threatened in America," Fulano said. "If it helps, I want to encourage you that what you're about to see will help take your mind off your troubles."

The helicopter crested the northern mountains. Beyond, the sun had almost completely set behind farther ridges. A murky valley lay below them.

"We're approaching the Spanish-French border," Gerrard said. "We won't cross it, of course. Without advance diplomatic clearance, even I don't have the authority to violate French airspace. But the surprise we want you to see is a custom in southern France that centuries ago drifted down to this area of Spain. It's quite remarkable."

The helicopter sped over more jagged ridges, crossing another dark valley.

But something was different. As Tess peered down, she realized, puzzled, that *this* valley wasn't completely dark. Hundreds of isolated lights flickered throughout the murky basin.

"What are those . . . ?" She shook her head. "They can't be from villages, not with the lights so small and so widely separated. I can't see anything else, but it's almost as if . . . I'm sure of it. The lights are coming from fields."

"That's correct," Fulano said. "What you see are bonfires. The local farmers and villagers are conducting a festival."

Gerrard pressed against his shoulder harness, leaning toward her. "Do you know what day this is? I don't mean the day of the week. I mean the date."

Tess had to think a moment. "June twenty-second?"

"Very good. And sometime between today and yesterday, the summer solstice occurred, the beginning of summer. What you're seeing are flames in honor of the new precious season, the growth of the crops, the fulfillment of the fertile promise of spring."

"The ritual is extremely ancient," Fulano added. "It's much older than Christianity, although of course like Easter, the true meaning of which is the resurrection of nature, Christian elements have been layered onto it. Those villagers are praying to Saint John."

Tess felt an inward jolt. In turmoil, she didn't know if the saint Fulano referred to was John the Baptist or John the disciple of Christ, but she was betting on the latter, the same John who'd written the final Gospel in the Bible, numerous epistles, and the Book of Revelation.

Her mind focused on the photographs in her purse, particularly the photograph of the Bible she'd found in Joseph's bedroom, a Bible from which Joseph had cut out everything except the works of John and the theories that so matched those of the heretics, especially the war between good and evil at the end of the world.

"The farmers and villagers are praying around those flames," Gerrard said. "They're holding crosses made from wildflowers and wheat."

Yet again Tess felt jolted. Flames. Wheat.

She recalled the grotesque statue: the torchbearers, Mithras slicing the throat of the bull, its blood cascading to fertilize the earth, the dog straining to intercept the blood, the serpent lunging to destroy the wheat that the blood caused to sprout from the soil.

A war between good and evil, and depending on which side won, nature would live or die.

With shock, she understood that the sacred festival in this valley was a remnant of Mithraism, that the heresy was more deeply rooted, more widely spread than she'd ever anticipated.

Nests. Father Baldwin had said he'd been searching for nests, particularly in Spain, although his attention was directed toward the Picos de Europa to the west, not the Pyrenees to the east. What he didn't know was that the nests existed not just in the Picos but all along southern France and northern Spain, and that the villagers had so absorbed Mithraism into Catholic traditions that they perhaps didn't even know the true origin and meaning of the fertility ritual they now performed.

Or perhaps they did know its true origin and meaning, and that made the ritual all the more awesome as well as terrifying. Like the villagers and farmers around the bonfires in the valley, Tess had devoted herself to nature, but Gerrard and Fulano—who'd devoted themselves to Mithras, the god of nature—controlled her, and maybe she and Craig would be the next sacrifices to the god.

The helicopter began to descend, approaching the isolated flames in the valley.

"We're not going back?" Craig asked.

"Not just yet," Fulano said.

"Why?" Craig's voice deepened.

"We have a further surprise," Gerrard said.

"This evening is full of them. I'm tired. I don't know if Tess and I can take any more," Craig said.

"Believe me, *this* surprise is worth it," Gerrard said.

The helicopter kept descending into the murky valley, and immediately Tess realized that some of the flickering bonfires had been arranged in a special pattern. They form a landing pad! she thought.

In the darkness, the helicopter's pilot used the squared-off section of flames to guide him toward a level section in the valley. As the bonfires flickered, the pilot eased the helicopter onto the grass, then shut off the engines.

"And now?" Craig asked.

"Something so sacred that very few have ever seen it," Gerrard said.

"You worry me. I'm from New York. Mountains, valleys, bonfires? To me, they're like Mars."

"Then we invite you to look at Mars," Fulano said. "I guarantee you'll be impressed. I correct myself. You'll be astonished. Open your mind. Prepare yourself for what will be the greatest memory of your life."

"Since you're my host," Craig said, "I take for granted that I can trust you. I also assume that as a host you feel an obligation to your guests."

"That goes without saying."

"All right, then, as long as we've agreed, let's see the surprise that'll be my greatest memory."

"Follow."

They stepped from the helicopter.

11

Tess felt cloaked with oppressive darkness while in a square that enclosed the helicopter, brilliant bonfires blazed. Their drifting acrid smoke conflicted with the fragrance of the grass and flowers in the night-shrouded valley.

Numerous villagers and farmers, all wearing festive garments, stood next to the flames, holding impressive crosses, woven from flowers and stalks of wheat. As the light flickered over those crosses, Tess faltered, stunned by the memory of what Priscilla Harding had told her. Before Christianity, before the tradition that the cross represented the execution of Christ, a prior tradition had associated the symbol of the cross with the glory of the sun. And now, with chilling certainty, Tess watched the flames reflect off the wheat of the crosses and knew absolutely that those crosses, composed from nature, were devoted to the sun—and to Mithras, the *god* of the sun.

Fulano took a torch from one of the villagers and gestured for Tess and Craig to walk to his right across the field. Gerrard took another torch and accompanied them as did the two Secret Service agents. But unexpectedly the group became larger, other men joining them from beyond the fires. These newcomers did not wear festive garments. They didn't carry crosses woven from flowers and wheat. What they wore instead was rugged outdoor clothing, and what they carried were automatic weapons.

Beyond the bonfires, the field became disturbingly black, il-luminated in patches only by the torches that Fulano and Gerrard held before them. Tess fearfully recalled the torchbearers in the statue that she'd seen in Joseph's bedroom. Her feet and ankles felt cold, the dew on the knee-high grass soaking her sandals and the lower portion of her long skirt. Panic made her want to tug at Craig and run. They might be able to escape in the darkness, she hoped. But despair took charge, making her realize that the guards would hunt them, that the villagers would join in the search, and the odds were that she and Craig would lose their sense of direction, running in circles in this unfamiliar valley, trying to avoid the bonfires until they were captured.

The field began to slope upward. Guided by the torches, she and the rest of the group passed beech trees, veered around boulders, and continued climbing, the dampness making Tess colder. The hill angled higher, and now she smelled the resin of pine trees.

At once the slope leveled off. Grass became rocks. She peered ahead toward where the torches revealed a narrow gap, concealed by bushes, at the base of a cliff. Stepping closer, she saw that the gap was the entrance to a cave. But a few feet into the cave, a rusted iron door formed a barrier.

Fulano handed his torch to a guard, removed a key from his pocket, and released a padlock on the door. With effort, leaning his shoulder against the door, he shoved it open, its hinges creaking. The night became eerily silent, the only sound the crackling torches and Fulano's footsteps as he disappeared beyond the door. Five seconds later, the silence was broken by the sound of something being cranked, then the sputter of an engine, then a roar as the engine came to life. The interior of the cave was abruptly illuminated by a dim bulb attached to the ceiling, and Tess saw that the engine was a kerosene-powered generator.

Someone nudged her back. Turning, Tess blinked in surprise at Hugh Kelly, who must have joined them during the trek up the slope. Where had he been? What had he been doing? Like the guards, he, too, wore outdoor clothing.

"Go in," he said. "You'll find shoes and a jacket. The cave can be slippery. It's also cold."

"I brought my sneakers," Tess said. She took them from her purse and pulled them on, her feet at last secure.

No matter, she trembled. The torches were set on the ground, twisted among the rocks, and extinguished. When she and Craig entered the cave, followed by Gerrard, Kelly, and the guards, she noticed woolen coats opposite the generator and put one on, buttoning it. Despite its insulation, she continued to tremble.

The narrow passage was barely head-tall. Proceeding, she stopped ten yards ahead just beyond a curve, frowning at another iron door.

While Fulano unlocked it, Hugh Kelly shut and locked the first door.

That's it, she thought. We're finished.

"Don't look so nervous." Despite the roar of the generator, Fulano's voice reverberated off the damp limestone walls. "That locked door is strictly for security precautions. After all, we're here at night, and remember, you're not the only ones at risk. Alan and I are attractive targets for assassins. I trust the villagers, but the darkness could very well hide enemies who may have kept track of our movements and would like nothing better than to catch us alone in this isolated area. Three guards have stayed outside to make sure that no one attacks us when we leave. As you may have noticed, Alan's Secret Service agents don't look happy about this trip."

"I did notice." Tess remained convinced that the guards cared more about Craig and herself than they did about Gerrard and Fulano. All the same, she pretended to follow his logic. "But what if something goes wrong outside? What if your guards are over-powered?"

"We try to contact them with walkie-talkies. If they don't respond," Gerrard explained, and gestured offhandedly, "we use a different exit."

"You've thought of everything," Craig said.

"We try to." Fulano nudged the farther door, forcing it open, its hinges screeching, its iron bottom scraping against rock. "And now the surprise."

"One of the greatest wonders in the world," Gerrard said. "Few people have seen it. Only those who deserve to, who have the capacity to appreciate it, who care about the planet, about its soul, and you, Tess, have the right. Because you do care. With a passion. You've proven that in your articles."

"So now"—Fulano shoved the door completely open—"you're about to see a mystery. Perhaps the greatest mystery. Something so sacred that after you see it, you'll never be the same."

"I can't imagine what—"

"No," Gerrard said. *"Don't* imagine. Don't anticipate. Just witness it. Just stand back and appreciate. You're about to be changed."

"The way my life has been going, I'm due for a change. For the better, I hope."

"For the better," Fulano said. "No question. You have my word. Absolutely."

Tess followed them through the door, clutched Craig's hand, and felt the guards behind her. Fulano paused to lock the second entrance.

It's getting worse, Tess thought.

Crude steps carved into the limestone led down to a deep, wide, towering cavern. Dim light bulbs next to the primitive stairway glistened off moist rock and guided the way.

Tess reached the bottom, overwhelmed by the vastness of the chamber. In awe, she stared this way and that at intricate rock formations. Stalactites hung from the ceiling, water dripping down from them, forming pools that she avoided. Stalagmites projected upward from the pools, their contours vaguely resembling the snouts of animals.

Her rapid breathing appeared as vapor.

"This cave has a constant temperature of fifty-five degrees," Fulano said. "Winter or summer. Thousands of years ago, a rockfall buried the original entrance, preserving the interior. In all that time, the secret of the cave was hidden. But during the 1800s, another rockslide opened a gap in the cliff. A local farmer, searching for missing lambs, wandered up the slope, discovered the gap, and decided to investigate, less out of curiosity about the cave—after all, such places can be dangerous—than out of concern that his lambs might have wandered inside. He soon reached a farther gap so narrow that his lambs could never have gotten past it. Dim sunlight from the entrance showed him that the cave was much larger beyond the narrow passageway, and he mentioned it to his family, then to other farmers after he'd found his lambs in a meadow later that day. Word gradually spread and eventually reached my valley, where my great-great-grandfather had an interest in caves. He decided to mount an expedition, came to this valley, and ordered his workmen to use picks and sledgehammers to widen the passageway. The limestone was brittle enough to allow them to accomplish his orders. He then used torches to investigate farther, and when he found what we're about to show you, he swore his workers to secrecy. As quickly as possible, he had an iron door secured into the rock walls at the entrance, and he alone carried the key to its padlock. Later a second door was added farther along. Those doors are not the ones through which we passed. Years ago, the originals rusted and disintegrated, replaced by others. In recent times, improvements were made, steps chiseled into slopes, light bulbs strung, their wires attached to the kerosene generator."

"But what did he find?" Craig asked. "And why did he want to hide it?"

"Not so much to hide it as protect it," Fulano said. "In a moment, you'll understand." He led the group across the chamber, entering a dimly illuminated corridor that twisted to the right, then the left, and took them lower.

Tess felt smothered by the dampness and the sense that the

confines of the cave created a pressure, making the air around her heavy. She stepped over pools of water, sometimes hearing water trickle from the ceiling. On occasion, cold drops pelted her head. One passage led to another, mazelike.

She rounded a bend. Another huge chamber opened before her. Fulano and Gerrard waited ahead, smiling with joy, their eyes glinting so intensely that reflection from the dim bulbs along the floor couldn't have caused the radiance in their expressions.

Craig stopped beside her. In back, Hugh Kelly and the guards emerged from the corridor, joining them.

"And now?" Craig sounded apprehensive. "Why are we stopping?"

"Because we've reached what we came to show you. Don't you see?" Gerrard asked, laughing. "Don't you *see?* Look around!" His laughter swelled, echoing throughout the cavern, his gleeful outburst magnified. "Look!"

Confused, Tess obeyed, slowly turning, directing her gaze in the direction of Gerrard's outspread arms.

Abruptly she did see, and the vision that awaited her caused her to clutch her chest, then to step back in astonishment, awestruck.

"Oh, my God." At once she said it again, louder, overwhelmed. "My God!"

Her knees became weak. She struggled to keep her balance, stunned to the core by what she was witnessing.

"They're magnificent!" she blurted. "They're . . . ! I've never seen anything like . . . ! It's almost impossible to believe . . . ! They're so beautiful I want to cry!"

Craig shook his head in astonishment, so overpowered with surprise and rapture that he was speechless.

All around and above them, on the walls and across the ceiling, animals seemed to race or graze, to swim or leap or simply pose to be admired. Paintings on the rock, so many that Tess couldn't count them or comprehend their complex flowing pattern, the animals frequently overlapping, their images static yet somehow in motion, a huge, eternal, rampant herd.

"Yes," Gerrard said, his voice sounding choked, "so magnificent, so awesomely beautiful that they make me want to cry. I've been here innumerable times, and their effect on me is always the same. Their splendor makes me ache. You realize now that I wasn't exaggerating. They're one of the greatest wonders in the world. To me, they represent the soul of the planet.''

Deer, elk, bison, horses, ibex, bears, lions, mammoths. More, many more, including species that Tess could not identify, presumably because they were extinct.

Some were engraved in the rock, the figures outlined with charcoal. Others were silhouetted in red, the lines either solid or composed of large dots. The animals were life-size. On the ceiling, an eight-foot-long deer had racks of spreading, many-pronged antlers that were almost equally long. The contours of the ceiling had been used to indicate bulging muscles in the deer's back and legs.

The style of the paintings was eerily realistic, as if the animals were alive and could at any moment leap off the walls. At the same time, the style was *sur*real, causing the magnificent creatures to look oddly distorted, some foreshortened, others elongated, a distortion that added paradoxically to the powerful effect. The animals curved gracefully around projections in the rock. They rippled dramatically in and out of cracks and fissures. An elk appeared to be swimming. A horse appeared to be falling. Moisture in the limestone made them shimmer. Breathtaking.

"Who *painted* these?" Craig managed to ask. *"When?* You said this cave was discovered in the 1800s. But before then, rocks had barricaded the entrance. How old are—"

"Twenty thousand years.''

"What?''

"These paintings come from a time when human beings had only recently appeared,'' Fulano said. "Who painted them? Our immediate evolutionary ancestors. A type of human called Cro-Magnon. Obviously their sense of beauty, their admiration for nature, was immense. In that respect, compared to our own disrespect for nature, perhaps our species hasn't evolved but regressed. Sometimes you hear these people referred to as 'cavemen,' an absurd expression because the Cro-Magnons never lived in caves. How could they have tolerated the chill and the dampness?'' Fulano shook his head. "No, they lived *outside* the caves. But for reasons that anthropologists haven't been able to determine, they sometimes went into the caves, *deep* within, and in chambers similar to this one, they painted the glory of the animals. It's my opinion that these chambers were their churches, that they came here on special occasions, perhaps at the vernal equinox and the summer solstice, to worship the miracle of rebirth and growth, to initiate children about to become adults and show them the mysteries of the tribe. The greatest mystery—life. A place of adoration, of sublime appreciation for what this planet is all about.''

Gerrard added to Fulano's explanation. ''This wasn't the only such sanctuary to be discovered during the 1800s.''

Tess nodded. ''I've heard about, although I've never seen, the paintings at Lascaux in France, and many others, including those at Altamira here in Spain.''

''But Lascaux was discovered in the 1940s,'' Fulano said. ''As far as historians believe, Altamira—three hundred kilometers west of here—was the first to be explored. In 1879. But my ancestor discovered *these* paintings ten years before. He knew instinctively that no expert in prehistory would believe in their authenticity. How could primitive human beings have produced such exquisite beauty? Scholars would conclude that these brilliant paintings were recent, cleverly forged. To prevent his discovery from being ridiculed, he kept it to himself, placing a door across the cave, preserving it for himself, his family, and special friends. His instincts served him well, for when Altamira was discovered, the experts scoffed. Only when other caves with paintings were discovered in France did anthropologists admit their mistake and accept the images at Altamira as authentic. Lascaux and Altamira are so impressive that they're often referred to as the Sistine Chapels of Paleolithic art. But I've seen Lascaux, and I've seen Altamira, and I tell you that they can't compare to what you've been privileged to witness. This is the *true* Sistine Chapel of Paleolithic art. My ancestor was wise in another respect as well. He understood that this cave, after tens of thousands of years of not being disturbed, was so delicate that if people flocked to see these images, the warmth from their bodies would affect its ecology. The soil on their shoes would leave contaminants. The breath from their mouths would add to the humidity on the walls. These paintings, preserved by a blessed accident of nature, would be destroyed by fungus and the soot from torches.

Only a few special witnesses could ever be allowed inside. The twentieth century proves that he was correct. So many tourists entered Lascaux that the paintings became covered with destructive green mold. The cave had to be sealed again, only experts allowed to enter and even then only after special precautions were taken, for example a disinfecting pool through which the limited observers had to step in order to kill the contaminants on their shoes. At Altamira, only a few can enter each day, and only then by appointment. But here, in this isolated cave in this isolated valley, even fewer are allowed to enter. The double doors provide an extra buffer, a way of keeping the outside air filled with pollen and seeds from entering the inner chamber. You were told that this would be the greatest memory of your lives. I assure you that, after a hundred years and more, your memories are shared by a precious minority.''

"And you haven't even seen the best part," Gerrard said.

"There are *other* paintings?" Craig raised his eyebrows in amazement.

"Yes, one more chamber," Fulano said, his dark eyes gleaming. "The best for last. Come. Appreciate. Worship."

"Believe me, I already have."

"Worshiped? Not completely. Not yet. It's just around this bend," Fulano said. "Prepare yourselves. The next-to-ultimate revelation will stun your . . . Well, why should I tell you what to expect? See for yourselves."

He led. They followed, and as Tess rounded the bend, she gasped, not only in awe but fear. So did Craig.

The chamber, like the previous one, was filled with paintings, images, lifelike portrayals of animals. But here the animals were exclusively bulls. Everywhere. And unlike the paintings in the previous chamber, the bulls weren't outlined in charcoal or red. These were multicolored, not merely silhouetted but completely detailed. Totally realistic. Their hooves were black, their haunches brown, their humped backs red. Their tails curved as if in a photograph. Their slanted, pointed horns, too, were black. And their eyes were so vivid that they seemed about to blink in rigid anger, furious that they'd been captured eternally on the walls and the ceiling, their legs thrusting, their muscles straining, their bodies arching, an example of—a celebration of—the strength of nature, the strikingly beautiful surge and power of the universe, which twenty thousand years later was on the verge of being destroyed.

"The colors come from powdered carbon, ocher, and iron oxide, mixed with animal fat and blood. The technique is known as polychrome," Gerrard said, "and there are only two other sites, Lascaux and Altamira, where it was used to such a degree. Immensely sophisticated. Superbly executed. The greatest artwork that human beings have ever created. Because the message is the greatest—the enormous vitality of nature. But as the green mold on the paintings at Lascaux makes clear, our interference with nature has caused its vitality to be weakened to the point of extinction. We have a sacred responsibility. At any cost, the sickness of the planet must be reversed."

Tess felt increasingly overpowered by what she was seeing.

And increasingly fearful.

Bulls. Like flames and crosses, so much of this nightmare had to do with bulls, and while her gaze pivoted along a wall, across the brilliant multicolored bulls, she suddenly froze at the sight of one bull that was larger than all the others. Instead of having been portrayed in red, black, and brown, it was monochrome, the white of chalk, like the bull in the statue, and its head was raised in agony, a spearlike barbed line projecting through its neck.

Tess followed the direction of the white bull's anguished expression and whimpered when she saw another locked iron door.

What had Gerrard just said? We have a sacred responsibility. At any cost, the sickness of the planet must be reversed. And earlier, Fulano had said that this chamber was the next-to-ultimate revelation. What was behind the door?

"This is the only example of a violent image in the cave." Fulano interrupted her urgent, panicked thoughts. "But my ancestor wasn't puzzled. He understood the necessity for the violence in the painting, and he also understood that the color of the bull, its whiteness, was a sign. He knew precisely what he had to do."

Tess gripped Craig's hand, watching Fulano unlock the door, then shove it open, the shriek of its hinges making her spine quiver.

"Somehow I don't think we're going to see more paintings," Craig said.

"You assume correctly," Fulano said. "What you're going to see is the truth."

Tess gripped Craig's hand much harder. In dismay, she hesitated. But Hugh Kelly and the guards urged her onward. With dread, her stomach cramping, she had to step through the door.

12

The cavern was dim, illuminated sparsely not by light bulbs but by torches. The cavern became darker when Fulano shut and locked the door, blocking the light from the bulbs in the chamber of the bulls.

"The floor is damp but level. You shouldn't have trouble maintaining your balance," Gerrard said reassuringly.

Their footsteps echoed. As Tess approached the first of the torches, she saw that it was made of stone and anchored into the cavern's floor. At the top, a basin was filled with flaming oil. The tongues of fire wavered as if her approach had caused a subtle breeze.

She stepped toward a second torch, and beyond in the darkness, she heard Gerrard and Fulano walking. Something scraped. A match flickered. She saw Gerrard lower it toward another torch, from which flames soon rose. Fulano did the same, lighting a farther torch. The two men moved around the chamber, continuing to light more torches until the darkness was almost completely dispelled. Even so, when they passed the torches, their shadows wavered eerily.

Fulano had described the cave paintings as the Sistine Chapel of Paleolithic art. But now, in shock, Tess found herself staring at a *true* chapel. She tried to retain her presence of mind, to analyze what she was seeing. The chapel's design, its columns and vaulted ceiling, looked Roman, but given what Fulano had said about the cave's having been discovered in the 1800s, Tess suspected that no matter the chapel's design, it wasn't ancient but instead had been built within the past hundred years.

It was chiseled from limestone and divided into three sections. To the right, three steps led up to an arched entrance and then an aisle with a bench carved out of the wall. On the left, three other steps led up to an identical aisle and bench. In the middle, a more lofty arched entrance provided access to a long open area, lower than the aisles and visible from the benches. The design was intended to focus attention toward a prominent object on a large square altar at the rear of the central area, and that object—Tess's heart faltered—was a bas-relief statue of Mithras straddling a white bull, slicing its throat. She wanted to scream. Her mind swirled. She feared that she'd go insane.

The statue was twice as large as the one she'd seen in Joseph's bedroom. Its white marble was weathered, cracked, and chipped, and she knew in her soul that this wasn't a copy, as Joseph's had been. No, this was the original. This was the statue that the small, determined group of heretics had managed to take with them when they used ropes to escape down the mountain the night before the massacre at Montségur.

"As I promised," Fulano said. "The truth."

"Come. Look closer," Gerrard said. He shifted between Tess and Craig, spread out his arms, and conducted them toward the chapel's central area. Before he entered, he stopped at a basin mounted on a pedestal and dipped his right hand within it. Water glistened on his fingers as he touched them to his forehead, his chest, then his left and right shoulder, making the sign of the cross.

But not the cross of Christianity, Tess knew. *This* cross was that of the sun god.

"A holy-water basin?" Her fear gave way to bewilderment.

"No doubt, it reminds you of Catholicism," Gerrard said. "But the ritual predates Catholicism. Like so many of our rituals, this one was borrowed—*stolen*—from us after Constantine converted from Mithraism to Christianity during the fourth century. After they persecuted us, the hypocrites then pretended that they'd also invented communion, the consecration of bread and wine, the sharing of the sacred meal. But unlike their false religion's bread and wine, which supposedly represents the body and blood of Christ, *our* bread and wine represents the fertility of, the bounty of, the earth. Similarly this water—which doesn't need to be blessed because simply by being water it's already holy—represents the glory of the rains and rivers that satisfy nature's thirst.''

"Or used to," Fulano said, "before poisons in the atmosphere turned the rain into acid. That water comes from a stream in this valley that hasn't yet been polluted."

They neared the altar. Tess shuddered at the sight of the dog, the serpent, and the scorpion trying to stop the sacrifice that would bring life back to nature. On the left of the dying bull, the blood of which was supposed to fertilize the soil, a torchbearer's flame pointed upward while that of the torchbearer on the right pointed down. Good and evil in conflict.

"So now it's time," Gerrard said.

Fulano joined them.

The Vice President continued, "I'm sure that despite the carefully constructed sequence of our revelation, the revelation itself is not a surprise. It was obvious to me that when you boarded Air Force Two, you suspected I was one of the heretics—to use the term you prefer—although for us Christianity is the heresy. It was also obvious to me that you suspected that *I* knew you suspected. So we engaged in word games, clever dialogues in which each tried to fool the other. But neither of us was convincing. Even so, the things you said affected me, Tess. Your profound environmental concerns, your obvious commitment to the planet. In Washington, when I heard that you threatened us, I agreed with a plan to have you guided toward me so I could personally arrange your death. At José's estate, your execution could easily have been accomplished. However, I'm no longer convinced that you ought to be killed. I see possibilities in your attitude. I think that your passionate skills as a journalist could be a help to us. You feel justifiably furious about your mother's death. As do I. That murder was senseless. Clumsy. Needless. But it happened. It can't be undone. So the question I need to ask is, to preserve your life, are you prepared to subdue your grief and work with us? Think carefully. It's the most important question you've ever been asked."

"Murder, blackmail, terrorism? Your methods are wrong," Tess said.

"But they're necessary, since no other methods have been successful," Gerrard said. "However, I appreciate your honest response. For the first time, you're not deceptive. You were tempted to lie, given the weapons aimed behind you, but you didn't. Remarkable. Perhaps there's hope, and I really would hate to order your death. You're a vital, healthy, athletic, well-intentioned, young woman—a perfect example of the life force we're trying to save. I'd sincerely regret destroying you."

Craig coughed.

"You have something to add, Lieutenant? Remember that the only reason you've been tolerated is your romantic association with Tess. If *you* were killed, she'd never cooperate."

"Exactly," Craig said. "Because we love each other, Tess and I very much want to stay alive. But suppose I manage to forget that I work for NYPD. Suppose Tess manages to forget that you bastards killed her mother."

Gerrard stiffened. "Proceed."

"If we agree to your terms, how would you know we weren't lying? How would you know you could trust us?"

"You've already answered part of your question," Gerrard said. "You and Tess love each other enough that you wouldn't jeopardize your future over something you can't control. The plan that our ancestors formulated hundreds of years ago has been achieved. We've infiltrated every major government and corporation, not to mention every important communication network and financial institution. You and Tess could never escape our attention. Our operatives would watch you constantly. You'd be killed the moment you tried to reveal our existence and urge nonbelievers to move against us."

Tess couldn't surmount her fear, remembering in turmoil that the night before, Father Baldwin had made the same threat. If you attempt to reveal the secret that the Inquisition never ended, our operatives—constantly watching you—will guarantee your silence. She felt trapped between one side and the other. Good and evil. But which side was good, and which side was evil? Both used similar, vicious, lethal tactics.

"All right," Craig said. "That makes sense. But according to you, I answered only *part* of the question. What's the rest of it? If

Tess and I promise to cooperate, how would you know you could trust us? How could we be confident that we'd be safe?"

"Yes," Gerrard said. "How indeed? At this point, I have to defer to José's judgment. My power is limited, even though I'm America's vice president. But José is the direct descendant of the leader of the heretics who escaped from the massacre at Montségur. *He* makes the final life-and-death decisions."

Tess and Craig spun toward Fulano.

The Spaniard narrowed his eyes. "You appreciated the paintings, the chapels of the animals?"

"Despite my terror, yes. They were unbelievably awesome," Tess said.

"And you understand their significance?"

"I do," Tess said. "They represent the soul of nature."

Fulano assessed her. "Then despite our differences, we may be more alike than you realize. Perhaps an accommodation can be reached." He frowned. "But in order to gain our trust, you need to make a sign of good faith."

"How do we manage that? What do you mean? What kind of sign?"

"You have to be baptized."

"What?"

"You need to convert."

"To *Mithraism?*"

"It's the only way," Fulano said. "If you become one of us, if you experience the mystery, if you respond to the powerful rite, you'd never dream of betraying us."

"Baptism?"

Fulano nodded.

Tess thought quickly. Anything to get out of here. Having my forehead splashed with water? A few prayers being said? That's nothing compared to what I've been through. She forced herself to appear to hesitate, to ponder, and finally said, "All right."

"Don't think you can fool us," Gerrard said. "This baptism isn't the type you're familiar with. It's not the same as Christianity's. I warn you. It's primordial, much more profound than you can imagine."

What could it possibly be? Tess thought. How different from

the baptism of Christianity? Total immersion in an ice-cold underground spring? Her fear of dying from hypothermia or of being suffocated was certainly profound. But baptism by total immersion was practiced by several Christian fundamentalist groups, she knew, and Gerrard had insisted that *this* baptism was totally different from Christianity's and by definition from fundamentalist versions of it.

At once, however, Tess remembered that total immersion wasn't limited to fundamentalist Christians. Various sects in India also practiced total immersion, and Priscilla Harding had explained that isolated groups devoted to Mithraism were known to have survived and to practice their rites in present-day India.

Total immersion? Tess grimly decided, as bad as that would be, the cold, the tug of the water, the feeling of helplessness, it still can't compare to what I've already been through.

"I appreciate your warning," she said, "but I've thought about it, and I agree. I'll do my best. I'll be baptized. I'll join you if that's what it takes for Craig and me to be left alone, to live without fear."

"Without fear, yes, but you'll still have to help us," Gerrard said.

"But only in nonviolent ways."

"Of course," Gerrard said. "As a journalist committed to protecting the planet."

"Nothing could stop me from doing that."

"Lieutenant, do *you* agree as well?" Gerrard asked.

"I'm with Tess," Craig said. "We share the same decisions."

"Then please step through that archway." Fulano pointed toward the rear of the chapel, toward an exit on the right beside the statue of Mithras on the altar.

Tess tried to demonstrate total resolve as she walked, muscles quivering, toward the right of the altar. Abruptly she faltered, hearing what at first was an inexplicable sound in the darkness beyond the archway.

With a clomping echo, something stomped.

Tess jerked toward Fulano, her face contorted with fright and confusion. "What was *that?*"

Immediately the stomp was followed by a violent snort.

"What *is* it?" Craig's husky voice became guttural. "It sounds like—"

"—an animal," Tess breathed.

"You were warned," Fulano said. "This baptism is more unusual than you expect."

"Primordial."

"Yes. Depending on your reaction, you'll live or die," Fulano said. "We'll know at once if you're converted because it'll be obvious whether you've accepted the baptism's power."

The mysterious unseen animal stomped what sounded like a massive hoof a second time and scraped it over the cavern's floor, the powerful echo reverberating from the archway into the chapel.

Then the animal snorted again, a gruff, moist, angry outburst.

Tess became paralyzed with terror.

But Hugh Kelly and the guards broke her paralysis, crowding relentlessly against her and Craig, pressing the two of them onward, forcing them through the archway.

Gerrard and Fulano had quickly entered before them, striking matches, lighting more torches, and as the flames rose, shimmering, they revealed what the cavern behind the chapel held.

Tess barely managed not to scream.

13

Trapped in a narrow pen carved from gray stone but with an iron gate at one end, stood the huge white bull that Tess had seen isolated in a field this afternoon as the helicopter descended toward Fulano's estate.

Tess suddenly knew where Hugh Kelly had been and what he'd

been doing since the helicopter had landed and why he'd gotten here ahead of them, mysteriously joining them on the slope outside the cave. He'd been ordered to arrange this.

As the torches flared, wavering from a breeze apparently created by the group's approach, the majestic white bull swung its angry head in Tess's direction, its bloodred gaze revealing its fury at having been imprisoned here for so long in the dark. Its nostrils widened, spewing moisture as it snorted once more in outrage.

The animal strained its neck and thrust with one horn, as if despite the distance it believed with proud desperation that it could reach and impale its captors.

"Dear God," Tess moaned.

"Yes," Gerrard said. "Dear God. That's the meaning of the statue. This white bull represents the moon, and because the moon brings light to the darkness, it symbolizes the triumph of good over evil. Obviously the moon is a counterpart to the sun, and so, too, this bull is a counterpart to—a substitute for—Mithras, the God of the sun."

Tess couldn't stop moaning.

"Your fear is understandable," Gerrard said. "But I hope that you also moan in reverence. After all, sacred rites have no effect if they don't induce profound emotion. Obviously this is a test. The two of you are about to be changed. I guarantee it. By all means, one way or another, life opposed to death, agreement opposed to defiance, you're about to be changed."

Tess trembled.

"Step closer," Fulano said. "Over here. Facing the bull."

Tess and Craig didn't move.

"Your hesitation doesn't encourage me," Fulano said. "You have to prove yourselves."

Hugh Kelly and the guards crowded Tess and Craig closer to the pen, compelling them to obey Fulano's orders. Ten feet from the face of the bull, Tess stared at its wrathful eyes.

But this time, when the animal snorted in outrage, hot moisture from its widened nostrils struck her face.

In horror, Tess rubbed at her cheeks, frantic to remove the burn of the acidlike specks. But something else horrified her even more.

Her bladder muscles threatened to fail. Peering down, she saw that a narrow stairwell had been carved within the cavern's floor and that murky steps descended toward a dark enclosure beneath the bull.

Gerrard rubbed his right eye, which was weeping again, the irritation having returned. He pulled a small plastic container from his pocket, bent his head, and propped open his eyelids, dropping contact lenses onto one palm. After placing the lenses into the plastic container, he raised his head.

His formerly blue eyes now were gray, glinting from the reflection of the torches.

Tess shuddered.

"Another secret. An inheritance from our ancestors," Gerrard said.

"Recessive genes. I know."

"Then you've learned a great deal. More than I expected. But now you'll learn even more. *Much* more. It's time. Step into the pit," Gerrard instructed.

Fulano had also removed contact lenses, revealing that his brown eyes actually were as gray as Gerrard's. They gleamed as brightly.

Tess shuddered with greater force.

"Take off your clothes," Fulano said.

"What?" Craig scowled. "Now just a minute."

"I assure you, the request isn't prurient," Gerrard said. "We have no interest in sex. It's an impure impulse that contaminates the spirit. We indulge in it reluctantly, only for the sake of producing children. To us, your nakedness would be no more arousing than seeing the natural nakedness of animals. But we do respect modesty. There's no need for you to undress before us. Take off your clothes away from our sight. In the darkness of the pit. Then throw your clothes up the steps. Otherwise they'll be sullied when you put them back on."

"Sullied? Why?" Craig glowered. "What are you talking about?"

"Because of your baptism," Fulano said. "Your reluctance continues to disturb me. Prove yourselves. Prove that you're worthy. Do what you're told. Step into the pit. Remove your clothes."

Hugh Kelly and the guards continued to crowd against Tess and Craig.

"We don't need your men to force us," Tess said. "We agreed. We told you, we want to stay alive."

"But only if you respond to the power of the baptism, and whether you do will soon be obvious," Fulano said. "Either you'll understand and appreciate the significance of the ritual, or else . . ."

"We'll be killed," Tess said.

Mustering her courage, Tess descended, leaving the wavering light of the torches.

Too soon, pressed against Craig, she reached the bottom. The pit was black, damp, and cold. Narrow. Constricting. Their arms bumped against each other as they reluctantly took off their clothes and tossed them up the steps.

Her eyes adjusting to the darkness, Tess raised her head, seeing reflected light from the torches through gaps in the top of the pit. Thick bars in an iron gate, wide enough so that the bull's hooves couldn't drop through them, were braced securely in the limestone rim.

Craig murmured, "What's supposed to happen? What kind of baptism . . . ?"

"You've seen the statue." Tess strained to keep her voice low. "Don't you realize?"

Abruptly Craig did.

She felt him tremble with horrified understanding.

One of her breasts bumped against his arm as she stared apprehensively upward. Despite her effort at a muted whisper, Gerrard must have heard.

"The blood of the lamb," Gerrard said above her. "According to Christianity, you have to be washed in the blood of the lamb. That's something else they stole from us. Their version of baptism. Then they substituted water for blood. But the blood of the lamb was originally the blood of the sacred bull. The white bull. Regardless of Christianity's changes, our tradition is pure. We still retain the sanctity of the age-old rite. It goes back to ancient Iraq. It reappeared in Greece, particularly in Crete, where legend has it that a pure-white bull arose from the sea and was eventually sacrificed by Theseus to the sun god—they called Him, Apollo—on the mainland at Athens. Later, in Roman times, converts were initiated into Mithraism through this baptism. Here, in Spain, the bullfight is a latter-day version of the sacrifice. In fact, at Mérida, a bullfight ring was constructed above an ancient Roman chapel devoted to Mithras, and in the bowels of that chapel, there existed a pit similar to this one, called a taurobolium, in which Roman centurions disrobed and were rebaptized before each battle—to give them strength in their fight with their enemy. The rite persisted in secret beyond the fourth century despite Constantine's conversion to Christianity. It persisted in the Middle Ages despite the efforts of the Inquisitors. It still persists. As long as nature endures, the rite will endure. Because of the rite's eternal majesty and power.''

"Then do it!'' Tess screamed. "Get it over with!''

Fulano's voice echoed, interrupting. "As the direct descendant of the man who guided his small group of survivors from Montségur, I take the place of my ancestor. I take the place of Mithras. I sacrifice the counterpart of Mithras.'' His voice became a chant.

Above, Tess heard the white bull rear and stomp in fury. She couldn't see but knew what was happening. Fulano—at the risk of his life—had mounted the imprisoned bull.

Gerrard's voice intruded, so calm that it was dismaying. "At the vernal equinox, this sacrifice represents the return of life to the planet. At the summer solstice, however, the sacrifice initiates youths from our sect into its mysteries. And on occasion, rare converts. They experience the power of baptism, and if they're worthy, they understand the necessity of the baptismal sacrifice.''

The frightened bull continued to snort, stomp, and rear in outraged protest.

Tess imagined Fulano straddling the bull, struggling to avoid its thrashing horns, to grab its twisting snout and thrust its head upward, exposing the neck, to plunge his blade in and slice it across, severing arteries, spewing . . .

A shower of blood cascaded. Hot, repulsive, thick and heavy, steaming, pungent, salty, bitter. It flooded in an unbelievable quantity through the bars of the grate. It plummeted, viscous, scalding, drenching, drowning, suffocating.

The bull roared, even though its throat had been slit. It bellowed in a final outburst of pride and bravery. Its knees buckled.

In terrified awe, Tess heard its legs thunk onto the metal grate, its huge, majestic body topple, sinking, thunking even harder onto the grate.

More blood gushed, soaking her hair, filling her ears, drenching her face, slicking her naked body, her bare feet immersed in a horrifying, ankle-deep, steaming pool.

She lost control. She sank to the floor. Craig tried to stop her, but he, too, was powerless, sinking from the force of the deluge.

"Oh, my God," he said.

"Now do you understand?" Fulano demanded, his footsteps clattering as he rose from the corpse of the bull and clambered over the side of the limestone pen.

Assaulted by insanity, her body immersed in blood, no longer shivering because the sacred bull's steaming life force warmed her, Tess blinked upward through sticky crimson fluid and struggled to focus her desperate thoughts.

She couldn't speak.

"Tell me!" Fulano shouted.

"The sacrifice"—her throat didn't want to work—"is supposed to teach us that life is precious." Her voice became hoarse, her words an extended groan. "The blood of the bull is so shocking that forever afterward we'll remember how truly final death is, and that nothing in nature should ever be killed unless it's absolutely necessary. That's why you don't eat red meat. That's why you're mostly vegetarians, because the crops come back in the spring, but an animal, each and every animal, is one of a kind, and if it's killed, it *won't* come back in the spring. If we kill enough of them, entire *species* won't come back in the spring. The planet is finite. Its bounty can be exhausted if we don't take care."

The chamber became terribly silent.

Blood dripped down Tess's body.

"You do understand," Fulano said. "Welcome. You're one of us."

Tess wiped at her blood-streaked mouth, tasting the salty crimson fluid, nearly gagging. When she inhaled, blood spewed up her nostrils. She fought to breathe. Furious, she remembered the painting of the white bull with the spear through its throat. After the glory of existence comes death, and because that glory can never be replaced, death must always be respected. That was the message.

But death, she thought. You bastards had no regard for death when you killed my mother!

You're hypocrites!

You're goddamned—!

A faraway echoing whump interrupted her furious, vengeful thoughts.

The whump, although distant, had sufficient force to waver the rock floor beneath her, although at first Tess thought it was just her knees that were shaking.

"What happened?" she heard Gerrard ask above the pit. "What was—"

Whump! A second jolt, closer, sent shock waves through the cavern. Somewhere a rock fell, clattering.

"It sounds like . . ." Fulano gasped. "A cave-in!"

"No! Explosions!" Gerrard sounded frightened.

"Find out!" Fulano ordered the guards. "Here's the key! Unlock the door! Tell me what's happening!"

Numerous footsteps raced toward the chapel.

At once Craig grabbed Tess's arm and lunged toward the steps. She charged after him, slipped on blood, and fell. Her gymnastic training made her tuck in her arms and twist her body to absorb the impact. Even so, she banged her shoulder, wincing. Immediately she scrambled to her feet and continued charging upward, joining Craig at the top.

The blood cooled on their bodies. Naked, they shivered and hurriedly dressed, shivering worse as the blood soaked their clothing. Ignoring the pathetic corpse of the white bull in the pen, they spun toward the entrance to the chapel.

Fulano, Gerrard, and Hugh Kelly were grouped at the archway. A gap allowed Tess and Craig to see the guards race across the chapel to unlock the cavern's door.

But the moment a guard used all his might to tug it open, he turned in dismay. "The lights are out!"

"Two outside doors, two explosions." Fulano clenched his fists. "The first explosion must have blown the generator."

"Whoever did it—" Gerrard started to say.

"You *know* who did it! Inquisitors!" Fulano said.

"But if the entrance isn't blocked, if they're coming for us, they won't be able to find us without the lights in the tunnels," Gerrard said.

"They'll be prepared! They'll carry flashlights!" Fulano said. "All they have to do is follow the trail of bulbs." He straightened and shouted to the guards, "Get into the tunnel! Close the door so the glow from the torches won't show where you're hiding! Shoot when you see their flashlights! They'll be easy targets!"

The guards snapped into motion, lunged through the door, and pulled it shut.

"Inquisitors!" Fulano said as if cursing. "How did they find us? How did they know where—?"

Gerrard spun toward Tess and Craig. "You! Somehow you *brought* them here!"

"How?" Craig demanded. "You know we couldn't have. You kept us prisoners from the time we left Andrews Air Force Base. If we'd used a phone on the plane, you'd have known about it. Then we boarded the *other* plane. Then we used the helicopter. There's no way we could have passed a message. We've done everything you asked, even to the point of being baptized. We've gone to the limit to prove we want to cooperate."

"No, somehow . . ." Fulano stalked toward them, his gray eyes bulging. "You were searched for weapons. You were scanned with metal detectors. How did—"

"Look at her feet! She's wearing the sneakers she had when she boarded Air Force Two!" Gerrard said. "She brought them with her. She carried them in her purse and put them on when she entered the cave. *That's* how they tracked us. *That's* how they found us. The sneakers must contain a homing device."

"Take them off!" Fulano said. "I want to see them!"

Tess stepped backward.

"I'm right!" Fulano shouted.

Tess stepped farther backward.

"Kelly," Gerrard told his assistant.

"Yes, sir?"

"Shoot them. We gave them our trust. They didn't deserve it. Don't just shoot them. Blow them apart."

"Yes, sir." Hugh Kelly pulled back a bolt on the side of his automatic weapon, then raised it, aiming.

In a frenzy, Craig dove toward Tess, shoving her into a pool behind a stalagmite. Stunned by cold water, they crouched protectively behind the rock.

But the shots they heard didn't come from Hugh Kelly's weapon.

Instead the shots came from *other* automatic weapons, rattling, muffled, distant, behind the door that led into the chapel.

Beyond it, men screamed in agony.

Abruptly the door scraped open, guards surging through, firing behind them, leaning their combined weight against the door, shutting it, locking it.

"They didn't use flashlights!" a guard yelled.

Fulano rushed toward the rear entrance to the chapel. "Then how could they have followed us here? How could they have seen the trail of bulbs in the dark?"

"They're wearing night-vision goggles! It didn't matter where we hid! *They* could see us, but we couldn't see *them!*"

"Take cover!" Fulano ordered.

The guards retreated, lunging toward the protection of torches and pillars. Some left a trail of blood. Tess heard their strident breathing.

Something banged on the opposite side of the metal door.

"They're trying to get through!" Gerrard said.

Something banged again. The lock held firm.

"They'll use explosives!" Fulano said. "Get down!"

Hugh Kelly had turned to view the commotion.

Taking advantage, Craig surged from the pool of water behind the stalagmite. Kelly heard him and whirled, but not in time. Craig reached him before he could raise his weapon and fire. Slamming Kelly, twisting him, Craig grabbed Kelly's chin from behind and jerked it upward. At the same time, Craig dropped to one knee, propped up the other knee, and banged Kelly's spine across it.

Sickened, Tess heard two brutal snaps—from Kelly's neck and

spine. As Kelly's lifeless body sank to the cavern's floor, Craig grabbed the weapon and aimed toward Gerrard and Fulano.

Too late. The sound of the struggle having warned them, they ducked through the entrance into the chapel before Craig had a chance to fire.

He cursed and started after them. But instantly he stumbled back, the force of an explosion making him fall. The blast was deafening, the metal door flying off its hinges, banging onto the floor. More rocks dropped from the ceiling.

Tess's ears rang. Nonetheless she heard guards shoot toward the entrance to the tunnel. From the darkness beyond the entrance, from the chamber of the painted bulls, other weapons returned fire.

Tess heard another explosion. Then *another*. In the cold pool behind the stalagmite, she winced and pressed her hands against her ears. Grenades! The Inquisitors were throwing grenades! The chapel filled with smoke and flames. Although her hands were pressed against her ears, the screams of dying men assaulted her.

The gunshots persisted, gaining in volume. More explosions rocked the cavern, more rocks falling. Through the entrance to the chapel, Tess saw a torch break, toppling, spewing its fiery oil across the floor. Bullets chipped pillars, ricocheting, rock shards flying.

As the shooting intensified, dark-clothed figures charged from the cavern of the painted bulls. Through the smoke, Tess saw that the figures wore goggles and that their faces were smeared with black camouflage grease. They held automatic weapons and fired in every direction, pausing only long enough to throw more grenades. The explosions shattered pillars. Guards dropped, blood bursting from their heads and backs. Others were crushed by cascading rocks.

In a rush, the survivors—Gerrard and Fulano among them—scrambled into the cavern behind the chapel. A few returned fire, but most fled in panic.

Tess tripped a man as he raced past the stalagmite. His chin banged hard against the floor.

Too terrified to resist the impulse of adrenaline, she lunged from cover and grabbed his weapon. Her father had never taught her how to use this type of gun, but she remembered that Hugh Kelly had pulled back a bolt on the side of his before he prepared to shoot. Evidently the bolt was a cocking mechanism, and assuming that the guard had already cocked his weapon, she responded defensively, aimed at the guard when he struggled to rise, and shot him, slamming him flat.

The spray of blood combined with the weapon's stuttering recoil unnerved her. The force of the volley yanked the barrel upward. She urgently told herself, remember to hold it down, to keep it level.

Spinning, determined, she looked for other targets. Craig? *Where was Craig?* In the chaos of the shots, the smoke, and the flames, she didn't dare pull the trigger for fear of hitting him. Then she saw him, flat on his stomach, shooting. Guards jolted backward, slamming into others, knocking them off-balance, coating them with blood.

Tess fired above Craig, hitting other guards. Meanwhile, in the chapel, the smoke and flames grew stronger. The gunshots came closer. Craig and Tess kept firing.

To her right, Tess noticed sudden motion. There, Fulano rose from beside the pen in which he'd slaughtered the sacred bull.

He reached beneath his sport coat, pulled out a pistol, and aimed toward Craig.

Tess fired sooner, stitching Fulano's chest with bullets. The direct descendant of the leader of the heretics jerked repeatedly, staggered, and toppled over the side of the pen, lying on the corpse of the great white bull.

But again Tess hadn't been able to control her weapon's recoil. Its barrel heaved upward. Her finger—still on the trigger—reflexively kept squeezing. Propelled, she twisted, and suddenly Gerrard was in her line of fire.

The Vice President wailed, holding up his arms as if to shield his chest, but the bullets struck higher, blasting holes across his handsome face, blowing apart his gray eyes. Viscous matter spurted. His head appeared to explode.

Then actual explosions threw Tess on the rocky floor, grenades detonating fiercely at the rear of the chapel. She fought to stand, knowing that there'd be more explosions, and that they wouldn't be in the chapel. They'd be closer. They'd—! She saw a grenade arc through the entrance to the cavern.

Abruptly she felt the breath knocked out of her, a figure hurtling against her, Craig, who tackled her and dropped with her, and the next thing, Tess struck the steps to the pit and tumbled down them, Craig twisting over her. She walloped her knees, her back, her skull, and hit the dark bottom, stunned, splashing into thick, pungent blood that heaved and splattered over her.

Immediately, as she regained sufficient presence of mind to clamp her blood-smeared hands against her ears, feeling Craig raise his arms and do the same, the grenade erupted with a stunning roar, its shrapnel splintering off the cavern's walls, a few fragments striking the upper steps of the pit, the thunderous echo swelling against the walls of the cave, more rocks cascading.

Immersed in blood, Tess raised her dripping head and listened to the burp of automatic weapons strafe the cavern. Above, there was only darkness, the grenade's rush of air having extinguished the torches.

"I think we finished them," a husky voice said.

"Make sure," another voice said.

Tess recognized its deep-throated resonance.

Father Baldwin. We're safe! she thought. She raised her face higher, about to shout to him, when Craig clamped a hand across her mouth and pressed her head down. Her instincts made her want to scream. But her love for Craig made her comply. She understood. He was trying to tell her something.

More important, he was trying to *protect* her. She acquiesced, slackened her muscles, quit struggling, and nodded. For whatever reason, his motives—however puzzling—were in her best interests.

Heavy footsteps entered the cavern.

"No sign of survivors," a taut voice said. "Those that weren't shot or killed by grenades were crushed by rubble."

"Keep checking!" Father Baldwin ordered.

The Inquisitor's voice was so muffled that Tess realized, her arms around Craig, that slabs of rock had fallen over the bull and Fulano's corpse and had fallen as well over the entrance to the steps that led to the pit.

"Complete kill," the taut voice said.

A rock toppled.

"But this ceiling's about to collapse."

"Rig the charges," Father Baldwin said. "Everywhere."

"I've already started."

"The statue's *my* priority. I'll set a bomb and blow it to hell. Thank God, at last we found the central nest. There'll be *other* nests, but this one's the most important."

"What about the woman and the detective? I still haven't found them."

"Probably buried beneath the rubble. They might even still be breathing. Five minutes from now, it won't matter," Father Baldwin said. "If they're somehow still alive, they'll die when the explosions bring down the ceiling. We owe them a debt. But they can't be allowed to know our secrets. Their reward for their service will be in Heaven. The charges?"

"I just finished."

"And I just finished planting a bomb at the foot of the statue. Like *it*, the bodies of the vermin will be blown to hell."

"Let's go." The taut-voiced man lunged from the cavern into the chapel.

Other footsteps scurried.

"The rest of the charges?" Father Baldwin demanded, his voice receding.

"Ready. We'll need five minutes to get out of the cave. That's how long I've set the timers."

"Hurry," Father Baldwin again demanded, his voice even farther away. "Set more charges as we leave. I want these caverns completely destroyed."

"No problem. We'll be able to see the fireworks from the bottom of the outside slope."

A final faraway scurry of footsteps.

Craig removed his hand from Tess's mouth. Their clothing soaked with blood, they squirmed up the steps and reached a slab of rock that lay across the exit. Groping, Craig found a gap and squeezed through, followed by Tess, who scraped her back on the rock. Although the chamber was dark, flames from burning oil in the chapel provided sufficient reflected light for them to be able to make their way through the rubble. Their wet clothes caused them to shiver.

"We have to get out of here," Craig said.

"How?" Tess hugged her gore-drenched chest. "Even if we reach the exit before the bombs go off, Father Baldwin's men will shoot us."

"We can try to dismantle the bombs."

"No. We'd never find them all."

"But we can't just stay here and wait to die," Craig said. "There has to be a way to—"

"I just thought of something." Tess gripped his arm. "Remember when we entered the cave and Fulano locked the doors? He left three guards outside."

Craig nodded. "And if the guards were overpowered, if they didn't respond to a message from a walkie-talkie"—his voice quickened—"Fulano said we could use another exit. There's another way out of here!"

"And it has to be close!" Tess said, heart pounding.

Craig sank against a rock.

"What's wrong?"

"In the dark, we'll never find the exit." He suddenly straightened. "Just a minute. I think I can get us some light. Stay here."

Desperate, confused, Tess watched him climb over rubble, searching. "What are you looking for?"

"A body. My clothes are too soaked with blood. My jacket won't burn."

"I don't understand."

"You will. Here. I found a . . ." Yanking a jacket off a corpse, Craig left the cavern and reached the flames in the chapel. There, he touched one of the jacket's sleeves to a blaze, igniting it. Hurrying, he returned, the fire spreading up the sleeve of the jacket. "The grenades knocked over the torches back here and extinguished the flames. But there has to be oil all over the floor. I can smell it." He dragged the burning sleeve across the floor, trying various places among the rubble, and suddenly flames grew, oil igniting among the fallen rocks.

The flames spread. Tess and Craig backed away. The chamber became illuminated.

"Over there. On the left." Craig pointed. "A tunnel."

As the ceiling groaned and more rocks fell, Tess scrambled over the rubble, frantic to reach the tunnel.

"Go slower," Craig said. "If you break an ankle . . ."

"I'm more worried about the bombs." A section of roof collapsed, its impact thunderous. "And being crushed."

They came to the tunnel.

"This is probably where Kelly and his men brought the bull in," Craig said. "The entrance from the chapel is too narrow for the animal to have gotten through. And the bull would have been so difficult to handle that whoever designed this tunnel would have made the passageway as straight and short as possible."

Craig was right. The fire from the oil in the cavern reflected into the tunnel and showed an exit twenty yards ahead. But Tess moaned when she saw that the exit was blocked by a metal door. She moaned even worse when she and Craig strained to open the door but couldn't.

"The damned thing's locked." Angry, exhausted, Craig leaned against a wall, blood dripping from his clothes. "We wasted our time. There's so little left."

"Maybe there's another exit." Tess's voice shook.

"Don't count on it. And even if there is, those bombs will go off before we find it."

"We've got to try."

Craig studied her with resolve. "Yes."

They rushed back along the tunnel, reaching the cavern. Another section of roof crashed. The force of its impact jolted them and made the flames from the oil waver.

"Over there. In back," Tess said. "Another tunnel."

"Any minute now, those bombs will—"

"The flames, Craig! Look at the flames!"

"What about them?"

"They're still wavering! They're leaning toward that tunnel. When we first entered the chapel, I noticed the torches waver, but I thought that was just because our movement created a breeze. Air's flowing into that tunnel. It has to be going outside."

Craig nodded. "But what if the hole's too small for us to—"

"It's our only choice!" The roof groaned again. "Let's go! Before—!"

They scrambled toward the tunnel at the rear. The moment they entered, another huge slab of rock fell, barely missing them.

They stumbled forward, the light diminishing.

"If this tunnel branches out into *other* tunnels, we don't have a chance." Craig breathed hard.

The light from the flames in the cavern became so weak that Tess had to grope along the walls. "Do you feel a breeze? Does it seem to be getting stronger?"

"Yes! But what am I hearing?"

Ahead, something roared, constant, louder as they approached.

The tunnel curved and slanted down, blocking the light from the flames. In total darkness, they kept groping along the walls. The roar gained volume, so loud that Tess could hardly hear what Craig shouted.

"What?" she yelled.

"I think it's a—!"

The blackness was absolute. She couldn't see him, grabbed for his hand, took another step, and abruptly lurched forward, the shock waves of repeated explosions shoving at her. The ceiling cracked, about to collapse. Propelled, she stepped into nothingness. With air instead of rock beneath her, she plummeted. The ceiling gave way, slamming down behind her. She screamed. Her stomach rose as she dropped. Clutching Craig's hand, she swooped toward the black, louder, closer, continuous roar.

The roar, she discovered, was an underground stream. Its icy current stunned her, drowning her scream. She went under, panicked, powerless, unable to see or breathe. Dimly, she understood that concussions behind her were slabs of rock hitting the stream, but the current's force sucked her away before the rocks could crush her. She tumbled beneath the rushing surface, straining to raise her head, hoping frantically that the breeze she and Craig had followed meant that the stream had an open space above it. But no matter how hard she fought, she couldn't reach the surface.

The stream gained speed. She banged against a polished curve in the channel, twisted, slammed against another curve, lost her grip on Craig's hand, struggled again to reach the surface, and suddenly felt herself dropping. Oh, Jesus, she prayed, unable to hold her breath, about to inhale reflexively.

The stream kept falling. At once, she burst through an opening, was hurled from the water, and flipped through air. The pressure of dropping made her chest heave. She gasped uncontrollably. Her lungs expanded, air rushing down her throat. The next thing, she struck a pool, propelled beneath it by the thunderous thrust of a waterfall. When she clawed to the surface, her arms thrashing weakly, she breathed in desperation and gradually realized that there were stars above her, that she was outside in the sweet, spacious night, that she was close to the rim of the pool.

A moment later, in a frenzy, she pivoted to search for Craig. His body floated toward her. Urgent, she swam and grabbed him. He raised his head, coughing, spitting out water, while she tugged him toward the rim of the pool. They lay on a grassy bank.

But Craig kept coughing, choking. He vomited water. In a rush, she turned him onto his chest, moved his head sideways, checked to make sure that there were no obstructions in his mouth, and pressed her hands on his back, squeezing his lungs, sensing water escape from his mouth. He coughed repeatedly. Then gradually his spasms diminished.

He began to breathe freely.

Only then did she slump back, exhausted. The air smelled fresh and clear. The moon and the stars were glorious. Despite the thunder of the waterfall, she heard a nearby stream flowing from the pool, trickling over rocks toward the valley.

Craig moved his head to study her. He coughed again and clutched her hand. "Thanks." He managed to smile.

"Hey, it took two of us to get out of there." She returned his smile, her heart swelling with relief that he was alive.

Then she, too, coughed up water. She shivered so badly that her teeth chattered.

Side by side, they held each other, trying to regain their strength.

Five minutes later, Craig roused himself. "That water was so icy . . ." He shook uncontrollably.

"Hypothermia?" Tess frowned.

He continued shaking, worried. "In these wet clothes, even on a warm night in June, we're both so chilled we could die from exposure. We have to get warm and dry. Soon."

Realizing the danger, Tess hurriedly glanced behind her toward the valley. No, she thought, we can't have survived what we did only to freeze to death. At once she mentally thanked God. "Everything's fine. No problem."

"What? The nearest village is probably miles away. We'd get delirious, fall asleep, and die before we managed to walk there, assuming we could even find it."

"I still say no problem." Painfully cold, Tess trembled from her head to her feet.

"You think all we have to do is rub two sticks together and build a fire?"

"No. Someone already did that for us. In fact a lot of people."

Puzzled, Craig turned to follow her gaze and let out his breath in wonder. Below them, across the fields in the valley, dozens and dozens of bonfires glittered in the darkness. Their glow was splendorous.

"The feast of Saint John. I'd forgotten," Craig said.

"Like tiny pieces of the sun. For once, flames are going to help us." Tess managed to stand, trembled, and reached for his hand. "Bright flames. Not dark. Come on, babe."

It took all her strength to raise him. Arm in arm, huddled against each other, clinging for warmth, they staggered down a grassy slope toward the fires.

"At least the stream washed the blood from our clothes," Tess said. "I guess in a way . . . It was like a baptism. Except that the second baptism canceled the first. The second was truly purifying."

"The thing is, our problems aren't over," Craig said.

"I know. Father Baldwin. What made you realize that he didn't want us to escape?"

"Just a hunch, but in my line of work, you learn the hard way to respond to hunches. I figured we ought to wait and see how much he wanted to find us in the rubble. Obviously he thinks we're a threat because of the secrets he told us."

"Right now, I don't care about his damned Inquisition. All I want to do is keep holding you. It feels so wonderful to be alive."

"Good fighting evil." Craig shivered. "In this case, it's hard to tell the difference between them. *Both* are evil. I'm sure of this—as soon as the Inquisitors learn we're still alive, they'll come after us."

Tess hesitated. "Maybe not."

"You've got a plan?"

"Sort of. I'm still thinking it through. But if they do decide to come after us, I'm ready to fight them. As far as I'm concerned, they committed an unforgivable sin."

"Because they turned against us?"

"No. Because they blew up the paintings. I'll always remember them—the deer, the bison, the horses, the ibex, the bulls. So awesome, so magnificent, so irreplaceable."

At the bottom of the slope, Tess noticed shadowy figures and realized that they were villagers huddled around a fire, holding their crosses woven from flowers and stalks of wheat. The villagers frowned at Tess and Craig, suspicious. But she raised her right hand, still wet from the stream, and touched it to her forehead, her chest, her left and right shoulder. The villagers nodded and motioned for Tess and Craig to sit.

The fire quickly warmed them, drying their clothes. Tess and Craig continued to hold each other lovingly and remained there throughout the night, sometimes dozing, only to waken and stare again, as if hypnotized, toward the power and magic of the flames.

14

Alexandria, Virginia

With Craig's comforting presence beside her, Tess stood in a cemetery near the city's outskirts and stared at her mother's grave. Tears misted her vision. The funeral had been yesterday, six days after she and Craig had escaped from the caverns and two days after they'd returned from Spain.

Much had happened. Following the night at the bonfire, their Spanish companions had escorted them across the valley to the nearest village. There, with great difficulty because of her unfamiliarity with the language, Tess had managed to use a phone and eventually contact the American embassy in Madrid. Her report had caused a half dozen helicopters to arrive by midafternoon, American and Spanish officials accompanied by armed guards hurrying out. From then on, she and Craig had repeatedly been questioned. They'd shown the investigators the obliterated, former entrance to the caverns. They'd taken the investigators to the waterfall that had saved them.

Soon other helicopters had arrived, bringing more investigators and guards. The interrogation had continued well into the night. After a few hours' sleep and a meager breakfast, Tess and Craig had wearily answered further questions, continuing to repeat the story that they'd agreed on before Tess had phoned Madrid.

The story was the core of Tess's plan to protect themselves from both the Inquisitors and the heretics. More than anything, she wanted to tell it to reporters, to make sure it was publicized, but when reporters did arrive, she and Craig were taken under guard via helicopter to Bilbao and then to Madrid, where the questioning continued at the headquarters of Spain's intelligence service, distraught American CIA officials joining in.

Reporters managed to learn enough from unnamed sources to publish and broadcast the story. It spread quickly around the world. Under pressure from numerous governments, Spanish and American officials finally admitted the truth of what they'd dismissed as rumors. America's vice president and the presumed future president of Spain had indeed been assassinated by terrorists while showing two American guests various cultural and geographical features in the province of Navarra in northern Spain.

The terrorists remained unidentified.

What the accounts did not include, of course, was the increasing frustration with which the grim investigators questioned Tess and Craig.

"Why the hell did you come to Spain? How did you enter the country? You don't have any passports."

"My mother was recently murdered." Tess continued to repeat what she'd answered so often. "Alan Gerrard is—was—a longtime, close, family friend. He invited my fiancé and me to accompany him on Air Force Two to Spain in the hopes that the trip would take my mind off my sorrow. His invitation was sudden. We didn't have time to get our passports, and I was too stunned by grief to think clearly, to refuse a request not just from a friend but from the vice president of the United States. Would *you* have turned him down?''

"But what were you doing in—how did you get to—*northern* Spain?''

"Before Alan began his official duties, he wanted to visit José Fulano at his estate near Pamplona. The two were friends. But I suspect that they might also have had some business to discuss. At any rate, we were taken along. Alan was quite enthusiastic, still trying to distract me from my grief. He claimed that he'd never forgive himself if we didn't have a chance to see that dramatically beautiful area of the country."

"A cave? At *midnight?*''

"Because of the feast of Saint John. Both Alan and José insisted on showing us the bonfires in the valleys. Then they ordered the helicopter to land so they could also show us the cave. It was special, they said, because it had Ice Age paintings that very few people had ever seen."

"Ice Age paintings?''

"Yes. They were beautiful."

"And that's when the terrorists struck?''

"The attack was sudden. I don't know how the assassins knew we were in the cave, but all at once there was gunfire. Explosions. I saw Alan and José shot several times. My fiancé and I raced down a tunnel. The explosions weakened the cavern's ceiling. It collapsed, but not before we managed to find that stream and escape."

"Seems awfully damned convenient."

"We were lucky. What would you prefer—that we'd been killed as well? There'd be no one to tell you what happened."

"The assassins. Who were they?''

"I have no idea. They wore masks. I could barely see them in the dim light in the cave."

And on and on. Although the interrogators tried to find inconsistencies, Tess and Craig stuck to their story. Much of it was true, and the Vice President's aides along with the Secret Service agents he'd left in Madrid verified those parts. What couldn't be verified and what the investigators had to take on faith was that Tess and Craig weren't able to provide information that could help identify the assassins.

Meanwhile efforts to retrieve the bodies proved useless. The interior of the mountain had completely collapsed. Leveling the mountain was out of the question. The corpses would have to stay entombed there forever with the massive peak as their gravestone.

Unidentified assassins. No hint of anything except the Ice Age paintings in the cave. Those two pieces of disinformation—a term she'd learned from her father—were the key to Tess's plan to protect her and Craig, and that disinformation was what she read in a newspaper as she and Craig were flown in Air Force Two back to America. The interrogation would continue in Washington, she'd been told, but she had no doubt that the investigators would soon release them, that she and Craig would be dismissed (presumably with lingering suspicions about them) as two innocent bystanders.

The newspaper she read on the flight to America was the international edition of *USA Today,* and in the economic section, she noticed an article that roused her spirits. Public outrage against the slaughter of elephants for their tusks had resulted in an international trade ban on ivory, with the consequence that the price of ivory had plummeted from two hundred dollars per kilogram to less than five dollars. Poachers no longer considered elephants valuable enough to massacre them. The species had a chance to be saved. At the same time, the article noted, other species were disappearing at the alarming speed of 150,000 per year.

Nonetheless the salvation of the elephants gave Tess hope, just as the brilliant sky, unusually free of smog, also gave her hope as she now wiped her tears at her mother's graveside.

She turned to Craig, her voice deep with mourning. "There's something I never told you. The night we sat at the fire in the valley?"

Craig put his arms around her.

She leaned her head against his chest and managed the strength to continue. "I began to understand why the followers of Mithras worship flames. The blaze rises from things that are dead. Old branches. Dry leaves. Like the phoenix."

Craig nodded. "Out of death comes life."

She raised her head. "The trouble is, the flames aren't immortal any more than the branches and leaves were. Eventually the blaze has to die as well, turning into, becoming . . ." With a sob, she stared again at her mother's grave. "Ashes to ashes, dust to dust."

Craig didn't respond for a moment. "Sprinkle ashes on a garden, though, and the earth becomes more fertile. The cycle of death turning into life continues."

Her voice sounded choked. "The miracle of nature. Except that my mother's gone forever."

"But you're still here. And you're the life she created."

"I'll try to do what I hope would have made her proud of me," Tess said. "So many years I avoided her, and now I wish so much that she and I could spend time together."

"Do you think she'd have minded being buried here instead of next to your father in Arlington National Cemetery?"

"No." Tess had trouble speaking. "My mother was a diplomat's wife. She knew the bitter rules. My father's career came first. She always had to stay in the background. But she didn't object. Because she loved him."

Craig kissed her tear-swollen eyes. "And I love you. And I promise you'll always be first, the most important part of my life."

Holding each other, they walked from the grave.

"I wanted revenge so bad," Tess said. "But when I killed Gerrard and Fulano, I didn't do it to get even. I didn't enjoy it. It didn't give me satisfaction. I hated it. I only did it to save us. That makes me feel clean somehow, or at least as clean as I'm able to feel under the circumstances. All the men I shot. All the blood. The ugliness. I keep having nightmares."

"I'll be there to share them with you."

They passed other graves, approaching their rented car.

"At least no one knows who really killed Gerrard and Fulano," Tess said. "The Inquisitors think *they* did. The heretics will think so, too. We won't be blamed."

"But you still believe they won't come after us?" Craig asked.

"It's a calculated risk, but yes, that's what I believe. When we were questioned, we never mentioned Father Baldwin and the Inquisition. We never talked about the heretics. We never revealed that there was a chapel in that cave. Both sides must have informants who know what we told the investigators. I'm hoping they realize that our silence about them is an act of good faith.''

"You want to leave it at that?" Craig asked. "You don't want to try to stop them?"

"We'd never be able to. I'm not sure which is worse, the heretics using terrorism to try to save the planet, or the Inquisitors using vigilante tactics to stop what they think is theological evil. Let the bastards fight it out. With luck, maybe they'll destroy each other, and people will get smart enough to save the world the right way, with love.''

They passed the final row of graves and reached their car. As they drove from the cemetery, Craig turned on the radio, and a news announcement made Craig stop abruptly at the curb.

Two days ago, when Tess's mother had been buried, there'd been a state funeral for Alan Gerrard. Earlier, as the constitution dictated, the President had nominated a new Vice President, subject to approval by both Houses of Congress. Despite the nation's turmoil, President Garth had decided that he didn't dare postpone his trip to Peru to attend a major drug-control conference. After all, as he said with deep tones of bravery in a nationally televised speech, he couldn't allow the drug lords to think that the Vice President's assassination made him afraid of possibly being assassinated himself. So he'd flown to Peru, and now the news announcer reported with barely subdued shock that Air Force One had been blown apart by portable ground-to-air missiles as the plane came in for a landing at Lima's airport.

Tess listened, stunned, struggling to absorb what she was hearing. A terrible question assaulted her consciousness. There'd soon be both a new president and vice president. But would either of those men have gray eyes?